D0057946

Books by Susan McBride

THE GOOD GIRL'S GUIDE TO MURDER
BLUE BLOOD

The
Good Girl's Guide to
MURDER

A DEBUTANTE DROPOUT MYSTERY

SUSAN
McBRIDE

AVON BOOKS
An Imprint of HarperCollinsPublishers

This is a work of fiction. Names, characters, places, and incidents are products of the author's imagination or are used fictitiously and are not to be construed as real. Any resemblance to actual events, locales, organizations, or persons, living or dead, is entirely coincidental.

AVON BOOKS
An Imprint of HarperCollins*Publishers*
10 East 53rd Street
New York, New York 10022-5299

Copyright © 2005 by Susan McBride
ISBN 0-06-056390-7
www.avonmystery.com

First Avon Books paperback printing: February 2005

Avon Trademark Reg. U.S. Pat. Off. and in Other Countries, Marca Registrada, Hecho en U.S.A.
HarperCollins® is a registered trademark of HarperCollins Publishers Inc.

Printed in the U.S.A.

10 9 8 7 6 5 4 3 2 1

This book is dedicated to my friends and family for being the best cheerleaders a starving artist could ever hope for. I love and cherish you all.

Acknowledgments

Many thanks to Robin Waldron, M.D. (aka Doc Robin) for coming up with a very interesting idea for murder, and to my web diva, Janell Schiffbauer, for answering my questions about web design.

Thanks always to the Deadly Divas—Letha Albright, Denise Swanson, and Lisa Kleinholz—for sticking together and making the impossible possible.

My eternal gratitude to Sarah Durand, editor extraordinaire, for her insightfulness and enthusiasm. Thanks also to Jeremy, Diana, and all the folks at Avon, who've made things so easy for me!

The
Good Girl's Guide to
MURDER

Chapter 1

"Put it down, or I'll kill you."

Marilee Mabry didn't even have to raise her voice, and the huge vase of flowers was hastily lowered. The elaborate arrangement from one of Dallas's premier floral designers, Dr. Delphinium, nearly hid the woman behind it, until she deposited the bouquet on the coffee table with a *clunk* and backed away.

"I'm sorry, ma'am. I was just trying to help with the party preparations."

Marilee scowled at the unadorned face and wild dark hair hanging down to where boobs should have been. *What was it with these New Age flower children? Hadn't they heard of straightening wands, padded bras, or Bobbi Brown?*

She flicked be-ringed fingers, motioning the girl away. "Please, do me a favor and go help somewhere else," she instructed, indifferent to the chill in her drawl, and watched the bewildered expression turn to dismay.

"I can't believe that you . . . you're not anything like I'd imagined . . . oh, forget it," the young woman stammered, then ducked her head and scurried off like a frightened rabbit.

Was she an intern?

A friend of Kendall's?

Though she looked at least a decade older than Kendall's eighteen.

Was she someone from Twinkle Productions?

Ah, one of *The Sweet Life*'s newer production assistants. She had to be.

There seemed to be bushels of those lately.

Marilee tapped a finger to her lips, thinking something about the shape of the hazel eyes and set of the mouth seemed familiar.

Hmm, a name was on the tip of her tongue, really.

Something with an *R,* wasn't it? Randa, Retha, Renée?

Heavens to Betsy, she couldn't expect to remember everyone!

There were always so many people wandering around her offices and *The Sweet Life* set these days, half of them unfamiliar. Her staff had grown so fast in the past six weeks—thanks to an infusion of crew from Twinkle—that she'd long since given up memorizing names and faces. Thank God this was Texas and calling everyone "hon" worked in a pinch.

Still it was disconcerting to feel that she had strangers among her inner circle. When they'd started out years ago, taping locally at one of the downtown stations, she'd had only a small crew, operating on a shoestring. She trusted department heads to do the hiring now, while she focused on hosting the show, on writing books, making videotapes, and developing related projects. Even if she wanted to—

and she didn't—she simply couldn't be all things to all people. She wasn't an octopus; she only had two hands, for God's sake.

Though that was the price of fame, wasn't it?

She sighed.

Never mind, she told herself and fiddled with the vase overflowing with artfully arranged Oriental lilies and green bamboo until it looked absolutely perfect. She stepped back to admire her handiwork, clicking tongue against teeth.

If she wanted anything done right, she still had to do it herself.

Wasn't that always the way?

Even married to Gilbert, she'd had to do everything: take care of the house, pay the bills, set up doctors' appointments, arrange vacations, and—perhaps trickiest of all—rear their daughter.

Dear, troubled Kendall, she mused with a shake of her head.

The girl had been a fussy baby and a demanding toddler; ripening into a needy teenager who required far more attention than Marilee could possibly give. Though it wasn't all Marilee's fault. Half that responsibility fell on Gil. Kendall had never received the affection she'd wanted from her father—or so the therapists had concurred—and, for that matter, neither had Marilee.

Kendall had been getting on her nerves all morning, whining about not being allowed to borrow any of Mari's best jewelry, complaining that her new pair of Jimmy Choos pinched her toes, and begging Mari to open the bottle of reserve stock Dom Perignon she'd been hoarding for tonight's big event "so I can have a little taste."

It was enough to give her an ulcer, if she didn't have one already.

Instinctively, Marilee reached for her third left finger, but it was bare. No wedding band to twist, not for six years, and still sometimes she tried out of habit.

Would things have been different for Kendall if there'd been no divorce? Was that at the root of her lack of self-worth?

Not that the divorce had been Mari's idea to begin with. Still, would she be where she was if it hadn't happened?

Absolutely not.

When she thought about it—really, truly, deeply—it seemed a wonder she and Gil had lasted as long as they did. More amazing that she hadn't smothered him with a pillow along the way, much as she'd been tempted. Always leaving his dirty clothes on the floor, mussing up the bathroom, pretending to slave away at the office, then disappearing for days on "business trips" when he was really off boinking his assistant, a former nurse's aide who looked like the love child of Pamela Anderson and Carrot Top.

She realized she was gritting her teeth and made herself relax.

That was then, Marilee.

This was *now,* and everything was different. Her life was her own, and she'd taken the reins in a big way.

No, a *colossal* way.

She let her gaze dance over the cadre of people—a mingling of staff and additional hired help—who moved purposefully within the cavernous surroundings, readying the place for tonight's big premiere. A warm buzz of voices filled her ears, as did the soothing strains of a Vivaldi violin concerto flowing from discreetly placed speakers. It would be an occasion to remember, a chance for friend and foe alike—yes, she had invited Gilbert and his hussy, had encouraged him to come for Kendall's sake, if only to stick it to them—and Marilee could hardly wait until the clock struck eight and guests began to arrive.

This was *her* time. She was on top of the world and suddenly understood how Martha Stewart must have felt when she rang the bell at the New York Stock Exchange, the day her corporation went public (before her trumped-up trial and conviction over a silly stock sale).

The thrill was undeniable.

She rocked on her heels and looked around her. Ah, how she loved her new sound stage! Each nook and cranny designed to her specifications by a team of architects, a brilliant contractor and his crew, and a slew of Dallas's top-notch decorators who fleshed out her vision. Needless to say, no expense had been spared. Twinkle Productions had been extremely generous in giving her what she wanted.

This was her dream. She deserved to be indulged, and she'd already made up her mind that there would be no more skimping.

She'd spent most of her married life doing that, anyway. Clipping coupons, creative decorating—translation: shopping for furniture at Goodwill—even making all of Kendall's clothes for a dozen years until Gilbert's surgical supplies company finally took off . . . and then so did Gilbert. With Amber Lynn, his secretary-whore.

Marilee pursed her lips at the mere thought of the auburn-haired bimbo with her collagen-filled lips and saline-filled breasts. She'd often pondered how delightful it would be to take a pin to the woman, stick her strategically, and let her leak until there was nothing left of her but deflated skin.

Beneath her rib cage, her heart did one of its funny flutters, and she felt suddenly woozy. She gripped the back of a nearby chair until her pulse settled down and the light-headedness faded.

What was wrong with her?

Did merely thinking of Gil and Amber make her dizzy?

Still jealous, Mari? Even with the divorce a half-dozen years behind you?

She shook her head, setting her freshly styled and high-lighted hair to shimmying around her face.

Jealous?

Hardly.

Gilbert would truly be sorry when he saw firsthand what she had become without him. He would regret casting her aside like a hunk of Grade-D beef and leaving her to fend for herself and Kendall without child support, alimony, or a familiar roof over their heads.

Not that she missed him, because she didn't. Gil had never been any great shakes, in or out of bed. Besides, she had her own stud muffin to keep her warm at night, a certi-fied personal trainer who kept her in shape, so to speak. His name was Justin Gable, and he was definitely "able" in so many ways: ador*able*, pli*able*, and dispens*able*.

So what if she wasn't in love him? Certainly not in that google-eyed way she'd once loved Gil (when she was too young to know any better). Was that a crime in this post-*Sex and the City* age?

Being with Justin meant that she wasn't alone, and that seemed like a victory in itself.

She might be nearing fifty, but she wasn't dead yet. She still had urges like any other red-blooded female. Why the hell not satisfy them with an eager young buck with six-pack abs and a hankering to please as opposed to a man whose sagging belly, red Corvette, and Viagra screamed, "Mid-Life Crisis!"

Besides, she'd kept herself up. A little Botox here, a nip and tuck there, and she could stop the clock for another ten years. She smoothed her hands over slim hips, feeling great about her looks, thinking she resembled Candice Bergen at her peak, the same streaky blond hair, thin build, and blue eyes. Marilee considered herself the epitome of growing older gracefully, still alluring enough to attract the opposite sex and to evoke envy in other women, even her own daughter. Would that it could last forever.

Knock on wood.

Justin dabbled in Chinese herbs, swore up and down that they had special healing powers and anti-aging qualities, but Mari didn't like to take pills or powders with odd names. She preferred not to touch tea or soda with caffeine, which made her heart race wildly and kept her up at night.

She had the genes of a survivor. That's all she needed to get her through from one day to the next. Not prescriptions or holistic remedies.

God knows she was looking forward to sticking around a long while and finally living her wildest fantasies.

And they all started with the party.

Marilee crossed her arms over her raspberry cashmere

sweater set and toyed with the vintage Mikimoto pearls at her throat as she surveyed the innards of the building that housed her production offices and television studio, converted from a warehouse in Addison, deep in the suburbs of North Dallas. Just six weeks ago, they'd started shooting new shows for her syndicated series here, a daily hourlong "how to" lesson for women everywhere who wanted the best without having to pay a high price.

"The Sweet Life with Marilee."

It was the title of the column she'd written for the *Dallas Morning News* since shortly after her divorce, since the bad old days when she'd had to use what skills she'd had—a wife's repertoire of cooking, cleaning, sewing, decorating—in order to survive when Gilbert had dumped them so unceremoniously.

Survive. That was the word for it, too.

The good ol' boy judge who'd presided over their divorce hearing had sided with Gil, deciding he owed her nothing but the savings bond for Kendall's college and whatever had been Marilee's at the start of their union (i.e., her own hair and teeth).

Gil had sold the place in Prestonwood, kicking them out on the street while he moved into an even larger abode in Northwood Hills with his then bride-to-be.

Marilee had packed up what little she and Kendall had owned, finding them a tiny subsidized apartment on the south side of the city. She'd scrimped and saved ferociously, relying on charity until she could get on her feet. She'd eventually found a low-paying job behind the counter at a dry cleaner, which got her home before Kendall decamped from the school bus. It was then she'd begun to write on a dinosaur of a PC while Kendall was asleep at night, churning out economical tips for making the best of what you had, always with a caustic slant. Because if you couldn't laugh at yourself when you were sewing kitchen curtains out of garage-sale table linens, then what was the point?

A twist of fate in the form of society maven Cissy Kendricks had earned her a meeting with the editor in chief at the *Morning News,* and she had a job by the time she'd left his office. Her column had been an instant hit, quickly selling to syndication and ultimately to *Good Housekeeping.* Then came the books and the talk-show appearances, a radio show, and finally *this.*

A fissure of excitement dashed up her spine, and she shivered, still amazed at how far she'd come. From a ramshackle chicken farm in the middle of Nowhere, Texas, to a mansion in Preston Hollow a hop, skip, and a jump away from Ross Perot's.

As a child, she'd had to don the same pair of shoes until they wore clear through, and now she owned a 15,000 square-foot mansion on some pretty high-class turf. She had over an acre of prime real estate for her organic farm—like *Green Acres* in the 'burbs—a seven-car garage, and the pièce de résistance, a big-ass closet (larger than her and Gil's old master bedroom) made to hold her uncountable pairs of Manolo Blahniks, Kate Spades, Michael Kors, and Stuart Weitzmans. No cardboard in those soles.

You've come a long way, baby, she told herself.

As for what she'd had to go through to get where she was . . . well, that wasn't something she needed to dwell on.

All the sacrifices she'd made had been worth it. No more

paying her dues. No more kissing ass. No, if anyone's ass would be bussed, it would be hers.

She smiled at that.

The sweet life, indeed.

About to get sweeter.

Nothing—and nobody—was going to screw it up.

Chapter 2

 Sometimes you do things because you want to.

Like eating a pint of Ben & Jerry's Chunky Monkey in one fell swoop. Or splashing through puddles after a rainstorm in old tennis shoes.

Sometimes you do things because you have no choice.

Like tetanus shots and dental appointments.

Or suffering through the party from hell with a guest list full of Dallas muckety-mucks.

I would have preferred root canal, to be perfectly honest. At least that involved anesthesia. If only I could be pumped full of Novocain before eight o'clock.

If wishes were laughing gas, huh?

Unfortunately, I was going to have to do this one stone cold sober. Well, until the champagne was served; then I aimed to drink like a fish.

The soiree I'd been strong-armed to attend was being tossed to celebrate the national syndication of *The Sweet Life with Marilee,* a local TV show that had skyrocketed in ratings and was on the verge of inundating hundreds of new markets across the country. The show's creator and host, Marilee Mabry, was a close friend of my mother's and had recently hired me to redesign her Web site. Basically, I was trapped between a rock and a hard case. So, much as I wanted to, weaseling out was no option.

I know, I know.

A party may sound like most people's idea of a good time, and, had it been a quiet dinner with a few of my buddies, I would have looked forward to going instead of dreading it the way I did the annual visit to my gynecologist (however nice she may be).

Events involving pals of Mother were never "quiet" in any sense of the word. They were noisy galas, extravaganzas, or over-the-top affairs whose invitations were coveted by every member of the Dallas glitterati.

Cissy Blevins Kendricks *lived* for such moments. Hell, she thrived on them. Call me a party pooper, but I, Andrea Blevins Kendricks, her only child and sole heir, avoided such gigs like rush hour on LBJ Freeway.

Which was one of the many ways we differed, despite our DNA.

Even to the casual observer, Cissy and I seemed way too dissimilar to be related. The fact that I had actually sprung from her loins surely belonged on the pages of *Ripley's Believe It or Not,* alongside the tale of Hillary Clinton giving birth to an alien baby (really, I saw the headline in the *Enquirer* when I was at the supermarket check out).

Cissy and I were like oil and water, night and day, the Rolling Stones and kidney stones.

I liked to be left alone, kept out of Mother's platinum world as much as humanly possible. I was comfortable with a far more low-key existence, living in my one bedroom condo, driving my years-old Jeep Wrangler, wearing blue jeans stained with chalks or acrylic paint, without standing appointments at the Plaza Park Salon or Elizabeth Arden's Red Door. In other words, my wants were few and my needs minimal. What I craved most was my privacy and the relative freedom to pursue the thing I loved most: my art, both on canvas and on the computer.

Don't get me wrong. I didn't aspire to be Henry David Thoreau, living off the land and all alone—with my easel, acrylics, and laptop—at Walden Pond. I had built a nice little nest in the northern suburbs of Big D, within reach of all the city had to offer but far enough away from my mother to enjoy relative tranquility (translation: at least a twenty-minute trip across town, depending on traffic).

I wasn't so much granola as Cap'n Crunch with lactose-free skim milk.

Cissy was mimosas and Eggs Benedict.

"Tranquility" was definitely a word that didn't exist in her vocabulary. Her days revolved around the seasons—the social seasons—her calendar filled with luncheons, sorority alumnae functions, fashion shows, cocktail parties, board meetings, and endless charity fundraisers.

Not exactly my cup of green tea.

I shopped with coupons and had no qualms about buying a bargain brand on sale. Labels didn't mean much to me.

I couldn't even recall the last time Mother had set foot in a grocery store, especially since Simon David delivered.

I'm not sure she'd ever even seen a coupon; though I'm damned sure she'd never clipped one. (She didn't even clip her own nails, for Pete's sake.)

If that wasn't enough proof for the pudding, there was always our opposing sense of fashion; or rather, my lack of one and her overabundance.

I felt uncomfortable in high heels and designer gowns with price tags that exceeded my monthly mortgage payment. My usual attire consisted of button-down jeans, T-shirts, and a well-worn pair of sneakers.

Conversely, my mother wouldn't leave the house unless she had on Chanel from head to toe . . . or Escada, Prada, Nicole Miller, whatever suited the occasion; so long as it was something she hadn't been seen in before, *God forbid*.

I was the apple that had fallen so far from the tree I'd landed in another orchard entirely.

Still, Cissy was nothing if not persistent. She kept trying to lure me over to the dark side, and tonight was merely another example of her handiwork.

As I said before, *sometimes you have no choice.*

So I wasn't at all looking forward to Marilee's swanky get-together at her new TV studio in Addison, even if it meant all the Dom Perignon I could swig and bruschetta out the wazoo.

Attending the gig was more like a payback, a debt I owed my mother because she'd helped bail an old friend of mine out of a sticky situation a couple months ago. My best pal from prep school, Molly O'Brien—"that scholarship girl," as Cissy had long ago dubbed her—got herself in a tangle that nearly cost her everything. Thankfully, all was resolved, in no small part due to Mother's connections, though I thought I'd paid my penance by attending a fancy gig at the Morton Meyerson Symphony Center. I'd even let her drag me to José Eber's salon for hair and makeup, and I'd put on a pair of Manolo Blahniks that redefined "torture" as far as my feet were concerned (forgive me, Sarah Jessica).

Little did I know that was merely a down payment. I'd hardly had time to recuperate when Cissy had plucked another IOU out of her red Hermès crocodile bag and waved it in front of my face.

Talk about a bad day at Black Rock.

The mere recollection was enough to bring on hives, and, the more I tweaked the details into focus, the itchier I became.

Dateline: Two weeks ago.

The setting: Trinity Hall, a wonderful Irish pub at Mockingbird Station.

The setup: Mother had lured me there for lunch, presumably to spend some quality time together, catching up.

I should've known that the choice of location was a Freudian slip on her part. I mean, an Irish pub? That might make some think of "Guinness" right off the bat, or even leprechauns and four-leaf clovers. For me, it conjured up "blarney," something my mother was so often full of, and that day proved no exception.

We had a nice enough conversation during our meal—a Gaelic club for me and, fittingly, a Blarney Cobb salad for Cissy—and, it wasn't until we'd finished dessert that she relayed her true intentions.

"There's a little favor I'd like you to do for me, darlin'," she drawled, reaching across the table to squeeze my nail-bitten fingers between her perfectly manicured ones.

A little favor?

Right.

Nothing was simple when it was Mother doing the asking.

"What's that mean, exactly?" I squirmed, feeling the Irish Cake I'd just consumed churn uneasily in my belly.

"I bumped into Marilee at Chanel this morning"—Cissy dropped by the boutique in Highland Park Village as often as I shopped at Tom Thumb for groceries, which was at least twice a week—"and she happened to mention that her latest web designer had quit on her, smack in the midst of redoing her site and setting up a video river to showcase the opening of her studio . . ."

"A video stream?" I suggested.

"River, stream, what does it matter?" She made a moue. "That was her sixth web designer to quit in as many weeks, and Mari was in a state of sheer panic."

I should've made a run for the hills right then, anticipating where Cissy was going with this. But, instead, I sat there in a food-induced stupor. Maybe the whiskey in the cake was to blame, since I wasn't exactly known for holding my liquor. (One hot rum toddy, and I was snoring like a baby.)

Otherwise, I would have used my head, made up some excuse about dashing off to meet a made-up new client or a just-remembered appointment for a high colonic and bamboo-shoot manicure. If it wasn't the whiskey in the cake, what else could have so thoroughly impaired my senses?

Didn't say much for my repeated showings on the Hockaday Headmistress List throughout my prep school years, did it?

"Well, I felt awful for her, simply awful," Cissy went on, gripping my hand more tightly, further preventing me from flight. "Marilee's had some bad luck since they finished her new studio a month or so back, a few minor mishaps. Her wardrobe mistress was bitten by a brown recluse spider that had somehow gotten in a box with a pair of Marilee's shoes. The poor woman's arm swelled up like a watermelon, and she had to take a medical leave for treatment. Then Mari's director got bumped on the shoulder by a falling boom microphone during rehearsal before a taping. Nearly dislocated the joint, Mari said, and narrowly missed hitting *her* in the head." Mother's eyes danced with worry.

"Mother, I'm sorry about Marilee's problems, and the fact that she can't hold on to a web designer but . . ."

"Yes, the Web site, that's where you come in, darling," she ran right over me, patting my hand. "Mari had planned to broadcast the party on the Internet to celebrate the syndication of her morning show, and now she's afraid it won't happen. She was near to tears. So what was I to do? I couldn't leave her in a lurch, not after all the poor dear's been through."

Mother flashed a most disarming smile that set off a warning bell in my head, like the Robot on *Lost in Space,* flailing his arms and screaming, "Danger, Will Robinson! Danger!"

Though, somehow, I knew it was too late already.

My eyes flickered over the shelves of books in the library area of the restaurant where we'd been seated, usually a calm and secluded place. But that afternoon, it seemed almost menacing, like a trap that had been set. I glanced longingly at the tables filled with other diners who chatted, ate, and laughed, all of them blissfully unaware of what was happening to me. The bribery, the blackmail, and coercion: wrapped up prettily and disguised as a mother-daughter luncheon.

"Help!" I wanted to cry but instead stayed silent, my butt glued to the seat.

Mother had that effect on people.

She would've made a brilliant snake charmer.

Or a damned fine secretary of state.

"Of course, I told Marilee not to worry," she said, honey-smooth, her lips curving coyly. "I reminded her that my darling Andrea was a genius on computers and could have her fixed up in no time flat."

My gut clenched. "You didn't?"

"Yes, sweetie, I did."

"*Muh-ther.* How *could* you?" I whined like a two-year-old, despite my best intentions. A well-modulated voice was often my best defense. When I sounded like Minnie Mouse with nasal blockage, I knew she had me licked. "Don't you think you should've called and asked me first?"

As soon as I'd said it, I realized how insane that question was.

"She'll actually *pay* you, Andrea."

I tried not to flinch as she took a jab at my penchant for doing so much pro bono web work, mostly for local charities. Often, my only compensation was the satisfaction I got from a job well done. Something I figured she'd have understood, considering the uncountable fundraisers she'd chaired over the years. She should've been proud of me, happy to think that, in some way, I'd followed her example.

Sure, Andy, sure. And Ivana Trump shops at Wal-Mart.

It was something I'd mulled over a million times only to reach this conclusion: the difference between my work and hers was that she'd married young and had a child by the time she was my age, and I was still unattached, despite my sparkling personality and the healthy—and mostly untouched—trust fund Daddy had left me. (I tried to use it only for emergencies.)

That had to be the gist of it; why she didn't accept my career as something I was passionate about, something I took very seriously. If I had a husband, nothing I did would rub Mother quite so wrong as my unforgivable state of singlehood.

"She'll pay you *money,*" she enunciated carefully as if I hadn't understood. As if that was the cause of my pink-cheeked frustration.

"That isn't the point," I insisted, knowing it was useless to explain. Because I'd tried more times than I could remember. How I wished she'd stop making decisions for me and realize I was old enough to live my own life.

Ha.

As if that would ever happen.

She'd been ruling my world since I'd emerged from the birth canal, dressing me in Florence Eiseman and enrolling me in Little Miss Manners classes before I'd graduated from kindergarten, so that five-year-old *moi* would know how to say "please" and "thank you" to well-to-do strangers who doled out extravagant birthday gifts at the lavish parties she'd arranged, ensuring that I'd develop a second nature about what fork to use in posh restaurants, when all I'd ever really wanted was a Happy Meal at McDonald's.

That I was an adult, sitting on the cusp of thirty, meant nothing.

I fiddled with the napkin in my lap, twisting it into tortured knots, determined to keep my voice under control.

I would not let her get to me.

But I was already grinding my teeth.

"You should have had Marilee call me, Mother, because I'll just have to phone her and tell her I can't take the job. I've got enough on my plate as it is."

"Is that so?"

"Yes," I told her definitively, meeting her eyes without flinching, as if that would be the end of it.

Wishful thinking.

She gently touched the nickel-sized freshwater pearl clip on her right ear, a finely plucked brow rising neatly over a clear blue eye, as she said ever so sweetly, "I'm told that Molly O'Brien's doing very well over at Terry Costa. They've had her cutting patterns, but I believe they're considering a few of her designs for next summer's collection."

Ah, geez.

My chest constricted when she brought up Molly's name, because it showed me how dead-set she was on bending my will to suit hers, yet again.

"Oh, and here's some more good news you haven't heard. Little David's been enrolled at St. Mark's this fall. On a full scholarship." She wiggled her slender fingers dismissively. "Don't look so stunned. It was nothing, really. I just had to talk to a few people, press a few buttons to put things in motion."

Talk to a few people? Press a few buttons?

David was Molly's six-year-old son. And St. Mark's was a private boy's prep with a waiting list a mile long. I wondered whose string my mother had yanked—and yanked hard—in order to pull off such a coup. And to think that she'd done something so unbelievable for the child of "that scholarship girl" showed that Cissy had endless surprises up her silk sleeve.

Too many for me to anticipate.

It was maddening. Infuriating. Discombobulating.

And oh-so typical.

I was tempted to wave my twisted napkin in surrender, because I knew—right then and there—she'd scored a TKO. *And the winner is Cissy Blevins Kendricks in the pink Chanel trunks!*

"Wow," I squeaked, surprised that Molly hadn't told me. That is, if Mother had even informed her of the news before springing it on me (probably not). "That was very"— *oh, rats*—"generous of you."

Generous was another talent Mother had honed to perfection. Only she usually expected something in return, particularly when her generosity involved friends of mine. Her good deeds had a way of turning around and smacking me upside the head at the strangest times.

At such moments, I thought of her as a subversive Mother Teresa without the vow of poverty and the ugly outfit.

So what could I do?

I opened my mouth, wanting like hell to say that I wouldn't be blackmailed, that I wasn't going to cave. But the only sound that emerged was a sigh of defeat.

"All right, all right," I moaned. "I'll fix the Web site for Marilee."

"And you'll attend the unveiling of her studio."

It wasn't even a question, not the way she said it. "Yes, I'll go."

Doomed, I tell you.

"Don't pout, Andrea sweetie. I'm sure there'll be eligible men there to make things more bearable for you." She had a familiar twinkle in her eye, the hopeful glint of a nearly sixty-year-old mother who wanted to live to see grandchildren.

Eligible men?

Good God, not this again, too?

I felt a headache begin its gentle throbbing at my temples.

It didn't seem to bother her that I'd been seeing someone steadily. A fledgling defense lawyer named Brian Malone who worked for the firm that handled all Mother's affairs. It was clear we were moving too slowly to suit her. I mean, it *had* been several months and my third left finger was still bare. Which Mother assumed made me fair game for her insufferable matchmaking.

"I'm not looking for eligible men at the moment," I reminded her. "Does the name 'Malone' ring any bells?"

"Not the kind of bells I'd like to hear," she said dolefully, and I was surprised she didn't start humming Wagner's "Wedding March" to rub it in.

Subtle.

"How fickle can you be?" I asked, knowing the answer already. *Very.* "I mean, you're the one who threw us together, remember? And you liked Brian well enough then."

"Darling, you've got it wrong. I like Mr. Malone very much . . ."

"But?" I prodded.

She sighed, giving me a very motherly look of concern. "But I don't like that he's taking advantage of you."

"Taking advantage?" What on earth was she talking about? Brian didn't borrow money from me. He had his own job, his own apartment, paid his bills on time (so far as I knew), and hadn't broken the law lately.

She glanced around, before bending nearer the table and lowering her voice. "Penny George tells me she's seen Mr. Malone's red car parked in front of your place. *Overnight.*"

Penny George was one of my elderly neighbors, a busy-body who served on one of Mother's church committees. I rolled my eyes. "Doesn't she have anything better to do than spy on me? It's none of her business besides."

"But it is mine, because you're my daughter." Cissy sighed again in that disappointed way of hers. "I thought you were smarter than that, Andrea. Surely you realize that men won't buy the cow if they can get the milk for free."

"For God's sake, Mother." Not that tired old analogy.

"Do you really want to drag God into this, sweetie? Because I don't think he'd approve, either. Nor would your father." She suddenly became fascinated with her wedding band, doing a little finger wiggle so I wouldn't miss it, diamonds gleaming. "Your daddy was a gentleman, Andrea, and I was a good girl. He never would have considered dallying with me, not before our engagement."

Dallying? Is that what she thought Malone was doing? Being ungentlemanly, getting the milk for free, tarnishing my sterling reputation?

Yeesh.

I reminded myself where she was coming from, an era very different from this one, full of traditions that had been trampled in the last few decades. Still, the fact that she was holding me to her impossible standards didn't sit well with me.

I looked her squarely in the face. "Mother, it's the twenty-first century. Queen Victoria is dead. My relationship with Brian is mutual. No one's doing any dallying."

"Is that right?"

"Yes."

She smoothed the napkin in her lap, murmuring, "Free milk is free milk, no matter the century."

I bit the inside of my cheek.

Let it go, Andy, let it go.

"Can we talk about something else?" I begged, because sex was the last thing I wanted to discuss with my mother.

"Something else? Well, hmm, let me see." She drummed her French manicure on the table. "All right, how about an interesting item I read this morning in the *Park Cities Press*?"

Neiman's at NorthPark was having a sale? A-line skirts were out of style? Collagen had been banned by the FDA? Ralph Lauren had been elected governor of New York?

I could hardly wait to hear.

"There was a rather large announcement on the wedding page," she began, cocking her head the way she did when she wanted to study my reaction, like a scientist intent on a petrie dish full of staph infection. "Seems your old friend Cinda Lou Mitchell just got remarried. That's number four, if I'm counting correctly. Amazing how some women can make commitments over and over while others"—she sighed and continued to fiddle with her earring, though her eyes didn't leave my face—"just keep draggin' their feet."

"Please, don't go there again," I moaned, thinking that hot bit of news hardly qualified as a change of subject. Though I realized it was merely her way of reminding me that my former Hockaday classmate—not someone I'd exactly call a "friend"—had managed four weddings and quite a few funerals (including geriatric hubbies number one and two) while I had yet to take a single stroll down the aisle as anything other than a bridesmaid.

"You really need to get out more, Andrea, instead of staying cooped up in your place with your paints and your computer. Practically the only men you ever see are the gas station attendants."

"I use self-serve."

"See what I mean?" She plucked at nonexistent lint on her blouse. "It'd be good for you to go to Marilee's party and meet people."

Meaning, go solo.

Malone-less.

I tossed my battered napkin on the table. "Okay, okay, I'll do it, if it'll make you happy." And settle the score, I nearly added.

Besides, unless I acquiesced, she would continue to torture me with tales of oft'-married, heir-bearing school "chums" with whom I'd purposely lost touch.

"I'd be pleased as punch." Her Cheshire-cat grin beamed across the table. She looked so damned self-assured that I knew she'd never doubted for an instant that I'd crumble under pressure. It was how things worked between us, more often than I wanted to admit.

And so it went.

That lunch was two weeks ago and as fresh in my mind as this morning's breakfast. (A wheat bagel and low-fat cream cheese.)

I scratched an itchy spot on my elbow, thinking maybe, if I did have hives, I could get out of this mess and stay home this evening, curled up with a pizza and Brian Malone.

Though I sensed that Cissy would drag me to Marilee's studio covered in calamine if she had to. It was embarrassing how easily Mother could manipulate me when it suited her, despite my best efforts.

I stared at the invitation to Marilee's party, stuck with a magnet to my refrigerator door. The elaborate creation of calligraphy, tissue paper, and handmade parchment looked out of place beside my grocery list and menus from Take-Out Taxi.

"Sucker," I muttered, shaking my head. "Chicken."

Telling my mother, "no," was a Herculean task. One I seemed to fail at, time and again, no matter what else I accomplished.

Though I knew I shouldn't be too hard on myself.

Cissy Blevins Kendricks wasn't the queen bee of Dallas society for nothing. The woman could make Ebenezer

Scrooge open up his rusty lockbox for one of her many worthy causes. If ever the U.S. government could bottle her powers of persuasion, it would eliminate the need for tanks and bombs and still cause plenty of "shock and awe."

"The gal's got it," as my father used to say.

And now she'd "got" me yet again, doing a job that I wasn't so keen on doing—attending a party I'd rather skip—because I couldn't turn her down.

Oh, and I was already suffering the consequences. Painful ones. From the moment I'd taken on Marilee's web design project, the woman had become a big fat boil on my derriere.

I'd had to put aside my other jobs in order to cater to Marilee and Marilee alone, as she demanded the upgraded site be ready to launch by the gala. I'd been working on it night and day, and I'd just finished the last of the major tweaks. She'd wanted lots of splashy effects, including flash animation and hues outside the "web safe-color palette" that would make it hard for viewers with older browsers to load or read correctly. She'd insisted on pages so full of data that it would've made for slower loading than I would have liked, and it took all of my reserve of tact and patience to work something out with her that seemed do-able to us both. There were times when I wanted to follow in the footsteps of her last six web gurus and quit cold turkey.

In calmer moments, I imagined killing the woman with my bare hands, though I realized I'd have to take a number. From what I'd seen on my visits to Marilee's studio the past few weeks, I wasn't the only one who envisioned her face on the target of a dartboard. She had earned her reputation as a difficult boss, often reaming people out in front of a crowd of others. Though I'd gotten off easy with minor nitpicking, probably because I was the daughter of her only true friend.

Still, I didn't want to extend my duties any longer than I had to. I kept reminding her that my work on her site was only temporary, until she could find a permanent webmaster to take over.

But I had a sinking feeling she wasn't looking too hard for anyone. Not when she'd had six web designers before me, each only lasting a week.

Thank goodness I'd gotten most of what she wanted done, though not all of it, by far. Since she'd insisted on web cams at the party tonight for a live stream, I had to go early and make sure everything was properly set up.

The worst part of it was that I had no one to blame but myself. I could've stood my ground and soundly rejected Cissy's proposal, and I hadn't. It was residual guilt. It had to be. I seemed inclined to do anything to avoid upsetting my mother after breaking her heart years ago, because I didn't want to see that happen again. I couldn't afford it.

God help me.

I'd been eighteen and had declined to go through with my coming out (back when "coming out" had meant *into society* and not *out of the closet,* just to be clear). I'd done it for all the right reasons—because it wasn't what I'd wanted, because my father had so recently passed away, because it had meant so much to her and so little to me— but she still had never fully forgiven me for becoming a debutante dropout.

The aftermath of that catastrophe continued to ripple

through my life, even a dozen years later. I had a feeling it always would.

"*She'll actually pay you, Andrea,*" I mimicked in my best imitation of Cissy's honeyed drawl and, scowling, I pulled open the fridge door to peer inside, scavenging for lunch, or at least something to tide me over until the soiree tonight. I was sure there'd be enough food there to feed every starving philanthropist in Dallas.

I pulled out a banana yogurt and plucked off the foil top, thinking a little food in my belly might brighten my mood. It nearly worked—that and Yo-Yo Ma on my CD player— and I was humming along to Yo-Yo's cello going at *Rhapsody in Blue,* when the phone rang.

I caught the number on my Caller ID as I snatched up the receiver and groaned, "What is it now? Did you betroth me to some Saudi sheik?"

"Andrea, darlin', is that you?"

"Hello, Mother," I started over, jamming a spoonful of Dannon past my lips, mostly because I knew how she despised my talking with my mouth full. "I had a feeling I'd hear from you."

Mother and I had this psychic connection. She always called whenever I felt the least like talking to her.

"Sweetie, do you have food in your mouth?"

"Me? Unh-unh," I lied and swallowed. "Don't worry, I'll be at the party," I assured her through another mouthful of yogurt, knowing that was the reason she'd speed-dialed my number. "I'll even comb my hair and put on a new pair of panties just in case I'm in a pileup and they take my lifeless body to the emergency room. 'Cuz, god help me, if I die in ratty drawers."

"Don't be silly." She didn't even chastise me for being a smart ass. In fact, she seemed altogether too tolerant of my attitude. Which didn't bode well. Something was clearly up. "I'll send the car around for you at eight-thirty."

"I don't need a car, Mother. I'm taking the Jeep."

"You might find it hard to shift gears in the dress you'll be wearing."

"What dress?"

"Well, I was shopping at Highland Park Village and happened to drop by Escada. They'd just gotten in some new things, and this little number just screamed your name from the moment I laid eyes on it. But you'll have to see for yourself. Come over, sweetie, and try it on, though I know it'll fit because they double-checked your measurements with your file at the Bridal Salon at Stanley Korshak."

My file at the Bridal Salon at Stanley Korshak?

What the heck was she babbling about?

For a moment, my mind went blank. Then it hit me like a stucco wall. Cissy had dragged me into the posh shop at the Crescent Atrium when I'd let her prod me into doing a trunk show charity event for a brain injury foundation, two or three years ago. I recall sometime after she'd mentioned having the wedding consultant Nina Nichols Austin hold on to my measurements, "for future reference."

Geez, Louise.

Enough was enough.

"What if I've already got an outfit in mind?" I told her, though I didn't. My closet wasn't exactly loaded with high fashion.

"What outfit?" she prodded. "A pair of sweatpants? Or

something speckled with paint?" She chuckled. "You're a card, darling. You remind me of your father's Aunt Edna who thought she was an opera diva and ended up in a mental hospital in Wichita Falls, singing *Aida* to her padded walls."

I reminded her of an insane (and deceased) great-aunt? Super.

"You'd better hurry, sweetie, I've got a date at the salon in about an hour, so I won't be home much longer."

"Mother, really, I don't need a dress . . . *Mother?*"

The dial tone hummed in my ear.

I swallowed a lump of yogurt and felt it slime its way down my throat to my belly. How had *that* happened?

Unbelievable.

I held the receiver for a moment, simply staring at it, amazed that I'd let myself get snared in yet another of Mother's webs. You'd think I'd have known better, but it was like *Groundhog Day,* the movie with Bill Murray, where the same things occurred over and over again. I'd say "like a broken record," only nobody had records anymore, just CDs with antiskid mechanisms.

Frustration bubbled inside me, and I seriously considered dialing Mother back and telling her exactly what she could do with the designer dress and chauffeured car, but that was the wrong approach entirely. I had to deal with this directly, take a stand for myself, like Daddy had always advised.

"Be a woman, not a weenie."

Okay, my father hadn't exactly put it that way, but I knew that's what he'd meant.

This was one of those situations that called for the Band-Aid approach. Better to rip it off in one quick yank than tug a little bit at a time.

I turned off Yo-Yo, grabbed my keys and headed down to Mother's house on Beverly Drive.

Chapter 3

 Ah, summer in Dallas.

Not exactly tourist season.

The days averaged a hundred degrees. Cloudless blue skies stretched from one horizon to the next, providing no relief from the blistering rays. Baking asphalt sent waves of heat simmering like a mirage. The sidewalks emptied, turning neighborhoods into ghost towns. Folks with any sense stayed inside and donned cardigans over T-shirts, the AC set to "arctic," not budging until the first cool front in October.

I tried to tell myself that it wasn't really *that* hot.

Mind over matter, see?

It worked for all of about a minute, until I touched the door handle of my Jeep, shimmering beneath the sun in the shadeless parking lot. I muttered, "ouch, ouch," under my breath as I got inside as fast as possible, still not prepared for the unbearably hot air that smothered me like an invisible electric blanket.

While the AC in my Wrangler took its time to cool off,

the back of my bare legs stuck to the leather and trickles of
sweat swam down my back. The steering wheel scorched
my skin, so I couldn't bear to touch it with more than the
tips of two fingers. I was already longing for Christmas,
praying for an early frost.

As if.

Maybe tunes would help, I thought and turned on the radio, bypassing ads and chatter. After some poking around,
I found an oldie by Alanis and sung at the top of my lungs,
trying to take my mind off the perspiration sticking my
shirt to my back.

"Life is a funny thing . . . isn't it ironic, don't you think,"
I crooned off-key and gazed out the windshield at the familiar route, though there wasn't much in the way of
scenery going south on Hillcrest from Belt Line, merely
row after row of brick ranch houses, high board-on-board
fences, occasional strip malls and shopping centers, gas
stations, a deserted park (it was even too hot for kids to
play).

It took a good twenty minutes before I rolled into Highland Park, one of the city's older residential areas and un-
questionably one of its loveliest, with stately homes that
reeked of old money, clipped green lawns with discreet in-
ground sprinkler systems that went off in the wee hours to
conserve water, and trees tall enough to provide shade, the
thick boughs stretching above cobbled driveways.

It was no wonder HP had been nicknamed "the Bubble."
It sat apart from the real world, from the images of crime
and poverty and war on the six o'clock news. Everything
was lush and beautiful—property and people—even in the
hellish Texas heat. I had yet to see a flower wilt or a Park

Cities woman sweat. Maybe part of the reason I'd never truly felt like I'd belonged. I wasn't near perfect enough, too quirky, too prone to human error.

I was the deb-to-be who'd worn Army fatigues and pink high-topped sneakers to afternoon tea at the Mansion on Turtle Creek. I was the quietly rebellious child who had preferred to paint rather than attend tennis lessons at the club, who'd left the state to attend art school in Chicago instead of going through rush at a proper Texas college, never to end up with my mother's treasured Pi Phi arrow pin.

"I'll just have to put it away and save it for my granddaughter," she'd insisted, which didn't exactly ease my conscience.

I squirmed in my seat the closer I got to the house on Beverly, and I realized that driving back to Mother's sometimes felt less like a coming home and more like a return to Cissy's turf.

It's not that I wasn't welcome—because I was, always—but rather I was a little like Cinderella in reverse. If I didn't escape back to North Dallas and my cozy condo before midnight, Mother might wield her magic wand and turn my Jeep into a Beamer, my flip-flops into spiky Manolo Blahniks, and my Operation Kindness No Kill Shelter T-shirt into a Carolyne Roehm gown.

I shuddered at the thought of it.

There were moments when I couldn't help but wonder if the hospital hadn't made a mix-up when I was born, and if a true Highland Park princess hadn't been raised in a modest home in Grand Prairie, all the while wondering why she dreamed of Gorham silver patterns and cocktail dresses with shoes dyed to match, while I lived in a 1920s-era mansion, dreaming of how to get away from exactly that.

There'd been no switch, of course, and I'd never really believed it.

Despite our bipolar existence, I did love my mother, and she loved me. I'd never doubted that for a minute.

I actually didn't mind going home once in a while. I likened it to staying in touch with my roots, so I would never forget the girl-trying-to-find-herself I'd once been and the independent woman I'd become. There was something about returning to the old house on Beverly that reminded me how lucky I was, despite the pains of growing up in the shadow of Cissy Kendricks.

The place had been my refuge back then. Strangely enough, I knew it had been Mother's as well and still was. A respite from her endless calendar of bridge clubs, Junior League, church, and charities. She and my father had bought the property soon after they'd married, when Cissy was fresh out of SMU with her "MRS" degree and Daddy with his MBA, someday to take over my Paw Paw's drug company.

I was raised there, had celebrated eighteen birthdays inside those French-papered walls before I'd moved out after prep school and headed to the Windy City. Four years away from Dallas—with only holiday visits home—had given me much more than I could ever put into words. I'd found a sense of who I was, the kind of person I was meant to be. I'd learned to be comfortable in my own skin without feeling the pressure to follow in my mother's—or father's—footsteps.

When I'd finally returned to Texas for reasons that only

partially concerned Cissy, I had lost much of my Southern twang but gained my own identity. No one in Chicago had cared that I was a Blevins Kendricks. No one had known about my trust fund. "Liberating" is the only word to describe it.

I never wanted to lose that, no matter what.

Despite the time I'd spent away from Mother's—both living in Chicago and in North Dallas—nothing much had changed. I'd thought at one point she might sell her place, but ultimately she couldn't bear to leave. "Too many memories," she'd told me, ones she wasn't ready to relinquish.

A part of me was relieved.

There was still so much of my father there, especially in his book-lined study that Mother hadn't touched except to allow for weekly cleanings. The leather of his desk chair smelled of his Cuban cigars and of the Old Spice he used to wear because I'd given it to him for Christmas so often when I was a child.

He'd hung several paintings I'd done in high school— Impressionist images of Mother's garden—on the wall behind his desk, bookending an original John Singer Sargent landscape. That simple act had made me burst with love for him, thinking that my art had meant as much to him as it did to me. I would never, ever forget that or anything else about him.

He'd been everything.

"Follow your heart," he used to tell me, so often that I repeated it in my head like a mantra whenever I needed a boost. "It's your life, pumpkin, so live it. Don't try to be someone you're not."

Someone, he'd meant, like my mother.

If I stood in his study, closed my eyes and breathed in, I could still imagine he hadn't left my life so abruptly, that he was with me.

I liked to believe that he was.

I imagined, too, that his spirit watched over Cissy so she was never alone. Okay, I'll admit that was one of the reasons I'd come home. Except for distant—and rarely discussed—family out of state, I was all she had left in the world. I worried about her, hated to imagine she felt lonely or neglected, regardless of how many people she surrounded herself with day to day.

Mother kept a small staff on hand, only a few of whom lived in, like her social secretary, the indispensable Sandy Beck. Cissy's dearest friend, if truth were told. Sandy was my fairy godmother and Mary Poppins rolled into one, having spent a good part of the thirty-odd years she'd been in Cissy's employ watching over me.

Beyond Sandy, there was the housekeeper, a part-time cook, the gardening and landscaping crew, and Cissy's sometime-driver (when she didn't feel like taking the wheel of her champagne-hued Lexus). Most came and went; keeping schedules that afforded them time to be with their own families.

I remember Mother remarking that the world had gone to hell in a handbasket when her former staff had started retiring—or dying off—and she'd had to replace them with a younger generation of employees who weren't about to give body and soul to tend to the needs of a widowed Dallas socialite.

"It's a different world," she'd said to me, and I'd agreed that it was. Some of it for the better, some not.

Occasionally, I found myself wondering if Mother and her ilk would ever completely adjust to the twenty-first century when they seemed so inclined to cling to a past where there weren't so many gray areas, where men behaved like men and women like Southern belles who knew the importance of finger bowls and never wore white shoes after Labor Day. (Though a belle wearing white go-go boots on the Dallas Cowboys' kick-line during football season was forgiven the faux pas.)

In some ways, I likened Cissy and her posse to the incredibly resilient Texas tree roach. No matter how much time passed or how many superpowered bug sprays came on the market, the critters adapted. Though I doubt they'd appreciate the comparison (Mother's friends, I mean, not the cockroaches).

Regardless, it made me smile, and, momentarily, I forgot the soaring temperature and my damp T-shirt.

The Jeep's old AC started spewing cold air by the time I turned onto Beverly Drive, though, at that point, I was beyond redemption. My face was pink and slick, and my bangs stuck to my brow. I hoped that Sandy had a pitcher of fresh lemonade in the fridge. It would take at least two glasses to revive me.

The thought made me want to move faster, but I found my progress impeded by a huge moving van that clogged the street, giving cars a narrow strip in which to pass around it. Adding to the congestion was a camera crew from Fox News.

Funny.

I raised my eyebrows.

It's not like I'd never seen an orange Atlas truck on Bev-

erly Drive before—or something akin to it—though it usually signified that someone had died and the heirs were
loading up the merchandise for auction. The folks who
resided in this part of Highland Park often stayed for gen-
erations. It wasn't a place for transients, other than the occasional pro sports figures who came and went, largely
ignored.

So I was curious about who was coming as much as who
was going, particularly if the new homeowners warranted
TV coverage.

Cissy hadn't mentioned anything about a neighbor moving out. I was less sure of who lived where since I'd left
home over a decade ago, but my mother had kept track.
She not only knew names but also who was related to
whom, who worked where or owned what company, and,
most important, who had eligible sons or grandsons of
marrying age.

Never let it be said that Mother didn't have her priorities
in order.

I pulled slowly past the enormous truck and the media
van, catching a glimpse of the movers drenched in perspiration, a dark-skinned woman with her head tied in a red
kerchief hovering at the massive front door of the residence, swinging her arms as if she were directing traffic. A
reporter with microphone in hand and a fellow with a video
camera wedged on his shoulder followed the woman's
every move as if she were a film star.

I squinted hard at her, reassured it wasn't Oprah. Otherwise, she didn't look familiar. Though I didn't watch
enough television to be sure she wasn't some kind of
celebrity. With all the reality shows hitting the airwaves,

she might've been the sole "Survivor" or someone who'd found love and a million dollars by smooching in a hot tub with a bevy of bachelors in front of the nation.

With a twist of the wheel, I swept up the curving drive that led to Mother's house, feeling anxiety flutter within my chest as I parked in front of the whitewashed terracotta lions that stood guard on either side of the front door.

For a moment, I sat in the car, fussing with my bangs and wiping sweat from my upper lip. My usual delay tactics.

Finally, I shut off the engine, pocketed the keys, and got out, ambling toward the carved front doors. I pressed a finger to the bell, hearing its clear chimes, and rested a shoulder against yellow limestone, the surface smooth and cool against my flushed skin.

I practiced saying, "No, thank you, Mother, but I don't need no stinkin' dress" several times before the door swung inward, and Sandy Beck stood smiling behind it, her lined face crinkling merrily beneath the cap of gray hair. Despite the soaring mercury, she wore an ever-present cardigan. This one was yellow with tiny pearl buttons.

"Andy," she said and opened her arms. "Always good to see you, sweetheart. Cissy said you might drop by."

Might drop by?

"I was summoned," I confessed before getting enveloped in a bear hug. Sandy rubbed my back, and I breathed in the scent of roses. "Seems she's intent on dressing me tonight for Marilee's bash."

Sandy tugged me into the foyer, frosty with conditioned air, and closed the door behind us. "Well, she does have good taste."

"She makes me feel like her toy poodle."

"Oh, please, Andy, you know Cissy would never allow a dog in her house. All that chewing and shedding."

I made a face.

"You're her only child, sweet pea"—my fairy god-mother wrapped an arm around me, walking me toward the curving staircase that would take me upstairs to Mother's room, where she held court—"so she can't help but . . . well . . ."

"Meddle?" I finished for her when she hesitated, keeping my voice low for my own sake. Mother had ears like a bat.

Sandy chuckled and gave me a squeeze. "I was going to say 'dote on you.' Now go on up and face the music. When you're done, I'll have a glass of lemonade waiting for you in the kitchen. You look like you could use a cold drink."

"What say we do the lemonade first?"

"Your mother's got an appointment at the salon, so you'll be down soon, I promise." Sandy gave me a gentle swat on the rump. "Scoot," she said, then shouted up ahead of me, "Andrea's here!"

"As if she doesn't know," I muttered, listening to Sandy chuckle as she shuffled off to the kitchen. Cissy had prob-ably stood at her sitting room window, watching for my Jeep.

Exhaling slowly, I paused and stood at the base of the stairwell, glancing up.

Let's get this over with, I thought and grabbed hold of the banister as I ascended.

My gaze fell to the worn pattern of the Oriental runner underfoot before I noticed the chips in my pale green-painted toenails. I hated that I was sticky and less than per-fectly groomed. I felt rumpled enough around Mother when I was combed and pressed, but felt absolutely frump-ish now, sweating through the armpits of my T-shirt.

I hesitated on the landing, lifting my chin and telling myself to buck up. I didn't have to stay any longer than it took to glimpse whatever dress she'd picked out for me, tell her "thank you but no thank you" firmly but sweetly, and be on my merry way.

Piece of cake.

The boards creaked as I reached the second floor, and my gaze swung left, settling on the door to my father's study. It was the first room I had to pass, so I poked my head in for good measure, inhaling his lingering scent and looking around me, at the leather-bound volumes on the book-shelves, at the enormous desk and empty chair behind it.

"Hey, Daddy," I whispered. "Wish you were here."

Boy, did I ever. My father had always been the buffer be-tween us. He could smooth things over like aloe on a burn.

"*Andrea?*"

My mother's drawl floated up the hallway.

"Darlin'? Is that you?"

"Yes, it's me," I replied sotto voce. Then I took yet another deep breath, straightened my shoulders, and headed toward her suite of rooms, my thongs slapping on the runner.

When I entered her sitting room, I saw her pink damask-covered chaise empty save for a folded newspaper. Filmy sheers muted the sun so that only an ethereal glow touched the antiques and watered silk paper that covered the walls.

"I'm in here, sweetie."

Her boudoir.

The inner sanctum.

When I was a child, it had been a "no-no" to go into

Mother's room uninvited. Though I used to sneak inside when she was out with Daddy. I'd go into her dressing room and fiddle with her cosmetics. Then I'd try on her shoes and parade in front of the mirrors, pretending to be a high society lady. Pretending to be Cissy.

But I'd grown up to be someone else entirely, hadn't I?

Life is a funny thing, indeed.

I forced my feet to move and crossed the threshold.

"Well, there you are."

"In the flesh," I said and smiled, catching sight of my damp and disheveled self in a gilt-framed mirror and wishing I hadn't.

Cissy approached, looking crisp in linen slacks and a short-sleeved blouse with a string of pearls peeking out of the opened collar, brown croc belt at her waist and matching croc slingbacks on her feet. She had not a hair out of place, the blond chin-length bob brushed back from her slim brow to frame her carefully made-up face, which broke into a smile as she approached with arms outstretched.

I tipped my cheek as she swooped in for a kiss, sweeping left to right, barely a butterfly's touch of her lips on my skin. Air kisses. Her specialty. At least I knew she wouldn't be leaving lipstick marks. That was for amateurs.

She backed away a step and clasped her hands together, looking me over. Her mouth parted, as if sorely tempted to comment, but I was pretty sure she wouldn't. Not if she wanted me to stick around.

"I'll fetch the dress," she finally said and vanished into the labyrinth that was her closet.

As I waited for her to return, I looked around me, inhaling Joy with every breath.

Mother loved pink, and her bedroom reflected it. Drapes of pearly pink damask, an embroidered raw silk duvet that softly shimmered; and buried beneath, pink Egyptian-cotton sheets with impossibly high thread counts rendering them soft as a baby's bottom. The furniture was antique, mostly French, the wallpaper imported, and gently worn Chinese silk rugs smothered the floor, so exquisitely done that you could hardly tell which side was up and which was down.

Such a far cry from my own bedroom, full of flea-market finds and sale-priced irregular sheet sets from Bed Bath & Beyond.

Atop her bureau sat a cluster of silver-framed photographs, and I went over to look at them, as if I hadn't seen them a dozen times before. Most of the shots were black-and-white chronicles of my parents' time together. Cissy and Daddy on the beach in Key West. At the palace in Monaco, a villa on the French Riviera, a yacht on the Mediterranean. In London and Kenya. Posing, laughing, smiling, dancing. There were several of Baby Andrea, cradled in Daddy's arms, him gazing down in adoration. One of Cissy and me, when I couldn't have been more than five. We were dressed identically in blue coats with big black buttons. Mother had on white gloves and patent leather pumps. I wore bobby socks with lace and patent leather Mary Janes. We each had wide blue headbands smoothing back our hair.

So long ago.

And what felt like a galaxy far, far away.

I ran a finger across our faces and felt a lump in my throat.

"Here we are." I heard the swish of plastic and my mother's voice as she swept back into the bedroom. *"Violà!"*

I'd imagined—okay, hoped for—a horrible monstrosity with yards of chiffon and ruffles, garish and overblown, something I'd have no trouble rejecting.

I turned around to see her fussing with a ripple of color spread atop the pink duvet. Tentatively, I stepped closer to see a short dress with skinny straps and gently ruffled skirt covered in tiny sequins. Deep pink, orange, and green splashed across the design like a painting by Monet.

Double rats.

It was gorgeous.

I felt my resistance weaken.

Stay strong, I told myself. *Be tough.*

"It's Escada," Mother reminded me, as if I'd forgotten our earlier conversation. She had her hands pressed together beneath her chin, almost prayerful. "Do you like it?"

Beside the dress she'd set a matching pink bag and heart-shaped pink slingbacks, also Escada, and I figured I could live for a couple months on what she'd shelled out for the ensemble.

"It's all . . . beautiful," I told her honestly, "but I . . . no, I can't." I was actually stammering. "It . . . it's way too much . . ."

"No, it's not," she interrupted, coming up behind me and snaking an arm around my waist. "Nothing's ever too much when it comes to my little girl. Let me do this for you, Andrea. Let your old mother have some fun, all right? I'd rather spend it on you now than have you give it all away to animal charities when I'm gone."

"Well, if you put it that way."

I stared at the lovely creation on her bed and nibbled on my lip, telling myself to be firm, to remember the reason I'd driven down here.

"Try it on," she urged, and I felt a little like Snow White being cajoled into biting the poisoned apple.

"Oh . . . no, I couldn't . . ."

"Sure you can, baby."

"But I'm all sweaty."

"Then stand in front of the full-length mirror, and we'll improvise," she instructed, nudging me in that direction. So I went, waiting with my arms at my sides until she'd removed the dress from its hanger and pressed it into my hands. I held it up against me, while Mother fiddled with my hair, drawing it off my neck in a makeshift chignon.

She leaned her cheek against mine. She smelled softly of perfume and powder. "You'll look like a princess," she whispered.

I felt like a child playing dress-up.

This wasn't right. This wasn't me.

And I thought of the girl in the tiny house in Grand Prairie—the one I'd been switched with at birth in my fantasy—and I figured she'd kill to wear Escada.

It was just one night, after all. Would it really be such a terrible thing?

Tipping my head, I studied my image, the sequins gently glistening in the light, little beacons screaming, "Take me, take me!"

"Well, what do you think?" she asked. "Isn't it to die for?"

My self-restraint shot to hell, I found myself saying,

"*Yes, yes, yes,*" like one of those libidinous shampooers on the Herbal Essence commercials. "Thank you, Mother," I further gushed, instead of telling her, "no dice."

Sucker, I chided myself. *Wimp.*

It was damned pathetic.

I did stand firm on something, however, convincing her that I didn't want her car to pick me up. I had to be at the studio early, in order to check on the web cams, and I was certain Mother wouldn't want to arrive ahead of schedule for the event. In her world, that was a fate worse than death.

So I was off the hook on that count. No chauffeured car for me.

Score one for the deb dropout.

Okay, a wee one.

In my ongoing battle with Mother, even the smallest victories counted.

Chapter 4

 Cissy headed off for her appointment at the Plaza Park Salon, where they'd primp and pamper her in readiness for Marilee's studio unveiling, and I sat with Sandy on the glassed-in sun porch with a great view of the terrace and rose garden, drinking lemonade and second-guessing my decision to keep Mother's gift.

"Am I analyzing this too much?" I asked Sandy between ice-cold sips. "With all that's going on in the world, it seems silly to worry about a dress . . . and a pair of shoes and a handbag . . . but I can't help feeling like I've been bribed."

"Well, sweet pea, you have." Sandy patted my knee, her eyes bright beneath soft folds of skin. I do believe she was enjoying this. "You surely have. And it won't be the last time as long as your mother's alive and kicking."

"So should I give it all back?" I heard the reluctance in my voice and blushed, because I knew she'd heard it, too. So much for standing firm on my convictions.

"Listen, Andy, I can honestly say that the rest of the world isn't going to care one way or another what you wear to Marilee Mabry's party. But if it makes you feel bad then don't do it. Leave everything upstairs for Cissy to find when she gets back."

I wrinkled my brow and pondered that one.

How disconcerted would I really feel if I donned a designer dress tonight? Who would I betray if I did? Cissy had reared me in fancy labels. It had been my choice to stop wearing them. Would it truly make a difference in the scheme of things? Throw the cosmos off-balance? Ruin my karma for life?

It wasn't like putting on leather pants with a PETA T-shirt.

Or serving blubber-burgers at a Save the Whales rally.

Right?

Sandy read the struggle in my face and tapped my leg more insistently. "Land sakes, child, stop agonizing over this. Rejecting that darned dress and making your mother unhappy will not solve anything, and you know it. So be a good girl, put on the pretty dress, and have yourself some harmless fun."

"It's as simple as that?"

"Yes."

Harmless fun.

"Okay," I said, because she made sense. I was making far too much of this. Some mothers baked apple pies. Mine went shopping with a vengeance.

"Glad that's settled. Now we can discuss less difficult topics, like peace in the Middle East and lack of funding for the arts."

"Ha ha."

Sandy grinned and tugged her cardigan tighter as the vents began to hum, blasting us with frigid air.

I reveled in the gooseflesh on my arms, deciding it was a far, far better thing to be cold than damp with sweat. With a contented grunt, I settled back in the cushioned wicker chair—a true Haywood Wakefield, part of the set clustered around me—and I gazed out at the gardens.

The riot of colors cheered me, as they always did. They'd been concocted by a hoity-toity landscape architect ages ago and were still Mother's pride and joy. The yard-workers must've been around recently as the hedges were neatly trimmed, the grass mowed and edges clipped, so that everything appeared crisp and symmetrical. I wondered how the crew avoided sunstroke, laboring beneath the unforgiving Texas sun.

Which led me to consider the musclemen I'd seen dragging furniture from the huge orange truck into the house I'd passed on my way to Mother's.

Who'd be crazy enough to move in the middle of summer?

"Did one of Mother's neighbors die?" I said.

"What on earth?" Sandy blinked. "Where did that come from, Andy?"

"The eighteen-wheeler up the street."

Recognition dawned on her age-softened features. "Oh, yes, that."

The cool way with which she'd dispatched that nonanswer made my antennae go up.

"So what's the story?" I cocked an ear and waited.

"There's no story, just new neighbors." Sandy shrugged, brushing me off, which only proved that I was right.

Something was up.

I leaned forward, propping elbows on knees. "If it's nothing, then why was there a camera crew from Fox News hanging around on the lawn? Is a rock star moving in? It's not a Kennedy, is it?"

"A Kennedy?" She chuckled. "Land sakes, Andy, but you've got the most vivid imagination."

Like I hadn't heard that a couple hundred times before, dating way back to my earliest school days when I'd drawn a Picasso-esque image of my third grade teacher on the blackboard during recess. (No, she wasn't flattered.) "So what's the big secret? And you still haven't told me who died."

"There's no secret." She fiddled with the bottom button on her cardigan, pushing it into the buttonhole then out again. "As for the other, Cissy must have mentioned to you that Ethel Etherington passed several months back?"

That was news to me.

"I don't think she did," I said, though admittedly there were times when I only listened to my mother with half an ear, if that.

"Well, she's gone, bless her heart."

"I'm sorry to hear it," I told her honestly, but I wasn't surprised. "So, old lady Etherington finally went boots up, huh? I thought she'd live forever. What was she? A hundred-fifty?"

"Andy." That earned me a stern look.

"At least a hundred?"

"Ninety-eight."

"Is that all?"

She wagged a finger at me.

Really, to call Ethel Etherington "old" was like saying

Methuselah was "getting up there." Even when I was a kid,
Mrs. Etherington had seemed ancient. I don't remember
much else about her, except that Mother had her over for
tea occasionally, usually with other church ladies who'd
dressed in gloves and hats and pearls, like someone's
maiden aunts. If there had been a Mr. Etherington, I'd
never met him. Maybe she'd been widowed early on,
which would account for the "missus" in front of her name.
I'd never heard her called anything else. I do know there'd
been no children.

"So when did the house go on the market?"

"Well, it took a while for it to get through probate. I
think it was finally put up for sale about three weeks ago. It
sold quick as a jackrabbit. Low mortgage rates, hot market
and all that."

"Who bought that old castle?" I asked, because that's
what it looked like, complete with turrets and a massive
carved front door that seemed big enough to allow a contingent of horsemen through. As a kid, I used to imagine it
was Camelot and that King Arthur lived behind its limestone façade.

"It's a nice couple from Tyler who'd been subletting an
apartment until now."

"Couple, as in a man and a woman?" I asked, because
you never knew these days and maybe that accounted for
Sandy's reluctance to broach the subject.

"For heaven's sake . . . yes, a man and a woman. Married and everything. There's also a young woman living
with them, a daughter who's about your age."

"Have you met them?"

"Not yet, no."

"But mother has?" I couldn't imagine Cissy not poking her nose into someone else's business, especially when they were fresh meat. Besides, someone had to be feeding Sandy her information.

"She has indeed."

Ah, just as I'd thought.

So Cissy had met the new neighbors. Still, if there'd been anything truly scandalous about them, surely she would've filled me in.

Or not.

Cissy could be closemouthed when she wanted to be. When it mattered. Though she could toss off a catty remark as well as anyone, with a blink of a false-lashed eye, she could become a human Fort Knox, protecting reputations as weighty as bars of gold.

Sandy was another story. I could always get her to open up if I badgered enough.

"So what did Mother have to say about them?"

"Well, really, she didn't stay there long, just took over some of her roses, because, of course, they're still settling in, as you saw. They'd had their things in storage, but the second truck was delayed. It finally showed up this morning."

Nothing yet explained the camera crew. And in Big D, the media didn't turn out unless there were bona fide celebrities involved. Or two-headed cattle.

"What's so special about them? Are they on the lam?" I asked. "Do they have leprosy? Dear God, they're not Yankees?"

"No, they're not lepers or Yankees, my word." She fidgeted, plucked at the pillow beside her. "Cissy says they're lovely people. Which is why your mother doesn't want us making a fuss." She sighed. "The Park Cities paper sent over a reporter yesterday, knocking on doors and asking how folks feel about having a family of color move into Highland Park. It's ridiculous, really."

Family of color?

The phrase sounded so odd, so antiquated, that I nearly laughed aloud.

I asked with mock gravity, "So what color are they? Magenta? Just tell me they're not vermilion. Or ochre, God forbid. Those ochre folks look so jaundiced."

"Don't be a smart aleck." She narrowed her brow. "They happen to be African American."

Ah-ha.

I flashed back to the woman standing in the enormous doorway, gesturing at the moving men, and I realized that I'd likely glimpsed the homeowner.

"So the media's interested in these people, not because they're celebrities, but because they're not white?"

Sandy clucked. "Crazy, isn't it? They're regular folk, Andy, just like anybody else. Their only distinction is bein' the first black family to own a home in Highland Park since the 1920s when the neighborhood was legally segregated, or so that reporter told me. An overeager pup named Kevin Snodgrass. Probably thinks he's gonna get the Pulitzer."

Legally segregated?

Wow.

I didn't know much about the neighborhood's history, especially going back that far. But I had noticed the people I saw tended to be pretty monochromatic, so I wasn't surprised at the revelation. But it bothered me nonetheless.

"Yeah, crazy," I said.

It was the twenty-first century, and I wanted to feel like things had come a long way, baby. And they had, I guess, in many respects.

Maybe not so much in others.

"So did Cissy talk to that reporter . . . Mr. Snake in the Grass?"

"Snodgrass."

"Yes, him. Did she give him a piece of her mind?"

Sandy shot me a Mona Lisa smile. "What do you think?"

Oh, the possibilities were endless. "Did she kick his booty out and slam the door in his face?"

Sandy laughed. "More like she told him it was about time they had some fresh blood on Beverly and new neighbors were welcome on her street so long as they paid their taxes, kept up their yard, and didn't kill anyone."

I pushed my hair off my neck. "She didn't say that, did she?"

"Her very words."

"*Oh, my gawd,*" I groaned, thinking the "didn't kill anyone" bit would probably end up in a headline. But I was proud of her, in a warped kind of way.

"Cissy said she likes Dr. Taylor very much . . . Beth's her name . . . her husband Richard is an investment banker . . . so much so that she's asked her over to the Dallas Diet Club meeting on Saturday afternoon."

"You're kidding?" I said, because that was a headline-maker in itself.

The Dallas Diet Club wasn't anything like it sounded. It had nothing to do with calorie counting, exercise, or weight loss. Several times each month, a small group of

my mother's friends gathered at the house of one, where
cards were played, gossip shared, and decadent desserts
devoured; goodies prepared by the finest pastry chefs in
Dallas, usually called "Death by Chocolate" or something
equally lethal-sounding. Cissy and her pals rarely let a new
member in, so this Dr. Beth Taylor didn't know how privi-
leged she was. There was practically a waiting list of
women who wanted to join. Had Ethel Etherington's demise opened up a spot? Because it pretty much took a
member's death for that to happen.

"So Mother's hosting?"

"Yes." Sandy didn't exactly look thrilled. "Which
wouldn't be any more bother than usual, except I'm told
that Marilee Mabry wants to bring her cameras and film
the Diet Club meeting for a segment on her show. She'd
like to feature some of the recipes, and your mother thinks
it's a grand idea."

"You're joking?"

"I wish I were."

Marilee was bringing a crew to tape at Mother's?

I sat with my mouth open, already envisioning the chaos
sure to ensue.

Marilee bossing around women who took orders from
no one. People tromping on Cissy's priceless silk rugs, sitting on her antique furniture, setting up lights, and rearranging rooms in order to get the best shot.

It was a disaster waiting to happen.

Oh, to be a fly on the wall. . . .

"Would you like sit on the sidelines with me, sweet
pea?" Sandy asked, and a slow smile tugged at her lips. "I
might need help with crowd control."

"You know, Sandy, I just may do that," I replied, returning her grin.

Might just take some of the sting out of having to attend the party this evening. Speaking of which—I checked my watch—I had to get rolling.

So I thanked Sandy for the lemonade and the reassurances, picked up the bags from Escada and headed home before my Jeep turned into a pumpkin-shaped BMW.

Chapter 5

 A better part of the day had vanished by the time I parked in front of my condo and walked through the front door.

So much for a quick trip to Beverly.

My goal to return empty-handed hadn't exactly panned out either, I mused, as I hung up the cocktail dress in its zipper bag on my closet door. I plopped down on the edge of my bed with the shopping bag and spent the next few minutes plucking out scads of tissue paper before unearthing the slingbacks and trying them on. I stared down at my feet, dangling over the edge, and a drawn-out sigh escaped me.

At least I wouldn't have to repaint my toenails. No one would see the chipped green while I was wearing these babies. I didn't even want to think of how much they'd cost. Nope, I wasn't going to dwell on how many bags of Iams I could donate to Operation Kindness with what Mother had spent to dress me up as the proper little heiress, suitable for public consumption.

It would be a completely guilt-free evening.

I'd spent the drive back to my condo convincing myself that, as long as I was going to have to suffer through this damned party, I might as well look good. Or as good as I got without being dragged to the salon with Mother, which was definitely not on my agenda this afternoon or any afternoon in the foreseeable future.

If I needed a trim, I either paid $9.99 at Fantastic Sam's or got out the kitchen scissors, which might be why my shoulder-length 'do often ended up in a ponytail.

It drove Cissy nuts.

Maybe part of the reason I did it.

I saw the red light blinking on the Caller ID, indicating voice mail messages, but I wasn't going to deal with anything more until I'd had a shower. I kicked off my party shoes and peeled my shirt off for starters, dropping my sweaty clothes in a pile on the floor.

The water felt great after the sticky hundred-degree air I'd been swimming through, and I stayed beneath the showerhead until my skin pruned, letting the lukewarm spray of water wash over me. I emptied my mind of all the thoughts that had accumulated along with the grime, and, by the time I stepped onto the bath mat and wrapped myself in a towel, I felt better about myself and the world in general. Enough to smile and hum a favorite Def Leppard tune as I pulled a comb through my hair and wiggled a Q-tip in my ears.

Amazing how something as simple as a shower can make you feel like a new woman, but it had and I did. So much so that I actually started to think that tonight might not be so dreadful, after all.

I dared to check my voice mail while I let my hair air-dry a little, finding a "call me" message from Brian Malone followed by four panicked rants from Marilee, wondering when I'd be arriving, asking if I'd remembered to do this, that, or the other. I pressed the "3" key to delete the lot of it, and then I dialed Brian's number.

"Hey, Kendricks," he said, picking up on the second ring, knowing it was me thanks to his own Caller ID. Little chance of anonymity in our brave new world, huh? "You still planning on going to that shindig tonight?" he grilled me right off the bat. "Or can we do dinner at Dragonfly and a movie after?"

Shindig?

It sounded like a Midwesterner's idea of how Texans talked, though Malone *was* a Midwesterner, I reminded myself. He hailed from St. Louis, Missouri, the "Show Me State," which explained why he always had to see something to believe it. He was a budding defense attorney with the prominent and enormous firm of Abramawitz, Reynolds, Goldberg, and Hunt, better known as ARGH around these parts. They covered the law from all angles: corporate, criminal, wills, and divorce. It was a one-stop shop for well-to-do Texans who found themselves in need of expert counsel.

The brain trust at ARGH had handled the legal work for Daddy's pharmaceutical company, on whose board Mother remained to this day. J.D. Abramawitz was a close friend of Cissy's and had arranged for Brian Malone to take on Molly's case when my friend had been accused of murder. As I'd later found out, Mother had requested Brian handle the matter in order to throw us together, hoping for a love match.

While there were definitely sparks, it wasn't a full-blown fire. Not the kind that made either of us want to say, "I do."

Not yet (much to Mother's chagrin).

We'd both agreed not to rush into anything serious, though we were sure having a good time doing the getting-better-acquainted routine.

It was definitely the most successful of any of Cissy's crazy matchmaking schemes, the vast majority ranking right up there with Hurricane Andrew in terms of disaster quotient. Like the time she'd set me up with the son of an oil magnate and GWH (Great White Hunter) whose fun idea for a date was to go to the shooting range. While he'd squinted an eye at the man-shaped target and squeezed off quick shots from a 9mm Beretta, he'd hissed through his teeth, *"Take that, Daddy! And that and that and that!"* I'd feigned a trip to the ladies' room, had made a dash to the parking lot, and burned rubber getting out of there.

Even the bluest of blue bloods could be freaks.

"Andy? You doze off on me?"

"Am I going to the shindig," I repeated, putting aside thoughts of the blind date from hell and getting back to Brian's question. I perched on the arm of the sofa, the towel tucked around me, a bare leg dangling. My freshly washed hair drip-dripped on my shoulders. "Unfortunately, it's not optional."

"Your mother won't let you get out of it?"

"Worse." I sighed. "She bribed me with Escada."

"The nerve of her."

"Exactly."

"I mean, how *dare* she?"

"It's despicable," I said, playing along, and he laughed, doubtless thinking, *"Poor little don't-wanna-be-rich girl."*

Still, he knew my mother, so he had to feel some pity.

I imagined his boyish, slightly crooked grin, and his unruly brown hair, tousled upon his forehead. It amazed me that I was attracted to someone so centered, so preppy, and so, um, white bread. Well, he *was* Ivy League—a Harvard law grad—so I guess he couldn't help it. Not a single tattoo or piercing graced his lean body. And, believe me, I'd done a fair amount of investigating in that respect.

Nope, Malone was entirely too presentable for my taste, which leaned toward longhaired poets with sad eyes, brilliant minds, and always-empty wallets. But, in spite of his passion for things buttoned-down, I liked him. A lot. He made me feel warm all over and tingly at the same time. A little like prickly heat.

"So you want me to go with?" he offered. "You know I own a tux, if that's an issue. It's Armani." Quick pause. "All right, it's a knock-off, but it looks real."

"It's not the tux. The issue is Cissy," I said, feeling horrible when I had to turn him down. "Mother insisted I go solo. She's hoping I'll meet an eligible bachelor."

"What am I? Chopped liver?" He sounded hurt.

"It's not that exactly. She *does* like you, Malone. It's just that"—how did I explain Penny George's spying and that stupid "milk for free" theory without completely humiliating myself and Cissy?

"Just what?"

I tried a different tack. "Think of my mother as the little socialite that could. She won't let up until I'm the ball on someone's chain." Preferably, someone with a pedigree

dating back to Plymouth Rock or with at least an oil well—
or three—in his pocket.

"She wants us to get married?" Did his voice shake, or
had I imagined it? "Is that what you're saying?"

I nervously played with the cord of my old Princess
phone. "Hey, it's not what Cissy wants, anyway, right? It's
what we want. And I don't plan to be anyone's ball and
chain"—I assured him, lest he started thinking I was implying anything—"not for a while anyway. I like things as they
are."

"Really?"

"Yes." I did want a ring on my finger someday. I just
didn't want it to be a rush job, even if that would make my
mother happy.

"Well, all right, then." He grunted. "How 'bout I crash
the party . . . put on my penguin suit, and pretend I'm with
the wait staff?"

"Cissy would kill you."

"Probably put a Jimmy Choo up my ass."

"A Ferragamo, at any rate."

"So the answer is 'no'?"

"Yes."

He sighed.

"Look, I'll do my best to sneak out early, okay? I'm hoping I won't have to stay any longer than it takes to get a
blister from my new shoes."

"Cissy got you shoes, too?

"And a matching handbag."

He whistled. "Whoa, Andy. That's some bribe. Like a
Winona Ryder shoplifting spree without the probation."

What a lawyerly thing to say. "Don't make me feel any worse," I grumbled.

"Give me a call if you make a jailbreak."

"It's a deal."

We said our goodbyes, and I hung up, grinning.

There was definitely something to be said for white bread.

In another twenty minutes, I had the sequined Escada zipped and my toes wedged into the pointy pink sling-backs. My minimalist makeup and hair wouldn't exactly have gotten me far in a pageant—at least not beyond Miss Congeniality—but it felt like plenty for someone not used to wearing much more than Chapstick. As much as I liked to paint, my preference was to put color on canvas, not skin. I'd seen enough women who looked like clowns to realize that less was often more, unless you had your eye on a gig under the tent at Barnum & Bailey.

Actually, I did know a girl who'd gone to Clown College in Sarasota. Last I'd heard, she was wearing a barrel on the rodeo circuit in Lubbock.

So maybe it did pay to overdo the Mary Kay, if you had that kind of aspiration.

My only goal was to get myself to Addison, do what I had to do—for both Marilee and my mother—and then scram at the earliest opportunity.

I teetered out the door of the condo in my high heels, greeting an elderly neighbor who was walking his dog in the still-smothering heat.

"Hello, Mr. Tompkins."

The poor man did a double take. "Andy, that you?"

"In the flesh."

"Flesh is right. Woo-doggy." He nodded and swiped his brow with a kerchief, though I wasn't sure if I'd inspired the beads of sweat or if the thermometer was strictly to blame. His pot-bellied beagle seemed more interested in the bushes, sniffing like mad and ignoring me entirely before lifting his leg.

Oh, well. Can't win 'em all.

"You look real spiffy," he said in his grizzled twang.

"Thank you, kindly." I lifted my purse in acknowledgment as I scurried down the sidewalk toward my car. I unlocked the door and jerked it open, metal hinges squealing. I tossed my purse across to the passenger seat and pondered for a moment how I was going to climb in gracefully.

"Woo-doggy." Charlie howled again more loudly.

I tried not to cringe, glad at least that the rest of my neighbors were tucked inside with their conditioned air. Though I caught a glimpse of Penny George in pink sponge rollers peering between her drapes from an upstairs window, the ratfink.

"You have a good evening, Charlie," I called out and scrambled into my simmering Jeep, settling myself behind the wheel without ripping a seam or having my dress ride so high that I flashed the old guy. A major feat considering my general lack of coordination, and I felt immensely pleased.

I glanced out the windshield as I started the car and saw the beagle wrapping the leash around Charlie's ankles. As I pulled out of the lot, I caught him in my rearview, still staring.

All that because I'd put on a skirt and lipstick?

I realized my neighbor was used to seeing me dressed-down, not dolled-up, so I wasn't surprised that he had trouble believing I was the same person. I liked to tell myself it really didn't make much difference what I looked like, but maybe I was a fool for assuming other people felt the same.

Beauty didn't go much beyond skin-deep in the heart of Texas. It was practically a state law that women look good enough to eat. As mouth-watering as chicken-fried steak smothered in cream gravy. Statuesque, big-haired blondes were as much a part of the landscape as longhorns and bluebonnets. Not surprisingly, pageants—and, consequently, plastic surgery—were a huge industry. If Miss Texas didn't take the Miss USA crown every year, the whole state was affronted. Correct me if I'm wrong, but I'm fairly certain that butt and boob tape—particularly important in the bathing suit competition—were homegrown inventions.

A fair number of the population—the prettiest of the pretty—were groomed to be beauty queens from infancy. Mothers didn't sing lullabies to lure these wee girls to sleep, they sang, "There she is, Miss America."

I remember a classmate by the name of Clancy Lee Carlyle who'd won the title of "Little Miss Lone Star" by the time she was seven. When our second-grade teacher had asked us what we wanted for Christmas, she'd blurted out, "World peace and nuclear disarmament!"

Okay, she'd actually said, "Whirled peas and new-cooler dismemberment." But Mrs. Overby had explained what she'd meant, making all the rest of us feel like dolts for wanting simple material things.

Silly old me. I'd craved an easel and a new set of finger paints.

Hardly things that would've scored points on the pageant circuit.

My daddy, bless his soul, had always tried to convince me that "beauty is in the eye of the beholder," and I'd wanted to buy the line. Badly. But I knew better because of people like Clancy Lee Carlyle.

And Cissy.

My mother had never met a can of AquaNet she didn't like.

I sighed and changed lanes, deciding it was the unfortunate but deep-seated wish of every woman to be the cheerleader or homecoming queen, even when well past prom age.

Okay, *almost* every woman.

Cissy was the one who'd had those dreams for me. My role, it seemed, was to dash them. Though every time I let her con me into wearing haute couture, like tonight, I gave her hope.

False hope, but hope just the same.

The Jeep's engine rumbled beneath my pink shoes as I slowed at a stoplight at Preston and Belt Line. The sky was still mostly blue overhead, though I could detect the vague tinge of dusk descending as the sun began its slow slide from twelve o'clock high. The glass of surrounding buildings reflected clouds softening to pink.

Still, it wouldn't be dark for an hour, at least. The days were definitely getting shorter, but not short enough to suit me. When summer got a hold of Dallas, it didn't let go easily.

I fiddled with the vents, adjusting the AC to blow on my face. A quick check in the rearview mirror showed the sheen of perspiration on my forehead. My eyeliner already looked smudged. Another reason I didn't like makeup. Sweat could too quickly turn me into Tammy Faye.

The light turned green, and I surged forward with the rest of the herd of four-wheeled cattle, catching the tail end of rush hour traffic. My gaze skimmed the lanes around me, finding Cadillacs aplenty. A swarm of white Sevilles surrounded me. Sitting high up in my Wrangler, I felt the urge to sing the theme from *Rawhide*.

My daddy used to drive a Caddy. A Brougham d'Elegance that he'd often bragged was inches longer than the Lincoln Town Car. It was definitely the biggest sedan I'd ever seen. Through my little girl eyes, it had seemed the size of a cruise ship. All it had needed was Gopher and Julie McCoy, and it could've been *The Love Boat* on wheels. I'd hated that car as much as my father had adored it. Though it was one of the few things he'd splurged on for himself. Nothing was too good for Mother or me, but Daddy didn't indulge himself, not often. Certainly not the way he could have (that so many of his friends did).

Case in point: he hadn't worn a Rolex like so many of his contemporaries (like so many of *my* contemporaries). He'd never seen the need. He'd told me once that "a watch is a watch is a watch," and, to prove it, he'd had the same stainless-steel Omega strapped around his wrist for as long as I could remember. He'd been wearing it when he'd died.

Now I kept it in a carved wooden box—one that used to hold Daddy's cigars—on the shelf of my nightstand, along with the paper strip from a fortune cookie I'd gotten from the Chinese take-out the evening after Daddy's funeral. The message: ALL IS NOT LOST.

At the time, I'd surely felt like I'd lost everything. It had taken me a while to realize it wasn't true.

My father had left me with so much. More than he would ever know.

Busy with my thoughts, I'd hardly noticed the countless restaurants on Belt Line that I'd bypassed, though the neon lights flashed in my rearview mirror. The colors set off nicely by the faded gray of the evening sky.

At the Midway intersection, I slipped the Jeep into the right-hand-turn lane and followed a slew of cars heading deeper into Addison. I glimpsed the antiques mall to my left, a big old box of a structure that housed aisle after aisle of treasures.

Marilee's studio wasn't much farther up, and it would've been hard to miss even if I hadn't known where I was going.

Though dusk had yet to bury the setting sun, the place glowed like a house afire. The tiny trees lining the front parking lot sparkled with a million tiny lights. Garlands of flowers entwined with more of the glittering bulbs gracefully draped the deep green awning stretching forth from the front doors.

I swung the car around, looking for an empty space, as a young man in white shirt, black vest, and bow tie ran out to greet me. Marilee even had nattily garbed valets for early birds, I mused, what with the party thirty minutes away. I was running a little later than I'd hoped, but there was still plenty of time to make sure the web cams were properly placed.

I slowed to a stop as the fellow approached my window and motioned for me to roll it down. Perspiration clung to his freckled skin, and I smiled at him. It was Dewey, an intern from UT-Dallas who was spending the summer earning college credits as one of Marilee's assistants. In other words, he was slave labor.

"Hey, Andy. I'll be happy to take care of this for ya," he said, looking eagerly at my dusty Wrangler.

And who was I to deny him his fun?

Or his tip?

"Thanks, Dew." I put the car in Park and unbelted myself as it idled, rumbling familiarly. As he popped open the door for me, I grabbed my purse and began my less than graceful slide out, accepting his proffered arm gratefully.

"You be careful in there," he advised, wiping sweat from his brow with a sleeve. "It's even stickier inside than out."

"Marilee's in a foul mood again?" I dared to ask him as I tugged down the hem of my dress so it covered my thighs or a small portion thereof.

"Let's say, I'd rather be out here sweating."

"That bad?" I grimaced.

"She already made someone cry."

"Who was it this time?"

"Her daughter." He sighed. "They had another fight. God knows what this one was about."

Kendall?

The girl could be a bitch and a half, but she was still no match for Marilee.

Poor thing.

I swallowed hard.

"Hope you have your thick skin on under that cute little

number. Try to have a nice evening, ya hear?" Dewey said
and grinned, looking pleased as punch not to be in my
pretty pink shoes.

He hopped into the Jeep quickly, and I almost dove in
after him. I kept my eyes on the taillights until I saw it
round the nearest bend, no doubt aiming for a bank of
empty spaces around back.

Didn't take me but another moment of standing on asphalt, breathing the remnants of exhaust, before I sucked in
my gut, gritted my teeth, and told myself that, if Marilee
made anyone cry, I was leaving.

Especially if it were me.

Chapter 6

 A couple of Marilee's regular security guys in blue suits and watch caps were taking a lap around the building when I crossed to the front doors. A tuxedoed man I didn't recognize stood inside, whisking the glass portals open for me as I approached. He checked my name off on his clipboard before letting me pass with a hesitant, "Um, good, um, evening."

As if even he didn't believe it.

"Lord help me," I said under my breath as I proceeded up the wide hallway toward the soundstage, the sage green walls on either side of me filled with framed poster-sized photographs of Marilee doing various things domestic: baking, gardening, scrapbooking, decorating, and stenciling.

There was even a shot of her in a yoga pose that had me wondering if someone hadn't done a bit of airbrushing to get that foot behind her head. Or else she was double-jointed. I marveled at the gorgeous lighting that made Marilee look amazingly ethereal, so calm and sweet, hardly resembling the demanding diva for whom I'd been working these past two weeks.

If only real life could be so picture-perfect.

But even supermodels had cellulite (seriously, I read it in *Cosmo*).

If Marilee had any cottage cheese on her thighs it would soon be public knowledge, according to the rumor mill. I'd heard the buzz around the office that an unauthorized biography was in the works, supposedly being written by a thus-far anonymous reporter who was well acquainted with her subject. If any dirt were unearthed, it would surely be gobbled up by the masses.

Thus far, Marilee had managed to stay under the radar. *The National Enquirer* still seemed unaware of her existence. But that surely wouldn't last long, not once *The Sweet Life* debuted on television sets across the nation.

I'd dug up articles and interviews online, mostly back issues from *D Magazine* and *Texas Monthly,* that didn't reveal much about my new client except that she'd built her business from scratch after a divorce had left her a penniless single mom. There was barely a mention of her life before that, except to say she came from a hole in the wall called Stybr, Texas, and had attended Texas Christian briefly before dropping out to marry her college sweetheart.

Still, I couldn't help but wonder if there wasn't more to it than that.

Because I'd come to realize that the image Marilee had created was based more on fantasy than reality. She peddled an illusion of herself as Earth Mother cum Household Whiz, and people seemed to eat it up. Everything she touched suddenly seemed in great demand. Her books and audiotapes sold like hotcakes. There were whispers that she was about to embark on a joint venture with a large retail chain—linens, cookware, furnishings, and paint, all bearing "The Sweet Life" brand—that would net her millions. Well, even more millions, considering her syndication deal was worth a bundle. She wasn't quite in Oprah's territory yet, but she was hell-bent in that direction.

Though all the money in the world couldn't buy friends.

Okay, real friends.

From what I'd seen, Marilee had very few people she trusted, besides her daughter Kendall (and even that seemed iffy).

And, of course, Marilee's staunchest supporter: Her Highness of Highland Park. The venerable Cissy Blevins Kendricks.

Now, *there* was a story to make an unauthorized biographer drool.

Mother had met Mari while volunteering at a food bank half a dozen years ago, shortly after Marilee's divorce. Marilee's finances had been tight, and she'd been fighting to stay off welfare. While my mother had filled up the food pantry bags, Marilee had started talking. She'd been working at the cleaners by day and writing at night. She'd even sent in samples of her proposed column to the *Morning News* without luck. To make a long story short, Cissy had stepped in and changed the course of Marilee's life forever. Though my mother didn't generally brag about her good deeds (to anyone but me), I never doubted she'd had a hand in Marilee's swift rise in Big D. Cissy knew all the right people, and Marilee hadn't known a soul, not then.

Now Marilee had the world knocking down her door.

My mother never publicly—or even privately—took credit for her involvement. It was just one of the many "projects" she'd thrown herself into after Daddy died.

When I'd asked Cissy what else she knew of Marilee's background, she'd fed me the "you know I don't like to gossip, darlin'" line before she'd spilled a few measly beans.

She told me that Marilee used to run around barefoot on a chicken ranch, hardly the Beaver Cleaver upbringing that Marilee alluded to in those interviews where she mentioned her childhood at all.

The "barefoot" part was tough to imagine.

The hard-edged businesswoman on display at the office would never run around without shoes much less without full makeup. I'd never even seen her wearing jeans, except on her show's gardening segment. Otherwise, it was most often twin-sets and trousers or Chanel suits, much like my mother.

In fact, I often wondered if Marilee hadn't mimicked Cissy's style on purpose in order to land on the annual "Best Dressed List" alongside my mother in the *Park Cities Press*.

Though I guess that wasn't a crime. You couldn't be tossed in jail for nicking another woman's fashion sense.

Cissy also confessed that Dallas's "diva of domesticity" had lost her mother when she was very young, which is why she was so intent on creating the perfect nest, for herself and for everyone else on the planet. Though the few times I'd seen Marilee with her daughter, they'd been bickering.

"She already made someone cry."

"Who?"

"Her daughter."

Ah, Kendall.

I barely knew the girl—well, young woman, since she was eighteen and out of school—but I felt sorry for her nonetheless. Not that she was the most pleasant person I'd ever met, but she had a good excuse for her shortcomings. It wasn't that I accepted the "blame the mother" theory that seemed so popular with Ricki Lake and Maury Povich, but, having rubbed shoulders with Marilee for two weeks, I believed that, in this case, it was true.

I had firsthand experience with a mother who was demanding, a true perfectionist, and it wasn't easy. I couldn't imagine that überdriven Marilee had much time for her daughter, and I was certain that Kendall was feeling particularly neglected with the attention the national syndication of *The Sweet Life* was raining down on her mom.

"There you are, Andy. I've been waiting for you. I thought you'd be here half an hour ago."

Every muscle in my body tensed at the sound of the voice. A somewhat refined East Texas drawl with an edge to it. Rather like Scarlett O'Hara with PMS.

Speak of the devil.

I drew my eyes from the photograph-lined walls and looked ahead of me, to the far end of the green runner where a woman sheathed in vintage black Valentino stood staring at me, hands on hips. She tipped her head, so the chunky highlights of light blond in her ashy hair glinted beneath the track lighting. Plenty of bling bling winked from her clavicle, ears, and wrists. Regardless, she didn't look happy.

"Sorry, Marilee. Traffic," I shot back, unwilling to let her get to me. I didn't want the word to spread that the charming Ms. Mabry had made two women cry this evening.

"Well, hurry up, then," she said, snapping her fingers. "Let's get going. We don't have much time."

"That's okay, since I don't need much," I assured her, following her quick footsteps into the belly of the studio.

Spotlighting shone from above, illuminating the enormous vases and pots of flowers that abounded. I heard the sweet sound of strings as a harpist tuned up from a corner of the soundstage. Polished silver candelabra filled every surface that flowers did not, and a cadre of staffers in black—the men in tuxes and the women in cocktail-length dresses—scurried about, lighting tapered candlesticks.

Large plasma-screen monitors hung here and there, where snippets from upcoming episodes of the *The Sweet Life* would play soundlessly throughout the evening. Gauzy sage green chiffon swags floated down from metal grids, in between pastel-hued bulbs that would shower the most flattering lighting on Marilee's guests. The whole atmosphere seemed surreal, as if I'd walked onto the pages of a decorating magazine. I felt like Dorothy awakening in a Technicolor Oz after starting out my day in black-and-white.

"Nothing can go wrong tonight, Andy," she said without breaking her stride, despite the height of her pointy-toed mules. "Everything *must* go as I've planned, though I do have a few surprises in store."

Hopefully, that excluded poisonous spiders and falling boom mikes.

"Surprises?"

"Don't worry. They have nothing to do with you. They're merely a gift to myself, sweet revenge, as it were. All you need concern yourself with is what happens online."

"We're in good shape, really. I set up the web cams a few

days ago," I reminded her, "so I just need to make sure they're all functioning properly."

She kept her back to me, tossing over her shoulder, "Is the site animation working?"

"Yes."

"What about the media clips I asked you to load?"

"Done."

I pretended that we hadn't already gone through this a million times before, an Oscar-worthy performance, if I do say so myself.

"And how about the blog?" she asked, referring to the web log where she kept in touch with her fans by posting messages daily. Okay, *she* didn't actually keep in touch; one of her production assistants did, pretending to be Marilee herself.

"It's already generating an amazing response," I told her. "Your fans are looking forward to seeing what goes on at this party. The e-vite you suggested was a stroke of brilliance. I'm expecting the number of hits from people wanting to catch a glimpse of you and your guests to surpass our expectations."

She stopped in midstride and turned around, the pinch of displeasure gone from her face. A slow smile crept across her impeccably painted mouth, and she lifted a hand, pointing a manicured finger at me. "Cissy was right. You are a genius, my dear. I couldn't have done it without you."

And the six webmasters before me.

Aw, shucks.

I felt a blush coming on. "Well, thank you, Marilee. It's been, um, great working here, and I think I've got things in good shape for my replacement."

"Replacement?" She narrowed her eyes. "What on earth are you talking about? I don't want to replace you, Andy. You're doing magnificently. You seem to understand just what I want, and I don't have to tell you over and over a hundred times."

No, just ninety-nine.

Crap.

That's what I'd been afraid of.

I reminded myself to stand my ground. "Um, remember I told you when I agreed to take the job that it would only be temporary. Usually I prefer to work with nonprofits. It's kind of a personal thing," I tried to explain.

But I wasn't even sure she'd been listening.

Her gaze shifted, her attention turned elsewhere.

"Carson!" she screamed at someone over my shoulder, the sudden rise in her voice causing my hair to stand on end. "What the hell are you doing with my homemade foie gras? Didn't you hear a word I said about putting it out too soon? And are those water crackers? Did I not *tell* you a *dozen* times that I wanted toast points?"

Only a dozen?

Without so much as an "*excusez-moi*" she whisked past me, leaving me standing there with my mouth half-open. I felt like one of the many potted palms set about, draped in twinkling lights. A mere prop for Marilee and nothing more.

Was she coming back?

Or had she deserted me for good?

I wasn't sure which to wish for.

I stayed put for a moment, gripping my purse in one hand and looking around, watching Marilee's staff scurry about, the men in tuxedoes with red rosebud boutonnières and the women in cocktail dresses. Marilee surely meant for their "uniforms" to convey elegance and class, but I found the effect rather funereal.

Was it an omen, I wondered, all those people garbed in black?

Marilee was nowhere in sight. She'd disappeared through a closed door, stomping after a fellow whose head was hairless as a cue ball.

Poor Carson, I thought and gave him a fifty-fifty shot of having a job after tonight. Marilee went through employees faster than Hugh Hefner did bunnies.

Carson Caruthers and I had never crossed paths, since I normally restricted my work to Marilee's office when I had to come in. I wasn't sure exactly what his position was beyond the fact that food was involved. All the names on the site had my brain scrambled, and the crew was so large it was hard to keep track.

Anxiously, I tapped my shoe against the floor.

What to do, what to do?

I couldn't wait for her to return, not that she would. It was closing in on twenty minutes to liftoff, and I still had to double-check the cams and the live stream on the computer. I didn't want to find a glitch in the system after the party had begun. Then the head on Marilee's platter would be mine instead of Carson's.

Hop to it, I told myself, deciding things would go a lot faster without Marilee looking over my shoulder and grilling me like the Spanish Inquisition.

After doing a quick inspection of the web cam locations and finding everything as I'd left it, I headed away from the soundstage, down a mazelike rear hallway, with various cubicles and offices shooting off right and left.

Though the overhead strip lights were on to illuminate my passage, most of the rooms appeared dark and deserted. The members of Marilee's production staff were either en route or out in the studio, buzzing around like worker bees under the close inspection of their queen.

My destination was the queen's office. I'd been there quite a few times in the past two weeks, and it was a sight to behold. The space was at least the size of my condo if not a couple hundred feet beyond. It was as plush and pretty as the pages of *House Beautiful* magazine, and I fleetingly considered hiding out there for the duration.

I approached the closed door, marked with a star (of course) and MARILEE MABRY lettered in delicate calligraphy. With a twist, I turned the knob and pushed my way in, reaching for the light switch and flipping it on.

Realizing, too late, that I wasn't alone.

Chapter 7

A sudden squawk emerged from the silence: a masculine, "Oh, Christ," along with a feminine squeal along the lines of "eeeek!"

Then two bodies popped off the butter-cream leather sofa, each grabbing at various items of loosened clothing, hastily buttoning and zipping.

I stood in the doorway, strangely mesmerized, not sure of what to do exactly. As far as I knew, this wasn't a subject covered by Emily Post.

So what's a not-so-good girl to do?

I gawked.

The man came toward me first—once he'd shrugged back into a dove-gray jacket, white shirt unbuttoned at the collar, sans tie—combing fingers through silky blond hair, face flushed but otherwise cool as the proverbial cucumber. He checked the red rose boutonnière in his lapel, reassuring himself it was there.

A red rose, I noted, *just like the rest of the hired help.*

If Marilee was making a statement by having Justin wear one, I wondered if he realized what that meant.

He approached, ducking his handsome head to avoid looking me in the eye. He murmured, "excuse me," before he rushed past, leaving only the faint scent of almonds in his wake, making an escape that would've done Houdini proud.

Before he disappeared entirely, I glanced with blatant admiration at his well-shaped posterior. It was plain enough to me why Marilee kept him around and showered him with expensive treats.

Woo-doggy, indeed.

But wasn't he playing it awfully fast and loose, messing with his lover's teenaged daughter?

I tried to come up with a good excuse for what Justin had been doing with Kendall—a quick check of her body fat that required both of them to disrobe, perhaps?—knowing that their activities had less to do with any real personal training than with cuckolding Marilee on her own sofa.

Tsk, tsk.

The young woman took her time setting herself to rights, adjusting a black under-wire bra and slipping her sticklike arms into a pair of spaghetti straps, before tugging a zipper up her side.

I summoned a calm I didn't feel and shut the door behind me. Stepping farther into the room, I shook my head with disbelief.

"Kendall, Kendall, Kendall," I murmured, for want of anything remotely witty. "What on earth are you doing with your mother's boyfriend? And in her office, too?" I clucked tongue against teeth. "You must be clueless or completely insane."

"Don't you know how to knock?"

The heavily made-up eighteen-year-old scowled as she fiddled with the elaborate French twist on the back of her head, trying unsuccessfully to tuck dismantled strands back in place. She looked like a skinny kid playing dress-up.

"Don't you know how to lock a door?" I said.

I mean, *duh.*

She stopped fooling with her hair and gave me a long, slow smirk. "What if I tried, but the lock was broken?"

Call me gullible, but I went back and checked the mechanism myself, and it seemed perfectly fine. "Nope, it works like a charm."

"Really? Silly me." Kendall laughed, and I lifted my eyes to hers, seeing something in them that made my toes curl.

Oh, my.

Suddenly, I had a darned good idea of her true intentions.

To get nailed being, uh, nailed. Only the wrong person had come along and caught her in a compromising position with Marilee's boy-toy.

She'd been shooting for her mother to appear and flip on the light.

Talk about an attention-getter.

That certainly would've done the trick.

"You must have a serious death wish," I scolded, pushing the door shut again and skulking toward the desk.

She ignored me and tugged at her pantyhose before stepping into a pair of lethal-looking Jimmy Choos. The spiked heels were stiletto-slim and at least four inches high. Kendall obviously liked to live dangerously in more ways than one.

If Marilee had made her cry earlier, she'd long since dried her tears. She didn't seem sad so much as spiteful.

"Want to tell me what's going on?"

"Bite me," she said.

"Not even if you were a Krispy Kreme."

So much for my attempt to reach out to a troubled teen.

It struck me then that there were good reasons people sent their kids to boarding school. If I were Marilee, I would've packed Kendall's bags and put her on a plane to the most remote location in Vermont long ago, and I wouldn't pay for her return ticket until she turned thirty.

Okay, maybe I was being a little harsh, but Kendall's tough-girl attitude made it hard to like her. Yet I couldn't help feeling sorry for her.

Perhaps that's how my mother felt about Marilee.

As my daddy used to say, that's called a "pair a ducks."

I set down my purse and pulled back the padded leather chair before sinking between its arms. As soon as I turned on the computer, I felt Kendall's presence behind me. I didn't turn until I had booted up the program and connected with the web-hosting network for Marilee's site.

"I apologize," she said quietly, a far cry from her snooty tone of moments before. "I didn't mean to snap at you. You're not going to rat me out, are you?"

From "bite me" to contrition in ten seconds flat.

Yo, Sybil?

I swiveled around so I could see her face. The heavy black liner around her eyes was smudged, whether from earlier tears or her tryst with Justin, I couldn't be sure. A tiny diamond glinted from above her right nostril, replacing the usual gold ring. So she'd broken out the formal nosewear. How classy. A small round mole dotted her right cheek where a dimple would have been, if she'd had dimples.

She had enough blush in the hollow of her cheeks to more than enhance her prominent bone structure, lending her a skeletal air. The black of her hair had inch-wide platinum streaks in it, reminiscent of Lily Munster. She managed to look fragile and frightening at the same time.

Kendall was so thin her exposed arms seemed all bones and taut ligaments. Her clavicle jutted out above the low-cut line of her cocktail dress, a flashy number that screamed Dolce & Gabbana. Size zero.

"You can relax. I won't blab about Justin," I promised, figuring the girl had enough troubles as it was. Besides, I figured, she didn't need me making things worse for her. Kendall seemed determined to screw up her life all on her own. "Look, I know you have problems with your mother, but . . ."

"Problems?" She snorted, cutting me off. "Problems are like one plus one equals two. It's not that simple. You can't possibly understand what it means to be the daughter of Marilee Mabry. Everyone assumes she's so perfect, that she does everything right, and it's so far from the truth it isn't funny."

"But maybe I do understand," I said. "A lot better than you think. It hasn't been easy being the only child of Cissy Kendricks."

"Give me a break." She twirled a strand of hair around a

knobby finger. The uncountable silver bands around her wrist jingled. "Your mother's a saint compared to mine. I'll bet she remembers your birthday and stays home on Christmas."

Well, she had me there. Cissy never missed a holiday or special occasion. Quite the opposite. She made a huge flipping deal out of every event. Overdoing was her problem, not forgetting.

Still, I found myself springing to Mama Mabry's defense. "But Marilee raised you single-handedly, Kendall, and she didn't have much to work with . . . financially, I mean. It had to be hard for her."

"Made her hard up, is more like it." The raccoon eyes narrowed. "I'll wager your mom has never stolen one of your boyfriends."

Cissy as Mrs. Robinson?

I think not.

Particularly considering the kind of guys I'd dated in my rebellious youth (i.e., before Malone), mostly artists and musicians who didn't fit any of Cissy's criteria for a son-in-law, the first of those being "gainfully employed."

I laughed until I realized that Kendall was dead serious.

"Oh." I quickly sobered up. "You mean Justin? That before he was with your mother, he"—I started, but she finished for me.

"Used to be with me."

"Ah," I said, ever the scintillating conversationalist.

"It's true." She stopped fiddling with her hair and sighed. "He'd still be mine if not for her." She braced her palms on the edge of the desk and glanced down at her hands. Her fingernails looked as ragged as mine. "If Marilee hadn't stepped in and waved her money in front of his face. She calls him our 'fitness guru,' but he mostly earns his keep by screwing Mummy dearest. I guess that makes me her pimp, doesn't it? I *am* the one who brought him home from the gym. Stupidest move I ever made."

Her jaw tightened, and I could see the angry beat of her pulse at her throat. "I thought it wouldn't hurt so much, the way he hopped so fast from my bed into hers, like it was nothing. But it does. It hurts a lot."

And Justin continued to hop like the Energizer Bunny, if what I'd dropped in on was any indication.

"If it hurts so much, why are you still sleeping with him?"

Her face froze, and something like fear flickered in her eyes before she blinked it away. Then she shrugged. "We care about each other. Mummy can't take that away from us."

"But doesn't it make you feel . . . I don't know . . . strange? Like he's using you? I mean, Kendall, get real." It popped out of my mouth before I could stop it.

Thank you, Dr. Phil.

"How does it make me feel to share a man with my mother? I don't know. Powerful. Wicked." She lifted her chin, defiant. "What? You think I should feel like a bad girl who needs a spanking?"

"How about used? Or guilty?"

"Used?" She bristled. "How do you know I'm not the one doing the using? And why should I feel guilty? My mother's never felt guilty for anything she's done to me."

I wanted to tell her that she was hardly the only girl I'd

ever known who'd had her boyfriend jump ship for a Sugar Mama, and she should get over it. But I was pretty sure that wouldn't exactly prove comforting.

I got the distinct impression they were in direct competition—Kendall and Marilee. I couldn't decide, though, if their struggle over Justin was as simple as two women vying for the heart of the same man or if it was merely a matter of them constantly trying to outdo each other, looking for attention—and affection—wherever they could get it.

How dreadful that must be, thinking your mother is your enemy.

Even in my tug of war with Cissy, I had never thought of us as combatants. We were more along the lines of Abbott and Costello, bumbling through our relationship, never quite sure of who was the comic and who was the straight man.

"I don't mean to come down on you, Kendall." I had no earthly idea what else to say. "You're right. I don't know what it means to walk in your"—I nearly said "Jimmy Choos" but settled for—"shoes."

"It sucks."

"I'm truly sorry for you . . . for everything you've had to go through," I said.

She glanced away.

Without knowing what else to do, I turned back to the computer monitor, more comfortable with the virtual world than with Kendall's real life.

"I'm sorry for everything you've had to go through," she mimicked, sounding like a drunken parrot. "Like I need your pity?"

Dear Lord, give me strength.

I swiveled to face her again. "That's not what I meant," I tried to explain, but gave up before I ventured further. Because I knew she'd take whatever I said the wrong way. She was that kind of kid. Mixed up, lonely, and looking for a fight to pick.

"Just because you had a perfect childhood doesn't make you superior," she vented, balling her hands into fists.

"My childhood wasn't quite so perfect as you think."

"Oh, no? Your father didn't walk out on you when you were twelve, did he? You never had to go on welfare, did you? Bet your mother never made your clothes . . . ugly things that everyone at school made fun of." Her eyes welled as she glared at me.

I sighed and shook my head, slowly turning to lay my hands on the keyboard, gnawing on my bottom lip, afraid to speak for fear I'd say something else to fuel her fire. Maybe even something I'd regret.

I was thoroughly convinced by now that Kendall needed serious therapy. "Have you ever, er, talked to anyone . . . professionally?"

"Like a shrink?"

"Yes."

"Let's see." She fiddled with the yards of bracelets clamped around her wrists. "I've been evaluated by social workers, child psychologists, psychotherapists, osteopaths, and psychic healers, either court-appointed or paid for by dear Mummy once the money started rolling in. I've been diagnosed as hyperactive, depressed, anorexic, bulimic, and suffering from posttraumatic stress disorder and abandonment"—her bangles jangled as she ticked off each count on her fingers—"not to mention having migraines, hormonal imbalances, and God knows what else."

She grimaced. "If those quacks had their way, I'd be on enough medication to stay constantly stoned out of my gourd. My mother would probably like that, don't you think? That's one reason I'm actually glad Justin's here, even if it means he has to be with *her* sometimes. He knows what's good for me and what's not, and I trust him more than anybody."

Directing her glare at me, she finished with, "So you still think I need to talk to a professional, Ms. High and Mighty? Or have I been dissected enough to satisfy you?"

Holy crapola.

I couldn't begin to respond. What could I have said?

Absolutely nada.

I couldn't conjure up a single word from my pretty extensive vocabulary to express my sorrow at what she'd endured in her short life. Kendall was right. I had no business even pretending I knew how she felt.

My silence obviously bugged her as much as a reply, because she leaned over the desk and hissed, "Cat got your tongue, Andy?"

Aw, geez. There she went stepping on my last nerve.

Sympathetic or not, I needed some space to do my job.

I felt real compassion for Kendall Mabry.

But I wanted her to go away.

"Look, I've got stuff to do," I told her. "And, if I don't do it now, your mother's going to kill me. So if you wouldn't mind"—I kept my eyes on the computer screen, though I could see her faint reflection in the glass, and it didn't look happy.

"Take a hike, scram, bug off, sayonara. Is that it?" Her voice shook. "That's like all I ever hear these days."

The "poor me" routine.

Alas, poor Kendall, I knew it well.

I refused to look at her for fear of getting sucked deeper into her act. I focused on the monitor as I clicked through the pages of *The Sweet Life's* Web site, hoping she'd get the hint and leave. At the moment, I was more afraid of incurring Marilee's wrath for not having the live stream on track than I was of Kendall's mood swings.

"You know, I could've done Mummy's Web site, if she'd let me," she said with a sniff. "I do all her research on the Internet, looking up recipes and stuff. I'm an expert at Googling. Can't be much harder to put up web pages."

I didn't have the patience for this.

"Can you drive a tractor, Andy? Because I can. And I can milk a cow and muck a stall, too. Not something everyone knows how to do. Hell, I can probably do all the things Mummy professes to doing so expertly on her show. Except I'm the real deal. Don't you think that's kind of ironic?"

I did my best to tune her out.

"Ignore me. Yeah. Whatever." She sighed weightily. "Maybe I'll go off the wagon and get rip-roaring drunk. Give the mayor a lap dance. If I wish really hard, maybe something crazy will happen tonight. Like poisoned food or falling lights."

"Great, great. Enjoy the party," I said through clenched teeth and gave her a backhanded wave. I half-expected some retort, an angry reply, but all I heard was the sweet sound of silence.

So I dug in, rapidly tapping the keyboard, checking the live feed from the web cams, seeing what I'd hoped to see: black-clad people bustling about various points of the sound stage, candelabra glowing, harpist playing, food being laid out on the buffet. Even the entrance to the converted warehouse was covered, and I saw an elegantly dressed couple arriving already. I made sure the feed alternated between locations with barely a few seconds' delay in between.

Everything looked fine.

Thank God.

Fifteen minutes later, I leaned back in the chair and exhaled slowly.

If anyone screwed up Marilee's evening, it wasn't going to be me.

Which reminded me . . .

I glanced around to where Kendall had once been standing only to find no one there.

The door to Marilee's office stood wide open and empty. *Phew.*

I'd been almost afraid she might hang around, waiting for me to finish, and I didn't feel like dealing with an angry teenager this evening. Particularly one carrying a chip on her shoulder the size of Mount Rushmore.

Hey, it was difficult enough keeping the "fun" in dysfunctional where my own life was concerned.

A small mantle clock tick-ticked the minutes from a shelf above Marilee's desk, and I saw the big hand pointing at the twelve and the little hand on the eight.

My eyes went back to the computer monitor and focused on the frame with the live stream. Guests began arriving in ever-increasing numbers. The front hallway beyond the double doors had turned into a river with schools of well-dressed salmon swimming upstream. I tried to pick out faces I knew, and spotted quite a few, including the Park Cities paper's society columnist Janet Graham.

The stream switched to the buffet, and I saw the bald-headed Carson emerging from the kitchen with a round silver tray in hand. I caught him glancing around to see if anyone was near—and no one was—turning his back, his shoulders and head jerking in one quick motion—oh, Lord, did he spit in the foie gras?—before he put the food down on the table.

Ix-nay the goose liver, I told myself, though I would have avoided it, anyway.

The live feed flipped again, this time to where several couples gathered inside the soundstage, on the set resembling a dining room, complete with repro Chippendale. There was Tincy Kilpatrick, oil heiress and philanthropist, and her husband, Oscar. While Oscar turned to fetch her a glass of champagne from a passing server, Tincy bent over the coffee table and picked up a small object—a crystal ashtray?—which she quickly slipped into her purse.

Oh, my.

Looks like Tincy Kilpatrick could add "kleptomaniac" to her curriculum vitae.

I wondered if Mother knew about her Big Steer Ball cochair's little idiosyncrasy?

Who was I kidding?

Cissy knew practically everything about everybody. She had ESP (extra-socialite perception).

Besides, it's not as though Tincy was the only member of the *beau monde* with sticky fingers.

I squinted at the monitor as the feed flipped to the kitchen setup, where Marilee was holding court with her blond boy-toy at her side. I could just make out Kendall standing with her arms crossed at the edge of the frame, glaring at the happy couple.

It was oddly addictive.

Like a soap opera with characters I actually knew.

Which made me feel a little too much like a voyeur for my taste.

So I left the computer and the lights on—for future quick checks of the stream—and tucked my purse into a bottom desk drawer before heading out into the madding crowd in search of champagne. I normally didn't drink beyond an occasional margarita, but I felt a sudden urgency to imbibe . . . heavily.

Fasten your seatbelt, I warned myself, as I tugged my dress over my thighs. *It's going to be a bumpy night.*

Chapter 8

 I tracked down Janet Graham at the beautifully laid-out hors d'oeuvres buffet.

Perched between floral arrangements overflowing with green bamboo and lilies were platters, plates, and bowls filled with puff pastry and tarts, minicrepes and caviar canapés, crab-stuffed artichoke hearts and portobello mushrooms as big as my fist. There was enough bruschetta to feed the Italian army, and cheese of every stripe. Nearby, another table laden with desserts tempted party guests with a sweet tooth.

Janet happened to be spreading a healthy dose of foie gras on a toast point, when I put a hand on her arm.

"Just say no," I advised in low tones.

She peered at me from beneath a fringe of flaming red bangs; looking for all the world like I'd gone nuts. "What on earth are you up to, Andrea Kendricks? Are you on another of your save-the-geese kicks?"

Leave it to her to remind me of that.

Okay, yes, I had a brief flirtation with an animal rights

organization called FOG (Free Overfed Geese). The four of us—if four can really be called "an organization"—had chained ourselves to a goose pen on the property of a billionaire-about-town who owned one of the city's sports franchises (the one with a ball made of pigskin, which also irked the other FOG members who were, not surprisingly, all vegans). The fellow recognized me and called my mother, who persuaded him not to summon the cops. Within the hour, Cissy showed up in her Lexus with Janet Graham in tow, supplying us with the press coverage we were demanding, which is how I'd ended up with my photo on the society pages—rather than the Metro section—with a headline that read, HIGHLAND PARK HEIRESS CRIES FOWL. After my mother convinced us to unchain ourselves— something about goose poop and bacteria—we'd decamped for the nearest Subway for vegetarian foot-longs.

I winced at the memory, wishing I could blame it on youthful idealism, but it had only happened a year ago.

"No, I'm not protesting anything political at the moment," I assured her. "I'm doing you a favor, believe me."

Despite my warning, Janet didn't seem any too eager to step away from the pâté. "This stuff supposedly comes from Marilee's own flock," she said. "So, as a journalist who plans to write about this party and its hostess in great detail, it behooves me to taste it."

"Well, unbehoove yourself." I hooked a thumb at the gray mess in the silver bowl lined with sprigs of watercress, deciding to impart the truth to my erstwhile journalist friend or risk her swallowing tainted goods. "Because not all the ingredients in there belong to a goose."

"What ingredients, Andy?" Her forehead wrinkled,

causing her dyed-to-match red eyebrows to narrow. "What the devil are you talkin' about? You haven't been smoking funny cigarettes again, have you?"

Good grief.

"No, I haven't been smoking anything, funny or otherwise."

My God, were all my past indiscretions common knowledge?

"Listen, Janet"—I watched her raise the toast point to her lips and realized desperate situations called for desperate measures. So I made a noise like I was about to hack up a furball and feigned lobbing it into the pâté. "Get it now?" I asked her.

"You're tellin' me that somebody spit in this stuff?"

I touched a finger to the tip of my nose.

She made a face. "Ugh. That's unsanitary. Shouldn't we hide the pâté? Or tell Marilee?"

"Tell Marilee?" I choked. "Do you really want to see the offender stuffed and roasted in her double-wide oven?"

"You're right. Bad idea." She set down the spreader and slipped the tainted toast point into a napkin, balling it up in her fist. For a moment, I feared she'd stick the wad into the pocket of her tangerine-colored pants suit, but instead she casually dropped it on the floor and nudged it under the serving table with her heel. As for the bowl on the buffet, she pushed it behind a vase of lilies and draped a linen napkin atop it. "Do tell me what's safe to nibble on, Andy? And, please, say the caviar canapés are free of bodily fluids?"

So far as I knew.

I nodded.

"So what's the dirt?" She asked as she feasted on fish

eggs. "Did Marilee make somebody mad in the kitchen? Like that'd be the first time she ticked off someone on her staff. She's got a turnstile on her employee door, they come and go so fast."

"She pissed off a guy named Carson. He does something with food on her show."

Her eyes got as wide as shooter marbles. "Carson Caruthers?"

"If we're talking about the same man, then he's bald as a cue ball."

"Right-o."

"She reamed him out in front of the rest of her crew," I dished. "Something about putting the foie gras out too soon and using water crackers instead of toast points."

"Good Lord." Janet appeared about to swoon. "He's the hot young chef that Twinkle Productions imported from Manhattan to take over the job as Marilee's food editor. I can't believe she'd risk yelling at him in front of the staff."

"They've got to be paying him an arm and a leg," I opined. "That's the only way she seems to keep people around."

Janet scanned the room before leaning nearer to whisper, "Marilee's on a power trip that she didn't pack for, Andy. It's like she's bound and determined to make as many enemies as she can. You should've seen her at Mrs. Perot's luncheon last week. I swear on my mama's grave that I haven't seen anyone put on such diva airs since that cut-rate duchess came to town. Marilee might as well have a tiara soldered to her forehead."

I snagged a champagne flute from a passing tray and

sipped, the bubbles tickling my nose. "What'd she do, if you don't mind my asking?"

"Tried to steal the spotlight, is all. Well, she did more than try, she succeeded," Janet said, her gaze roving about the room all the while. "She played demure until Mrs. Perot was about to hand over a nice-sized check to the Salvation Army fellow, all dressed up in his uniform. Then right as the *Morning News* photographer was about to snap a photo, Marilee popped out of her seat, flung herself in front of Mrs. P., and whipped out a big ol' check of her own. Bigger than Mrs. Perot's by at least a zero. So guess which picture made the paper?"

"You're kidding, right?"

Janet drew an *X* across her heart to prove it was no lie.

Marilee might've mimicked my mother's style of dress, but she certainly lacked Cissy's finesse.

"Unbelievable," I said between sips.

"I've been doing some research on Marilee's rags-to-riches story, and there's a lot more to her than anybody knows," Janet went on, keeping her voice low.

"Like what?" I asked, licking my lips after another swallow of Dom, then setting aside my glass.

"Her mother died when she was ten, and her father practically abandoned her on the chicken farm. He'd go on benders, hit the road and not come back for weeks at a time. A few of the neighbors felt sorry for her, tried to help out. Gave her feed for the fowl, left her casseroles and hand-me-downs."

Though I'd heard about the loss of her mother, the rest was certainly a chapter of Marilee's life I hadn't been privy to, and I wondered if growing up so quickly is what had turned the woman into such a control freak.

"Her father left her to fend for herself when she was ten?" I felt a lump in my throat just thinking about it. "Didn't anyone bother to call in social services?"

Janet waved dismissively. "Oh, hell, Andy, that was back in the early sixties, and we're talking a *rural* community. Stybr, Texas. A teensy-weensy bump in the road between Tyler and Longview. The kind of place that still had a one-room schoolhouse until about five years ago. Sometimes the village did raise the child in those days, or close to it. I found one of Marilee's old teachers—and I mean *old*—and she told me the girl showed up for class like clockwork until she was sixteen. So she wasn't truant. Though she did disappear for a spell before she was set to graduate. I'm still digging into that. By then, her daddy had lost the farm to taxes and no one's sure where she went. I heard she lived with an aunt, taking care of the woman during an illness, before she went back to Stybr long enough to finish school so she could get into college and get out for good."

I realized suddenly how little I really knew about Marilee Mabry, and I wondered if Mother was even privy to the whole sordid story.

The idea that Marilee had been left to raise herself—off and on—when she wasn't yet a teenager, amazed me. I couldn't imagine being alone at that age, not for a day much less for weeks at a time. I thought of how she must have felt, frightened and more than a little lost. Maybe even unloved.

"Her father's long since passed away, and so have many of the neighboring farmers who'd known Marilee Haggerty when she was a kid. Most of her peers have taken off, too, but I've been able to dig up a few old-timers, and the one teacher who remembers her. But I'm not having much luck tracking down her aunt."

"Why don't you confront Marilee? Could be the reason no one knows about where she went is because no one's ever asked her."

Janet nearly spit out a mouthful of fish eggs. "Confront Marilee? Hmm. Maybe I'll just douse myself in lighter fluid and throw myself on the grill at Burger King. It'd be a lot less painful."

"She wouldn't tell you, would she?"

Janet sighed. "No, dammit. I'd naively assumed she'd scratch my back since I've been scratching hers for the past few years, putting her name in my column until it became a household word, at least in this city. Oh, she'll be sweet as pie to me if I ask about her show or her books, but if I try to dig too deep into her past, I'm hearing a dial tone just like that"—she snapped her fingers, the tips painted the same bright orange shade as her pants suit. "She could've made something up, and I wouldn't have questioned her. Now she's got me wondering what she's hiding."

"Hmm," I said, because it did seem odd that Marilee would turn down free press, especially with *The Sweet Life* so soon to premiere in the national arena. "I'd imagine she'd like the ink, even if it had to do with her less-than-perfect childhood. Really, what could a teenaged girl have done thirty years ago that was such a big deal?"

"I have my theories, and I aim to find out if I'm on the money. Then she'll be sorry for the kind of ink I'm gonna give her," Janet murmured and turned away, becoming extremely interested in the bruschetta.

Abnormally interested.

"She'll be sorry? What's that supposed to mean? Are you planning a feature article for the paper? Like an exposé? Something down and dirty?"

"I can't exactly . . . maybe I shouldn't . . . oh, hell." She stuffed a bite of bruschetta in her mouth and looked off in the distance.

"Janet, hey, it's me, Andy, remember?" I wiggled my fingers in front of her nose. "What's going on? You know you can tell me anything."

"Oh, gosh, I think I see Bootsie Ann Wyatt standin' over by the plasma screen, if you'd excuse me, sugar . . ."

I put a hand on her arm to keep her from bolting.

"Janet Rutledge Graham."

Calling her by her full name—or at least three of them—was the surest way I knew to take her to task. Get her to spill her guts.

But she clammed up instead. Her mouth pinched into a line so tight it would've taken a crowbar to pry it open.

Which was strange and so unlike her, at least with me.

I'd known Janet since we were kids, though she was three years my senior. As I'd often felt like one of the lone individualists at the Hockaday School, I'd admired those who didn't mind standing out. And Janet never failed to set herself apart from the crowd, even in our uniform of plaid skirts and knee socks. Her hair changed color regularly. Some mornings it was blond; other times, a brassy orange or shoe-polish black. She wrote for the school paper, but her true love was drama. She starred in virtually every play or musical until she graduated and went off to UT-Austin, where she ended up majoring in journalism. And I always thought she'd end up in New York on an afternoon soap or an off-Broadway stage.

While I was still in Chicago at art school, Janet began working at the Park Cities paper, covering lots of Mother's causes on her beat, everything from school board meetings to Girl Scout cookie sales to weddings. Cissy sent me plenty of clippings, all with Janet's byline, until the prolific Ms. Graham was promoted to "society editor."

When I returned to Dallas, Janet was the first to hear the news from my mother, which quickly turned to fodder for her column.

"Our favorite debutante dropout's back in town! You can take the girl out of Texas, but you can't take Texas out of the girl, which is why Andrea Blevins Kendricks decided to pack her bags and return to Big D from the Windy City," she'd written about my homecoming.

I'd called her at the paper shortly after, asking why she wasn't reporting for the *New York Times* instead of fawning over socialites at sorority alumnae teas, and she'd confessed that she adored her job, that going to the endless string of galas and luncheons with high society was akin to the very best theatre. "It's real drama, Andy, better than fiction," she'd gushed, as if I hadn't recognized that fact very early on with Cissy as my role model.

We kept our friendship up-to-date by meeting for lunch once in a while; but her world revolved around gossip, and she knew I really didn't care much about the blue bloods who were the gristmill for her columns. So we didn't talk shop much, mostly we'd yammered about men and the lack of them in our lives.

But I was curious about her suddenly nosing around in Marilee Mabry's background, more so because she didn't want to tell me. Unless there was some reason she didn't want *anyone* to know what she was up to, like it was some deep, dark secret.

Wait a dad-gummed minute.

A light bulb flickered.

Could it be?

Despite the growing hum of voices, I could hear a tiny warning bell go off in my brain.

"You're the one writing the unauthorized biography, aren't you?" I ventured to ask, and Janet's cheeks turned near as red as her hair.

"I plead the Fifth," she said.

Which could only mean one thing.

I'd struck crude.

I downed the champagne that remained in my flute and set it aside, leaning a hip against the edge of the buffet table, shaking my head.

"Oh, my God." The realization struck me silly, and I grinned like an idiot, looking up at her. "It *is* you. You're writing the book about Marilee. And it's going to be down and dirty, isn't it?"

Janet's crimson curls flew this way and that as she quickly looked around us, making sure no one had overheard. Then she grabbed my hand and squeezed hard enough to wipe the smile off my mouth.

"You've gotta promise to keep mum about this," she quietly pleaded. "Or Marilee'll be down at the courthouse with her lawyers, filing some kind of injunction to keep me from doing this project. And it's important to me, Andy." Her skin looked suddenly pale against the vivid tangerine of her jacket. "This could make my career. It could be my ticket to *Oprah*. I could finally meet Katie Couric in person," she whispered, breathless.

Katie Couric was Janet's idol.

I wasn't so sure that much of her fascination with Ms. Couric didn't have to do with the hairdo, which Janet did her best to mimic in every way except the ever-changing color.

Despite the longish bangs that kept falling into her face, I managed to hold her eyes and swear solemnly, "I won't say a word about the book. You know me better than that, for Pete's sake. Besides, who would I tell? My mother?" I laughed.

She didn't.

"You think I'd tell Cissy?" Now *that* was funny. "I don't think I've confided in my mother since I was twelve and got my period."

And that was definitely a moment I'd rather forget.

"Promise me you'll keep quiet." She gripped my fingers more tightly, so that I momentarily lost sensation.

"Girl Scout's honor. Cross my heart and hope to die, stick a needle in my eye. My lips are sealed." With my free hand, I feigned locking my mouth shut and tossing the key.

"All right. I believe you." Janet sighed and let go.

And not a moment too soon.

I'd been on the verge of crying "uncle." I massaged my white knuckles to get the circulation going.

She turned her head, scanning the room and the ever-growing crowd that loitered about, chatting and drinking. "Speaking of Cissy, has she arrived yet? I figure I would've seen her if she'd made her grand entrance already."

"It's barely a quarter past eight," I reminded Janet. "Way too early for Mother to be fashionably late."

A slow sweep of the studio—the parts I could see—revealed a contingent of politicians from city hall, half the population of Highland Park, and lots of designing types from artsy Deep Ellum boutiques and swanky Lovers Lane antiques shops, men too well dressed and styled to be hetero; unless a few metrosexuals had slipped through the cracks (translation: men purportedly attracted to women who spent nearly as much time at the salon as the gym).

My gaze skimmed over plenty of blondes with hair teased and sprayed to such proportions they looked like bobble-head dolls. Such was the Texas way.

I caught a few strains of the harpist playing something Mozart when Janet gasped and grabbed my arm.

"Ah, it's Babette von Werner and her grandpa . . . oops, I mean, her hubby."

"You gonna write that in your column?"

"Not unless I want to get canned, since Fritz von Werner's company just bought out the newspaper." She snorted. "But it's the God's honest truth."

And that was no lie.

Babette was a slender woman in her forties, while her spouse was at least twice that. Flashing laser-whitened teeth, Babs nodded her "hellos" as she pushed her beloved (and very rich) Poppy von Werner in his wheelchair. I admired her maneuvering skill, especially since she was wearing high, high heels and a backless white Versace gown that showed off her perfectly bronzed skin, absent of strap marks.

"Have they been on vacation? Lolling about the Mediterranean on his yacht, perhaps?" I asked Janet, who knew the comings and goings of virtually every member of the philanthropic set in Dallas.

"You're talkin' about her tan, right?" My society columnist friend bent nearer. "It's spray-on, Andy. She stands in a booth and turns around while a machine shoots out the paint. It's all the rage."

"I wonder if they use Benjamin Moore or Behr," I quipped, but Janet's eyes were already on another pair entering the studio.

Her elbow winged into my side. "Ohmigawd, I can't believe they're here!"

"Who . . . who?" I sounded like a stuttering owl.

I tried to follow her line of vision, but the arriving guests multiplied by the minute; a never-ending stream of big blond hair, so many red lipstick smiles, and enough beading and glitter to make my eyes blur. It was getting louder and louder, too, setting off a faint ringing in my ears. Voices had risen well above the "hum" level and nearly drowned out the sounds of the harp altogether.

"I'd heard a rumor they might show, but I didn't believe it. I wonder what Marilee's got cooking? Damn, where is my photographer? He was supposed to show up right at eight."

"Who, for God's sake?" I asked again, stomping a foot on the floor and barely missing Janet's toes.

"Them." This time, she pointed.

All I saw was a rather plain-looking middle-aged man in

a dour gray Brooks Brothers suit and a younger woman with the biggest red ponytail I'd ever seen, like Barbara Eden's hair from *I Dream of Jeannie*, only on steroids. It poured out of the top of her head like a fountain, and I wondered how many bobby pins it had taken to hold that critter on. I figured at least a bucket.

"Gilbert and Amber Lynn," she hissed.

Okay, I'd heard of Gilbert and Sullivan.

Gilbert and Amber Lynn rang zero bells.

"Who are they?" A little champagne surely couldn't have impaired my brain that much. The names sounded familiar, but I couldn't grasp exactly why they were so important to Janet.

She nudged me. "How can you not know them, Andy? You work for the woman. It's Gilbert and Amber Lynn *Mabry*. Marilee's ex-husband and his trophy wife." Janet's whole body was aquiver, like a racehorse raring to spring from the gate. "Sorry, Andy, but I've gotta scoot. There's definitely a story here, and I'm gonna find it."

I watched her maneuver her way through the crowd, nodding here and there as she went, careful not to snub, always the consummate pro.

It amazed me, too, that she never took notes. She was afraid doing so would inhibit the people around her. So she locked every observation, every bit of overheard dialogue, into her head. She didn't even write up the piece until the next morning, after she'd had time to let things simmer.

A bespectacled man in black tie paused near me. "Champagne, ma'am?" he said, proffering his loaded silver tray.

I nearly told him, "no, thanks," then I realized I'd have

to stick around until Mother arrived, which could mean a while yet.

"Yes, please," I told him, snatching a flute before he sidled away, muttering something about having to open another case.

Apparently, I wasn't the only guest hoping the Dom would make it easier to get through Marilee's soiree.

So I looked around me and sipped, figuring I'd hang back and observe until Mother showed up. After that, I'd linger just long enough to pay off my debt to her—oh, let's say, at least twenty minutes. Then I'd duck out to meet Malone somewhere quiet.

Someplace far away from demanding domestic diva Marilee Mabry.

From Mari's ex-hubby Gilbert and trophy wife Amber Lynn.

From part-time lovers Justin and Kendall.

From angry food editor Carson Caruthers.

And from Tincy Kilpatrick philanthropist cum ashtray thief.

Chapter 9

 I hung on to my glass as I purposefully slipped away from the crowd that had gathered around the buffet tables. A bouffant-haired woman layered in pink chiffon stood with her hip glued to the chocolate desserts display, "ooh, ooh, ooh-ing" with delight as she masticated.

Then I spotted the back of a slim woman in a black minidress, dark hair twisted into a knot on the back of her head. She had a black pashmina wrapped around skinny shoulders, so I couldn't see much else.

Kendall, I thought, and wove my way in her direction. I wanted to apologize for ignoring her earlier. Didn't want the girl to get a complex.

"Hey," I said and tapped a thin shoulder. "I'm sorry I"—was all I got out as the woman turned around, and I realized my mistake.

There was a similarity in their features, but this woman was older than Kendall, at least my age as opposed to eighteen. She had no ring in her nose, but did sport a tiny mole on her cheek. Her eyes were hazel, her face broader, and her skin tone a pale cocoa as opposed to Kendall's porcelain paleness. Quickly, I owned up to my error.

"I'm sorry, I thought you were someone else."

"That's okay," she said, smiling sheepishly and looking at me as if I were someone she thought she should recognize, too. "Do you work here?" she asked.

"Sort of," I said, then quickly ended further conversation with a fast "It was nice to meet you." Though we really hadn't met at all.

No time for detours.

I tiptoed along the fringes of conversing groups, hoping no one would notice me. I tried to convince myself that wearing designer duds enabled me to blend in so seamlessly that I was invisible, as innocuous as a dust mote.

"Andrea, lamb, is that you? Why, child, you look good enough to serve for supper. Come and give me a hug."

Rats.

I shot a smile at the woman who called my name, but hesitated long enough to take a deep, wet sip of Dom. When there was nothing left to swallow, I wiped a hand across my mouth, set the empty glass down, and wobbled on my high heels toward the reincarnation of Norma Desmond.

"Darling." Tincy Kilpatrick held out her arms to me, her satin evening bag dangling from a wrist. I could see it bulging in the middle, like a small snake that had swallowed a baseball.

"Good evening, Mrs. K," I said to her, and let her smother me against her breasts, her purse whacking me squarely between the shoulder blades. I clenched my teeth and wondered if the stolen bauble would leave a bruise.

"Where's our darling Cissy?" she asked, drawing back so I could clearly see her penciled-in eyebrows and the spidery legs of her false lashes.

"If she comes a minute before nine o'clock, I'd be surprised," I told her with a grin plastered to my face. I was feeling pleasantly giddy from my champagne buzz, seeing things through booze-colored glasses. "Nice party, huh? Have you tried the pâté?"

Bad, bad girl.

Perhaps I was channeling Kendall.

"Good God, no." Tincy put a hand to her heart and toyed with the enormous diamond dangling from her throat. "Oscar and I are doing low fat, low carbs these days. High cholesterol, you know. Don't want to keel over from clogged arteries, like Norbert Dobbs at the symphony gala last week. Splat!"—she clapped her hands together, making me jump—"face down in his steak tar-tar. It was a dreadful sight to see."

I'm sure Mr. Dobbs wasn't thrilled about it, either.

"Poor Mrs. Dobbs," I said.

"Oh, aren't you the funny one! Norbert wasn't married, not to a woman. *He was the Dior buyer for Neiman Marcus,*" she whispered with an arch of her eyebrows.

"Ah."

"But enough about Norbie." She patted my arm. "Your mother tells me you're working for Marilee these days." Her painted mouth tightened, a slash of crimson on white. "How's that going? Have you been tempted to lace her coffee with arsenic?"

"The job's going . . . great," I said, finding it way too easy to grin and lie. "Working for Marilee has been an, er, interesting experience."

"Interesting how?" A penned-on brow arched skeptically.

Run, my brain screamed. *Run like the wind.* "Oh, goodness, I didn't realize the time." I glanced at my wrist, but I wasn't wearing a watch. I hoped she didn't notice. "I'm actually working tonight, doing a live stream of the party on the Web site, and it's about time I headed back to the office to check on a few things. So if you don't mind . . ."

"Of course, not, dear. Go, go." She air-kissed my cheeks before shooshing me off, her bulging handbag swaying from the crook of her elbow. "I didn't mean to monopolize you, child. It's just that we so rarely see you out and about. Besides, I think Oscar needs rescuing, so I'd better scoot myself. Ta."

"Ta," I said, sounding like a parrot.

Polly wants a fat-free Carr's water cracker.

Moving off behind a lit-up palm, I peered between the silk fronds, swaying on my pink heels as I watched Tincy head toward the harpist, where a large man in a Stetson stood with his hand on Oscar's shoulder, pinning him in place. The big guy was the head of the Republican Party in Dallas—he'd tackled my mother more than a time or two in the past—doubtless trying to get Oscar to commit some Texas-sized bucks for the next gubernatorial election.

Free and clear.

Without further ado, I took off in the other direction, skirting the wall-less living room on the soundstage toward the pseudokitchen.

A growing throng of guests had gathered in this most

spacious part of the set—where Marilee would do all her cooking segments—and I shouldered my way through the edge of the group as the chimes of silver on crystal turned everyone's attention toward the room's center.

If I teetered on the pointed tips of my shoes and angled my head just right, I could catch glimpses of Marilee with Justin, standing at her heel. His grim expression didn't reflect someone having fun. I wondered if he were worried about my popping in on him and Kendall earlier, afraid Marilee would find out?

Behind them, on a large granite island, sat a huge vase of Asian lilies. On the other end had been placed an enormous silver candelabra, its sage green tapers brightly burning. Above, silky green sheers dangled from the lighting grids, resembling graceful wings set aflutter by the occasional flow of air.

"Could I have your attention, please?" Marilee called out, her voice overwhelming the ebb and flow of conversation until it came to a halt. "Can everyone hear me?"

A chorus rang out in the affirmative.

"Good." She smiled gracefully and pushed an errant strand of streaky ash-blond from her brow. "If you'll bear with me a moment, I have a few things to say. I'd like to start by thanking each and every one of you for coming tonight to celebrate a new phase in my own life . . . and *The Sweet Life,* my baby, if you will. Certainly my most treasured creation."

Polite applause and a few "Hear! Hear!s" ensued, but I noticed one person standing to the side of Marilee who hadn't joined in.

Kendall's face crumpled, crestfallen, like a child whose

sucker has been swiped, though I couldn't say I blamed her after just having heard her mother tell a roomful of people that a TV show was "her baby."

Ouch.

"Things have certainly not been easy for me," Marilee went on, her smile faltering, "but I've learned great strength from my adversities. I had to scramble to survive for years and years, but that determination is what got me where I am today. And now I think I finally have everything. My column, my books, the TV show, and soon a new line of products to be launched in conjunction with Smart-Mart. Yes, it's true! I know you've heard rumors, and I'm confirming them all."

Another smattering of applause rippled through the ever-gathering throng, and a tall man wedged himself in front of me, completely blocking my view.

"Um, excuse me . . . excuse me." I tapped his shoulder to no avail. The fellow didn't even turn around, just kept flicking at my finger like it was a bug.

You, sir, are no gentleman.

Scowling, I scooted further around bodies taller than mine, trying to find a better vantage point.

"I can't tell you how good I feel tonight, so strong and emboldened. I've a few more things to get off my chest, but first a toast." Marilee reached for a bottle behind her, which she then handed to Justin to open. He turned his back and worked on the cork.

"A 1973 Dom Perignon Oenotheque," Mari announced gleefully. "I've been saving it for years, for just such a special occasion, and nothing's more special than this. Sorry, but there's not enough of this to go around, so y'all get the

'93. A very good year, too, so don't whine," she teased, and her audience tittered. She turned to her boy-toy. "Honey, would you, please?"

Justin swiveled as he freed the cork, and Mari grabbed a trio of flutes for him to fill. She passed one over to Kendall and took another for herself, while Justin kept the third, though he didn't seem any too eager to drink it.

"Here we go," Marilee said and raised her glass. "I've been waiting a long time for this, so bear with me if I go on for a bit."

Tuxedoed waiters wove through the tightly knit audience, making sure everyone had fresh bubbly on hand.

I'd already had my quota for the evening, if I wanted to remain upright. So I waved away the tray-toting fellow and maneuvered closer to the front, stepping on someone's toes while an unseen elbow pressed into my ribs.

My bra strap slid down my left shoulder, and I pushed it back up. I tucked my hair behind my ears and figured which way to go next.

"To everyone at Twinkle Productions for having such faith in me and my vision . . ."

I wove my way around to a false wall against which a humongous stainless steel refrigerator was anchored. A working fridge, too, for I could feel its humming as I pressed up against it for a better view. Kendall had backed up and was near enough to touch. I watched her tip the glass to her lips and drain it.

". . . to my lawyers for making sure I didn't get screwed by Hollywood, at least not unwillingly . . ."

That one got some laughs.

Still feeling the tail end of a bubbly buzz, I squinted at

Marilee in her black vintage gown, grinning with her wide red mouth, nodding at the faces in the crowd. The glow in her eyes bordered on the fanatical.

". . . lest I forget, an enormous thanks to my former husband Gilbert for dumping me for his, er"—she cleared her throat—"secretary and running off with everything we owned, giving me no choice but to start over, all by my lonesome. Without you, dear Gil, tossing me onto the street and forcing me to dream my own dream, I'd still be clipping coupons and shopping at thrift stores."

What was she doing? Was this the "surprise" she'd mentioned earlier? A public drubbing of her ex?

I only hoped it would be as quick as it was merciless.

But Marilee wasn't finished. She turned and tipped her glass toward her blushing blond boyfriend who stood at her elbow.

"And, finally, here's to my sweet, sweet Justin, my fitness guru and oh-so-significant other, for working so *hard* night after night to give me what Gil rarely could during our marriage. All those nightly workouts have certainly kept me in such good shape, so thank you, sweetheart. You deserve everything I have and more."

I groaned.

Please, I silently begged, *someone make her stop.*

And Marilee did stop . . . talking, that is. She leaned over and kissed Justin hard on the lips. A big, juicy clench that caused the gathered guests to let out a collective gasp.

Kendall did more than gasp. Her empty champagne glass sipped from her fingers, hitting the floor and smashing to smithereens. Her head down and arms clasped around her middle, she shoved past me, nearly knocking me down in her effort to escape.

Marilee glanced over but didn't even flinch. She ignored the broken glass and her fleeing child, as if nothing had happened. Though Justin looked increasingly upset. He ran his hand through his hair and shifted on his feet. Part of me expected him to race after Kendall, but he didn't. No doubt afraid of getting in trouble with Marilee.

I thought about going after Kendall myself, since no one else felt compelled to do it; but I ended up keeping my spot beside the fridge. Like a rubbernecker on the freeway, I couldn't turn away from the accident-about-to-happen. Which is what this felt like, with Marilee playing Joan Collins in a bad scene from *Dynasty*.

"You bitch! How could you?"

The shriek erupted from somewhere in the belly of the crowd, and I clung to the refrigerator to keep from being swept to the floor as several bodies surged forward, heading for Marilee: a woman with a bobby-pinned fall the size of Niagara flopping from her crown and a man in gray Brooks Brothers.

Gilbert and Sullivan.

No, no, Gilbert and Amber Lynn.

"You heartless crone!"

Letting loose another cry, the woman flung herself at Marilee with all her might, knocking the nearly full glass from Marilee's hand and pushing her back against the granite island. Marilee called for help, but no one seemed to be doing much of anything except Gilbert, who ineffectually pawed at his outraged wife.

Justin jumped out of the fray.

Gil did manage to snag the back of Amber Lynn's dress, holding her in place as she flailed her arms and shrieked. "Honey, honey, please," he begged. "Don't play her game. Let's just leave."

Marilee scrambled to escape but merely inched sideways along the enormous length of granite.

She spun around for a moment, gazing frantically at the enormous vase and the blazing candelabra, probably contemplating using one or the other as a weapon. But each was nearly as big as she was, so she looked around her, at the crush of guests forming a wall of gawkers, pinning her in place.

"Get that woman out of here!" she demanded, but no one moved, not an inch. No one seemed quite able to figure out whose side they were on.

"Get away from me, Gil!" Amber Lynn swung at her own husband, catching him with a right hook beneath the chin. He wobbled, letting go of her, and stumbled back into the stainless steel dishwasher.

"Ahhh!" Amber Lynn charged Marilee, letting loose a cry like a Confederate war general, while Gilbert nursed his jaw—and doubtless saw stars—relegated to the sidelines to stand and watch like the rest of us chickens.

If I hadn't been so fascinated by the unfolding scene, I would've scrammed as things began coming apart at the seams. Instead, I kept my front row seat for the wrestling match as the two women tussled against the granite island.

"Justin!" Marilee screamed to no avail. "Justin, help me!"

I looked around but didn't see her blond boy-toy anywhere, just his untouched champagne glass sitting on the counter by the sink.

"Aaaaaah!"

Amber Lynn snatched up the neck of the 1973 Dom Oenotheque and swung at Marilee who ducked in the nick of time. The bottle hit the vase of flowers instead, taking it over the side of the island and crashing to the floor, glass shattering, spewing water, champagne, and stems.

A handful of partygoers complained loudly as hems and cuffs were splashed. The incident didn't amuse Marilee, either.

"You owe me three hundred fifty dollars for that bottle," she screamed and went after Amber Lynn.

I braced my back against the fridge as Marilee caught Amber in a death grip, rolling her toward the end of the granite island with the silver candelabra.

"You husband-stealing whore! You silicone-enhanced tramp!" she shouted and grabbed hold of Amber's shoulders, forcing her to bend backward. Amber kept shaking her head, her faux ponytail swinging precariously close to the burning wicks on the candelabra.

Dangerously close.

Until, with a "whoosh," the hank of hair ignited into a fireball.

Amber screamed and threw her hands up to her head as soon as she realized her fall was aflame.

Someone bellowed about extinguishers while another voice cried for "water!" But it was Gilbert who ran to the rescue. He snatched the fake hairpiece from his wife's head—bobby pins be damned—and flung it up, up, and away.

Which might have been the end of things if the burning hank of horsehair hadn't caught on the green swag dangling above the granite island.

The beautifully draped fabric went up like a dry Christmas tree. Flames licked at the pastel-colored spotlights and the acoustically proper foam-tiled false ceiling.

Oh, my God—my thoughts clicked into gear—*the place was on fire.*

I'd imagined this would be the party from hell.

And now it was.

Literally.

Chapter 10

 Above the crowd, the once-green fabric swags crackled as hungry orange flames chewed through them, releasing sparks of ash into the air, embers that floated and flickered like fireflies, showering the guests packed below.

Tilting back my head, I stared, in utter disbelief.

I rubbed my itchy eyes, tasting smoke as I swallowed.

Could this really be happening?

"Fire . . . fire!"

"We're all gonna dic!"

The very real and very frightened screams of the party guests swelled in my ears, and I felt my heart boogie, adrenaline crashing through my suddenly sober veins.

This was no bad dream.

It was a nightmare.

I clenched my hands in and out of fists, trying desperately not to panic.

"Everyone stay calm . . . please, proceed in an orderly

fashion!" Marilee shouted, though no one seemed to pay attention but me.

Gilbert had found a fire extinguisher and aimed it at the burning swag. He pointed upward but his aim was shaky, and he shot foam on several party guests before he threw down the red tank, giving up and grabbing for Amber Lynn.

Right on cue, the fire alarm sounded, its ring so loud and angry that I had to raise my hands and cover my ears.

I was thinking that it might be a good idea to sneak out the back hallway instead of joining the crush of people manhandling one another to break free of the faux kitchen. They looked like a herd of wildebeests, stampeding across the Serengeti toward the lobby of the studio, where an EXIT sign glowed red above the arch that led to the front doors.

Hungry flames crackled overhead as the fire licked at the lighting rods, the heat causing bulbs to burst in an erratic succession of pops, like a bag of microwave Orville Redenbacher, only louder.

Time to get the hell out of Dodge, I told myself, cringing at the clanging alarm and raised voices that pounded my eardrums.

I'd barely taken a step away from the kitchen setup and toward the rear hallway—in the direction that Kendall had fled moments before—when I felt the plop-plop of water on my head and gazed up again.

With a "whoosh" the gentle spray turned into Niagara Falls, dumping a geyser down upon me as the sprinkler system switched on full force. Water pounded my face and slapped my bare shoulders, causing my skin to sting.

I might have felt like Debbie Reynolds in *Singin' in the Rain* if only I'd been armed with galoshes, a slicker, and umbrella. Somehow, getting drenched—and painfully so—didn't make me want to break into song. There was nothing "glorious" about this.

Slip-sliding through puddles, I made my way off the soundstage. My hair was plastered to my skull, and melted mascara muddied my vision. All I wanted was to find someplace dry.

No one followed my flight through the hallway toward where the offices were situated, but I realized soon enough that I'd made a smart move. I'd barely stepped onto the stretch of wall-to-wall Berber, when I realized the waterfall had stopped. At least, it wasn't raining on me anymore. I turned my head and pushed wet bangs from my eyes to see it still coming down behind me, beyond the arch of the hall.

The alarm still ringing at unbearable decibels, I gritted my teeth, hurrying toward Marilee's office, relieved when the noise seemed to lessen the farther I scurried from the soundstage.

By now, the sequined fabric of my dress had turned into a suit of armor and felt as heavy as a ton of scrap metal. My ruined shoes squished against the carpet as I raced for Marilee's sanctuary. I desperately desired to get behind the computer, figuring the sprinklers had shorted out a web cam or two. Though I was sure the Web site viewers had gotten their money's worth—especially since the live stream was free—courtesy of Marilee's obnoxious toast.

Once I checked on the system, I'd grab my purse and get lost. Marilee's soiree was officially *finito,* and my mother had never even shown up. Which didn't sit well with me at the moment.

I approached Marilee's office door, which stood wide open.

When I'd shut it before, hadn't I?

Stepping inside, I closed it behind me and was relieved to hear the alarm only dimly. The cacophony muffled enough that I could pretty well ignore it. The clamor was certainly no worse than a car alarm going off on the street.

I quickly flipped on the ceiling light, my focus strictly on the desk and computer. I didn't dare settle in Marilee's chair, not in my current state of saturation. A real-live SpongeBob Squarepants. Instead I crouched down over the keyboard and tapped away until I'd tallied the score as far as what was working and what wasn't. The two cams located in the studio kitchen were on the fritz, all right. Another cam showed bodies swarming out the front doors.

I made the decision to fold the live stream altogether. I doubted Marilee would disapprove, considering she'd embarrassed herself pretty thoroughly already.

With a few keystrokes, I disconnected.

Then I shut down the system.

This shindig's done, and so am I.

First, home, I thought. A hot bath. Afterward, if I asked real nice, maybe Malone would bring over a pizza.

I slid open the bottom drawer in the desk, removing my purse, doing my best not to leave puddles anywhere except the carpet.

Somewhere beyond the walls, I heard sirens, and I knew I should get my dripping arse outside with the rest of the evacuees. It probably wasn't kosher for me to be inside the building at this point, even if the fire had been put out and no one was really in danger.

"Goodnight, Gracie," I said under my breath and took a couple steps toward the door when something stopped me.

"Uhhh."

What the hell was that?

I had to strain to reassure myself that I hadn't imagined it.

"Is someone here?" I asked, my heart doing a nosedive as I looked around me, seeing nothing but the expensive furnishings in Marilee's sitting area.

Wait.

Two objects resembling small black birds lay dejected on the floor.

Were those Kendall's black Jimmy Choos?

I took a few steps nearer, rounding the kidney bean-shaped coffee table, spotting a blob of crimson on the carpet.

Blood?

Man, oh, man, oh, man.

I swallowed, making myself go closer still, only to realize that the red blot was no stain. It was the broken bud off a rose boutonnière.

What was going on?

A chill went through me, one that had less to do with my drenched state than my fear that I wasn't alone. "Hey, is anyone here?"

"Uhhhh."

There it was again.

I swallowed hard and tentatively crossed the Berber, stepping around the leather sofa and seeing a closed door that I knew led into Marilee's private loo.

"Kendall? Is that you?" I asked in my loudest voice, leaning my cheek against the wooden panel and placing a hand on the knob, which I turned without resistance.

I pushed the door open and spotted a black shape, crumpled on the tiled floor. I smelled a rank odor before I saw the puddles near the toilet bowl.

Ohmigod.

My purse slid from my grip and landed at my feet.

This wasn't good. Not good at all.

"Kendall?"

I crawled toward the unmoving form and peered down at the dark hair with the near-white streaks, at the pale, pale face with tear-stained cheeks and vomit-stained Dolce & Gabbana dress. Her eyes remained closed, lips parted just wide enough to emit another feeble moan. Her stocking-clad legs splayed beneath her short skirt, and her arms sprawled on the tiles, limp as a rag doll.

I reached for her hand, and the silver bracelets jingled as I pressed it between mine. Her skin felt so cold.

"Kendall, can you hear me?" I said and attempted to push back the sterling bangles to check for a pulse at her wrist, but there were six inches of them at least, too many to deal with. Instead, I placed my fingers at the side of her neck, right below her jawbone. All I could feel was my own heartbeat, pounding through my ears.

She couldn't be dead, I told myself. *She wasn't.* Dead girls don't groan. She'd just had too much to drink, got sick, and passed out, right? That had to be it.

I leaned over her. "Sweetie, wake up, please."

Ahh.

Was that an exhaled breath?

Or had I imagined it?

Damn.

What to do? What to do?

Sliding around her, I cupped her head in my hands and set it on my lap, brushing the hair from her face, bending down to touch my cheek to her lips, hoping to feel her breath on my skin.

But I couldn't tell, didn't know what was real and what my adrenaline-crazed mind was making up.

I shook her shoulders gently—"please, honey, wake up"—until I realized I could be doing more harm than good. Reaching out, I snatched a plush towel from the rack and set her head down upon it.

C'mon, Andy, think.

I considered grabbing my cell from my purse and calling 911, until common sense reminded me that help was nearer than a phone call.

I thought of the sirens I'd heard and figured a shiny red truck with hook and ladder was parked out front already with firefighters running all over the place.

"Hold on, okay?" I begged Kendall and squeezed her lifeless hand before slipping out of my heels and scrambling to my bare feet. I didn't want to break my neck if I took off running. "I'll go get help and be right back," I said over my shoulder as I sprinted from the bathroom and took a curve around the sofa.

The door ahead of me, I had a hand outstretched toward the knob when the lights flickered.

On. Off. On.

Like the lighting at a disco.

I flung open the door.

Off went the lights.

Only they didn't go back on again.

Damn.

Panting as if I'd run a marathon, I stood with the black surrounding me, waiting for my eyes to adjust.

You've got to be kidding, right?

Was this some kind of cosmic joke? Bad karma from wearing Escada?

I tried to stay calm as I fumbled forward, my fingers guiding me into the hallway. Lapsed Presbyterian that I was, I found myself praying that nothing else would go wrong, wondering what the hell else could.

Because, so far, this night had been one freaking disaster after another.

Chapter 11

 I couldn't see a thing, not the tip of my nose much less my hands stiff-armed in front of me.

A vague breeze, like a rush of warm breath, blew across my cheek, and something hard hit my shoulder, enough to spin me around. Flailing awkwardly, my knuckles brushed against the wall, and I flattened myself against it, turning my head, first left and then right.

"Who's there?" I called out, still feeling the sting in my shoulder, my nerves all but shot to hell.

I listened for the soft patter of footfall on the carpet, but all I could hear was the noise of my heart, pounding as ferociously as a symphony bass-drum crescendo.

Whoever it was had been in a hurry.

And obviously knew his or her way around, because I didn't hear any loud thumps or mangled cries of someone banging into a solid object.

Where was I?

After a moment to get my bearings, I gravitated toward the emergency exit that led out the back of the building, feeling spooked and wanting out of there. I fumbled my way to the door, nearly crying with relief when I found it and pushed it wide. Greedily, I breathed in the muggy night.

Looking out, I spied the rows of cars Dewey had parked and the stars blinking down from high above me. But I didn't spot a single human.

Then I stopped, stepped back, and let the door close, shutting myself in.

If I'd gone out, it would've locked behind me, and I was more afraid of leaving Kendall alone inside the building than anything else.

So I turned around.

The alarm had been disabled—thankfully—and so had the sprinklers, the absence of sound in the dark further dulling my senses, making everything so ungodly still. Though there was quite a racket going on inside me. My thoughts were darting in every direction, and my heart seemed ready to leap from my chest.

Here and there, I squished in puddles I'd left on the carpet during my retreat; though I couldn't see as far down as my toes, I was sure my feet were dyed as pink as the fabric of my discarded slingbacks.

Mentally, I kicked myself, knowing I should have followed Kendall when she'd run out after Marilee's tirade, hating that I'd been unkind to her earlier. I'd virtually ignored her so she'd let me be.

Why was it so hard to do things at the moment but so easy to look back and wish we'd done them differently?

As I groped my way past the maze of offices toward the once-burning kitchen, I muttered every four-letter word I could think of. I don't know that it made me feel any better, but somehow it soothed my nerves.

I turned what I felt to be the last corner when voices floated toward me, growing louder the nearer I moved toward what should have been the hallway's end.

When I saw rays of bright light floating through the gloom, I didn't waste a second. I started calling out, "Help! I need help, please!"

Every minute was precious.

I kept wondering if I'd left Kendall for dead, or very close to it.

What if she'd stopped breathing? How long could a person go without oxygen? Wasn't it something like five minutes?

"This way . . . I'm over here!"

The rays of light swung at me, and I squinted as bright white beams filled my eyes until I squeezed them closed and saw spots behind my lids.

"You injured, ma'am?" someone asked, sounding miles away.

"I'm fine . . . except for some temporary blindness."

"Oh, yeah, sorry about that."

They lowered their Maglites.

I blinked until my vision cleared. "There's a girl who's in trouble . . . Kendall Mabry . . . she's sick . . . she won't open her eyes . . . I'm not sure if she had too much to drink or what, but she's not good . . . not good at all"—I ran out of breath.

"Stay put, ma'am, please, we're almost there," a second equally masculine voice advised, as if I was going anywhere—the words accompanied by the *slop-slop* of their boots as they slapped through water, wading toward me.

I suddenly felt the earth move under my feet. Well, small vibrations as the firefighters stomped ever closer.

Within moments, hulking shadows emerged from the pitch, moving near enough for me to make out slightly more than their dim silhouettes.

"I'm afraid she might be . . . oh, God, please, let's hurry." I pulled at the heavy cuff of the nearest coat as I explained exactly where Kendall was and how to get there through the winding hallways. Until it seemed I had talked too much, for too long, and so I turned, ready to take them to Kendall myself.

But a gloved hand caught my arm, holding me still.

"Stay put, ma'am," Fireman Number One insisted. "Can't have you running around without shoes in the dark. You might get hurt."

What the hell did he think I'd been doing before they found me?

A walkie-talkie crackled, and Fireman Number Two radioed for the EMTs to get inside pronto. His coat brushed my shoulder as he headed off in the direction of Marilee's office, his heavy gear making him clunk as he ran.

"I should really go back . . . she needs someone with her . . . I shouldn't have left her alone," I said, panic rising, and my teeth started to chatter.

Though Number One wasn't letting loose. "I can't let you do that, ma'am. It's not safe."

"But, I need to . . ."

"We'll take care of her, ma'am. Trust me."

Like I had any choice.

I stopped struggling, and he released me.

It seemed forever before the paramedics finally appeared, paddleboard and gearboxes in tow. My firefighter-jailer gave them split-second instructions before they jogged off to save the day.

They'd make sure Kendall was okay, wouldn't they?

More beams of light weaved, voices swarming all around me. The orange stripes on their coats glowed through the gloom.

"Ma'am? Let's get you out of here, all right? I don't want you walking through the water in your stocking feet, not in the dark. You could cut yourself on debris."

Debris?

Like Amber's crispy-fried hairpiece?

"Okay," I said into the shadowed face, wondering how he was going to get me out if I didn't walk.

I figured maybe he'd sweep me off my submerged feet into his burly arms and whisk me from the building à la Richard Gere and Debra Winger in *An Officer and a Gentleman*.

"You got something on under that pretty dress?"

"What?" Was he asking if I had on panties? "Yeah, of course, I've got on something." Was my savior a perv? It would be just my luck, wouldn't it?

"All right then, upsy daisy, little lady," he said, making me feel all of five years old. Without warning—unless I counted his loud grunt—he grabbed my waist and tossed me over his shoulder like a sack of potatoes.

I would've squealed with surprise had he not knocked the air from my lungs by that less than delicate maneuver.

So much for the Gere/Winger scenario. The only way my hanging across his torso could have been construed as anything romantic would have been if I were wearing burlap and had REAL IDAHO stamped across my tush.

"You okay, ma'am?"

At least he was polite.

"Oooph," I expelled, sounding weird upside down, as though I had plugs on my nose and couldn't breathe.

My head hung down his back, my legs dangling against his chest. His hands held my thighs to keep me in place, and his shoulder jabbed into my gut as he marched through the studio. I could only hope that my aforementioned panties weren't on display.

Or worse.

Grabbing a coarse handful of coat, I hung on for dear life, gritting my teeth to keep my jaws from clunking together, unable to see anything but the back of his boots from my vantage point and wondering if this night wasn't near about the lowest point in my life, or somewhere in the direct vicinity.

The slosh of water and the chatter from walkie-talkies tickled my ears, and I could feel the movement of others around me, occasionally brushing past without warning, setting my hair to standing on end.

When he pushed open the glass front doors, and we emerged into the night, even more racket greeted us. Raised voices and shouts and the hum of engines. Humid air descended with the force of a damp blanket. Somebody called my name, but I couldn't tell whom, not with the blood rushing to my head. Nor could I see, considering my vision was limited to the pavement.

"Down you go," Mr. Fireman uttered and lowered me to earth far more gently than he'd swung me up.

"Please, take care of Kendall," I said instead of a "thank-you," but I'm sure he understood.

He nodded, his big fireman's hat bobbing, before he walked away and was swallowed by the crowd. So many people in so little space. Uniforms running around, weaving in and out of the mass of evacuated party guests. A hook and ladder truck, several police vehicles, and an EMT van clogged the parking lot. The squad cars had their bubble lights going, swirling blue and red across wide-eyed faces.

Pausing to catch my breath, I glanced at those hunkered around me, folks who looked as frightful—and frightened—as I felt. I wanted to find Marilee and tell her about Kendall, but I found myself turning back to stare at the building, waiting for them to bring her out. I had to know she was all right.

My toes curled against the warm asphalt, and I wrapped my arms around my middle, not sure of what to do. If I'd been abducted by aliens and released in the middle of a cornfield, I wouldn't have felt any more confused.

"Andrea, sweetie?"

My shoulders stiffened.

I brushed wet strands of hair from my cheeks, glancing up at the purple tint of the evening sky. Passing cars sent waves of light flashing over the parking lot again and again. Moths attracted to the glow of streetlamps swam happily within the soft orange haloes.

Everything else seemed to go on as normal, but I wasn't deceived.

"Andrea? For goodness' sake! We just arrived to find the fire trucks and the police. I was petrified something had happened to you. Who was it that carried you out? The strapping fellow who had you slung over his shoulder. Is he single, do you know?"

The cultivated drawl asking those absolutely inappropriate questions made me want to laugh out loud. Or cry with relief. I was torn between the two, though I was leaning toward crying.

"And you thought there'd be no eligible men here tonight. How wrong you were, sugar. There are plenty of them. You should listen to your mother now and then."

Chapter 12

When I faced her, it was all I could do not to burst into tears.

As always, she looked magnificent, dolled up in ivory Chanel and matching satin pumps, not a hair out of place. Though *she* certainly appeared out of place in the parking lot full of drenched partygoers who'd had the misfortune of arriving on time and witnessing the fireworks—and waterworks—in Marilee's make-believe kitchen.

"Sweetie?"

My expression must've looked as soggy as the rest of me, because she opened her arms, and I stepped inside.

Until she held me, I hadn't realized how badly I was trembling. She rubbed her hands over my arms, trying to warm me up. Considering that my mother was not what you'd call "a hugger," this was powerful stuff.

"Andrea, good Lord, where are you shoes? And your purse?"

I drew back and sniffled. "Inside," I confessed, hating how choked up I sounded, hating that I felt so out of control. Maybe it was the alcohol I'd drunk before I'd stumbled upon Kendall, but I felt precariously close to meltdown. "The shoes are a disaster. And I'm sorry about the dress." I plucked at the drooping sequins.

"Who cares about a dress and a pair of shoes? As long as you're safe. You weren't injured, were you?" Her fingers clung to mine, and I thought I felt her tremble, too.

"No," I assured her.

"Thank God." She tucked her hand beneath my chin, and I pressed my cheek into her palm for the longest minute. Then she made a clucking noise and started in, "I ran into Janet Graham, and she filled me in. My word, it's a wonder no one was hurt." She lowered her voice. "I still can't believe there was a fistfight between Marilee and Amber Lynn, that their misbehavior started a fire. Good heavens, what were they thinking?"

Obviously, they weren't thinking at all.

She pressed her mouth into a hard line, pausing before she added, "The fire chief said they're not letting anyone back in until daylight. Marilee's beside herself. She yelled at the police first, telling them she wanted Amber Lynn arrested. Then she started howling for Justin, but no one seems to know where he'd gone. After that, she rattled on about set repairs and tape delays. I think Dr. Cooper gave her a shot of something to calm her down, thank heavens."

"Did Marilee even ask where her daughter was?"

"What do you mean?"

Glancing back at the doorway, I said quietly, "Kendall's in bad shape, Mother. She was on the floor of Marilee's bathroom, dead to the world. Okay, not *dead* dead, at least I hope not."

Cissy's hand went to her throat. "Was she burned in the fire? Smoke inhalation?"

"No, none of those things."

"Then what?"

I shrugged. "I don't know. Maybe she had too much to drink. Or it could be alcohol poisoning, an allergic reaction." I'd seen Kendall chug the one glass from the 1973 vintage poured for Marilee's toast, but I had no clue if she'd had more beforehand.

"Drugs?" Cissy suggested.

I hadn't seen any signs. No spilled pills on the floor, no coke residue, nothing obvious. But then I remembered the litany of physical and mental ailments Kendall had professed to have, and I wondered if she might be taking a medication that didn't mix with alcohol.

"I hope it's not drugs," was all I could muster in Kendall's defense. I hated to think she'd made herself sick to the point of unconsciousness.

My mother clicked tongue against teeth. "Marilee's always had trouble with that girl. I hope she hasn't done anything to hurt herself again."

Hurt herself *again*?

The idea of that merely made me feel worse.

"Kendall tried to talk to me earlier. She was upset after having some kind of argument with Marilee before the party"—I left out that Dewey the valet had been the one to impart that bit of info—"and she did seem . . . out of sorts, but I was busy checking the live stream and blew her off. Maybe if I hadn't . . . if I'd just let her *vent*."

"Andrea Blevins Kendricks, you stop that this minute." She fussed with the clumps of hair clinging to my brow.

"You're not responsible for the rest of the world, though you always seem to believe that you are. Ever since you were a little girl, you've had the need to rescue things. Stray animals, endangered species, misfits . . ."

"If you'd only seen her," I tried to explain my guilt. But any remaining words caught in my throat as I saw the front doors bang open and a firefighter rush out.

"Stand back," he shouted and held the nearest door wide for someone behind him.

A uniformed cop jumped in for the assist. "Step aside, y'all . . . step aside," he demanded and waved his arms madly at the crowd of people. Like Moses parting the Red Sea, he created a path for the paramedics who emerged next, the paddleboard clutched between them, Kendall's limp form lying atop it.

They rushed her to the EMS van and maneuvered her inside. Before the doors were closed, I saw Marilee crying as she was helped into the back.

Sirens roared as the van took off, weaving into traffic on Midway.

All I could do was watch, my insides tied in knots.

"Where are they taking her?" I asked. "Which hospital?"

"I'm not worried about Kendall as much as I am about you. C'mon, let's get you home," Cissy said, ignoring my questions, and folded an arm across my shoulders. "Fredrik's waiting with the car, and there's nothing you can do besides. We need to get you into dry clothes before you catch pneumonia . . ."

"Mother, it's at least ninety-five degrees."

"Don't fight me on this, Andrea."

But I dug in my bare heels. "I'll only go with you now if

you'll take me to the hospital afterward," I said. "I need to check up on Kendall, whether you come with me or not."

Even in the dim of night, with the freaky red and blue lights of the police car pulsating, I saw her eyes widen. She lifted her chin and gave her head a toss. "My, my, but you must get that stubborn streak from your father's side of the family. I certainly doubt it came from any of the Blevins clan. We're all very reasonable."

I didn't have the strength to tell her she was full of hooey.

"Is it a deal?"

She sighed, creasing her smooth powdered brow. "How about this? While you put on something dry, I'll find out which hospital they've admitted Kendall to and then I'll have Fredrik drive us. Is that all right with you?"

"It sounds . . . reasonable."

"Well, thank heavens."

Dewey had my keys, and it took me a few minutes to find him. So many of the partygoers were hounding him to get their cars so they could leave. When I told him I just needed my key ring and would pick up the Jeep the next day, he seemed relieved.

I'd have to return anyway to claim my purse, which, thankfully, held my cell phone, a tube of old Mary Kay lipstick, and little else of importance. Maybe I'd have Malone bring me, which seemed preferable to asking my mother.

By the time I picked my way across the parking lot, Cissy's car was waiting. It wasn't the champagne-colored Lexus she normally drove but the antique Bentley that had belonged to my Paw Paw (and usually sat in the garage).

Cissy only used it on rare occasions, which was good for Fredrik, her chauffeur, as he didn't like to work more than part-time. He did the Mr. Mom thing while his public-relations-executive wife locked in sixty hours a week for a downtown firm, an arrangement that baffled my mother.

Fred pulled the Bentley's back door open for me, and I smiled wanly into his clean-shaven face.

"Bad party, huh?" he said.

Let's see. Spit in the pâté. The hostess engaged in fisticuffs. A fire followed by a drenching from the sprinkler system. The hostess's daughter on the floor of the bathroom, barely breathing.

"It stank worse than Livarot," I told him, earning a blank stare. "Um, it stank worse than Limburger?" I offered instead, and his expression said, "Gotcha."

It would've been hard to come up with anything that could've made the evening any worse except famine or pestilence. We'd pretty much covered fire and flood.

As Fredrik shut me in, I slid across the soft leather to where Cissy waited for me with a blanket, an old plaid thing we'd used for picnics when I was a kid. The sight of it made me teary. Daddy had always kept that blanket in the trunk, and we'd used it for countless Fourth of Julys for viewing fireworks from the grass at the country club.

When I scooted close enough, Mother wrapped it around my shoulders and said, "It'll be fine, you'll see."

She meant Kendall.

And me.

"I hope so."

Fredrik turned on the radio, the button preset to the classical station and talk radio, all Mother would listen to. A soothing Beethoven sonata purred through the speakers.

Still, I shivered, unable to shake the image of Kendall's bloodless face from my head. The coldness of her skin.

Cissy tugged the blanket more snugly around me.

"I ran into Babette von Werner a few minutes ago and would you believe her tan came right off onto her snow-white Versace?" She was trying to take my mind off things, I realized, though it wasn't going to work. "You can't imagine how upset she was when she saw that the god-awful burnt orange had washed off onto her dress. She practically tossed Poppy out of his wheelchair and into the limo. Then they tore out of the parking lot like a shot. Wonder if she'll sue the spa who spray-painted her?"

Ordinarily, I would have found that tidbit amusing. At the moment, my smile muscles didn't seem to be working.

A media van pulled into the parking lot just as we exited.

I leaned my head against the seat and closed my eyes.

Cissy seemed to get the message and didn't attempt to engage me in conversation except to comment that Laura Mercier made a fabulous waterproof mascara guaranteed not to smudge like whatever brand I was wearing.

Needless to say, I didn't thank her for the beauty tip.

Within another fifteen minutes, we'd reached my condo. Fred parked the Bentley and opened the back door on Mother's side, offering her his hand and helping her out. Then it was my turn, and I scooted across the seat with the plaid blanket wrapped around me. Like a butterfly who refused to leave her cocoon, I wiggled free of the car, my naked feet hitting the pebbled sidewalk. Cissy kept reaching out for me as I waddled forward, as if afraid I'd topple over onto the patch of green lawn.

Fredrik had my key chain and reached the front door ahead of Mother and me. He made sure we were safely inside before he mentioned he'd wait in the car. After depositing the keys in my hand, he promptly exited, leaving us alone.

It felt great to be home, and I stood for a moment, unmoving, simply looking around at my tiny living room with its sand-colored walls and eclectic furnishings. Even the air I inhaled smelled reassuring, like my favorite vanilla candle with a hint of burned bagel.

"If you'd rather not go to the hospital, it's all right, sugar." Mother trailed a finger along the bookshelf lined with hardcover mysteries. "I'll go with you in the morning."

"Just give me a minute," I told her.

"Sure, sweetie. Take all the time you need."

She strolled into the kitchen, probably to take a peek in my fridge to see if I had enough to eat, or maybe to do the white glove test on my appliances. (An exam I would surely flunk.)

At the moment, I was too wiped out to care what she did, so long as it kept her occupied.

What I really wanted most was to throw off the blanket; shed my wet and impossibly heavy sequined dress and equally damp underthings; hop in a steamy tub, and forget that this night had ever happened.

What I *needed* to do, before I could ever consider relaxing in a scented bath, was to find out where Kendall had been taken by the ambulance and go see her for myself. I had to be sure she was all right, before I could truly breathe.

Discarding the blanket that had draped me like a human crepe, I went into my bathroom and peeled off the limp Escada dress and everything underneath it. I splashed my face with warm water and dried myself with a fresh towel, rubbing my skin from head to toe until the goosebumps were erased.

On went dry bra and panties, cargo pants, and faded PEROT FOR PRESIDENT T-shirt, flip-flops for my feet. Unruly tendrils curled around my face; the rest of my hair I combed back straight and bound with a clip.

My eyes looked red-veined and irritated, and I worked out my contacts and put them away. I slipped on my wire-rims, which completed my transformation from "Woo-doggy" to Marian the Librarian. But I felt like myself at last.

When I emerged from my bedroom, Mother was on the telephone, uttering things like, "Am I related? Well, technically speakin', no, but I chaired the committee that raised funds for the new equipment for the cardiac wing so you could call me a fairy godmother to the whole danged hospital . . . hello? Hello?"

She slammed the receiver down and looked up.

"Kendall's at Medical City," she said and tugged at an earring.

That was in Mother's neck of the woods.

"How is she? Is she okay?"

"Silly privacy laws." She frowned. "No one would tell me a danged thing even after I reminded them I'd chaired the donation drive that had raised the funds to replace every dad-gummed defibrillator in the place."

Okay, I knew she was pissed off, because "danged" and "dad-gummed" were the closest to four-letter words she ever got.

"You ready?" she asked.

"As I'll ever be."

"Then let's go." Like a woman on a mission, she scooped up the plaid blanket and her Chanel evening bag before hustling me toward the door. "If there's one thing I've learned after all these years of charity work"—she drawled as she waited for me to lock up—"it's to never conduct business over the phone if you can do it in person. That way, no one can put you on hold, forcing you t' listen to Barry Manilow. And they most certainly cannot hang up on you."

"I'll remember that," I murmured, climbing into the Bentley behind her.

Mother was full of such practical tips. Perhaps someday she'd write it all down in a book and call it: *Who Moved My Brie?*

Or, *What Color Is Your Prada Suit?*

Maybe I'd send Bill Gates a copy for Christmas (in a box marked C.O.D.), a little repayment for all the trouble I'd had with his various Windows systems through the years.

I had a feeling he could benefit from Mother's wisdom as much as anyone.

Chapter 13

 I'd never much liked hospitals.

(Except for doctors and nurses, did anyone really?)

It was more than the overbright hallways where the slap of shoes on vinyl flooring echoed far too loudly. It wasn't even the thought of green Jell-O and Ensure being passed off as meals, the cloying stench of cleaning fluids, or the annoying voice over the intercom intermittently "paging Dr. Green . . . paging Dr. Green."

For me, it was something else entirely, tied to my own ugly experiences.

Once I set foot inside any place with "medical center" in its name, my mind would fill with frightening scenes from my childhood, appearing in flashes, like short flicks directed by David Lynch or Quentin Tarantino.

They always began with one particular long-ago incident from Mrs. Cannon's first-grade class. *Cut to homemade mail receptacles strapped to the back of the chairs,* used to exchange Valentines. *Zoom in on mine,* a brown

Neiman-Marcus box wrapped with toilet paper. *Cut to a line of girls in plaid skirts,* queued at the opened door, ready to head to lunch. I'm there, standing in front, the line leader, leaning casually with my hand on the doorframe, my thumb folded into the wedge of space between the hinges. *Quick shot of my smile* as I imagine the beans and franks on the hot lunch menu; fast forward to the next frame, where I'm howling like a banshee after Holly Hertel stepped out from the line behind me and yanked the door closed.

Yes, while my thumb was still in it.

Hello!

See blood drip to the linoleum as Mrs. Cannon races me down to the nurse's room near the principal's office. *Light as bright as a klieg* hovers over me at the hospital, and a doctor assures me "this won't hurt a bit." *Hear my heart pound with terror* as a needle the size of a turkey baster bears down on my wounded digit.

Thankfully, that's when everything fades to black—rather like the electricity in Marilee's studio. There was another flick, one that dealt with a jump-rope exercise gone bad and more blood (this time, from my head). But I won't get into that.

Instinctively, I rubbed at the scar running across the back of my right thumb as I followed Cissy to the admitting desk at Medical City.

While she scored information from the volunteer at the counter, I squashed down the flashbacks. I didn't want to see them again, didn't want to be reminded of why being in this place made my pulse race and my palms sweaty.

Grow up, Andy, I told myself, but it didn't seem to matter. Things like that stuck with a person, no matter how old they got.

"Kendall's having some tests done before being moved to a private room from the ER," Mother said, nudging me toward the elevators. "I know Mari must be a total basket case."

Stuffing my hands in the pockets of my cargo pants, I trailed behind the click of Cissy's high heels. We passed a smiling group of women in green scrubs and more than a few grim-looking folks in cut-off shorts or blue jeans, looking lost.

No one gave Mother more than a passing glance, despite her attire, and I wondered if the hospital's proximity to Highland Park had made visitors wearing head-to-toe Chanel commonplace.

The elevator button pinged, and I slipped behind Cissy into the small space that already held a man in a wheelchair and a fellow in blue scrubs transporting him.

Not a word was uttered until the lift stopped moving with a *ping* and the doors opened up again.

"This is us, sugar," Mother said, and I followed her out.

At least she knew her way around, so we didn't have to mess with confusing signs and arrows. Her committee work for the hospital had paid off in more ways than one.

Past an empty nurses' station, we found Marilee in a small waiting room, sitting on a lumpy sofa amidst discarded coffee cups and magazines. Though she slumped with her head in her hands, she must've heard us approach because she slowly raised her chin, revealing a face ravaged by tears.

"Cissy," she said, breathing my mother's name in an exhaled breath. "My dear, dear friend. I'm so glad you're here. I can't find Justin, and I'm a total wreck."

In a snap, my mother turned into Florence Nightingale, sending me to fetch a fresh cup of coffee for Marilee. She drew a folded handkerchief from her Chanel bag and pressed it into Marilee's hand, confirming my long-established impression that Mother's purses were like a magician's hat, producing whatever was needed in a particular emergency. Whether it be a needle and thread or a breath mint.

While I moseyed over to a table with a much-used coffeepot, I heard a lot of "there, there's" as Mother settled onto the sofa and began patting Marilee's shoulder.

"How is Kendall? Have you seen her?" I asked when I returned with the black coffee. I offered it to Marilee, though she was sobbing too much to drink. So I cleared away a mess of magazines on the knee-high table and put down the cup in front of her.

"This night . . . *gup* . . . has been . . . *gup* . . . so awful." She hiccoughed between every other word so that it was difficult to understand her. "How could this . . . *gup* . . . happen to me? It was supposed to be a celebration . . ."

"What did the doctors say?" I tried again, interrupting her pity party. "About Kendall," I added, so there was no mistake.

With most of her makeup now on Mother's linen kerchief, Marilee's face appeared haggard; crisscrossed with lines I hadn't noticed before. She seemed older than she had just an hour or two earlier. All her smugness drained, she appeared the very portrait of a distraught mother, reminding me of Picasso's *Melancholy Woman* with her head bowed, her skin a bluish shade.

"In the . . . *gup* . . . emergency room . . . they asked if she . . . *gup* . . . took any drugs . . . *gup* . . . like Ecstasy. Her heart wasn't beating normally, they said. They had to stabilize her cardiac rhythm before they could . . . *gup* . . . do a tox screen and a . . . *gup* . . . blood alcohol test." She gulped in air, trying to stop her hiccups attack, while Mother kept patting. "But Kendall doesn't . . . do drugs," she spoke slowly, and, this time, without "gupping" mid-sentence. "Not since Justin's been around, I'm sure of it. Unless, she did this to hurt me. To pay me back." She moaned. "What am I going to do with her, Cissy? *What?*"

They had her heart rhythm stabilized and were running tests. That much registered in my brain, which could only mean one thing.

Kendall was alive and breathing.

That was what I'd needed to hear.

My legs wobbled beneath me, and I eased myself into a vinyl-cushioned chair, listening to Marilee moan on and on about her ruined party and the damaged set.

"I'm wondering now . . . I can't help but consider . . . the recluse spider in my shoebox . . . the crashing mike that would have struck me if Jim hadn't jumped in its way . . . what if Kendall had something to do with all of them? Perhaps she wants me to fail. Could that be it?" she asked my mother. "She's always been so needy. I could never give her enough of me."

Kendall was needy?

Obviously, Marilee hadn't looked in the mirror lately.

I tuned them out and looked around me, at the television hanging from the wall, the nine o'clock news anchors moving their mouths but the volume too low to hear. Had video and sound bites from Addison already hit the airwaves?

Did the whole city of Dallas know about the fire at *The Sweet Life*'s studio, started by a burning *I Dream of Jeannie* hairpiece?

Had anyone contacted Gilbert about Kendall? I wondered. Did he realize his daughter nearly died while his wife was going after Marilee with a vintage bottle of champagne?

And what about Justin?

Where was Marilee's young lover?

He'd disappeared during the wrestling match between Marilee and Amber Lynn, and I'd half-expected to find him with Kendall. Only she'd been all by her lonesome when I'd stumbled upon her in Marilee's bathroom.

Or was she really all by her lonesome?

I hadn't exactly peered into closets or poked behind furniture. Could Justin have been with her when she got sick and passed out? Would he have left her there on the floor when the fire alarm went off, afraid someone might find him with her limp body and accuse him of debauchery or worse?

My mind was on overdrive.

I squeezed my eyes shut and pictured Justin uncorking then pouring the special bottle of Dom Perignon that Marilee had saved for her special occasion. He'd poured a glass for himself, but he'd never drunk it. Marilee had barely touched hers either, because she'd been too busy fending off Amber.

But Kendall . . . she'd downed her full glass like a fraternity boy attacking a beer bong. What if Marilee's expensive bottle had something wrong with it?

Hey, I'd gotten sick off yogurt that was only two weeks past expiration, not thirty years.

"There you are, Marilee. My God, I've been so worried." *Speak of the devil.*

Justin swept into the waiting room, an unruly lock of blond fallen onto his brow. He drew his hands from the pockets of his dove-gray jacket, reaching out for Marilee, who shakily rose from the couch.

"Where *have* you been?" she railed at him. "I couldn't find you when the fire started or later in the parking lot. I was afraid something had happened to you, too."

"To me? Oh, no, no. I was never in harm's way." He stroked her hair, calming her, seemingly oblivious to the fact that Mother sat on the sofa, mere feet away, and I sat just across the coffee table. "You know how I hate parties, so I slipped out back for some air. I didn't even know there'd been a fire until I heard the sirens and ran around front. By then, the ambulance was rushing off with you in it. A cop told me they'd taken an unconscious woman to Medical City, so I assumed *you* were hurt. Then I found out it was Kendall."

"Oh, Jussie, I'm so sorry. I didn't realize . . . didn't mean to insinuate that you'd deserted me on purpose," Marilee blubbered. "I'm just so worried about Kendall. Do you think she drank too much? She wouldn't have taken drugs, would she? The emergency room doctors asked about Ecstasy."

"Drugs? No." He shook his head. "Never."

"You're right. She's put those days behind her, thanks to you." She placed her palms against his chest, staring up at him. "They said her heart stopped, or nearly stopped, but they've got it beating normally again. After they draw blood and run some tests, they'll bring her up to the private room I arranged for her. She'll have to stay overnight."

"That's probably best."

"I hate to consider that she might have done something . . . to harm herself. She's so sensitive, so temperamental. Whatever I said that made her lose control earlier . . . you saw her drop her glass, didn't you? What if I'm responsible? What if this episode she's had is my fault? No matter, she'll blame me, won't she?" Marilee pressed her face into his chest, and Justin drew her close, tucking her head beneath his chin.

His gaze slid my way, and, for a moment, I met his eyes before he looked off, as if he hadn't seen me at all.

"This isn't your fault, Mari," he said, his voice muffled against the puff of her blond hair. "Kendall brings these things on herself. It's what the Chinese call 'Ming.' It's her fate . . . her destiny . . . to cause chaos in her own life and the lives of others."

"You think so?"

"Yes, babe, I do."

I wondered what the Chinese word was for "excuse me while I puke"?

Mother made a face and discreetly slipped off the sofa. She came around to where I sat, leaned low and whispered in my ear, "What a bunch of hogwash. That boy must've swallowed a trough."

Scary that Mother and I were thinking the very same thing. Thank goodness it didn't happen often, but, when it did, it unnerved me.

I got up, ambling toward the Mr. Coffee.

Cissy followed.

"Young Mr. Gable wasn't looking for Marilee after the fire"—she insisted, hovering at my shoulder—"and I should know, because I found her easily enough once Fredrik got the car far enough into the parking lot to let me out. Marilee was in the center of it all, as usual, hollering like she'd had a bad bikini wax. Anyone with ears would've pinpointed her in a second flat. It was a lot harder trying to find you. No one told me you were still inside the building." She poked me in the ribs and asked, "Did you see Justin before that nice fireman carried you out?"

Fleetingly—and I mean, *fleetingly*—I considered confiding that I'd walked in on Justin and Kendall in Marilee's office, shagging on the sofa before the party started.

Then I nixed that idea, afraid that Cissy might blab to Marilee out of some sense of loyalty. And I'd given Kendall my word that I wouldn't squeal.

Since it sounded like basically everyone in Kendall's life had let her down at some point—her father, her mother, her off-and-on-again lover—I didn't want to add my name to the list. She needed to learn that not everyone was out to betray her.

"Justin could've been inside the building, but I didn't see him, no. I didn't see anyone else except Kendall."

See being the operative word.

I could still feel the darkness around me, the sense of disorientation as I'd fumbled my way down the hallway. But I hadn't been alone. Someone had been there, had bumped into me without apology. If it were Justin, I would've needed night goggles to ID him.

But it could've been.

I pushed my glasses tighter on my nose and looked across the room.

Marilee clung to the lapels of Justin's jacket.

Empty lapels, I realized.

Where was his rose?

"What is it?" Mother asked, noting my hesitation.

I rubbed a hand over the nape of my neck where my short hairs prickled. "I'm not sure, but I think Justin might have gone back to Marilee's office after Kendall."

"Well, did he or didn't he?"

"There was a broken boutonnière on the carpet by Kendall's shoes."

I thought again about who'd knocked into me in the hallway, the brush of air against my skin, and I suddenly remembered breathing in the scent of something sweet and soft.

Almonds.

"What's wrong, sugar?"

I shook my head. I couldn't explain to her when I wasn't sure myself. "It's nothing, never mind."

"What about that broken rosebud? You think it's Justin's? He isn't wearing a boutonnière now."

"It doesn't mean anything, Mother. Not really," I said, and I could read her disappointment. "All of Marilee's male staffers wore them in their lapels. Any one of them could have been in the office at some time during the party."

"That boy is up to no good," she whispered.

"Well, you can't make up what didn't happen." Still, there was something I was sure of. "Justin wasn't out back," I told her, keeping my voice down. "I would've seen him when I pushed open the rear exit door. No one was out there. Just rows of parked cars."

Cissy sucked in her cheeks. "But it's possible he was with Kendall."

"How?" My mother seemed awfully eager to pin something on Marilee's junior Romeo.

"He could've slipped her a Mickey," she hissed in my ear, "in the champagne."

"What?"

"A *Mick-ey*," she reiterated, emphasizing each syllable, as if I'd bought deaf and dumb in a two-pack at the Horchow outlet store. She snapped her fingers, rings twinkling beneath the green fluorescent glow. "It's so easy these days, what with the Internet and all. You can order anything. He could've used that date rape drug. What's it called? PHD?"

My right eyelid twitched.

Like the night hadn't been long enough already.

"It's GHB," I told her. "Not PHD." Though, come to think of it, I had once gone out with a PhD whose tales of academe nearly rendered me unconscious.

"You sure it's not GHP?"

"Yes, I'm sure. That's my health insurance company."

"GHB. Okay, yes." She whispered like we were coconspirators. "I've seen warnings about it on TV. I even watched an A&E special about that Max Factor heir who went around sprinkling it in women's drinks so he could"—she frowned—"have his way with them. All that money and not an ounce of charm." She clicked tongue against teeth. "Such a waste of a trust fund."

As if she wouldn't have been matchmaking up a storm had the guy lived in Big D, at least before his mug shot appeared on *America's Most Wanted*.

"I don't trust Justin Gable, not as far as I can spit." Mother was on a roll. "Marilee thinks Kendall's jealous of her relationship with that boy, but what if Justin's equally envious of Kendall? She stands to inherit when Mari goes. So perhaps Justin wanted to get the girl out of the way, so he could be first in line if anything happened to Mari?"

"You think Justin spiked the champagne . . . or whatever . . . so Kendall would be out of the picture for good?" It was hard to say without laughing. And people thought I had a vivid imagination. "Look, Mother, this isn't an Agatha Christie novel. Regular people don't do that kind of stuff."

Not the people I knew.

"I am well aware of the difference between reality and fiction, thank you very much, Andrea."

"You sure?"

I was tempted to remind her of a certain "Count Vladimir from Romania" whom she had entertained and introduced around on the party circuit last spring before he was arrested for fraud. Turns out he was a bankrupt day trader from Baton Rouge pulling a con.

Surprise, surprise.

"The world is a far different place than it used to be, so

much more violent," Mother said, a reminder of why I avoided watching the nightly news. "It's enough to make you want to stay home with all the locks bolted and the alarm set." Lines puckered around her mouth. "Why, last week, Buffy Winspear was robbed, for heaven's sakes."

"What?" I hadn't seen that one coming. Buffy Winspear was a sixty-year-old perennial fundraising chairwoman who ran with Mother's crowd, so the fact that she was victimized didn't exactly put me at ease. "Geez, Mother, was she hurt?"

"She had the DVD player stolen right out of her Escalade while she was at Pilates."

"Her Escalade?"

"Fresh off the lot and loaded."

I struggled to keep my eyes from crossing.

Slowly, I exhaled. "Buffy's *car* was burgled?"

"They broke a window, but they didn't take anything else. Luckily, her Liberace CD collection was untouched."

Luckily?

A tiny ache tweaked my temples.

"Listen to me, Andrea," she said in a hushed voice. "Men are ruled by testosterone, not common sense or reason."

Was she talking about Buffy's burglar or Justin?

"They do things out of anger when they're pushed too far, usually by a woman."

I pressed my fingertips against the throbbing above my eyes.

"Think of that case in California, where that husband bought a boat, killed his pregnant wife, and dumped her into the bay. Fool claimed to be fishing on Christmas Eve." She flipped her head. "Good Lord, who goes fishing on

Christmas Eve? He should have said he was doing some last-minute shopping, because he surely couldn't use golfing as an excuse. It's what OJ told the police, so that alibi was taken."

"Mother, you can't copyright an alibi."

"Just listen to me, Andrea."

I gritted my teeth.

Good God.

Calgon, take me away. And make it ASAP.

Chapter 14

 I squished my eyes closed and opened them again.

Even took off my glasses and rubbed the lenses with the hem of my T-shirt. Pinched the bridge of my nose before I put them back on. Unfortunately, nothing had changed—Marilee was crying into Justin's shoulder and Cissy was yapping about the shortcomings of homicidally inclined husbands, though at least the smudged fingerprint was gone from my peripheral view.

"You would have thought he'd learned from OJ, but he tried to run to Mexico with $10,000 in his pocket, his hair dyed blond, and with that awful beard. If he'd lain low, maybe someone besides his own poor misguided mother would have believed him. Good heavens, Andrea, have you paid attention to a word I've said in the last five minutes?"

My eyes had glazed over, so numbing was her monologue. If I never heard another word about OJ—other than the indisputably innocent breakfast juice—I could die a happy woman.

Cissy cocked her head and stared at me. "Sweetie, you don't look well. Perhaps you should sit down."

If I didn't look well, it was because I felt like a zombie. Too much bombardment of external sensation and not enough chance to absorb it.

"Come along." She took my arm and led me back to the chair with the blue vinyl cushion. Out of the corner of my eye, I saw a figure sweep past us and charge up to the nurses' station.

A trim fellow in khakis and a Polo tee, brown hair curling at the collar.

He leaned against the counter and rattled off quite plainly to a ponytailed woman in scrubs, "I was told the victim from the Addison fire was transferred to a room on this floor. I think it might be someone I know . . ."

Even if I hadn't heard his voice, I would've recognized that backside. Like an in-season plum, small but firm.

"Brian?" I called out, getting to my feet, despite Mother's attempts to keep me glued to the chair. "Hey, Malone?" I tried again and, this time, he turned around, giving me a full frontal of the concern on his bespectacled face.

He rushed over with all the eagerness of a puppy whose owner has returned from an extended vacation. "Oh, my God, I was so worried," he said, grabbing my arms and pulling me close. His chin caught my glasses, knocking them askew.

Grace was not his forte any more than it was mine.

"I saw on the news about the fire at the studio," he went on in a rush. "They mentioned a woman being transported to Medical City by ambulance, and I tried to call your cell.

Then I tried your condo. When you didn't answer either phone, I panicked."

"I'm okay," I assured him as he rubbed his hands over my shoulders. "It wasn't me. It was Marilee's daughter, Kendall."

"I'm so relieved I could kiss you."

"So, what's stopping you?" I quietly asked.

He caught his hand at the nape of my neck and bent toward me, his mouth on a direct trajectory to mine.

Mother cleared her throat.

A foghorn could not have given off a louder warning.

Abort, abort.

Abruptly his lips changed course and landed on my forehead. He clumsily patted my arms before stepping back to introduce a couple feet between us. He brushed his palms on his trousers and uttered, "Uh, hello, Mrs. Kendricks. How're you doing, ma'am? I'm sorry, but I didn't see you there."

I straightened the glasses on my nose and frowned, finding it hard to believe that a man who spent his days learning the ropes as a defense attorney for one of the most powerful firms in Dallas could be so cowed by a woman wearing size-six Chanel.

It's not as though she was packing heat. The only concealed weapon she carried was a Charles of the Ritz touchup stick. Though she did carry a good deal of weight with his bosses, which might well account for his awkwardness around her.

"I'm sorely offended by your remark, Mr. Malone. Didn't see me, hmm? And with me dressed to the nines. Perhaps you ought to have your vision checked. You may require a stronger prescription," Cissy said, sounding miffed.

I could tell she was toying with him, but I'm not sure it was all that clear to Brian.

This was her "alpha belle" routine, a test she put each man through with the balls to date me, which doubtless had something to do with my still being single.

Brian ran a finger under the collar of his shirt, eyes bugging at me, pleading silently for help.

Unfortunately, I was running low on ammo at the moment, so I did what I could, which amounted to giving my mother the evil eye. For all the good it would do. At this point in our lives, she was used to my dirty looks.

Footsteps sounded on the floor, and a sturdy female in a white coat strode into the waiting room. She clutched a rather substantial manila folder in her right hand. A badge was clipped to her breast pocket, and a stethoscope coiled around her neck. The overhead fluorescents lent a yellow tinge to cocoa brown skin, but otherwise her attractive features appeared rather stoic. She looked cool and composed in contrast to the frazzled state of everyone else in the room.

She also looked vaguely familiar, though I didn't know why.

"Mrs. Mabry?" she asked, glancing about the room with dark eyes. For a moment, her gaze settled on my mother, and her mouth parted slightly.

Cissy nodded.

What was that about?

"Over here." Marilee quickly rose to her feet, Justin

propping her up with his hand beneath her elbow. "I'm Marilee Mabry," she said. "How is Kendall, Doctor . . . ?"

"Taylor."

"Dr. Taylor, yes, where is Kendall? What's going on? When can I see her?"

"Perhaps you'd like to talk privately," Dr. Taylor suggested, the cue all too clear to me. "I can find an empty room."

I gently prodded my mother, thinking we should go. "C'mon, let's go check out the vending machine," I said, though Cissy didn't budge an inch.

"Would you like us to leave, Mari?" my mother asked.

"No, no, please, stay," she said, then faced the doctor again. "I want them here, if you don't object. They're as close to family as I've got." She clutched at Justin, and her eyes moistened. Her mascara had further smeared after her latest histrionics, giving her the appearance of a rabid raccoon. "So, you may talk freely about my daughter. Will she be all right? Did you find out what caused her to pass out? Where is she?"

"Let's take it one issue at a time, Mrs. Mabry." The doctor raised a pink-palmed hand. "First off, your daughter's on her way up as we speak. Her vital signs are weak but stable, and she is conscious, though she'll be extremely groggy when you see her. I won't allow visiting for long. She needs to rest. She's had a rough evening."

Marilee nodded. "Yes, yes, I understand."

"As far as what happened"—Dr. Taylor crossed her arms over the manila file, her brow crinkling beneath tight brown curls—"we're still piecing that together. I'm hoping you all can help us figure out some of the puzzle." She glanced our way again. "Are you certain you want me speaking openly? There are privacy rules that I'm supposed to follow . . ."

Mother sniffed. "Here we go again."

"I don't give a damn about the rules!" Marilee bristled, clutching her hands to fists. "For God's sake, get to the point. What's wrong with my child? Why did she collapse?"

The ponytailed woman in scrubs watched from the nurses' station. She picked up a telephone receiver then put it down again.

"Let's start with Kendall's medical history, or at least what we have from the records available," Dr. Taylor resumed in a soft, controlled tone. "Though it doesn't appear she's been seen here recently, she was examined in the past by several different specialists—most notably, a psychiatrist, a podiatrist, and a gastroenterologist—at this facility. We don't have all the notes at our disposal, but we have enough." She paused, pursing her lips, before she went on. "There are well-healed scars at her wrists which indicate a suicide attempt . . ."

"That was years ago," Marilee cut her off, sounding tearful. "Kendall was out of control then, torn apart by the divorce and feeling neglected. She only wanted my attention."

Scars at her wrists.

My God.

I pressed my eyes closed and envisioned the silver bracelets lined up on Kendall's forearms. Put there to hide the evidence of a failed suicide attempt? I never saw her without rows of bracelets, wrapped around her like Slinkies, and now I knew why.

"My daughter has not tried anything of the sort since," Marilee insisted. "So I won't believe it if you tell me that's what this episode was. She's thrilled about my show. She loves being at the studio. She's as happy as she's ever been."

Thrilled? Happy?

Kendall?

I considered the young woman with whom I'd argued in Marilee's office. "Thrilled" and "happy" were definitely not words I'd use to describe her. I could think of others that suited her better: sullen, moody, confused, and manipulative.

"Hold on a minute, Mrs. Mabry. I'm not implying that Kendall's collapse was self-inflicted, perhaps not intentionally. Please, bear with me." The doctor shifted on her sensible pumps, gripping Kendall's records with both hands. "The notes show that your daughter was diagnosed with depression and an eating disorder . . ."

"Again in the past," Marilee interjected. "She's cured of those."

"Really?"

"Yes, Doctor, really."

I rolled my eyes, wondering how a mother could think her daughter was "cured" when she looked like a human toothpick.

"She reportedly suffered from bulimia." Dr. Taylor flipped open the chart in her hands and glanced at the pages within. "Which caused erosion of the esophagus and decay to her tooth enamel. About six months ago, her gastro prescribed Prevacid for acid reflux, at the same time her podiatrist placed her on an antifungal for an infection . . ."

"Because of her ugly toenails," Marilee jumped in. "But that was all before."

"Before what?"

Marilee turned to her blond beau and stroked his arm. "Before Justin. He weaned her off her prescriptions, you see. All the pills she used to take for her stomach, for her nerves, and to get to sleep. She said they made her feel funky, like her heart was jumping out of her chest." Justin stood like a mannequin, his chiseled features impassive. "Jussie's a certified personal trainer, and he's studied ancient Chinese nutrition."

The doctor sucked in her cheeks, looking irritated rather than impressed. "So you're a holistic healer, Mr. . . . ?"

"Gable," Marilee said for him. "Justin Gable."

"What kind of a regimen was Kendall on, might I ask?"

"I didn't do anything illegal," Justin began, but Marilee cut him off at the pass.

"He started her on a liquid juice fast several months ago to detoxify her system." Marilee held on to Justin's arm, though I noticed he kept clenching and unclenching his fingers. "Kendall rarely touched alcohol anymore, and she was eating healthier, gaining a little weight back. Justin had her on herbal supplements. She finally felt her energy return."

"Herbal supplements?" Dr. Taylor cocked her head. "Like what?"

When Justin didn't respond, Marilee turned to him. "Go

on. You tell her. I can't remember all the names of those things."

"Yes, do tell, Mr. Gable. I'm very interested to hear."

"Kendall took only what she needed." Justin seemed reluctant to answer, his eyes frequently casting down toward his shoes. "Antioxidant vitamins, ginseng for energy, and echinacea to treat infection and inflammation. Sometimes, maybe deer velvet," he added, voice softening to a near whisper.

"Deer velvet?" the doctor repeated. "I'm not sure I'm familiar with it."

"It simulates the immune system," he said. "It can also, um, improve sexual function." He blushed.

Marilee looked at him.

"But the deer velvet was merely intended to build up her resistance to bacteria and viruses," Justin added quickly. "Kendall was so prone to colds."

Right, resistance to bacteria, I thought and wanted to utter, "ha!"

"It's important, Mr. Gable. What else was she on?" Dr. Taylor pressed, making notes in Kendall's chart with a pen from her lab coat pocket.

He rolled his head back, glancing at the ceiling. "She took kava kava on occasion, for her anxiety and mood swings."

"Did she have any this evening?" The doctor's brown eyes watched him closely.

"She was nervous about the party, so it's possible. I don't keep the herbal supplements under lock and key, okay? Occasionally, I've made her protein smoothies from my own recipes, but she had access to whatever she needed, and she knew what levels were safe for her."

"Safe for her, huh?" Frowning, Dr. Taylor shook her head and scribbled. "Anything else, Mr. Gable? Any other supplements you've given her lately?"

Even white teeth pulled on his bottom lip. "Kendall has taken ma huang. But it's not like I forced her."

"Ma huang? That's ephedra, right?"

"It's a purer form, yes."

"So it's more potent?"

"Yes."

"The substance was banned for sale by the FDA," the doctor said.

"But it's still available," he insisted and smoothed his hands over his lapels before he shoved them in his jacket pockets. "Anyone who wants to can find it on the Internet, and it's safe when used appropriately. The FDA's being unreasonable, and it won't stop people from getting it. Kendall used it to keep her appetite down . . ."

"Her appetite?" the doctor scoffed. "She can't weigh much more than a hundred pounds."

"She also used it for flare-ups of her asthma. Sometimes she'd get short of breath if she exerted herself."

"I see." But it didn't sound as if Dr. Taylor "saw" at all. "So you assumed the shortness of breath was respiratory? Are you a pulmonologist, too, Mr. Gable?"

"No." His nostrils flared.

"How much was she taking?" The doctor flipped Kendall's chart closed and shoved it under her armpit. She looked like she wanted to smack Justin upside the head with it.

"Never more than the recommended dosage," he said and pushed the lock of hair off his brow. His eyes avoided Marilee. "I advised her to go off the ma huang every few weeks to give her system a chance to breathe. I assume she followed my instructions. It's not my fault if she didn't. I'm not her keeper."

"Since we detected toxic levels in her system, I'd have to agree with that assessment, sir. How could you expect her to follow such an unsupervised regime, and when you didn't even know her medical status?"

"Toxic levels? No way. It's not possible." He scratched his forehead, doing a good impression of befuddled. "Believe me when I say that I had no idea, Doctor. I can't imagine Kendall would do something so foolish, but, then again, she's rather impulsive and has a tendency toward self-destructiveness."

I waited for the doctor to respond, half-expecting her to throw the book at him for practicing holistic medicine without a license (if there was such a thing).

But she surprised me.

"This conversation has been highly enlightening, I must say, particularly as it relates to Kendall's well-being." She kept her tone even, but her body language radiated disapproval. She had her hands on her hips, chart tucked away on the right side. "First, I believe you actually did her a favor, Mr. Gable, by taking Kendall off the Prevacid and the antifungal, which she should never have taken at once. The combination would've been as dangerous to her system as the kava kava and ephedra—excuse me, ma huang— you've been doling out to her, sir. I'm surprised she didn't collapse prior to this evening considering the severity of her heart condition. She should have been seeing a cardiologist to monitor her arrhythmia."

"Arrhythmia?" Justin's voice went up like Mickey Mouse. "What are you saying? Kendall didn't have a heart problem."

"Oh, yes, she did. And I'm tempted to include the police in our debate here about whether or not what you did for Kendall was negligent at best, criminal at worst . . ."

"The police? There was nothing wrong with my advising Kendall about herbal remedies," Justin countered, his face suddenly sapped of color, his eyes wide with fear.

"Hold on a minute here!" Marilee wailed. "Kendall's a grown woman. Justin didn't do anything against her will, and he had no more idea about any heart condition that I did. If she had a problem, surely I would have known. I've sent her to more doctors in the past few years than I've seen my whole life."

I considered the litany of problems Kendall had professed to suffering, and I wondered how anyone could've honestly believed she was healthy or sound.

"I've been diagnosed as hyperactive, depressed, anorexic, bulimic, and suffering from posttraumatic stress disorder and abandonment—not to mention having migraines, hormonal imbalances, and God knows what else."

It was all I could do not to shout, "Kendall's a frigging mess! Can't you see that?" Though I figured Marilee had been too busy worrying about her career and her love life to take a good hard look at her own daughter.

I bit my tongue.

Malone must've seen my shoulders stiffen, as I felt his

hands settle on either side of my neck. He gave a gentle squeeze, and I leaned back against him.

"Kendall might've seen a lot of doctors, but apparently none of them ever administered an ECG, according to her records," Dr. Taylor said, slipping the chart from beneath her arm and patting it with the palm of her hand.

"An ECG?" Marilee looked puzzled.

"An echocardiogram. We use ultrasound to evaluate the heart for abnormalities. When Kendall was brought in, we hooked her up to both an ECG and an EKG, an electrocardiogram, because we detected an arrhythmia," the doctor explained. Then she lifted her chin, looking squarely at Marilee. "What we found was that Kendall has a prolonged QT rhythm . . . her ventricular heart rhythm is off more than a few beats."

"And that's not good?" Marilee asked, not looking so good herself.

"No. In fact, it's very bad. It's called long QT syndrome. It's often inherited. Certain drugs and"—Taylor's eyes went to Justin—"herbal supplements are contraindicated and can lead to shortness of breath or more serious complications, like syncopal episodes . . . passing out," she clarified. "Which is likely what happened to her tonight."

"Maybe you're wrong. Maybe it wasn't the herbs. She was drinking," Justin interjected. "She had champagne."

"No," Dr. Taylor stated emphatically. "It wasn't the champagne that did this to her. It was the high dose of ephedra"—she waved a hand dismissively as Justin started to correct her—"the ma huang, whatever you want to call it. She had a large enough dose in her bloodstream to knock a heart-healthy person off her feet. But someone with long QT"—she shook her head—"I'm surprised it didn't kill her. She could've gone into sudden cardiac arrest. It would've looked exactly like a heart attack on autopsy, and no one would've been the wiser."

Chapter 15

 A pair of orderlies rolled Kendall past us and into a private room.

She was hooked up to an IV and a beeping monitor that scooted along with her, and I glimpsed her face on the pillow, dark hair on white. Her skin had the translucence of skim milk, beyond pale with a tinge of blue.

Marilee followed the doctor and orderlies into the room. She moaned all the while, calling, "Kendall? Darling, it's Mummy. I'm here for you."

Justin started to follow, and I put a hand on his arm, refusing to let go when he tried to pull away.

"Why don't you let them alone, just for a while? They don't need you getting in between them, not now."

"You have no clue how important I am to them, do you?" he said, staring hard at me. "I watch out for them, care for them in a way no one else around them does. I make sure Kendall's lies don't get out of hand, and I keep the peace between her and Mari. I would never hurt either one, despite what you think. I'd rather cut off my right arm than harm a woman."

Nice sales pitch, buddy, but I wasn't buying.

I didn't back off. "You've already hurt them plenty, and not just with your herbal mumbo-jumbo," I replied, "by sleeping with mother and daughter. Don't you get what that does to Kendall? It tears her up inside."

"You think I did this to her on purpose? You think I'm the reason she's here?"

"Aren't you?" I asked him.

He looked over at the door of the room into which they'd taken Kendall. Then he shrugged off my hand and muttered, "I need some fresh air. It's too damned stuffy."

He sauntered off in his athletic stride, though I didn't admire any part of him, not anymore.

I found myself hoping he wouldn't come back. Kendall didn't need him around.

Good riddance, I mused and moseyed back over to where my mother and Malone idled in the waiting room, the television flashing silent images above them.

"What did you say to him?" Cissy asked.

I told her, "Nothing."

She obviously didn't believe me, but I didn't care.

So the three of us stood there, not really talking, just glancing at one another awkwardly, none of us quite sure of what to do.

Brian finally made a move, slipping away and heading over to the Mr. Coffee. I saw him pick up the glass carafe and examine what was left at the bottom before he returned it to the warmer.

He wandered back, hands in his pockets. "Don't think I

want to chance drinking that poison, although at least I'm in the right place to do it, huh?"

Mother's face lit up, and one of her tweezed-to-the-bone brows arched. "Poison, did you say?"

"Oh, God, please, no," I said. "Don't go there again."

"Go where?" Malone gave me a puzzled look.

"She thinks Justin tried to snuff Kendall," I told him.

"Snuff her?" he repeated.

"Mother has this cockamamie theory that he slipped a deadly dose of ma huang into her champagne to knock her off so he could be first in line for Marilee's money."

"Cockamamie?" Cissy sniffed. "It's a banned substance, sweetie, weren't you listening? And did you see how fast he took off? Doubtless afraid that the police would be called in."

"He went out for some air . . ."

"Oh, yes, for some air. The same excuse he used for disappearing during the fire, hmm? Either he's sufferin' from a severe lack of oxygen, or he feels guilty about somethin', and you know I'm right. Did you see how reluctant he was to admit which herbs he'd given that poor girl? Then he blames it all on Kendall. If she'd died, no one would've been the wiser. Those are Dr. Taylor's words, not mine."

"Well, he could've denied it altogether."

"Are you defendin' the boy?"

Malone cleared his throat. "What a minute, ladies. Are you seriously suggesting that there was an attempt to commit an actual crime?"

"Yes," Mother said in duet with my, "No."

Brian's gaze swung from Cissy to me. "Well, which is it? Because if you think that what happened to Kendall involved foul play, we should call the police."

"Yes," Mother said again, more loudly, nearly drowning out my, "No."

"Stop it." I scowled at her, stamping my foot, before I faced Brian. "Look, even if Justin gave her a big enough dose of ma huang to make her sick, there's no proof it was an intentional act. And I mean, not even a molecule. If the champagne was spiked, which is what Miss Marple here thinks happened"—I jerked my chin toward Mother—"any evidence was destroyed in the fire. Kendall's glass broke when she dropped it, and Amber shattered the bottle of 1973 Dom when she went after Marilee."

"Wait a minute." Brian stopped me. "Did you say she broke a bottle of 1973 Dom? Whoa, don't tell me it was the Dom Perignon Oenotheque?"

"Uh-huh."

His hand went to his heart. "Now there's the real crime. Busting up a bottle of a sweet year like that. Do you know what that goes for on the open market these days?"

"As I was saying"—this time, I glared at him—"there is no proof. Zero, zip, nada, nothing."

Brian said to Cissy, "She's right, Mrs. Kendricks. You can't accuse a man of attempted murder, much less intent to do bodily harm, if you have no witness and no evidence. Unless Kendall wakes up and tells a different story, there doesn't appear to be cause. If the emergency room personnel had found evidence to suggest foul play, they would've already called the police. From what Dr. Taylor said, I assume they're figuring this was accidental. That Kendall took the supplement of her own free will. And she is eighteen, not a child in the eyes of the law."

"Aren't you off-duty, Mr. Malone?" Mother muttered, and Brian's brows went up.

He couldn't seem to decide whether to be offended or amused, though I saw the corner of his mouth twitch, threatening to curve.

I decided to end this once and for all. "Okay, hear me now, Mother, and hear me good. The doctor didn't ever accuse Justin of trying to poison Kendall with ma huang. Maybe he was stupid to put her on a holistic regimen without knowing her health condition, but there doesn't seem to be malice involved."

"Are you so sure he didn't know about her heart condition?" she asked.

"No one *knew* before tonight."

"Really? And you're so certain because you're psychic?"

"Right now, I'm closer to psychotic." I pressed my fingers to my forehead, feeling the ache again. I forced myself to relax my jaw to keep from grinding my teeth. "Marilee certainly seemed surprised. She had no clue about Kendall's arrhythmia . . . the QT syndrome. And, if she didn't know, how could Justin?"

Malone crossed his arms, watching the exchange between my mother and me like a spectator at a ping-pong match.

"But, Andrea, you're not grasping the big picture." She held out her hands as if she were lying about a big fish she'd caught. "Justin and Marilee, Kendall and the ma huang. Don't you see it?"

"No," I admitted.

What I saw was my attractive sixty-year-old mother,

dressed to the gills, standing in the midst of a generic-looking hospital waiting room, making up stories to kill the time. At least, I hoped that's all she was doing. Or else she'd finally inhaled toxic levels of Joy and her brain was as fried as okra.

Cissy tapped a pump on the vinyl floor, rat-a-tat-tat. "All right, I'll explain it to you," she said. "The girl is under Justin's spell. She takes whatever herbal hooey he puts in front of her, and suddenly she collapses? You heard Beth. If Kendall had gone into sudden cardiac arrest and expired, an autopsy would've ruled it a heart attack. Wouldn't that have been awfully convenient for Mr. Gable?" She smugly crossed her arms.

But it wasn't Mother's preoccupation with her "Justin's a killer" theory that had piqued my interest.

It was what she'd called Dr. Taylor.

"Beth?" I repeated. "That's mighty friendly terms to be on with a doctor you just met. Or are you two already acquainted?"

Cissy preoccupied herself with unclasping the entwined *C*'s on her Chanel evening bag. Then she jabbed a hand in and fished around. "Beth Taylor is my new neighbor."

"The one who just moved into old Mrs. Etherington's place?"

"With her husband Richard, yes."

I remembered the woman I'd seen in the doorway with the red kerchief on her head, directing the movers like a traffic cop while a reporter from the local news shoved a microphone in her face.

No wonder she'd seemed familiar.

"Small world," I murmured, because sometimes the

Park Cities and its surrounds did indeed feel like a very small town, where everyone knew everyone, where you couldn't escape who you were, no matter how hard you tried. Not as long as you lived.

"She's attending the Dallas Diet Club meeting tomorrow afternoon, or did Sandy already tell you?" Cissy slipped a compact from her satin pouch and checked her reflection in its tiny mirror, frowning as she added some powder to her nose and forehead. "Marilee's crew will be there, taping for a show."

"After this? Won't Kendall's situation change her plans?"

My mother stared at me for a long moment, then laughed in that soft silvery way of hers. "Marilee doesn't change her plans, darling. You should know that by now as well as anyone."

"Not even for her daughter?" I asked.

"Not even if Mari herself were run over by a Mack truck. She's worked too hard for what she has. If she had to crawl to an appointment on her hands and knees, she'd do it. Besides, things seem to go wrong if she doesn't stay on top of them. I told you there've been some mishaps at the studio, and she wants to keep a close eye on everyone."

"You don't like Justin, do you, Mother?"

She feigned nonchalance and checked her manicure. "Let's just say I've checked up on our Mr. Gable and learned some interesting tidbits about him. And, even if I hadn't, I've seen too many women of a certain age fall for younger men and end up brokenhearted, not to mention a good deal lighter in the pocketbook. He's up to no good. He's a player."

"He's playing Kendall, all right," I said, nodding. "He's got her completely under his thumb, acting like he's the only one who cares about her. She feels neglected by her mother and her father, so a little of Justin's attention goes a long way." I flicked my arm in the direction of Kendall's room. Marilee and the doctor were still in there, though the orderlies had emerged a while before. "She's so confused. She needs a friend, someone she can trust, and I'm not sure there's anyone," I blathered on. "I want to see her before I head home."

Otherwise, I knew I wouldn't sleep.

"Give Mari another minute with her, sweetie."

"Kendall needs to know someone's on her side." I still felt guilty about the way I'd handled my encounter with her in Marilee's office, not completely sure that it didn't relate somehow to what had happened.

"It's not your fault," Cissy said, not for the first time that night, and she tucked her finger beneath my chin. "Please, don't blame yourself for anything Kendall has done."

I nodded.

Though understanding and accepting are two very different things, and I hadn't quite done either.

"Er, if you gals don't mind"—Brian interrupted, reminding us both that he was there—"I'm going to hit the cafeteria and get us some coffee that doesn't look like it came from the La Brea tar pits."

"Thanks," I told him, as he slid his hands down my arms and rubbed them. "Hot tea would be great."

"Mrs. Kendricks?"

"Coffee with cream and sugar, Mr. Malone, if you please."

He nodded. "Sure thing. Be right back." He headed off, taking the same route out of the waiting area that Justin had. I kept my eyes on him until he'd rounded the corner into the hallway.

My mother leaned over and whispered, "You're staring, Andrea."

"Am I?"

She gave me a look like I'd committed a fatal error contrary to Emily Post's chapter on "Staring is a No-No Unless You're Comatose."

Maybe sooner or later she'd come to realize I was hopeless at following the rules to her "good girl's guide" and would let me be.

The door to Kendall's room flew open, and Marilee rushed out, her black gown flowing behind her. Tears streaked her blotched face. "I can't take this," she cried. "I just can't take this, not after everything else. The spider, the falling boom, the fire, and now *this*. Why, Cissy, why? I want to go *home*," she whined. "Justin can drive me." Her eyes darted about, frantic when she couldn't find him. "Where *is* he?"

Mother took her arm, and Mari collapsed against Cissy's smaller frame. "C'mon, hon," she cooed. "Let's make a trip to the ladies room and get some cool water on your face. Then we'll track down the boy."

The boy?

I put a hand over my mouth.

Their footsteps clack-clacked away, past the empty nurses' station, finally fading around the corner of the hallway.

I pulled myself together, crossed the floor to Kendall's

door, and pushed it open wide enough to see Dr. Taylor standing at bedside, gazing down at the young woman lying so still beneath the white sheets.

"Can I come in?" I asked, and Beth Taylor's head jerked toward me.

"Just give me a minute, okay?" She busied herself, glancing at the blipping screen that monitored Kendall's heartbeat. Then she turned to me and nodded. "It's all right."

I entered, letting the door swing closed behind me.

"You're Cissy Kendricks's daughter, right? Andrea, isn't it?" she said, her brown eyes taking me in. "So you're the only Highland Park heiress in the history of the Hockaday School to refuse to debut?"

If I hadn't felt so worn out, I would've groaned at her description. "I doubt I'm in the textbooks yet," I said.

She smiled sympathetically. "Some people are born to break molds."

"And others are born to pulverize them."

"Your mother is one of a kind herself, you know. I like her already. She's the first of our new neighbors who dropped by to meet Richard and me."

"She likes to lead, not follow."

"So I've noticed."

Beth Taylor had a face that was striking even with minimal makeup. Her bone structure seemed carved from stone, but concern softened the dark of her eyes. I'd seen it there when she'd been looking at Kendall.

"I hope you like living on Beverly," I found myself saying. "I grew up on that street, and there's a real sense of community, despite what you might think from all the goings on." I thought of the reporter from the suburban paper, Kevin Snodgrass, who'd been interviewing the neighbors, according to Sandy. "It's downright embarrassing."

She shrugged, but her expression turned cooler. "It'd be nice if color didn't matter, wouldn't it? But I've learned the hard way that it does, a lot more to some people than others."

"I'm sorry," I said. "I can only imagine what that's like."

I knew what it meant to be an outsider, but not because of the shade of my skin.

Her starched sleeve crinkled as she reached out to pat my arm. "No need for you to apologize. No one person's responsible, Andy. It's just the way things have worked for a long time, and we have to hope it's getting better with every generation."

Speaking of getting better.

My eyes shifted away from Beth Taylor, over to Kendall's bed. "So is Kendall really okay?" I asked, because part of me still didn't buy it.

"Well, she should be now," the doctor said. "We've got her on a beta blocker for her arrhythmia. I heard you're the reason she got to the hospital so quickly. Without you, she could very well have died. It just amazes me, the things young people do to themselves, despite all the warnings."

"I'm just glad I found her in time." I hated to think what would've happened if I hadn't.

"I'm more worried about Marilee," Dr. Taylor said. "LQTS is more common in young adult women, but it can be present in middle-aged females. And it's just as deadly. I can just about guarantee she has some degree of the long QT herself, since her daughters have been positively diagnosed."

"Her daughters?"

Her dark eyes widened momentarily. "Did I say that? I meant 'daughter.' Kendall." She rubbed a hand over her jaw. "It's been a long day, a real ball buster."

For us all.

"Can I see her? Just for a bit?"

"I shouldn't be allowing her visitors, because she needs her rest. But I'll give you a few minutes, okay?"

"Thanks."

Dr. Taylor perused Kendall's monitors once more before she left, letting the door swing shut behind her.

I slowly approached the bed and reached over the railing to Kendall.

An IV clung to the back of her small hand, taped there with a clumsy *X* of adhesive. Gingerly, I touched her fingers, slid mine underneath and held them.

Her skin was warmer than it had been when she'd lain on the cold bathroom tiles, and I sighed with relief. The persistent "blip-blip" of the heart monitor sounded better than any Mozart piano sonata.

"You scared the heck out of me, Kendall," I said and felt the sudden urge to laugh until I cried. "Please, don't do it again, all right?"

"Hmmm."

The sound of her voice was so tiny, I wasn't sure at first that I'd heard it.

"Kendall?"

She fluttered her eyes, driving them open to mere slivers, enough to glimpse the foggy brown of her iris. Tears caught in her lashes.

She moved her mouth again. *"Mummy."*

I leaned closer over the railing.

"Kendall, it's me, Andy Kendricks. Your mother's coming right back. She was just here." I didn't care if I was lying if it comforted her.

"Hurt . . . me," she breathed.

"Hush, you're okay," I said. "You're all right."

"Mummy . . . help," she exhaled the words before her eyes fell shut, squeezing a tear down her cheek.

I set her hand gently down on the sheet and brushed her cheek dry with my finger. My eyes went to her other hand, and I turned it upside down so I could see the scars.

My chest ached powerfully.

Kendall had been right about one thing. I didn't understand.

She was a girl with a broken heart, and I prayed that what had happened tonight was truly a mistake, an accident, not the result of a troubled eighteen-year-old wanting to take her life.

Again.

It was hard for me to imagine sinking that low, feeling that desperate to want to escape. Figuring that killing yourself was the only answer. As many insecure moments as I'd had growing up, I'd never gone there. I guess I was lucky.

"If we're lucky, something crazy will happen tonight. Like poisoned food or falling lights."

I'd nearly forgotten Kendall's remarks. What a strange thing to say, looking back, and I wondered if she was merely being flippant or prognosticating?

"Hurt me. Mummy help."

Who hurt her? Justin?

"What really happened, Kendall?" I whispered, getting

no answer but the drip-drip of the IV bag into the tubing and the blip-blip of her beating heart.

Whatever the truth was, we'd have to wait.

I stared down at the sleeping face, feeling hopeful Kendall would explain when she recovered in the days to come.

Good God, girl, I mused. *What did you get yourself into?*

I went up to the nurses' station and spoke with the pony-tailed girl in pink scrubs whose nametag read: ALICE PECK. She listened without blinking as I suggested they keep an eye on any visitors to Kendall's room, notably a fellow named Justin Gable.

Nurse Alice indulged me with a nod and assured me she'd personally monitor the comings and goings regarding Ms. Mabry's room. After all, it was a private bed, paid for by *The Sweet Life*'s Marilee Mabry herself.

I did a quick survey of the surroundings, the wide brightly lit hallways, the circular desk, and the waiting room, but I saw no sign of Justin. I had wanted to point him out to Nurse Alice, but ended up giving her a brief description instead.

"Good-looking blond man with bedroom eyes and a square jaw, about five foot ten inches tall and all of it lean muscle."

"And you want me to keep this guy *out* of Ms. Mabry's room?" Nurse Alice stared at me like I was crazy.

"Right."

I didn't know if Kendall was afraid of Justin or not. I just didn't want to take any chances.

Alice sobered up and promised to talk to Dr. Taylor.

"Thank you."

Chewing on my lower lip, I trudged over to the waiting area. Neither Marilee nor Justin had returned, and I wondered if they'd already gone home. Maybe my mother had left Marilee washing her face in the rest room, because Cissy was present and accounted for. I saw her standing near the muted overhead TV, conversing in a fairly civilized fashion with Malone. I wanted to believe they were sharing a bonding moment. Unfortunately, as I approached, I caught the gist of their conversation and realized it wasn't the kind of harmless chitchat I'd hoped.

"I would appreciate it very much if you'd take Andrea off my hands," I heard Cissy tell him as he held onto a small red tray filled with Styrofoam cups.

"Take her off your hands?" The tray rattled, causing coffee to slosh over the rims. "How do you mean, Mrs. Kendricks?"

"What do you think I mean?"

"Mother." I stepped between them as fast as I could.

What the hell was she doing? Forcing him into a lifelong commitment right here in the hospital waiting room? If she started in on her "getting the milk for free" lecture, I was going to have to bean her with the sludge-filled Mr. Coffee.

Cissy brushed me out of her way and wagged a finger at Brian. "I mean for you to take my daughter's hand and . . ."

"Mother," I hissed, through gritted teeth, about to throw myself atop her and tackle her to the ground.

". . . get her out of here," she finished. "Andrea obviously needs to go straight to bed, so if you could drive her home, I'd appreciate it since I'd like to stay at the hospital a while longer and keep Marilee company."

One of these days, I will kill her for this, I promised myself, letting out a held breath.

Malone did one of those sigh-coughs, practically doubling over with relief. "Get her out of here? Yes, ma'am, no problem there. I'll do that right now. Take her straight to bed . . . um, tuck her in tight . . . drive it right home . . . aw, hell, you're right, it's getting late." His cheeks stained pink, he wandered away, setting down the tray and digging in his pocket for his keys, as if he couldn't wait to get going.

Neither could I.

But first things first.

I glared at my mother so fiercely even she shifted on her feet. "Not funny," I mouthed, but she merely raised her eyebrows, as if to say, *"What did I do?"*

When she knew damned well.

It was like she had a severe maternal form of Tourette's. And meddling in my life was the tic.

Chapter 16

Brian didn't exactly put me to bed, as directed by Attila the Mom.

He didn't "tuck me in tight" or "drive it right home," either.

Not that I'm complaining. I really did have a headache, and he looked as drained as I was from hanging out with Cissy at the hospital for the past hour or so.

All in all, it had been a truly miserable evening. It ranked right up there with a blind date I'd had with a thrice-divorced real estate mogul who lived with his mother in a Turtle Creek high-rise. He had a roomful of Star Wars collectibles obtained through eBay, complete with full-sized cardboard cutouts of Han Solo, Luke, and Obi-Wan Kenobi. I didn't mind so much when he suggested we watch the first episode of *Star Wars* on DVD, but the setup quickly escalated from bad to worse when he asked me to don a Princess Leia wig and "talk Jabba" to him. I'd feigned a sudden attack of PMS cramps and made a getaway worthy of a Jedi knight.

Since returning to Dallas from Chicago after art school, my romantic life hadn't exactly been chock-full of men with whom I'd wanted to settle down and make a commitment. In fact, I'd considered swearing off the dating scene altogether, for a while, anyway; figuring life was too short to keep chasing Mr. Right when maybe he didn't exist.

Then I'd met Malone, something for which I had to give Cissy credit (even if she was regretting the arrangement for whatever old-fashioned reasons).

Granted, he didn't fulfill all the superficial criteria on my "perfect boyfriend" wish list, but he did pass the sanity test with flying colors.

So he wasn't creative or poetic. Maybe he was a tad too responsible and stable for my tastes. But he was also gentle and compassionate; characteristics I'd never associated with a defense attorney.

And tea and sympathy were smack at the top of my wish list tonight.

He even offered to draw me a bath—full of my favorite Crabtree & Evelyn lily of the valley-scented gel—but I'd spent enough time being waterlogged in sequins. Despite how great bubbles sounded, I preferred to stay dry.

So, he made me hot tea and then he nestled beside me on the sofa, stroking my hair as I babbled on about what had happened at Marilee's studio. My mind felt so jumbled with the night's events that I needed to sort them out, and talking helped, at least a smidge.

He kept dozing off then snorting indelicately each time I nudged him awake, until I finally gave up and let him snooze.

Well, I never said he was perfect.

Another thing I liked about Malone was that he could sleep through anything, including tornado sirens or the telephone ringing. It was a gift, one that I hadn't been dealt. I'd inherited my mother's horrible ineptitude for falling—and staying—asleep. My brain didn't turn off easily, and it certainly wasn't shutting down tonight.

I lay my head on his chest, though my eyes were wide open.

If I shut them, I saw things I didn't want to see.

The blood red rose, the discarded shoes, the crumpled body.

I felt things I didn't want to feel.

The bump against my shoulder, the breath on my cheek as someone pushed past me in the pitch-dark hallway.

Believe me, I desperately wanted to convince myself that Mother's suspicions about Justin were nonsense, but I couldn't help wondering if Justin *had* been responsible for Kendall's collapse.

He'd had no boutonnière in his lapel at the hospital. He'd lied to Marilee about where he'd been during the fire evacuation. He'd been doling out herbs to Kendall to cure whatever ailed her, like a holistic Dr. Feel-Good.

I know, I know. As Malone had said, it didn't necessarily make him guilty of anything. But still.

"Hurt . . . me. Mummy . . . help."

Was it worth reading anything too deeply into Kendall's gibberish? She'd been sedated, for God's sake. I was acting like my mother, looking for hidden meaning when there probably was none.

Right?

I peeled myself away from Malone and scooted off the

sofa, heading into my tiny spare room no bigger than a walk-in closet. I didn't even bother with the light as I slipped into my desk chair and booted up the Dell.

Within minutes, I was online, Googling for "long QT syndrome."

Site after site appeared, and I began clicking on them, one by one, squinting at the screen in the dark of the room, my eyes moving across the text that appeared as I tried to grasp all that I read, feeling ignorant for knowing absolutely nothing about this condition. I'd never even heard of it before tonight.

I picked up a pencil and took some notes in the light of the monitor, scribbling down what seemed the most pertinent facts.

Long QT syndrome, aka Romano Ward syndrome, meant the ventricular heartbeat was prolonged, causing an arrhythmia (Torsades de Pointes). One in 50,000 people was suspected of having LQTS and 3,000 deaths a year were blamed on it. When the arrhythmia occurred, a syncopal episode (passing out) was often the result; or it could cause sudden death. LQTS could be genetic or caused by certain medications that prolonged the QT rhythm. But there were no routine genetic tests to diagnose it, not yet. Though it had been determined that if one parent was known to have LQTS by ECG, then there was a 50 percent likelihood that any offspring would have it. Only research labs did testing, and those results often took years to return. Common drugs could initiate the Torsades de Pointes, including antidepressants, antibiotics, and anti-inflammatories. Ephedrine was clearly listed on the "contraindicated" list. There was an increased risk of LQTS for females during adulthood, while males often experienced symptoms in childhood. Because it was hard to diagnose without an available ECG, otherwise healthy folks who died unexpectedly—with "sudden cardiac death of unknown etiology" listed as the cause—could be victims of LQTS. In order to find the disease in a dead person, the body fluids (blood) would have to be tested for a known gene mutation.

My God.

I wondered if Kendall's arrhythmia was genetic. And, if so, did Marilee suffer from it, as well? Maybe, like Kendall, without even realizing that she was ill?

Just for kicks, I did a Google search for "ma huang" and came up with more Web sites than I could count. Whatever ban the government had placed on ephedra-related products didn't seem to be stopping sites around the world from selling the stuff.

Scary, I thought as I shut down the computer, and I put a hand to my chest, feeling my own heartbeat, waiting for it to stutter. But it didn't.

My mind even more clogged with "who knows" and "what ifs" than before, I dragged myself back into the living room and insinuated myself into my former position against Malone's chest. He grunted, shifting slightly, but didn't awaken.

I closed my eyes, willing myself to sleep, but instead the kitchen scene at the party replayed itself in my head, again and again.

There was Justin holding the 1973 Dom Perignon. He'd turned away for a moment, shielding the bottle from view. Then he'd faced the crowd again to publicly uncork the pricey vintage.

What if the bottle had already been uncorked? What if

someone had opened it ahead of time and spiked it with ma huang?

I had watched Kendall gulp down her glass before she'd dropped it. The flute had hit the floor and splintered into pieces. She'd ducked her head as she'd run past me, crying. But I remembered something else. The way she'd clasped her arms around her belly.

Was it the ephedra that had her doubled over? Or was her reaction merely a response to Marilee's hurtful remarks?

Oh, man.

What was I doing?

My eyelids flipped up like window shades, and I stared at the ceiling, listening to Brian's even breathing, sure I was going nuts, which was probably genetic. My mother had obviously plunged over the deep end, cooking up theories that were more ridiculous than sublime.

It had become a hobby, like knitting or crosswords.

She and her pals liked to sit around, playing cards and dreaming up nonsensical answers to questions nobody asked but them. Okay, them and possibly John Hinckley.

For instance, they believed that the e-mails were invented to subvert the art of writing proper thank-you notes. Another popular idea with the Dallas Diet Club was that pop stars like Britney Spears and Madonna were puppets of Victoria's Secret, mere tools to sell lingerie to prepubescent females.

Their most idiotic hypothesis was that JFK's assassination had zilch to do with politics, Oswald, or the School Book Depository. Instead, they'd decided it was a botched plot by the Sixth Avenue mafia against, not Jack, but *Jackie* for exclusively wearing Oleg Cassini during her White

House years and forcing pillbox hats on every woman's crown, causing a wave of bobby pin-induced migraine headaches.

"Cockamamie," I muttered.

In the morning, everything wouldn't look so suspicious, I decided. Everything seemed worse, more dramatic, in the bleak of night.

Having reached that conclusion, I raised up on an elbow, reaching over to slip Malone's glasses from their cockeyed perch on his nose. Then I did the same with mine, putting the pair in a tangle of wire frames onto the coffee table.

That was the third beautiful thing about Brian Malone.

He was as blind as I was without his specs.

Minus our glasses, neither one of us could see what the other really looked like in the unflattering light of dawn.

As far as I was concerned, it was a huge bonus to have a boyfriend with 20/50 vision.

Ranked right up there with not having to wear a Princess Leia wig or talk like Jabba the Hut—whatever the heck that meant—in order to flick his Bic.

Normalcy.

I liked that in a man.

Almost as much as a sense of humor and firm lips that knew how to kiss. And Malone knew how to kiss, all right.

Curling up against his chest, I closed my eyes and, eventually, drifted off.

Chapter 17

The white noise of the shower awakened me.

It sounded like rain, only the sun streamed through the partially opened louvered blinds. Which is when I realized Brian was already up.

I squinted at the coffee table, then reached out with my fingertips to detect only one pair of glasses.

As long as he had a head start, I wasn't going to worry about my bad breath or tangled hair. Besides, I had no reason to rush. It was Saturday. And, even if it wasn't, it's not as if I had a job to rush off to. My office was no farther away than my desktop PC.

So I sighed and snuggled deeper into the malleable old sofa cushions, cocooning beneath a crocheted throw that a woman had knitted me as payment for setting up a Web site for her nonprofit group, a bunch of former Pan Am flight attendants better known as CRAP, short for Crocheting Retired Airline Personnel, an acronym that had earned them a feature in the *Dallas Morning News,* which was picked up by AP and reprinted in *USA Today.* Just goes to show that being brassy can pay off. They made, well, crocheted things for women and children in shelters. Hats, sweaters, scarves, and blankets.

I pulled the throw up to my chin, and a pink pseudocabbage rose tickled the skin at my throat, so comfortable that I didn't want to move.

I must've dozed off, because when I opened my eyes again, the shower was off and I smelled toast. Yawning, I fumbled for my glasses on the coffee table and put them on. I finger-brushed my hair and ignored the foul taste on my tongue.

Wrapping the throw around me, I struggled off the sofa and shuffled into my tiny kitchen to find Malone there, wearing his khaki pants and Polo T-shirt from the day before. He stood at the counter, buttering a pair of browned slices of wheat bread.

"I love a man who can cook," I said as I settled down at the table, into one of the refinished oak chairs I'd picked up at the Junior League rummage sale for five bucks a pop. All they'd needed was a bit of elbow grease to bring out their natural beauty (not so different from the rest of us).

He brought the toast over on a chipped Pier One plate, and I greedily reached for a slice. I'd forgotten to eat at Marilee's studio opening, though I had swallowed my share of champagne as the dull ache behind my eyes reminded me. I was such a wuss when it came to liquor.

"You should go back to bed, Andy, unless you've got something pressing on your agenda. You deserve a day off after last night."

His hair was still damp from the shower, brushed back from his clean-scrubbed face. I could see the glint of my reflection in his glasses and wondered if he could see himself in mine.

"I was hoping you'd drop me off at the studio to pick up my Jeep. My purse is there, too." I hesitated, wondering if I'd assumed too much. "If you wouldn't mind."

"No, it's fine." He swallowed a bite of toast and brushed crumbs off his fingers. "I'll take you over on my way home. Better still, I'll hang around, wait for you to do whatever you need to do."

It was clear by his tone of voice that he was worried. Mother had doubtless scared him to death with her tales of mishaps on Marilee's set.

After the fire and Kendall's collapse, I was feeling a little jittery myself.

Still, I put down my toast and touched his hand with buttered fingertips. "Nothing to worry about," I assured him. "I'll grab my purse and the Jeep, then I'll be out of there. Besides, I promised Mother I'd come down for her Diet Club meeting this afternoon. Marilee's crew is filming a segment for her show, and I want to make sure Cissy doesn't have a meltdown if someone spills on her Persian rugs."

He laced his fingers together with mine. "Be careful, Andy. I mean it."

"Don't worry, Mr. Defense Attorney." I dredged up a smile. "I promise to call you if someone dies."

Funny, but he didn't smile back.

A half-hour later—after I'd had a hot shower and two Extra-Strength Excedrin—Brian pulled his Acura coupe into the parking lot of Marilee's studio in Addison.

The place was nearly as full as it was a dozen hours before but, instead of a hook and ladder truck, paramedics vans, and police cruisers, a host of repair trucks filled the yellow grids. HARVEY & SONS WATER DAMAGE RESTORATION read the painted side on one, FEINSTEIN ELECTRICAL REPAIR another. Though my favorite was BIG BOY'S STEEL ERECTION. A flatbed truck held stacks of lumber, and I tried not to dwell on the number of trees that had sacrificed their lives to rebuild Marilee's studio kitchen.

The front entrance had yellow CAUTION tape stretched across it to keep us regular folks away. A big white sign on the glass front doors read, USE BACK ENTRANCE! The repairmen obviously had a different set of instructions entirely, and strutted back and forth, dragging gear inside and hauling small dumpsters swollen with debris out.

There was no sign of any media activity, and I figured the news jockeys had gotten enough tape after the fire to last them a while. Besides, they'd surely had more fun poking their mikes up the nose of Marilee's party guests in their drenched designer attire than they would interviewing the fix-it guys in their wife-beater shirts and crack-baring blue jeans.

"Doesn't look to be much damage from the outside," Brian said.

"It was pretty much contained to the one set," I explained. "The sprinkler system kept it from spreading, I guess, but there was water everywhere."

Besides, the worst of the damage wasn't caused by the fire or the artificial rain, I mused, thinking of Kendall.

I asked Malone to drive around to the rear, and I glimpsed my Wrangler parked against a chain-link fence without a lick of shade. I hated to think how hot the inside was. Though it was barely past ten, the sun crept ever upward in the sky, unfettered by clouds of any kind, save for a few feckless wisps no more solid than gauze.

Before I got out of the car, Brian grabbed for my hand. "I'll be working at home all day, so I'm easy to find."

I squeezed his hand and said, "Um, just what kind of trouble do you expect me to get into?"

"Well, if you're going to your mother's, it could be any number of things."

"You never learned how to look on the bright side, did you?"

"I'm an attorney, Andy," he said, as if I'd forgotten. "If I looked on the bright side, I'd be out of a job."

"Right."

I bent over the console for a kiss, and it was worth the glove box digging into my hip. Just a good old-fashioned lip-lock, nothing French. Perfect for ten o'clock in the morning.

Reluctantly, I slid off the Acura's leather seat and out the door, giving him a loose-fingered wave before he slowly drove off.

When the little red car disappeared around the corner of the warehouse, I stood on the warming asphalt with the sun hot on my neck, and I stared at the rear exit door, propped open with a brick. I drew in a few calming breaths, before I tucked my hair firmly behind my ears and headed in.

Goosebumps rose over my skin as I entered, and it wasn't because of the air conditioning, humming from the vents. At least the electricity was running in this part of the building, a vast improvement over the last time I'd been here.

Though now well lit, this was the path I'd taken last night after I'd discovered Kendall in her mother's office. It seemed odd to retrace my steps and recall how frightened I'd been, fumbling in the darkness.

It was reassuring to hear voices, to see office doors that stood wide open with lights on within and people at their desks.

I wondered if Marilee had ordered her staff to come in this Saturday morning, to keep on top of things despite the mess on the sound stage. I'm sure she didn't care if Twinkle Productions had to pay her staff and the repairmen overtime, so long as they returned the place to perfection as soon as possible. Marilee wasn't exactly what I'd call patient. I figured it was a blessing that she planned to take her crew to film at Mother's.

Heads looked up as I passed, but no one smiled or waved.

Usually when I'd scheduled appointments with Marilee, the folks I encountered looked preoccupied, or maybe harried was a better word.

This morning, they just looked grim.

Not exactly the kind of place I'd want to work, day in and day out, unless I was a masochist. Marilee was not my idea of a dream boss, and I couldn't wait until she hired a permanent webmaster to take over my job.

As I approached Marilee's slightly ajar office door, I heard raised voices and hesitated in the hallway, not wanting to interrupt, particularly since I anticipated Lady Mabry's mood would be foul. I wondered how many brown noses had already tried to tell her, "Nice party," only for her to pop them in the kisser?

Okay, an exaggeration. But Marilee did take failure personally—or rather, took it out on every person—and last night had been the Mother of All Bombs.

I waited outside, not meaning to eavesdrop, but I couldn't help overhearing Marilee's angry drawl raised in disagreement with the equally angry voice of a man. It didn't take me long to figure out who the man was, not once he laid into her about Kendall.

"She's my daughter, too, for Christ's sake," he growled. "How dare you not call me from the hospital. I didn't even know what had happened to her until I saw a piece on the news this morning where they mentioned her by name."

"She's your daughter, too, huh?" Marilee snorted. "Is that why you dumped her on me after the divorce? Why you didn't go for shared custody and never wanted her for more than a few days at Christmas? My God, Gil, I had to take you to court to get any kind of child support, and what I got barely paid for a bag of groceries."

"That's not fair . . ."

"You're damned right it wasn't fair. Nothing about our divorce was fair, not to me."

"You would've preferred we'd stayed married when we couldn't stand to be together anymore, when we were fighting like cats and dogs over every little thing . . ."

"You cheated on me, Gilbert. Don't forget that. You cheated on me, and you cheated Kendall out of having a father . . ."

"You nearly killed me, Mari," Gil snarled back. "How the hell was I supposed to live with a woman who just about nagged me to death. Nothing I ever did was good enough for you. I could never do anything as perfectly as you, from the laundry, to raising our daughter, to the way I touched you in bed . . ."

"Shut up . . . shut the hell up!"

"I couldn't imagine for the life of me why you were so adamant that Amber Lynn and I attend your party. It was for Kendall's sake, you said, so she'd see the two of us on friendly footing, see us both as equals." His laugh was harsh. "I thought that you'd actually gotten over us and were extending the olive branch. Now I know you only did it to embarrass Amber and myself . . . and Kendall. You are the most self-indulgent bitch, and someday you're going to get exactly what's coming to you . . ."

"Get out!" Marilee shrilled at the top of her lungs. "Get the hell out! And, by the way, you owe me three hundred and fifty dollars for that bottle of champagne your trophy wife broke . . ."

"That was my vintage Dom, wasn't it? You stole it from the house before you moved out . . ."

"Before you kicked me out . . ."

". . . so you owe *me* three hundred fifty dollars . . ."

"Over my dead body!"

"We'll see about that."

I glanced up the hallway, half-expecting to catch heads popping out of doorways, wondering what was going on.

But I didn't spot a one.

Maybe they were used to Marilee shrieking like a banshee.

The door flew open, and a body came barreling out. I didn't have time to get out of the way, and Gil clipped my shoulder as he rushed by.

He didn't bother to say, "Sorry."

I rubbed my arm as he stalked off, gathering my courage before I turned back to Marilee's now-opened door.

Not knowing how else to announce myself, I knocked lightly on the jamb before ducking my head in and saying, "Yoo hoo? Marilee, it's Andy Kendricks. Are you busy? I'm sorry to bother you, but I need to collect my purse."

When she didn't answer, I dared to step in.

I cleared my throat. "Marilee?" I tried again.

I didn't see her at first.

She was huddled on the butter-cream-colored sofa, wearing slacks and a blouse that very nearly blended in. Her head hung down in her hands.

"I don't mean to intrude . . ."

"It's all right." She sniffled, raising her chin and wiping the back of her hand across her cheeks. "That was just my ex-husband, making an ass of himself." Her face showed strain in the lines at her mouth and the hard set of her jaw. "The only good thing that's happened this morning is the fire inspector proclaiming the fire accidental and allowing us to start repairing the damage. I've got the men working on twenty-four-hour shifts so we don't lose too much time. Thank God we're taping at your mother's this afternoon." She paused. "What was it that you came here for, Andrea?"

I'd been standing in the middle of the room, saying nothing, my hands clasped in front of me, afraid to interrupt or to speak until spoken to (blame it on being indoctrinated by Little Miss Manners all those years ago).

"What did I come for?" Thank God, she was giving me an opening. "My purse," I told her. "A pink Escada bag on

a chunky silver chain? I dropped it last night when I"—
how should I phrase it?—"stumbled upon Kendall."

"Ah, the purse, yes." Marilee slowly rose from the sofa,
smoothing her hands down the front of her silk pants. "I
wondered who that belonged to. There was no ID in it, just
a cell phone and a tube of lipstick. I nearly punched one of
the numbers on speed dial to see who answered."

"Then you might've rung up Cissy," I said.

"Ah, dear, dear Cissy," she murmured and went around
the couch to a closet.

She pulled open the louvered doors to reveal shelves of
mannequin heads wearing ash-blond hair in a variety of
'dos. No wonder she never had a bad hair day. I glimpsed
scarves and gloves of every hue as she reached in and
emerged with my pink bag.

"Here you go, honey." After she closed the louvered
doors, she crossed the room to give it back.

I took it from her and, without thinking, unclasped it and
checked inside.

Yep, everything seemed intact, even the pair of quarters
I'd thrown in just in case my cell phone did one of its dying
acts.

"Okay, well, thanks, Marilee. I'll see you later at
Mother's," I said and started to leave. Then I stopped. "I
was wondering how Kendall was doing? Is she feeling better this morning?"

*Has she talked about what actually happened before she
passed out?* I wanted to ask, but didn't.

"I assume you've already been by the hospital," I continued when Marilee didn't immediately answer. She had her
arms crossed and seemed to be staring off into space, or

maybe she was listening to the distant noise of drills and hammers. "Kendall? How is she?" I gave it another shot.

"Kendall? Oh, she's fine, yes, thanks for asking." She waved a hand. "I haven't had time to go by the hospital yet. Too much going on here . . . too many things that require my attention, as you can well imagine."

Too many things that required her attention . . . as opposed to her sick daughter, I was tempted to mention but bit my tongue just in time.

"I did call the nurses' station on her floor, and they assured me she was doing much better. She's doing well on her medication and her heart rhythm is back to normal. She was having a can of Ensure for breakfast, I believe."

"Good. I'm glad she's better."

"Yes, we're very relieved. I think Justin was up all night, pacing the floor, worried sick about Kendall. He took off early this morning. He said something about going to the hospital to check on her."

"Justin went to Medical City by himself?" *For crying out loud.* I just hoped that Nurse Alice had talked to Dr. Taylor about restricting Kendall's visitors and had kept Justin out of the girl's room. I still wasn't convinced that he wasn't some kind of threat to her, to her emotional stability at the very least.

"Yes, he went alone." She rubbed her arms and sighed. "He's such a sweet man, and he cares so much for both Kendall and myself. You can't imagine how far he'd go in order to take care of us. He's so devoted."

Oh, yeah? I can do more than imagine. I saw for myself how much he cared for Kendall, right on that sofa.

I had something to ask her, and I wasn't sure how to put

it. So I figured I'd blunder dead ahead. "Um, Marilee? I was wondering about something. I looked up long QT syndrome on the Web last night, and it's often passed down from a parent to a child. So if Kendall has been diagnosed with it, there's the possibility that either you or your ex-husband has the mutated gene as well . . . and the arrhythmia that goes with it. Have you ever had an ECG to check?"

"Please, Andrea, don't worry about me." She placed a hand on her chest. "I am fine, really. I've had checkups for insurance purposes for the past several years, and the physician for Twinkle Productions just gave me a clean bill of health. So let's blame this one on Gil, shall we?" Her jaw tensed. "He is responsible for so much of Kendall's pain as it is."

The phone rang, screaming like a child for attention, and Marilee hustled over to her desk to pick it up. "Why, hello, Mr. Mayor." Her drawl turned so molasses sweet that it's a wonder she didn't go into sugar shock. She perched a hip on the edge of her desk and twirled the cord around her finger. "Yes, yes, I'm fine, just fine, and we're already at work rebuilding the set. Things should be back to normal in a few days' time. No, no, the fire department didn't fine us, though you're a doll to offer to intercede . . . hold on a sec." She put a hand over the mouthpiece and glanced at me, as if finally remembering I was there.

"Listen, hon, would you do me a big favor and scoot into the kitchen to see how Carson's coming with the desserts for the Diet Club. Tell him we're going to have to start packing up and heading to your mother's house within the hour."

"Sure, I'll tell Carson," I said.

"You're a life saver." She shot me a prom queen smile before turning back to her phone call.

Not that I wanted to hang around the place, but I was curious as to what the damage really looked like in broad daylight. I'd only seen the set in the dark. Actually, I'd mostly seen rubber boots sloshing through several inches of water on the floor as the nice fireman had cavemancarried me to safety.

Anyway, Marilee had basically given me a hall pass to roam around, so I figured I'd use it.

As I wove through the tunnel of hallways, moving from the back of the building toward the front, the cacophony of power tools grew louder until I felt a permanent buzzing fill the back of my ears.

Yellow tape blocked my path out into the studio set, though I wouldn't have wanted to go farther anyway. Klieg-type lighting had been brought in with thick orange and black cables running to a humming generator. Men in plaid with hard hats and tool belts swarmed like bees, crawling up ladders, sawing plywood in half, using nail guns, and wet-dry vacuums, cleaning and replacing and restoring what the fire and the sprinklers had wrecked.

Dangling the purse from my wrist, I put my hands over my ears and stood to watch for a moment, impressed by all that testosterone in action. Several of the fellows nodded in my direction, and a wiry fellow with a long gray ponytail streaming from beneath his yellow hardhat graced me with a clear view of his butt crack as he squatted to check out an electrical circuit.

Oh, I'd say I saw a quarter-moon, maybe a half-moon. A

little early in the day for a lunar sighting, but it gave me something to honestly grin about for the first time in twenty-four hours.

After a few minutes, I'd had my fill of men wielding power tools, and I took a back route to the test kitchen, where the actual food was prepared for Marilee's show.

Until I'd spent time here, I hadn't realized that Marilee had next to nothing to do with the actual cooking, baking, or craft projects that appeared on the episodes of *The Sweet Life*. Now I knew firsthand that people like Carson did the real work, and Marilee took the credit.

There were dozens of staff whose sole purpose it was just to figure out how to make puppets out of fabric remnants or how to turn burned-out light bulbs into Christmas ornaments by adding bric-a-brac and glitter.

Marilee merely had to stand in front of the cameras with the pieces of a project laid out before her—and a finished piece hidden behind the counter on a shelf—chatting casually in her down-home drawl about how she'd had to figure out this simple idea of using old dishtowels to create stuffed animals for children when she couldn't afford to buy toys for her baby daughter all those years ago.

And the viewers bought it all, ate it up, if the ratings were any indication.

Ah, the magic of television, I mused, as I crossed beneath the open archway that led from the hall into the kitchen. *Nothing was ever as it seemed.*

I stopped in the doorway, looking around for Carson's bald head, surprised to see so many bodies running about. I'd thought maybe everything but the offices would be shut down until the studio kitchen was repaired, but apparently life—and electricity—went on in the test kitchen as well.

In some ways, the setting seemed a mirror image of the tableau I'd viewed with the workmen. A handful of people purposefully moved around the stainless-steel island and between the stainless-steel appliances. Mixers whirred, food processors spun, oven timers dinged. And an apron-wearing Carson Caruthers reigned above all, shouting instructions, pausing to stir a pot, stopping a mixer to check the consistency of batter. His placid-looking face seemed at ease, despite the hustle and bustle.

"Come on, gang, chop-chop," he rallied the troops, clapping flour-whitened hands.

"Get those rum balls out of the fridge, Debbie, please."

"But Marilee said she wanted them to chill at least two hours," a ponytailed worker bee spoke up, before Carson shut her down with a growl.

"I don't give a damn what Marilee said, you got that?" His placid expression turned fierce, caterpillar eyebrows scrunching together, creasing his hairless brow. "She may sign our paychecks, but the woman doesn't know what's best for my chocolate rum balls or anyone else's balls, for that matter. Did she graduate from the Cordon Bleu? Ha! I'll bet she couldn't bake her way out of a box of Betty Crocker. Did she study pastry and chocolate-making in Italy with the famed Luca Mannori?" He wagged a finger. "No, no, no, I think not. So if anyone brings up her name again in my kitchen, they're going to be sorry," he promised and drew a floury finger line across his throat. "Sliced and diced, and set to stew in the crock pot."

"Um, then I guess I'm the first ingredient," I said and took a step farther into the room, hugging my pink evening bag to my belly as all eyes fell upon me, and not in a friendly way. "Because that person I'm not supposed to mention under penalty of death wanted me to remind you that you'd better have things packed up and ready to drive down to Highland Park within the hour."

"Is that so?" Carson squinted at me, wrinkled up his nose, and asked, "And, to quote the venerable Roger Daltrey, who the hell are *you*?"

Chapter 18

 Once we got formalities out of the way—and got ourselves out of the way of the kitchen crew—Carson's face relaxed, and I decided he wasn't half bad looking. He reminded me of Kojak in disguise as a chef, a tough guy in an apron.

"I've seen you around the last couple of weeks, haven't I?" He crossed well-muscled arms and leaned against the wall in the rear hallway, nodding as he checked me out. "Usually you're with Marilee, so I wasn't sure if you were cozy with her. And I only came down from New York a few months ago, so I'm still learning how things work around here. Who I can trust."

"My mother is a good friend of Marilee, but I'm just an innocent bystander," I assured him.

"Your mother?"

"Cissy Kendricks. The show is taping at her house this afternoon. She's one of the founding mothers of the Dallas Diet Club."

"Ah, gotcha." There was a hint of Brooklyn in his accent, which you didn't hear much in Dallas. He ran his fingers over his smooth pate, smearing a bit of flour on his skull. "I don't understand this whole Diet Club thing. How's it a diet club if all they do is eat desserts?"

I grinned. "My mother and her friends were tired of everyone they knew being on Pritikin or Atkins, so they formed the Diet Club as revenge. It's really an antidiet club, and there's a waiting line a mile long to get in. Pretty much someone has to die to make room for a new member."

"You're kidding?"

"If you make it exclusive, they will come," I told him. "At least in the Park Cities."

"The Park Cities?"

"Highland Park, where my mother lives, and University Park, where Southern Methodist University is located. Pretty much, that's where the Old Money is."

"Ah, like Park Avenue in Manhattan."

"Exactly like that, Mr. Caruthers."

"Carson, please," he said, smiling right back at me. He had such nice straight teeth, and I was a sucker for a good smile. "Mr. Caruthers is my old man, and he still lives in Flatbush."

"Okay, Carson." I had to glance down, away from his thick-lashed blue eyes.

A guy who could whip things up in the kitchen and not look half-bad without hair on his head made a dangerous combination. Just to have something to do, I fiddled with the rectangular silver links on the Escada bag.

"Look, I don't want you to get the wrong impression about what you heard in there a few minutes ago," he picked up the slack. "It's not that I hate the Divine Ms. M, it's just that she rubs me wrong. She tends to interfere with my creative process. I realize she's the star of the show—hell, she *is* the show—but she's really no more than an actress. You've been around long enough to know how things work, right? Everyone else does the crafts and the cooking and the gardening, and she just pretends in front of the camera." He rubbed his palms on his chocolate-smeared apron. "You ever been to her house?" he asked.

"No." My mother had, but I'd never had a reason to go.

He set his hands on his hips. "Behind this freaking enormous mansion, she's got at least an acre of land. She's got a pen for the geese, a hen house for chickens, incredible gardens, and even a man-made pond for her organic catfish that's bigger than the Y's swimming pool. But you think she gets her own hands dirty?" He shook his head. "No way. Just like here, she's got people who take care of everything. Marilee's forte is running things with her mouth, if you get my drift." His own mouth screwed up, like he was chewing on the inside of his lip. Then he lifted his hands, gesturing surrender. "But who the hell am I to comment, right? I'm just a minion."

I remembered what Janet Graham had told me, that he was some big deal in New York until *The Sweet Life* had lured him here to take over as the food editor. I got the feeling he was second-guessing his decision.

"I saw Marilee come down kind of hard on you last night before the party," I told him, and his eyes rounded. "Is it tough for someone of your reputation to be working for a woman who's so . . ."

"Bitchy?" he finished for me and chuckled. "Hey, pardon my French."

"I was going to say 'controlling.' "

He shrugged. "Same difference. Technically, I don't work *for* Marilee. Twinkle Productions hired me, not her. But she pretty much pushes the buttons. If she doesn't like someone, pffft"—he jerked a thumb across his throat—"so I'm always on my toes, mostly trying to avoid her so we don't come to blows. Sometimes it works. Sometimes not so well. But I keep tellin' myself that this show is good exposure, and I've gotta put up with the woman, even when she's yanking my short hairs." A deep purple stain rose upward from his neck, as if the mere thought of Marilee getting on his nerves was enough to pump up his blood pressure.

"Do you know Kendall well?"

He squinted. "Marilee's kid?"

"You heard about what happened to her, I presume."

"She got hurt during the fire at the party?"

"Um, sort of. She's in the hospital," I told him. "She had a bad reaction to something she ingested."

His eyes widened. "Ingested? As in something she *ate*? Not here? Please tell me it wasn't something from the buffet?"

Like the foie gras? I felt tempted to ask, but refrained.

"No, no, the doctors think she had too much of one of those herbal supplements she's been taking"—at the behest of Justin Gable, Chinese herbalist and personal trainer. "Though maybe it was the champagne, that special vintage Marilee had been saving." And had apparently swiped from her ex-husband. "Was that particular bottle stored in a public place? In the kitchen maybe, where anyone would have access to it?"

"Yeah, yeah, there's a wine refrigerator, and a humidity-controlled wine closet. Neither one is locked, if that's what you're asking. The Dom, it was a 1973, right?" He scrunched up his forehead. "Did the bottle go bad?"

"Um, in a way," I said. "But she's all right. Kendall, I mean."

"Glad to hear it. She's a little off, but she ain't had it easy." He glanced toward the kitchen, where voices and the clang of pots and pans kept floating out. "The girl hangs around a lot. She likes to tell people she's Marilee's assistant, but I think it's in name only. Marilee can't keep a real assistant to save her life. I've seen two, three of them come and go already, and I haven't been here that long."

"So Kendall helps out?"

"I wouldn't say 'helps' exactly. She comes into the kitchen sometimes, probably to get out of her mother's hair. So I'll let her run the mixer or stir batter, simple stuff like that. I feel sorry for her. She seems lonely, you know, despite that bad-ass attitude she wears like a badge."

"Yeah, I know what you mean."

"She's way too skinny, too," he said with a small laugh. "I told her no man likes a woman who's a sack of bones. But she got me back for that. Told me she already had a boyfriend"—he raised his hands—"who knows, right? Said she was gonna get this guy to marry her one of these days."

Marry her?

"Did she tell you his name?"

Carson shook his head. "Nope, but she said it was serious, and she didn't want her mom to know 'cuz dear Mummy wouldn't be happy about it."

Serious? Unhappy Mummy?

Was Kendall referring to herself and Justin?

I couldn't imagine what other man she'd be talking "relationship" about.

Poor delusional child. Particularly since Marilee stood in the way of Kendall's being with young Mr. Gable, publicly anyway.

"Just out of curiosity, does Justin Gable spend much time on the set?" I asked.

"Marilee's sweet-meat?" His dimples came out in full force. "The buffed-up blond dude who doesn't say much?"

"That's him."

"Why? You like him or something?"

"More like or something."

Carson scratched his nose, adding a pinch of flour to his proboscis. "Guy comes into the kitchen whenever he feels like it, uses the fruit and yogurt to make up smoothies for himself and Kendall, sometimes Marilee. He adds all kinds of powders and shit, pardon my French. I did hear him tell Marilee once that she should do a segment on the show about holistic healing."

"What'd she tell him?"

I got another shot of his even white teeth as his mouth split. "I think she gave him a pat on the head and told him to go wait for her in the yoga room, like a good puppy."

Oh, wow.

I couldn't imagine Justin liked getting brushed off like that.

Would it have pissed him enough to slip ma huang in her champagne?

"Carson!" someone yelled from the kitchen, and the bald man's head turned.

"Hold your pants on, would ya?" he shouted back before looking back at me. "This place is like Grand Central Station, you know, so many people always coming and going. Even Marilee's ex-husband wandered in."

"Gilbert Mabry was in the kitchen?"

"He asked for a glass of water and took some headache powder. Then he wanted directions to Marilee's office. He said he got lost." Carson shook his head. "Guy had to be lost in space to ever hitch his wagon to the likes of her." He jerked his chin at me. "You say you're just temporary help? Consider yourself lucky. Being here is more penance than pleasure sometimes. You met Renata?"

"No."

"You should," he said. "You'd like her. She started working here when I did, about six weeks ago. She's doing production work, has to put up with a lot of crap from Marilee. I hope she stays." He brushed at the front of his apron.

"Her name's Renata?"

"Yeah. Renata Taylor. She's a pretty girl." His cheeks flushed. "Got some gorgeous black hair and an attitude as cool as a summer melon."

Sounded to me like Carson Caruthers had a crush.

"*Carson!*" The cry came louder this time.

Carson turned and yelled back, "Coming!"

"You've got to go," I said, a master of the obvious. "Guess I'll see you down at Mother's."

He stuck out a hand, and I shook it. He held on a little longer than was necessary. "I'll be there with the chocolate," he told me.

"Just don't spit in any of the desserts, okay? Especially

if my mother and her friends will be eating them," I said as I wormed free of his grasp.

"Spit in them?" he repeated as I started walking off, up the hallway. "Pardon my French, but what the hell's that supposed to mean."

"The goose liver," I called over my shoulder. "I was manning the web cams at the party."

"Web cams at the party? Oh, shit," I heard him say, obviously catching on. Bright boy.

Grinning, I took a corner fast, without paying attention.

And ran smack into another body, hurrying along as fast as I was.

"Oomph," we expelled simultaneously, the impact knocking us each back a few steps. Papers fluttered from my co-bumper's arms, drifting drunkenly to the floor and settling in a cloud atop the Berber.

It took a few seconds to shake it off and then I bent to help her out. "Oh, geez, I'm sorry. I didn't see you."

"I didn't see you either . . . damn, look at this mess."

A curtain of dark hair hid her bowed head as she crouched down, quickly picking up pages scattered between our feet. I squatted, too, doing my best to help her get them off the carpet and back into her arms.

Glancing at the sheets as I rounded some of them up, I saw topics for future episodes of *The Sweet Life,* call sheets for the crew, and what looked like insurance papers. I thought I glimpsed the name "M. Mabry" on them, but it was such a quick peek, I wasn't sure.

"Thanks," she snatched what I'd gathered from my hands, shifting the papers into some semblance of order as she rose from the floor.

I followed suit, standing up and finally getting a good look at her.

Loose black curls cascaded from a center part, tumbling past her shoulders. She had smooth café au lait skin, and I envied her for it, being pretty colorless myself despite a smattering of freckles. Her hazel eyes quickly assessed me, and she smiled, accentuating the mole in the crease of her cheek.

There was something familiar, too, about the shape of her eyes, the set of the mouth, and I recalled meeting her before, albeit informally.

"You must be Renata," I said, figuring she had to be the woman Carson had mentioned (and who'd made him blush). "You're a production assistant, right? Actually, I believe we've bumped into one another before."

"Last night at the party, right?"

"I mistook you for Marilee's daughter," I said.

"Is that so?" Her mouth tightened, eyes incredulous, and I sensed that she was another of Marilee's staff who felt ambiguous about the "Divine Ms. M," as Carson had dubbed her.

"I'm Andy Kendricks. I've been doing web design work for Marilee for a couple weeks, but I'm only temporary."

"Kendricks?" she repeated, and her frown softened into a look of surprise. "As in Cissy Kendricks on Beverly Drive?"

"Guilty as charged."

Her face broke into a full-fledged grin. She shifted the mess of papers into the crook of her left arm, extending her right. "Yep, I'm Renata Taylor," she said, and I shook her proffered hand. "Your mother's my new neighbor."

"Your neighbor?" I couldn't imagine the woman could afford to live in Highland Park, particularly on Beverly Drive, earning a production assistant's wages.

"I'm living with my folks until I have time to find digs of my own." She shrugged. "They have plenty of room besides."

"Taylor? As in Dr. Taylor? Your mom's a doctor at Medical City, right?"

"Beth Taylor, yes," she said. "My dad's an investment manager at Bank of America."

"So you're from somewhere in East Texas?"

"Somewhere about says it." One of those silent, awkward moments passed before she shuffled the papers in her arms so she could look at her watch. "Oh, hell, I've gotta run. We're taping a segment outside the studio at . . ."

"My mother's house," I cut her off. "I'll see you there."

Renata scooted off, and I ambled up the hallway toward the rear exit to fetch my Jeep, my brain reaching for something that had been bothering me since I heard the girl's name.

It wasn't until I stepped outside into the god-awful heat that it hit me.

First year Latin. Mrs. Bishop.

Renata.

It meant "rebirth."

Deep, I mused.

My father had insisted on naming me Andrea because it meant "courageous" in Greek, or at least that's the spiel he'd given me when I was a little girl. Sometimes I wondered if he'd made it up, like a bedtime story, so I'd feel special (it had worked).

Though, deep in my heart, I wanted to believe it was true, and I hoped I could somehow live up to it.

Chapter 19

 I had some time to kill before I headed to Mother's, so I decided to stop by Medical City and check on Kendall for myself.

It wasn't far from Cissy's house, anyway, and it made me nervous to think that Justin had gone to the hospital alone. What if he'd gotten into her room, despite my warnings to Nurse Alice? What if he'd tried to scare her into keeping quiet about what really happened before she collapsed? Whatever that was.

Another thing bothered me, too.

The fact that Marilee hadn't even visited her daughter today—had merely called the nurses' station for an update—galled me. I figured that Kendall could use a friendly face, and I was pretty sure mine was as friendly as it got.

As I headed south from Addison, my radio off, I found myself wondering how much Kendall actually recalled about last night. The shock of the high-dose ephedra on her heart could have affected her memory, right? There was a good chance we'd never know if Justin gave her the herb or if she administered it to herself before she got sick and blacked out on the bathroom floor.

Though I felt surer than ever that he was the one who'd pushed past me in the darkened hall as I'd left Marilee's office to search for help.

Because of the smell.

Almonds.

I'd noticed Justin's scent when he'd stepped around me, desperate to make a quick escape after I'd caught him with Kendall on Marilee's sofa.

I breathed in the very same smell in the hallway after the lights went out. It had to have been Justin.

Which led to yet another question. If he had been with Kendall when she collapsed, why hadn't he done anything to help?

Because he was afraid?

Or because he was responsible?

My mother's honey-smooth drawl invaded my head, and I recalled something she'd said at the hospital.

"He went out for air again, did you see? Which is the same reason he told Marilee he'd left the party. Either he's sufferin' from a severe lack of oxygen, or he feels guilty about somethin', and you know I'm right. Did you see how reluctant he was to tell the doctor what herbs he'd given that poor girl? And if she'd died, no one would've been the wiser."

Her words had seemed crazy when she'd uttered them, but I found they made more sense, the more I mulled over them.

I hated to sound judgmental—and hated even more to side

with my mother—but Justin hadn't exactly won me over.

It amazed me to think that he had both Mabry women so snookered.

I turned up the AC and pushed down harder on the gas pedal.

Within thirty minutes, I'd reached Medical City from Addison, taking the long way and avoiding Central Expressway. I hated highways and suicide lanes that threw you into traffic without a running start.

It was eleven and already hot enough to toast a bagel on the asphalt. Even the covered parking lot felt sticky when I parked the Jeep and got out, heading for the sliding glass doors that led inside.

An older couple sat in the waiting room, perched side by side on the blue vinyl couch where Marilee and Justin had huddled the night before. The television played on, the sound still too low to hear.

Nurse Alice was nowhere to be seen when I reached Kendall's floor. In fact, the nurses' station was unmanned at the moment, and I walked straight past, heading for Kendall's door.

I pushed it open and peered inside, prepared to find her sleeping.

What I found instead was an empty room and a bed that had been stripped.

No IV on a pole. No monitors that blinked and beeped. *Where the hell was she?*

My heart dribbled like a basketball as I rushed out of the room, looking around for anyone in scrubs and finally spotting a dark-skinned woman in green emerging from a room up the hall.

I ran up to her. "Kendall Mabry," I breathed in a rush. "She isn't in her bed. She can't have checked out already, could she?"

"Hold on a minute, hon," she said. "Come on with me to the desk and we'll see what's what."

The tag pinned to her ample breast read, NATTIE BUMPUS. I followed on her heels and waited while she glanced through paperwork on a clipboard and then pulled a manila folder from the stack.

"Kendall Mabry, you said?"

"Yes."

"Looks like you just missed her. Seems she was discharged against medical advice at ten-thirty this morning."

"Do you know if anyone was with her?"

Nurse Nattie flipped through more pages. "Dr. Feinstein was on call when she left, because Dr. Taylor's off today, and he noted Ms. Mabry was accompanied by her uncle."

"Her uncle?"

"A fellow named Gable."

Unfortunately, I knew it wasn't Clark.

"Are you sure?"

Nurse Nattie tapped the papers. "Everything was done by the book. We couldn't keep her against her will, even though Dr. Feinstein tried to discourage her from leaving. She's eighteen, so she doesn't require a parent's permission. He did emphasize the importance of taking the Inderal for her heart condition and following up with the cardiologist recommended by Dr. Taylor. Hope she follows through."

Kendall left with Justin.

I leaned my palms against the counter feeling weak in the knees.

Did the girl know what she was doing? Or had she been coerced?

Good God, Kendricks, I told myself. *Get a grip. It's not any of your business. You don't even really like Kendall, do you?*

Maybe I didn't. But I felt a strange sense of responsibility for her.

Sort of like that old proverb, that if you save someone's life, they become a part of you.

I got in the Jeep and headed out of the Medical City parking lot, pulling over to the shoulder before I exited the grounds altogether. I opened the pink Escada bag and retrieved my cell phone, dialing up Marilee's office extension. When she answered, I raced to get out the words, "Kendall's not at the hospital . . . she checked out against medical advice. They say that Justin was with her."

"Andy, it's okay," she assured me. "They're both here, at the studio. Kendall's a little shaky, but she's fine. She and Justin insisted on helping, so I sent them to the kitchen to assist Carson with the desserts for the Diet Club."

"Kendall's there?"

"Yes."

My shoulders sank with relief. "And she's okay? Should she be out of bed?"

"Like I said, she's shaky. But she promised to go home and rest after she's done in the kitchen. Justin's promised to stay with her. She'll be okay so long as she takes her medication. You're sweet to worry. I'll tell her you called."

She hung up, and I sat behind the wheel for a moment, just staring at the cell phone in my hand. I tried to convince myself to shake it off, to let Kendall be. As Marilee said, she was fine.

Before I put my phone away in my shoulder bag, eschewing the Escada, which I tossed behind the seats, I dialed Janet Graham's cell. I wanted to see if she'd be dropping by Cissy's for the taping. I found her at her office, finishing up the piece about Marilee's party.

"Come by, Andy, would you? I could use a ride to your mama's place," she said, and I told her I was on my way.

Put Kendall out of your mind, I instructed, as I drove away from Medical City toward Greenville Avenue.

The newspaper office was Janet's home away from home. I knew she often went in on Saturday mornings. Said she got more done when the place was quiet. That's when she filed her column and picked out photos for the Tuesday edition. Though she had the option of sending in her pieces by modem, she'd confessed she liked the kick of being part of a real-live newsroom.

The *PCP* came out on Tuesdays and Fridays, unlike the *Dallas Morning News,* which was a daily. The suburban rag was widely read in the Park Cities, with nearly 70,000 subscribers. Hardly chickenfeed. And Janet was a big reason for their ever-growing readership. Highland Park socialites knew they'd made it when their names were mentioned in Janet's pieces on the society pages, to which a whole section of the paper was devoted.

I figured maybe we could do lunch from the vending machine before we hit Mother's house. I could use a little fortification—even plastic-wrapped chicken salad—if I was going to have to face Cissy and her cronies.

The lot at the stucco-walled building was nearly empty, so I had my pick of spots. I pulled the Jeep right up to the concrete base around the only tree left alive near the pavement. Despite the bad angle, I managed to cover at least the trunk and the windshield in the shade. By Dallas standards, that was a primo parking space.

I rolled my window down a crack and locked up, just in case someone thought the pink Escada evening bag on the back seat was worth stealing.

The *Park Cities Press* kept a large suite on the second floor, across the hall from an orthodontist's office. The door was clearly marked and unlocked, and I entered to find an empty receptionist's desk. But lights were on, and, though I'd hardly label it a beehive of activity, a few warm bodies were in evidence, tapping away on keyboards or huddled over copies of the paper. Where bodies weren't, computer monitors displayed bouncing balls and shooting stars on the screen savers.

Janet's cubicle had a window view, which made her almost as important as the editors who had actual offices with doors and walls.

She peeked around the corner as I strolled the aisle in her direction. Did I mention that her cherished window has a view of the parking lot?

"Hey, girl, I've been watching for you," she said and grinned. Her bright red hair was piled on top of her head with a smattering of sparkly butterfly clips. "Hang on for about twenty minutes, and I should be ready to head over to Beverly."

"I thought we might get a bite first. You hungry?"

"I've already got a head start on you, honey," she said and pointed to the sandwich wrapper and half-eaten Milky Way on her desktop—if there really was a desktop beneath all the papers. Countless invitations and photographs from parties she'd attended were pinned to a stretch of cork-board. An ivy plant with brown leaves sat on the top shelf that ringed her gray cage. A handful of gold Godiva and silver Ethel M boxes attested to her popularity with the people she wrote about. They adored her because she never said anything negative. Not to their faces and not in her column, anyway.

I noticed, too, plenty of photographs of Marilee, as well as a rather plump folder marked MABRY. The notes for her tell-all book, I surmised, wishing I could take a peek.

Janet must've sensed where my eyes had gone as she picked up the file and shoved it inside her right-hand drawer.

"Go on and get yourself something while I finish up, okay?" she said, and I nodded, as she sat back down in front of her computer and started tapping away.

I tried to read over her shoulder. "So you're writing about Marilee's party?"

"Yep."

"Are you mentioning her fight with Amber Lynn?"

"I'm calling it a 'colorful reunion of the two Mrs. Mabrys.' It sounds much more civilized."

"So what are you calling the fire?"

She paused. "Um, just a fire, Andrea. Or I could use 'conflagration' if it'd make you happy."

"No, fire's good."

I left her alone and wandered off in pursuit of a sandwich. I tried to remember where the vending machine was the last time I'd met Janet here to take her to lunch, only to be told she couldn't go out, that she was waiting on this fax or that phone call. So we'd ended up dining on pimento cheese on white bread wrapped in a triangle of plastic.

Yum.

I took a right when I should've taken a left, and I ended up in a room with a mock-up of the paper displayed on the walls. Had to be the upcoming issue, I decided, because there were still some blank spots on the computerized printouts.

Out of curiosity, I stepped closer, until I could read the front-page headlines.

My heart ground to a halt when I saw the words printed below the bottom fold:

GUESS WHO'S COMING TO DINNER . . . AND STAYING?

Whoa, Nelly.

As if that wasn't bad enough, below the screaming black letters was a photograph of a dark-skinned woman with a red kerchief wrapped around her head, standing in a massive front doorway.

It was Dr. Taylor, pretty much as I'd glimpsed her when I'd been driving to Mother's house yesterday morning.

Un-frigging-believable.

I hunched over, squinting at the copy, noting Kevin Snodgrass's name on the byline. The story played heavily on what Sandy had told me about Highland Park being legally segregated until the 1920s, then went on to say that no non-Caucasian had owned a home in the area until Dr. Beth Taylor and husband Richard had purchased the Etherington home on Beverly Drive.

I read on.

Apparently, Dr. Taylor and her husband moved from Tyler, where she ran a medical clinic and he worked as an investment banker at Republic Bank. It alluded to Beth growing up in a small town near Longview and having had an older brother, Ronald Hull, who—according to public records—had been honorably discharged from the Army and had died in a traffic accident some twenty-odd years ago. Ron had been the single parent of a little girl, whom the Taylors had adopted and raised as their own.

Renata, I realized, though Snodgrass didn't print her name.

The things you learn, huh?

I wondered what that must feel like, to lose your daddy so young and end up with your aunt and uncle as parents? I guess it wasn't something you blurted out to strangers upon first meeting, was it?

Snodgrass went on to note that the Taylors confessed to having always loved Dallas and even talked about moving to the city many times before they actually did it. As fortune would have it, Beth was offered a position on the staff at Medical City several months ago, and they decided to go for it. She sold her share of the clinic to her partner in the practice, and Richard easily found a job with Bank of America in Big D.

"We visited lots of neighborhoods, but picked Highland Park because it was the most beautiful area we'd ever seen, so many gorgeous old houses and big trees," Dr. Taylor had remarked. "We're sure we'll love it here. So many other professional people are our neighbors, and those I've met already seem so friendly."

Snodgrass surmised that it must be difficult being the first blacks to reside in HP, though Beth had responded—crisply, I'd imagine after meeting her—"It's overdue, don't you think?"

There were also quotes from some of the neighbors, most notably one "Cissy Blevins Kendricks, Big Steer Ball Co-chair and Society Hall of Fame Best Dressed."

"It's about time we had some fresh blood on Beverly," Mrs. Kendricks insisted, adding, "New neighbors are welcome on my street so long as they pay their taxes, keep up their lawn, and don't kill anyone."

I smiled.

Mother was nothing if not quotable.

Stepping back from the paste-up of the front page, I shook my head, finding it hard to believe that the paper was doing a story on a black family moving into Highland Park in the twenty-first century. What was wrong with this picture? And I don't just mean the shot of Beth in her red kerchief. That hokey headline stolen from the old Sidney Poitier film was laughable.

God help us all.

"Um, excuse me, but I don't think you're supposed to be in here."

Slowly, I turned around to find a tall man filling the doorway. He had on jeans and a Polo shirt, untucked. Coffee let off steam from the Styrofoam cup in his hand.

"Sorry," I said, "but I guess I got lost. I was looking for the vending machines."

"Out the door and take a left."

"Thanks."

He turned sideways to let me pass, and I felt his eyes on

me as I veered off in the opposite direction, nearly running straight into a room with three vending machines, one for sodas and two for everything else. I rounded a small veneer-topped table and plastic chairs, smelling the stale odor of cigarettes and spotting a dirty ashtray despite the sign on the wall that ordered NO SMOKING.

I pulled a few bucks from my purse and fed the machine, settling on a tuna sandwich. Then I got myself a can of Diet Pepsi and headed back to Janet's cubicle.

She was fiddling with the text on her screen, deleting a sentence here or there, fine-tuning things.

Grabbing hold of a loose chair, I pulled it up to her desk, unsure of how to clear any space to set my food and drink without using papers and photos as coasters.

But she waved a hand, wriggling fingernails painted a deep pink to match her dress. "Make yourself comfortable, sugar," she drawled. "I'll just be another few minutes, really. I'll be meeting my photographer there and he can bring me back when we're done. We'll have to go over his shots anyway and get them page ready."

"So fast?" I said as I freed the tuna from the plastic wrap and popped my soda.

"Honey, everything these days is digital."

"I saw the front-page layout for Tuesday's edition," I confessed to her, explaining that I'd wandered into the wrong office en route to the vending machines.

"So you caught the piece on your mama's new neighbors, huh?" She stopped messing with her keyboard and swiveled around. "What'd you think about that?"

From the way she looked at me, I could tell she didn't think any more of it than I did.

I chewed thoughtfully on a bite of sandwich that tasted a lot like Play-Doh. Not that I'd eaten Play-Doh recently, but one never forgets. As I swallowed, I shook my head in disbelief, just as I'd done when I'd seen the mock-up. "Guess who's coming to dinner and staying?" I nearly choked just repeating the words in the headline. "What lame brain came up with that?"

"Ace reporter Kevin Snot-Ass himself." She blew out a breath, setting her red bangs to fluttering. "What a genius, huh?"

"A regular Einstein."

"Yeah. I'd rate this one right up there with his story about the SMU coeds who stripped at night to earn money for tuition. What was that headline? Oh, yeah"—she made a grandiose gesture with her hands, and I could envision the letters in bold as she spelled out the banner—"LAP DANCING THEIR WAY TO AN MBA."

"No."

"Yes, it's true." Janet laughed, a sound amazingly like a snorting pig.

Which got me to giggling, too.

I mean, really.

What else could we do?

Chapter 20

 Five minutes later, I'd finished half the tuna sandwich and Janet had wrapped up her coverage of Marilee's party, so we headed out to the parking lot and climbed into my oven-like Jeep (so much for finding the sole shady spot).

Destination: Cissy's.

As I slipped on my Ray-Bans, Janet set a plump Louis Vuitton bag in her lap, one with the LV monogram in all sorts of Day-Glo colors (ugly as hell, I thought). But it matched her deep pink sleeveless shift. A Ralph Lauren, I knew, because the tag was sticking up.

Out of habit, I reached over and flipped it under for her.

She didn't even flinch.

It was just one of those things that friends do for each other without even thinking, like spotting chives between front teeth, pantyhose tucked into underwear, or toilet paper stuck to a shoe.

On the way over to Mother's, I told Janet what had happened to Kendall after the party came to a fiery end, including the girl's previously undiagnosed heart condition and the fact that she'd truly come *thisclose* to dying. I also filled Janet in on how Justin Gable factored into the whole mess; his turning into Kendall's health guru and feeding her herbs like kava kava and ma huang, which the doctor had suggested could've triggered the nearly fatal attack of long QT syndrome. And I told her that the physician who'd made the call on Kendall's condition was none other than Dr. Beth Taylor, the new neighbor of Mother's featured in Kevin Snot-Ass's front-page feature in the Park Cities paper.

"Small world," she said, just what I'd thought when I'd found out myself. "Sometimes I think living in Dallas is incestuous. Everyone's related to someone else, or they're friends of friends. Like six degrees of separation."

In my case, it was six degrees of Cissy Blevins.

Speaking of, I mentioned to Janet, "Dr. Taylor will be at the Dallas Diet Club meeting today, and maybe it's a good thing since people around Marilee seem to keep getting hurt."

"Like the wardrobe lady bitten by the spider"—Janet was nodding—"and the director whose shoulder was nearly knocked out of its socket by a boom mike. Now this thing with Kendall. Don't bad things come in threes?"

"Let's hope that's the end of it."

"So Justin was giving Kendall harmful herbs?"

"Maybe not harmful to healthy people," I said, "but dangerous for someone with Kendall's arrhythmia."

"You think he knew?"

"I don't see how. Especially if Kendall had never undergone an ECG, which Marilee insisted was the case."

"So her collapse was accidental?"

"No one's quite sure how such a big dose of ephedra got in her bloodstream. Mother thinks Justin is responsible for attempted murder," I admitted and found myself gripping the steering wheel harder. "I thought she was full of hot air at first, but I'm not so sure anymore. He's behaving pretty oddly and he seemed awfully reluctant to tell Dr. Taylor what supplements he was giving Kendall. Marilee let the cat out of the bag, though, so he couldn't avoid the truth when Dr. Taylor cornered him. Then I found out he helped Kendall leave the hospital this morning against medical advice. I'm worried for her, Janet. I can't help it. She's such a confused kid."

"Justin signed her out?"

"He claimed to be her uncle."

"No?"

"Yes."

"He is a piece of work, isn't he?" I glanced away from the road to see Janet tapping her chin with her forefinger. "Makes you wonder, doesn't it? When did all the bad stuff start happening with Marilee's crew? After she met Justin, or before?"

"After." So far as I knew. "Kendall brought him home a couple months ago, right? The incidents have all happened in the past six weeks, since they've been working in the new studio."

"And the plot thickens," Janet murmured.

"You know something about him?" I asked, because Janet always knew something about everyone. That was her gift, just as it was my mother's.

"I've been doing some digging on Justin for the book

about Marilee," Janet confessed as the Wrangler bumped over the road toward Cissy's house. "But you have to promise not to breathe a word. I'm still double-checking facts."

"Didn't I promise to keep mum about this book already?" Did she want me to swear on a stack of Bibles or something?

"Say it."

"Cross my heart and hope to die."

Geez. What were we? Six?

"All right, here's what I've got on Justin so far. It looks like Marilee Mabry isn't the only rich older woman he's latched onto in the past few years, or so my sources tell me."

Her sources being other society columnists across this great state of Texas, women and men who knew more about the doings of the wealthy than the police or the FBI ever would.

"He romanced Kathryn Bremer in Houston just last year."

"Bremer?" I echoed. "As in Bremer Plastics?"

"One and the same. Kathryn's a sixty-year-old billionaire widow, just ripe for the picking."

Bremer Plastics was one of the companies my trust owned stock in, and my shares had split since college more times than I could count.

"And before that it was a divorcée named Helen Stapleton of San Antonio."

"Don't tell me. Stapleton Electronics?"

"Yep."

"Wow." I glanced at the stereo system in my Jeep, which had that very name stamped above the CD player.

"Justin has a very smooth MO for slithering into the lives of these women. He apparently gets a gig as a personal trainer at the gym where these women work out. Then he weasels his way into their trust, into their homes, into their beds, and, finally, into their bank accounts."

"Did he steal from them?"

"Not outright, no, which is why he's so slippery." She squirmed against the seat belt and reached over to flip the AC up higher. "If he had, I'm sure someone would've pressed charges by now. Nope, seems like our boy Justin gets these women wrapped around his little finger"—she hesitated—"or other parts that aren't so little. My sources say he takes care of them, slowly encroaching on their entire lives, managing their lifestyles, their eating habits, until they feel like he's essential to their well-being. He cajoles them into giving him things, cars, money, stocks, even small percentage shares in their companies."

"Marilee certainly acts like she depends on him," I said, thinking of the way she'd behaved at the party and at the hospital last night. Clinging to him, freaking out when he wasn't there, leaning on him. The same way Kendall did. "I think he's got both mother and daughter wrapped around his little, er, finger."

"That's precisely what he does." Janet braced a palm against the dashboard. "He'll get as much as he can out of them before he figures he's overstayed his welcome. Justin's no dummy. That's why he targets widows and divorcées, preferably with no children. Still, he's gotta be afraid that, one of these days, someone's going to realize he's a con man and file fraud charges or something. Until then, he's basically no better than those gypsies you see on television, pulling roofing scams. Like Old Man River, he just keeps rolling along."

So Justin Gable was a con man.

A gigolo, a liar, and a thief.

Mother's instincts had been dead-on. Or were they instincts?

"Let's just say I've checked up on our Mr. Gable and learned some interesting tidbits about him. And, even if I hadn't, I've seen too many women of a certain age fall for younger men and end up brokenhearted, not to mention a good deal lighter in the pocketbook. He's as smooth as they come, and I don't trust him as far as I can spit."

I considered what she'd said about Justin at the hospital, and I wondered if Mother already knew what Janet's sources had confided to her. That Justin had a way with rich older women.

Still, it didn't necessarily make him an attempted murderer.

Or did it?

He'd sure seemed nervous when Dr. Taylor had mentioned calling the cops.

What if Kendall had found out what he was up to? Maybe she suspected a scam and had threatened to rat on him. But then why would she suggest to Carson that she had a serious boyfriend she intended to marry? Was she secretly blackmailing Justin? Did she want him badly enough to force him into a commitment? What was really going on with them?

The more I tried to figure out Kendall and Justin's relationship, the more it made my head spin.

I couldn't wait to get my hands on Kendall and try to

find out what really happened between them last night. That is, if Justin hadn't convinced her to keep mum about it. Damn, I wish I'd gotten to her at the hospital first.

The Jeep jostled beneath us, as I pulled onto Beverly Drive, grateful for the huge shade tress that lined the street and draped their branches over us, reducing the sunlight to mere splotches.

There were no orange moving vans in sight, just the usual assortment of Lexuses, Beamers, and Jags parked in front of circular drives, and yardworkers mowing lawns and clipping shrubs, sweating in the heat.

Besides the sweaty guys with the weed eaters, not a living soul was visible, which was as it should be at midday with the temperature hovering around 100 degrees.

"You think we beat the crowd? I'd love to get there ahead of Marilee's crew and watch them set up," Janet was saying as I rolled the Jeep onto Mother's long circular drive, but a fast glimpse around the bend suggested the crowd had us beat handily.

"My gosh," I exclaimed as I drove nearer and saw the extent to which cars and trunks had this cobbled artery clogged.

A veritable army of vans and SUVs jammed the curve of the drive directly in front of the mansion. Two of the vans had their rear doors opened and crew members paraded back and forth, carrying equipment and boxes of who knew what.

I stopped the Jeep and considered running around to the rear alley behind the house and parking by the garage.

But Janet had already unfastened her seat belt and was grabbing at the door handle, itching to get out. "Oh, wow, this is going to be great," she gushed. "A Diet Club meeting being taped for national television. It's like being allowed into the pope's bedroom at the Vatican."

Watching a bunch of aging socialites eat desserts as rich as they were and play a few hands of bridge was like visiting the pope's boudoir?

Only in a parallel universe.

And a very freaky universe, indeed.

I put the Wrangler in Park as Janet popped her door with a creak and flew out, leaping to the ground like a gymnast. She fairly skipped across the cobbles heading toward the house in her bright pink outfit.

In contrast, I took my time getting out. First, I rolled my window down to let in the hot air and then I slipped my Ray-Bans back into my purse, before I hopped down and followed on Janet's fuchsia heels.

I squinted at the mass mingling of cars on the drive, looking them over and spotting several I recognized as belonging to Mother's friends from the Diet Club. Buffy Winspear's recently burgled white Cadillac Escalade and Millicent Maxwell's (also white) M-class Mercedes among them. No doubt several of the women would have had their drivers drop them off, despite living up the street.

I circled the parked vehicles twice before it registered that Justin wasn't here. Despite Marilee saying he was taking Kendall to the Preston Hollow mansion once they left the studio, I'd suspected he'd make an appearance.

Yet, there was no sign of his shiny silver BMW Roadster, a gift from Marilee.

I paused in the shade of a catering truck with THE SWEET LIFE painted on its sides, a chill passing through me, despite the trickle of sweat that slid slowly down between my shoulder blades.

Why did I feel that Kendall was in danger still? Instead of picturing the girl at home, safe in her bed, I imagined Justin driving her into the woods to finish her off, after his attempted snuffing last night had failed.

Stop it, Kendricks, I told myself, wishing my mother had never uttered a word about Justin craving Marilee's money enough to want Kendall dead.

Wishing I hadn't heard what Janet Graham gleaned from her sources about the Boy Wonder's past December-May romances that were nothing but cons.

Damn.

Maybe I was suffering from an anxiety hangover, but I felt in my bones that the worst wasn't over yet. My stomach churned, tying itself into a tight figure eight (the only knot I could recall from the sailing class my mother had made me take when I was eleven).

I leaned back against the catering truck and sighed, trying to convince myself that everything would be okay, that the taping of the Dallas Diet Club would go off without a hitch, then Marilee and her crew would be on their merry way.

Please, no more fires, I prayed. And no more water. After the drenching from the sprinklers at Marilee's, I wanted to stay dry for a while. Spare me a plague of locusts, too, though I figured I could count that one out since Mother had the house regularly sprayed for pests.

I pushed away from the truck and wiped the perspiration from my brow with the palm of my hand. Then I trudged through the cars toward the front door.

Maybe nothing would happen. Maybe this afternoon

would be blissfully dull. It was a typical, hot, cloudless summer day. Probably the worst that could happen would be if the air conditioner went out.

Sure, it would suck, but it wouldn't kill anyone, would it?

With that pleasant thought in mind, I ascended the stone steps, past the whitewashed terra-cotta lions standing guard on either side of the opened door, and I crossed the threshold to the cool of inside.

Though I'd expected to find some disarray, what I saw when I entered bordered on chaos.

The marble tiles in the foyer had been covered by plastic and plywood. I poked my head into the living room to see furniture rearranged and most of the rugs rolled up, priceless antique knickknacks removed from fireplace mantels and tabletops, replaced by fresh flowers in vases used as props on Marilee's set.

Atop more plywood sat what looked like small transformers or large battery packs sprouting snakelike cables connecting umbrella lights, more lights on tripods, and microphones on metal arms reaching up toward the ten-foot ceilings.

Crew members purposefully moved about, having taken over Mother's house like an occupying force.

I spotted Cissy, Buffy, Millicent, Beth Taylor, and the other members of the Diet Club being primped and powdered by several of Marilee's makeup artists.

My mother turned her head, sensing my presence, and gave me her "what have I gotten myself into" look: wrinkled brow, down-turned mouth, and eyes that rolled heavenward.

I felt a sudden urge to laugh, but stifled the impulse behind a tight-lipped grin. It wasn't fair to wallow in her regret, was it?

She crooked a finger at me, beckoning, but I shook my head, surveying the treacherous path I'd have to take to reach her.

I didn't see how I could cross the living room without risking life and limb, so I followed the plastic matting from the foyer through a hallway that led past the main staircase and into the kitchen.

Before I'd even passed the butler's pantry, I heard the chalkboard-scratch howl of Marilee's drawl, raised in heated argument with the hard-edged Brooklynese of Carson Caruthers.

Despite my misgivings, I made my way into the one room in the mansion that Mother rarely visited, finding Sandy Beck standing on the sidelines in a navy cardigan, keeping a watchful eye on the proceedings. I put a hand on her shoulder, and she started, turning quickly to see who it was. She relaxed when she realized it was *moi.*

"What's going on?" I whispered.

"World War Three." She jerked her chin toward the clutter to our left. "They're setting up to shoot here in the kitchen, and Marilee's not happy about something."

"Ah," I murmured and looked over at the white cardboard boxes covering the countertop near the double sinks, the chocolate creations that had once filled them—obviously the desserts Carson had cooked up in Marilee's studio kitchen—now sat upon various tiered plate stands, dressed up in chocolate shavings, fresh fruit, artistic glazes, and powdered-sugar designs resembling lacy doilies. They looked prettier than some people I knew and all too ready for their close-ups, more so than the ash-blond woman with the makeup bib around her collar, a frown on her blood-red lips, and a serving knife in hand, poised to carve what appeared to be a fancy pie.

"I told you I wanted to feature all chocolate, so what the hell is this doing here?" Marilee snarled at Carson, his smooth pate sweating under the ceiling lights.

"It's a Brandy Pecan Pie, and I'll drizzle it with dark chocolate. So it's close enough to qualify," he explained, barely raising his voice. "We've got a Dark Chocolate Mousse Pie, a Chocolate Almond Torte, a Raspberry Fudge Trifle, and the Death by Chocolate, so I don't think one pecan pie is going to ruin the segment."

"Are you saying you know what's better for my show than I do?" Marilee squawked, waving the serving knife. "How dare you!"

"I'm the food editor, *capisce*? Give me some credit, lady, would you?" A red flush spread up the back of Carson's neck. "Now put the knife down and step away from the pie. Don't make me have to hurt you."

"This is my show, I can do whatever I want, and you'd better get that through your shiny skull if you want to stick around, *capisce*?" Marilee thrust the utensil deep into the heart of the Brandy Pecan Pie. "Now get this thing out of here before we shoot!"

Carson winced and clutched his fists over his apron-covered heart, as if feeling the pie's pain. With a sigh, he removed the offending dessert with the serving knife sticking out of it and took it over to the sink.

Marilee busied herself rearranging the desserts set in

front of her. When she'd finished, she whipped the makeup bib from her throat and yelled, "Renée, Renée! Where are you, damn it?"

"I'm right here, Mrs. Mabry." A breathy voice piped up, and I saw Renata warily approach her boss. "What do you need?"

"Throw this away"—Marilee pushed the paper bib into Renata's hands—"and get me some dental floss, would you? If I'm going to chat with the Diet Club ladies while I sample dessert, I'll need backup in case anything gets stuck in my teeth. That's your job, Renée, to make sure my teeth are clean."

"It's Renata," the young woman enunciated, her smile fading as she crumpled the bib in her fist.

"Whatever," Marilee brushed her off with a flick of her wrist. "What are you standing there for? Go fetch my floss!"

Carson stepped up and stood in front of Renata protectively. "Hey, don't talk to her like that. She's not your flunky."

"Really?" Marilee laughed.

Renata opened her mouth, but no words emerged. She turned on her heel and dashed off through the butler's pantry toward the foyer. I wondered if she wouldn't keep going right out the front door.

I noticed that Carson was watching her exit as well.

"Lovely woman," Sandy muttered under her breath. "I don't know how your mother stands her. Or how anyone else puts up with her, for that matter."

I thought of the six webmasters who'd worked for Marilee before me, and I said, "Most of her employees seem to last about a week."

"That long?"

Several members of the crew made adjustments to the umbrella lights beaming down on the desserts and on Marilee, who stood behind the counter, waiting until they were satisfied with the setup.

"Quiet on the set!" someone shouted, making me jump, and then two men armed with shoulder-held cameras rolled tape. One seemed to be focused on Marilee while the other zoomed in on the pies and cakes. A woman crouched on the floor held handwritten cue cards, though Marilee didn't appear to need them.

"I've got a very tasty show planned for y'all," Marilee said, beaming into the camera. "Yes, it's your good pal Marilee Mabry again, and today I'll be visitin' with a group of ladies who call themselves the Dallas Diet Club. I'm gonna share some of their wonderful chocolate dessert recipes with you, so you can truly live the sweet life without a lot of muss and fuss. In fact, our featured recipe for Death by Chocolate cake even uses ready-made mixes to minimize your time and effort. After all, that's what the Sweet Life is about. Making your busy lives easier without breakin' your back or breaking the bank."

Next, they shot Marilee putting together the ingredients for the Death by Chocolate cake, all the bowls already filled with precisely measured ingredients. They even had a bundt pan greased and filled with batter for her to slip into Mother's stainless-steel oven—despite never turning the appliance on—and, *voilà!* out came a perfectly baked cake, cooled and easily removed from the pan. The only thing Marilee actually did herself was to shake the sifted powdered sugar onto the finished cake.

"Cut!" the director yelled, his shoulder still in a sling from the boom mike accident. "Let's move it to the living room, ladies and gentleman."

I saw Carson and his food crew begin unpacking Tupperware containers from large coolers. They removed already-sliced pieces of Death by Chocolate and positioned each one on a china plate. After carefully topping each slice with perfect chocolate curls and a drizzle of raspberry glaze, they set them all on a tray to take into the living room for the segment to be taped with my mother, Millicent, Buffy, Beth, and the rest of the Diet Club. Several of his crew gathered teacups and saucers and filled a china coffee pot from the percolator that had been brewing on the counter.

"You need any help?" I asked Carson, and he looked at me blankly, though I couldn't blame him for forgetting my name, what with all the Marilee-inspired chaos.

"Andy Kendricks," I reminded him. "This is my mother's house."

He blinked as recognition dawned. "Oh, yeah, sorry, my brain's kinda fried at the moment. Thanks for your offer"—he shifted the tray on his hip—"but I've got it covered. Though you could do me a favor."

"What?"

He leaned in so close I felt his breath on my skin as he whispered, "How about running over the Divine Ms. Mabry with a train, preferably one that has an extremely large caboose?"

I smiled. "Can't help you there."

He winked. "Then get out of my way so I can deliver the poison."

He and his crew scrambled through the swinging door that led through the dining room. As fast as that, the kitchen emptied, leaving behind a few of Marilee's staff, who began to pack away the cups, bowls, pans, and utensils used in the baking segment.

Sandy had already headed into the living room, and I followed suit. I didn't want to miss seeing my mother's star turn.

The umbrella lights beamed and the cameras were rolling when I finally edged into the room. A crowd gathered on the plywood, behind colored cables, focused on the women comfortably seated in front of the Italian-marbled fireplace. Marilee and the half-dozen members of the Diet Club perched on Louis XVI-style chairs and love seats arranged in a semicircle. The china pot of coffee sat upon a silver tray atop an upholstered ottoman in between. The cups and saucers rested on side tables, as linen napkins and floral plates with slivers of Death by Chocolate occupied the ladies' laps, so each of them could nibble on the cake while Marilee asked them questions about the origins of the Diet Club.

"So you started the group several years ago?" she asked my mother.

Cissy nodded and began to explain how the group got together. Marilee picked up her fork and shoveled in healthy bites of cake, nodding as she did so, as if to say, "mmm-mmm good."

I noticed that my mother's friends seemed too nervous to eat and merely picked at their perfect slices of Death by Chocolate. Playing with their food, as it were. Beth Taylor didn't even pretend to fiddle with the dessert, instead calmly sipping her cup of coffee, her dark eyes taking in the goings-on.

". . . so that's how the Dallas Diet Club got started, and we've been meetin' several times a month, schedules permitting, ever since. We play a few hands of bridge, then eat dessert and chatter. It's been a godsend to us, because we're all so busy with charity work and . . ."

Marilee came half out of her chair, gagging.

"Sugar, are you all right?" Mother asked her, leaning forward in her seat and reaching over.

"Ahhh." Marilee dropped the dessert plate and her fork to the floor with a clatter. Her eyes went bug-wide and her hands went to her chest, clutching at her blouse, like she couldn't breathe.

The other Diet Club women suddenly pushed their cake plates off onto the coffee table.

"She's choking!" someone said as Marilee toppled off her chair to the floor.

I saw Beth Taylor leap up from the sofa before pandemonium struck and moving bodies got in my way.

"Call 911!" one of the crew yelled, as I pushed my way through the crowd and emerged to see Marilee lying on the rug with Beth Taylor bending over her, hands pushing at Marilee's chest, while everyone else looked on.

If she'd been choking, why was Beth doing CPR instead of the trusty Heimlich maneuver?

Had Marilee had a heart attack?

I suddenly flashed on finding Kendall, lifeless on the bathroom tiles, and my knees felt wobbly all over again.

"Stand back, everyone, give them some space!"

There was barely a sound as Dr. Taylor worked on Marilee, doing CPR without pausing, sweat glistening on her face. With a sigh of exhaustion, she finally gave up, rocked back on her heels and looked up, her dark eyes filled with defeat.

Sirens swelled, coming nearer.

"They're here!" someone shouted from across the room. "I can see the ambulance at the end of the drive."

Beth Taylor shook her head.

My gaze fell to Marilee, sprawled upon the rust red of the Persian Serapi rug, her mouth slack and eyes unblinking, staring up at the ceiling. The floral plate lay at her feet, bits of cake still sticking to its shiny surface.

"Why are you stopping?" Cissy prodded Beth. "Don't give up."

"It's too late," the doctor said. "She's already gone."

I heard someone start sobbing.

And it hit me like a fist, squarely in the chest.

It's too late . . . she's gone.

Marilee Mabry was dead.

Chapter 21

 It was a long two hours before Mother got her house back.

I would have said, "back to normal," only nothing felt remotely normal at that point, not after what had happened.

One hundred twenty minutes of being sequestered in the dining room with the members of *The Sweet Life* crew who'd been present for the shoot, while police officers with clipboards made the rounds, getting everyone's contact info before letting them leave, one by one.

I sat beside Cissy for the duration, patting her hand, the anxiety palpable among the several dozen others gathered around the Chippendale dining table. Long faces stared blankly, others whispered to each other, asking, "What will happen now? Is it over? What about syndication?"

Because the show would not go on, would it? Could there be a *Sweet Life* without Marilee?

All the while, voices drifted in, along with an occasional shout or bump against the wall, as the crime scene technicians combed through the living room and kitchen, bagging and tagging everything they considered to be evidence, including, I was told, all the cakes, pies, and mousses, the coffee pot, the cups and saucers, and crumbled remains of the Death By Chocolate that Marilee had been eating when she'd keeled over.

The deputy chief of police in Highland Park, a woman my mother's age named Anna Dean, had arrived on the scene along with two police cruisers not five minutes after the paramedics had given up trying to resuscitate Marilee with portable defibrillators.

The petite gray-haired Deputy Dean stood no taller than five two, but looked plenty intimidating in her blue uniform with the shiny brass badge. With mind-numbing efficiency, she'd assessed the situation and called for the medical examiner and crime scene technicians from Dallas before ordering her officers to corral us all in another room, away from the scene of death.

No one had dared call it a "crime scene" yet, but I got the distinct impression that's how it was being viewed.

I overheard Dr. Taylor telling the deputy chief it was paramount that Marilee's body fluids be drawn and tested for the gene mutation that causes long QT, in addition to checking her stomach contents and the cake and coffee she'd ingested.

Which got me to wondering if there was some kind of connection with what had happened to Kendall. Could last night have been a practice run for somebody wanting to kill Marilee? Or was it a mistake?

It didn't take much to convince me that Marilee's death was no run-of-the-mill heart attack; something that Deputy

Chief Dean all but confirmed once her officers had sequestered the lot of us in Mother's dining room.

The woman in blue hooked her thumbs in her duty belt, her right hand perilously close to her holstered weapon as she addressed the question that was foremost in everyone's head. "As of now," she told us, "we're calling this a suspicious death. So give your name and address to my officers and don't make any plans to leave town. We might need to follow up with formal statements, you understand." Her narrowed eyes surveyed the large group seated around Mother's enormous Chippendale table. "Any questions?"

No one uttered so much as a peep.

As the hours wore on, I patted my mother's hand and fought back tears. Tears for Kendall as much as for Marilee.

What would Kendall do when she heard? I wondered, my chest clenching at the thought. She was so fragile already. Would the police wend their way over to Marilee's residence to break the news? If that was the case, I felt a grudging relief that she wasn't alone. As much as I didn't like Justin, it would be worse if Kendall had no one.

As soon as I could get away from the house, I was determined to head over. In spite of the conflict between them, Marilee had been pretty much it for Kendall in the way of family. I was afraid of what Kendall might do; truly fearful she'd turn self-destructive when it really hit her that her mummy was gone.

And what a way to go.

Death by Chocolate.

Isn't it ironic . . . don't you think?

The lyrics of that Alanis song kept running in a loop through my brain, which I guess was a lot better than thinking about Marilee's body sprawled on the rust-colored rug, her unseeing eyes staring at the ceiling.

Thankfully, by the time the police finished up, there was no body to be seen. Hell, there wasn't even a rug between the Louis XVI loveseats, just bare wood with a vague rectangular outline on the varnished planks. Though I wasn't an eyewitness to the rug's removal—or the body's, for that matter—I heard they'd rolled up the Persian Serapi and had hauled it away in the crime lab's van.

I heard other things as well.

Like the fact that the deputy chief had spoken to Carson Caruthers privately, before she'd allowed him to leave. She'd chatted with Beth Taylor again, then Renata and Janet, too.

Guess she'd saved Mother and me for last.

We were the only ones remaining in the dining room when Deputy Chief Dean ambled in and sat across the table, arms folded on its edge. She broke the tension by chatting with Mother for a few minutes about an upcoming fundraiser for the Widows and Orphans Fund, before she eased into questions about Marilee, how long we'd each known her, if she'd been in ill health or if she'd had any problems with particular employees that we were aware of.

I admitted that Marilee wasn't exactly beloved on her set, but that I couldn't imagine anyone who'd actually resort to murder. I did spill what I'd heard about the spider incident and the falling boom microphone, though the deputy chief nodded like those were old news.

It was Mother who brought up Justin Gable and his romancing Kendall before worming his way into Marilee's life. As I cringed in silence, she shared her theory with the deputy chief that Justin was responsible for Kendall's near-fatal dose of ma huang.

For some reason, that prompted Anna Dean to look directly at me, locking her narrowed eyes on me like a bomber pilot zeroing in on a target. "You were over at the studio this morning, is that true?"

I slid my hands into my lap, wedging them between my knees. "I had to drop by to pick up my evening bag and my Jeep. I'd left them both there after the fire."

"Were you in the kitchen while the food was being prepared for the shoot?"

Okay, who'd blabbed? Carson? Renata? It could've been either one, I guessed.

"I wasn't in the kitchen for more than thirty seconds," I said, finding myself blinking rapidly, while Deputy Chief Dean stared like an eyelid-less gecko. "First, I ran into Gilbert Mabry . . . well, he ran into me, coming out of Marilee's office. They'd been arguing." I winced. "I really hadn't meant to eavesdrop, but they were shouting."

"About what?"

I sighed, knocking my knees together, hating to be put on the spot. "He was mad that she hadn't called him from the hospital to tell him about Kendall. She told him he'd been a crummy husband and father. He accused her of stealing a three hundred fifty dollar bottle of 1973 Dom Perignon from his stash in their basement before their divorce . . ."

"Hold on a second." The deputy chief pulled a slim notebook from her breast pocket, licked her forefinger, and flipped through the pages until she found what she was looking for. "The 1973 Dom Perignon Oenotheque that Kendall Mabry drank before she collapsed?"

I glanced at my mother, who appeared to be listening as intently as the policewoman. She had her arms crossed, her head tipped, and her lips pressed into a thin line that worried me.

"Yes, that bottle," I confirmed before resuming my story. "After Gilbert left, I went in to Marilee's office to get my purse. I asked about Kendall and then I asked Marilee why she didn't get tested for the long QT. I read about it online, and it's usually genetic."

"So I've been told. Dr. Taylor was pretty insistent about that, so we'll have the lab check it out. We're putting a rush on the results, and I'm gonna lean on them myself, so we should have preliminaries pretty fast."

"Marilee mentioned having physicals for insurance purposes, for her TV show, and that nothing serious had ever turned up. She got a call from the mayor, so she blew me off, but not before she suggested I go to the kitchen and remind Carson that they had to pack up and leave within the hour."

"Carson Caruthers?" Anna Dean asked, her notebook still out.

"Yes." I wet my lips. Mother hadn't shifted position, and I figured she'd have a fairly painful crick in her neck by the time I was through. I didn't think I'd mention Carson's remark before he took the cake out to the living room: *"Get out of my way so I can deliver the poison."* He'd been joking, after all, and I couldn't see getting him in any trouble because he had a dark sense of humor.

"You saw Mr. Caruthers at the studio earlier?" the deputy chief prodded.

"Yes," I picked up where I left off. "Carson and I went

into the hallway to talk. The kitchen was too crazy. He said it was like Grand Central Station, that even Mr. Mabry—as in Gilbert—had been there already, getting some water to take his headache powder."

The deputy chief thumbed through a few pages, nodding. "Mr. Caruthers noted that Justin Gable and Kendall Mabry visited the kitchen as well, helping them finish up with the desserts."

"I wouldn't know about that, not personally." Though Marilee had told me as much on the telephone. "The only other person I saw was Renata Taylor. We bumped into each other before I left the building. She had her arms full of papers." I squinted, trying to recall what I'd seen. "Call sheets for the crew, scripts, medical insurance papers."

"Anything else, Ms. Kendricks?" Anna Dean asked, eyes pinning me down, like she could see I was holding back.

"There is one thing, maybe," I started, wetting my lips. "It's about Justin Gable."

"Yes?"

"It's just that he's . . . never mind." I clammed up and glanced down at my lap.

Oh, man, how I itched to confess what I'd learned about Justin's past from Janet in the car coming over, but I couldn't. I'd promised I wouldn't repeat a word, but it was killing me to keep it in.

"The boy's a con man," Cissy stepped in. "He's left a trail of lovesick older women from Galveston to El Paso, perhaps even points beyond. He steals their hearts and then their money. Marilee was just another notch on his bed post."

I raised my eyes to stare at my mother, my heart pumping. So she had known, just as I'd suspected.

The deputy chief smiled dryly. "We're running a background check on him, so we'll see what turns up. By any chance, did Marilee Mabry know about his past relationships?"

Mother glanced at me sideways before she admitted, "Yes, she knew. Because I told her."

I stared at her, wondering what else she'd been hiding from me.

"How did she react?" Deputy Dean asked.

Cissy tugged at the tail end of her scarf. "I thought she'd be upset, but she wasn't. She took it in stride, told me that it didn't matter what Justin had done with other women. She insisted she didn't care, because she wasn't in love with him. He gave her great pleasure and he doted on Kendall, was how she put it, and she said that's what mattered at this point in her life."

"Thank you for your candor, Mrs. Kendricks." She nodded at Mother, then at me. "Thank you both for your cooperation. I'll be in touch."

"Will you be going over to see Marilee's daughter now?" I asked. "If so, I'd like to come. She'll need a friend." And I didn't count Justin as one, I left unsaid.

Anna Dean shook her head. "I don't think that's a good idea, Ms. Kendricks. I've already asked Dr. Taylor to ride along, because of young Ms. Mabry's heart problem. What we don't need is an audience."

An audience?

Mother pressed her pump into my shin, and I sighed.

"Okay. But please tell Kendall I'm around if she needs me." I fished into my purse and withdrew one of my business cards, which I passed across the table to Anna Dean. She scooped it up and slipped it in her breast pocket.

The deputy chief apologized again for the inconvenience and the mess—since the police wouldn't let the crew remove any of their equipment, and they'd confiscated the tape from the shoot. She did request that we stay out of the living room, at least for another day or two, until they had some answers from the medical examiner's office.

She pushed away from the table and stood.

Before she'd taken a step, I blurted out, "You think she was murdered, don't you, Deputy Chief?"

For an instant, I didn't think she was going to answer me. Then she said, very deliberately, "They don't hire me to investigate what I *think,* Andrea, just what I *know.* And I'll know soon enough in this case. We should have some preliminary blood work back before long," she remarked, then excused herself.

Mother gave me one of her looks.

But I didn't care if I'd been rude.

Anna Dean was more than suspicious about Marilee's death.

So I wasn't the only one.

"I'm pouring myself a brandy and then retiring to the sun porch," my mother said as she rose from her seat.

"You never drink before five o'clock," I said.

"I've never had anyone die in my living room, either," she tossed over a shoulder as she sashayed off.

My cell phone let loose a muffled ring, and I reached

over to free it from the purse at my feet. The number was Janet Graham's work extension, and I braced myself as she went into a breathless monologue about how exciting the past few hours had been and how she'd already gotten a thumbs up from her editor at the paper to do a piece about Marilee, a three-part feature on her life and death. Which, she added, would be great publicity for the book she was writing.

As she rushed on, I hung my head, wishing we could do this afternoon over again, only with a different ending. Like with Kendall.

"Tell Cissy I'll be sensitive to her situation, being at the center of this whole mess, okay? I don't want to take advantage of our friendship . . ."

I imagined her frantically typing up a story with the headline:

DEATH BY CHOCOLATE (REALLY)

Or maybe:

THE DALLAS DIE-IT CLUB

Oy.

"My photographer showed up late as usual, damn him, but this time it was a good thing . . . he snapped a few shots of them removing the body . . ."

I dropped my forehead to the table, holding the phone loosely to my right ear, barely listening.

Last night was bad enough, but this was worse than I could've dreamed.

I still couldn't believe Marilee Mabry was dead. No matter what I thought of her, it was strange to realize I'd never see her again. She was like a tornado, sucked up into the clouds, there one minute and gone the next. A force of nature silenced.

Poor Kendall, I thought again. *Poor confused and lonely girl.*

"Mother told the police about Justin," I confessed, hoping she wouldn't think I'd betrayed her. "She knew about him, Janet, everything. At least as much as your sources."

"Crap," she murmured. "I was planning to do a sidebar about Marilee's boy-toy and his prior relationships. I'd wanted it to be an exclusive."

"I'm sorry." What else could I say?

"Hey, it's not your fault. And just because the cops know doesn't mean our readership does. Oops, gotta go, but I'll call you tomorrow and see what's shaking. I'm thinking of taking a trip out to Gunner tomorrow. I've finally got a lead on the aunt Marilee supposedly lived with for a while when she was sixteen. There's a woman named Doreen Haggerty in a nursing home there that has to be her. You want to keep me company?"

"Ask me later, okay?"

"Sure, Andy, sure. Hey, tell your mom I'm sorry about everything."

"Right."

When I hung up and put away the phone, Sandy was escorting the last of the police contingent to the front door.

I followed in my mother's footsteps and headed to the stillness of the sun porch.

She reclined on the chaise, cradling a brandy snifter. From the few drops remaining, it appeared she'd made a good dent already.

"Not quite happy hour, is it?" I said as I collapsed onto the cushioned sofa.

"We've never had anyone pass away at a Diet Club meeting," she murmured and rolled the remainder of the brandy around in the bulb of the glass. "Bunny Beeler did break out in hives once from eating a cookie made with peanut oil, but it wasn't serious. Do you think there was something in the cake, Andrea? It couldn't have been the coffee. We all drank from the same pot."

"Once they get the tests back, we'll know for sure. If it was a natural death, then nobody's at fault."

"But if it's not?"

"Then it's homicide."

"Oh, God." She brought the snifter to her lips and knocked back the liquor till she was on empty. Then she pressed the glass to her forehead. "I should never have let Marilee bring her crew into my home. It was a mistake, and I should have turned her down when she suggested the idea. What if someone poisoned her, Andrea? Dear Lord, I hope they don't think I had anything to do with it."

I hated to be the bearer of bad news, but I'd never been less than brutally honest with her. Okay, maybe once in a while. But not over something as important as this. "They'll probably suspect everyone close to Marilee, at first."

"I can't believe this," Cissy moaned. "I'm a Daughter of the Republic of Texas, a member in good standing of the Society of the Bluebonnet Ladies, and a direct descendent of Sam Houston himself. Could the police honestly believe I would have killed someone in my own home? On the very rug your dear daddy bought me at auction in London the year before his heart attack?"

She looked distraught, too much so for me to poke fun at her. I didn't feel so hot, either. "No one's going to suspect you, Mother. You were one of the few people who didn't have a beef with Marilee. You were probably her only real friend in this world."

Setting aside the bone-dry snifter, she reached for the ends of the Hermès scarf looped gracefully around her neck, dabbing at the damp on her cheeks. "You know, Andrea, it's not like I haven't lost my share of friends. When you get to be my age, it's something you expect, though you never grow accustomed to it. But Marilee was such a ball of fire. I can't believe she's really gone." She pursed her lips, looking off for a moment, out the window at the rose gardens, now bathed in late afternoon light. "She was a survivor, a fighter, and so terribly driven. She may have upstaged Mrs. Perot at the Salvation Army luncheon, but she didn't deserve *this*."

I pictured the worried faces lined up around the dining room table: Carson Caruthers and his kitchen crew, Renata Taylor and the other production assistants, the director with his arm in a sling, and a dozen others. I thought, too, of Gilbert and Amber Lynn, and I wondered how many of them felt that Marilee got exactly what she deserved.

Something Beth Taylor had said about Kendall swam into my head.

"She could've gone into sudden cardiac arrest. It would've looked exactly like a heart attack on autopsy, and no one would've been the wiser."

It would've looked like a heart attack.

A natural death.

No one the wiser.

And I wondered if someone close to Marilee had hoped to get away with murder, by betting she, like Kendall, had the potentially fatal arrhythmia.

Someone who stood to profit from Marilee's death, particularly if he were romancing Marilee's confused and emotionally needy daughter—perhaps mesmerizing the girl with talk of a future, of marriage.

Someone like Justin Gable, perhaps?

Mother had nearly demolished her second glass of brandy when my cell started ringing. I figured it was Malone, wondering what was going on, but it was Deputy Chief Dean, and she didn't sound any too happy.

"Ms. Kendricks, would you mind driving over to the Mabry residence," she said, sounding a lot like my mother when she states a direct order in the guise of a question.

"What's wrong?" I scooted to the edge of the wicker seat, and Cissy's tear-filled eyes peered at me over her snifter.

"Kendall's been asking for you. Said you're the only one she can trust since you saved her life." Deputy Dean cleared her throat. "Um, she refuses to believe her mother's dead. Said she wants to talk to you. That she trusts you."

"Oh, wow."

"I wouldn't bother you, Ms. Kendricks, except she's adamant, and Dr. Taylor thinks it best you come. Kendall's refusing to allow the doctor to administer a sedative until she sees you."

"I'll be right over."

"There's just one other thing."

I waited for her to finish.

"You haven't heard from Mr. Gable lately, have you?"

"Justin? No." It's not as if we were pals or anything.

Anna Dean hesitated. "The thing is, we can't seem to locate him anywhere. Looks like he packed up in a hurry and took off for parts unknown."

Talk about a heart-stopper.

Justin Gable was MIA?

To quote the Farmer in the Dell when he stepped on a fresh cow patty:

"Shit."

Chapter 22

 I left my mother in Sandy's capable hands—after refusing to take her with me—and I headed over to Marilee's address in Preston Hollow, only about a five- or ten-minute drive, depending on traffic.

Then I hit the Mockingbird and Hillcrest intersection and saw a backup that looked like the lines at the emissions testing facility.

I smacked a palm against the steering wheel in frustration, then rolled down my window and craned my neck out to see the holdup. Squinting through the sun and inhaling exhaust, I finally spotted the accident smack in the middle of the cross streets.

A bright yellow Hummer had apparently rear-ended a relic of a Chrysler, turning the Chrysler's trunk into an accordion. No one seemed to be injured, though the driver of the rusty sedan apparently had a few words to share with the driver of the Hummer, choice words, if his hand gestures were any indication.

At least the police were already on the scene with their

flares and orange cones. They were doing what they could to restore order to the busy cross streets. I figured they'd have a lane open before the tow truck showed up. Or so I hoped.

I ducked my head back inside the Jeep, rolled up the window, and grabbed my wildly colored M. Avery Designs handbag from the passenger seat. Snatching out my cell phone, I speed-dialed Brian Malone, since he'd told me he'd be working at home all day.

Two rings trilled, then three, before someone picked up. "Hello?"

The voice that chirped those two syllables wasn't Malone's unless he'd gone soprano since I saw him that morning. "I'm sorry, I must've hit the wrong button. I was looking for Brian Malone."

"Oh, no, you've got the right number. He's here, just buried in briefs." I could hear the laughter in her voice, and I bristled. "Can I ask who this is, please?"

Like she couldn't tell from the Caller ID?

"It's Andy . . . Andy Kendricks," I said impatiently and took a page from Carson Caruthers, asking, "Just who the hell are you?" But she wasn't listening anymore, she was calling out to Brian in a too perky tone, *"Bri . . . hey, Bri, it's someone named Andy . . . a girl."*

I tapped my fingers on the steering wheel, gritting my teeth, not in the mood for anything even remotely like this. I needed support, and I wanted Malone to provide it. So who was the bimbo who'd picked up his phone?

All I knew for sure was that it wasn't me.

Finally, Malone came on the line. "Hey, Andy, I was just . . ."

"Buried in briefs, I know," I tried not to snap. "I thought you were *working*."

"I am . . ."

"So who's that? Your answering service?"

"Naw, it's Allie Price. She's an attorney at ARGH. We're on a case together, Bishop v. Bishop? Remember? I told you about it. Two brothers who used to be in partnership, doing a little money laundering on the side, until one of them slept with the other's wife and suddenly they're at each other's throats . . ."

Take a breath, I told myself. *Chill. Don't say anything stupid that you'll regret later when you're not so shaken up.*

"She sounds blond." I already pictured her looking very much like Reese Witherspoon. "She is, isn't she?" It came out before I could stop it. So much for my good intentions.

"Who? Allie?"

No, Toad, the Wet Sprocket.

"Yes, Allie"—for Pete's sake—"unless there's another woman in your apartment besides her."

"No, no, of course, there's not . . . and, yeah, she's blond, but what does that have to do with anything"—he hesitated, cleared his throat—"Whoa, Andy, you almost sound like you're . . ."

"Upset? Because I am upset," I ran right over him before he could piss me off any more than I was by using the dreaded "j" word. "I just came from Mother's, and it was no garden party, Bubba."

"Bubba?"

"I said I'd call you if someone died at the Diet Club taping, right? Well, they did. Marilee Mabry. So if I seem worked up, that's why, okay? I'm on my way over to see

Kendall, because the police are there with her, breaking the news."

"Marilee Mabry is dead?"

"Yeah, Bri," I sneered, "she's roadkill. And now I'm stuck in traffic on the way over, and Kendall won't let Dr. Taylor sedate her until she hears the bad news from me, because she thinks they're all lying . . . and, to top it off, Justin Gable is missing . . . which makes him look guilty as hell . . . for all we know, he could've murdered Marilee. But never mind." I felt tears prick my eyes, and something caught in my throat. I had to swallow hard to get rid of it. "I won't keep you another minute, since I'm sure you and your associate are chomping at the bit to get back to your briefs."

Malone started to stammer out a response, but I was finished.

I hit the "end" button, switched the ringer off, and tossed the phone onto the passenger seat.

For crying out loud. What had I just done?

Bad move. Really bad move, I decided, but it was too late to take any of it back, and I honestly didn't care. A minor tiff with Malone meant little compared to what I was sure to find at Marilee's house.

I dropped my head and pressed the balls of my hands against my closed eyes to keep from crying. I had kept it in at Mother's, for her sake as much as mine, and suddenly I felt the trembling begin.

Don't crumble now, Kendricks, I told myself. *No wimping out, you hear? Kendall needs someone to lean on. And you're it.*

Horns honked behind me, and I raised my chin to see the

police waving traffic around the accident scene. From the persistent *wonk-wonks,* I realized the line of cars behind me wasn't any too happy with my slow response.

My hands shaking, I put the Jeep in gear and lurched ahead, sweating buckets despite the AC spewing cool air at me.

As I drove toward Douglas Street, I kept catching my eyes in the rearview, telling myself I could do this.

Courage, I reminded myself, was my first—not my middle—name, at least according to Daddy.

I would be strong if it killed me.

After taking enough deep breaths to qualify for a Lamaze certificate, I felt calmer, saner, and as much in control as I was going to be under the circumstances. My mind kept running over everything that had happened in the past twenty-four hours, trying to figure ways that I might've changed the turn of events, to stop them from falling like dominoes until Marilee was dead, too preoccupied to notice the mansions I passed on the way to the wrought-iron gates that marked the entrance to Marilee's property.

If Ross Perot had been out on the sidewalk in an undershirt, walking his dog, it would hardly have registered.

I sped up the length of pebbled driveway toward the sprawling house that resembled a Mediterranean villa only in some greedy builder's mind. A tiled roof and a splashing fountain did not a villa make. It was a Dallas palace, pure and simple.

I didn't bother to aim for a shady spot, merely jerked the Jeep to a stop squarely beneath the merciless sun, right behind two squad cards from the Highland Park Police Department and a Mercedes S-series with vanity plates—DOC TEE—that had to belong to Beth Taylor.

My eyes scanned the rest of the drive. The silver BMW Roadster wasn't visible. I don't know why I'd expected to see it, since Justin had taken off.

Snatching my keys from the ignition and grabbing my purse and cell from the passenger seat, I left the Jeep to boil and strode through a smaller set of iron gates to the enormous carved front doors. I pushed my finger on the bell once, then again, until I heard the click of the lock.

One side of the arched pair of doors pulled inward, and I found myself nose to nose with the deputy chief. Her slim brow wrinkled beneath her no-nonsense salt-and-pepper hair.

"Hit traffic?" she asked, which sounded nicer than "took you long enough to show up."

"Accident at Mockingbird and Hillcrest."

"Oh, yeah, heard that one radioed in after we got here." She gestured for me to enter, and I stepped past her into Marilee's home, the first time I'd set foot in the residence.

"How's Kendall?" I asked as she shut the huge door behind me.

"She's in denial, won't even speak to us."

My chest ached, knowing that, no matter how much Kendall had fought with her mother, she would miss Marilee like hell. As much as Cissy drove me insane, I couldn't imagine the day when she would no longer be around.

"Where is she?"

"Upstairs. Dr. Taylor's with her." She grabbed my arm as I started for the stairwell. "First, Ms. Kendricks, would you mind coming with me. I just want to make sure we're on the same page."

Though I desperately wanted to see Kendall, I didn't argue. She had a gun and a badge, and I had neither. My mother hadn't raised a fool, that's for sure.

So I followed Anna Dean into an enormous living room area with high ceilings painted with frescoes and expansive paned windows that looked out onto Marilee's kingdom. Just an acre, Carson had told me, but it reminded me of visiting Colonial Williamsburg when I was a kid.

"Impressive, huh?" Deputy Dean said.

"Yeah, very." I would never have expected to find such an extensive backyard farm in such a posh section of North Dallas. Though I'd seen photographs of Marilee's spread on the Web site for *The Sweet Life,* it was pretty amazing to finally view it with my own eyes.

She'd gotten permits from the city to raise geese for pâté, chickens for eggs, honeybees, and even organic catfish in a pond that sparkled beneath the late day sun. What had Carson said? That the pond was as big as the pool at the Y. I realized now that he hadn't exaggerated. There were rows, too, of organic vegetables. Plenty of them. I recalled from the Web site that, among other things, Marilee grew potatoes, French beans, tomatoes, Japanese eggplant, arugula, Thai basil, and cucumbers.

Quite a spread, I mused, for a woman who never had a hair out of place or a chip in her manicure, despite dipping her fingers into plenty of pies. Which reminded me of another comment Carson had made, that Marilee had done little of the work herself on her backyard farm, like on the set, always leaving the dirty work to someone else.

"Did she give her staff the day off?" I asked, because I hadn't detected anyone else around, except a few blue uniforms.

"According to young Ms. Mabry, an animal caretaker came by this morning, and we're trying to track him down," Deputy Dean told me. "Apparently, a number of the staff had worked the party at the studio, and she let them off until tomorrow as compensation."

"So no one else is in the house but Kendall?"

"Yep."

"Which means no one saw Justin leave?"

"Unfortunately, no." The deputy chief set her hands on the back of a wing chair, looking past me out the windows. I followed her eyes and spotted a few of her officers out back, poking around the henhouse. "Before Kendall clammed up, she did say that he brought her home from the studio once the crew had packed up and taken off for your mother's. She claims she went upstairs to lie down and promptly nodded off. When she got up several hours later, she couldn't find him. She noted the drawers and closets in his room were tossed. That's, uh, his quarters as opposed to the room he sometimes shared with Mrs. Mabry. A large Coach duffel bag is allegedly missing and so is Mr. Gable's car. We've got a BOLO out on him now."

The only "bolo" I knew about was the string tie Paw Paw Kendricks had worn around his neck.

My bemusement must've been easy to read, because Anna Dean clarified, "A be-on-the-lookout-for."

"Ah." I rubbed my arms as regret washed over me. I found myself thinking how different things might've been today if someone had called the police last night from the hospital. It was one of those rare times when I wished I'd listened to my mother. "So you think Justin knew what would happen at the taping this afternoon? That he"—I wet my lips, finding it hard to get out—"may have caused her death and had his escape route planned ahead of time? I know he's a gigolo, but do you really think he's a killer?"

I considered that my mother and her cronies could've gotten sick if they'd done more than pick at their own slices of Death by Chocolate. Though I wondered how much damage a high dose of ephedra could've done to an otherwise healthy heart, as opposed to Marilee's badly wired one?

"As for whether or not Justin Gable is responsible for Marilee Mabry's demise, your guess is as good as mine." She shrugged epaulet-covered shoulders. "I try not to deal in the hypothetical. I prefer to wait until I have solid evidence pointing to a suspect. But Justin Gable is certainly acting guilty by running. We're doing a quick check of the house and grounds now, with Kendall's consent. We found some interesting items in the kitchen and Justin's bath. Seems Mr. Gable was in such a hurry to scoot that he left a stash of his herbal supplements. If tests link them to the cake that Marilee Mabry was eating when she died, I'd say he's in big trouble."

Death penalty-type trouble, I imagined.

Was there any kind worse?

"We also located his passport and around a thousand dollars cash stuffed down into a pair of Tony Lamas in the closet."

"His passport?"

Anna Dean rubbed her jaw. "Makes you think he's either coming back or not going far, doesn't it?"

Or that he hadn't planned this out very well. And he was supposedly so good at cutting and running.

I stuck my hands in the pockets of my shorts, just to have something to do with them.

"Has anyone contacted Gilbert Mabry?"

"That's my next stop," the policewoman confirmed. "I want to tell him myself. Sometimes a person's reaction to such news can be very, uh, enlightening."

I nodded, but my thoughts weren't on Gilbert Mabry or the possibility that he'd break down and confess to poisoning a cake. "So Kendall wants to see me alone? Will Dr. Taylor stay in the room with me, just in case?"

I was still afraid for Kendall's health. I couldn't begin to imagine what it would do to her when it sank in that Marilee wasn't coming back.

"Don't worry. Dr. Taylor and I will be waiting outside the door."

"Okay."

She pushed away from the wingback chair. "Let's go."

She strode purposefully toward the foyer and began to ascend the stairs.

At the bottom of the steps, I froze for a moment, taking in a deep breath, trying to slow my racing heart.

You can handle this, Kendricks.

My daddy had always told me that I could handle anything, if I had to.

Courage.

I reached for the carved mahogany balustrade and went the way of the deputy chief, marching upward until we reached the plush-carpeted second-floor landing.

"She's in her mother's room," Anna Dean told me before

we reached a closed door with an officer standing outside it. He pushed it open for Deputy Dean and me to enter.

The bedside lamps glowed softly, but no other lights had been turned on. With the drapes fully drawn, the room seemed far from cheery. A suitable gloom, I thought as I took a few steps in and saw Beth Taylor rise from a chair near the king-sized canopied bed. My gaze quickly focused on the girl who sat beneath the gauze canopy, pillows plumped behind her and covers drawn over bended knees.

The doctor and the deputy chief exchanged nods. Beth squeezed my shoulder as she passed, but didn't say anything. The door clicked softly after their exit, leaving me there with Kendall, alone.

"Hey," I said tentatively, feeling my chest ache as I approached and her face came into focus in the gleam of the scallop-shaded lamps. Shadows underscored her dark eyes. Her hair fell in lank waves on either side of her face. She looked like a street waif, weary and impassive, as if she'd bottled up all her emotions to keep her heart from shattering.

I settled beside her on the edge of the bed, close enough to touch her hand. But I didn't. "I wanted to come over even before I heard that you were asking for me. I figured you could use a friend."

She drew her arms up to her chest, clutching tight to a battered Snoopy doll that appeared to be missing the black ball of his nose.

"I can't believe it, Andy," she whispered. "I can't believe that Mummy's dead. It doesn't make sense. I saw her before she went to Cissy's, and she was her usual old self, bossing everyone around, yelling at Carson for this or that. Maybe they made a mistake. Maybe it wasn't her at all."

"I'm sorry, Kendall."

"I trust you, Andy. Mummy told me that I would've died if you hadn't gotten me help last night." She hugged the Snoopy even tighter. "I'm so used to people lying to me, but I know you wouldn't do that."

I saw the flicker on her face, the desperate hope that I would change fate with a few words. But I couldn't.

"Yes, it's true about your mother. She's gone. I was there when it happened. I'm so sorry," I said again and reached for her then, caught one of the hands that clutched the Snoopy and drew it into mine, holding fast.

"She's gone . . . she's really gone. She's not coming back?"

"No."

She pressed her lips together, nodding to herself, admitting to herself that it was so, that her mother was gone for good. Her fingers trembled in my grasp, but I saw no tears yet. I was sure they would come. I just wasn't sure when.

"I'm here for you, okay? Please, believe that."

"Are you?" Fear rounded her eyes. "Because it's not like anyone's ever stuck by me before."

"Yes," I told her. "I am."

"I want to believe you," she said softly. "But I believed Justin, too. He made plenty of promises and then he left me, just like Mummy. He swore he'd stay with me forever, but he lied." Tears welled, and I waited for her to let loose, but she didn't.

"Maybe he was scared."

"Of what?"

I bit my lip, not certain of how to respond. I finally told her, "Justin seemed very frightened when you were in the hospital. He was worried that you'd taken too much of the ma huang, and he thought people would blame him. Do you remember what happened, Kendall? Was it his fault or yours?"

"Justin said I took too much?" Her forehead creased. "But I don't remember taking any yesterday, Andy. I was feeling too jumpy already, because of the party and all. Justin knew I didn't like the ma huang, that it made my heart race. Sometimes it made me so dizzy I'd nearly fall down. Mummy wouldn't take it because she said it made her feel bad, too."

"Really?"

"She didn't even like caffeine in her coffee. Even your mother knew that, Andy. Everyone on Mummy's crew knew."

Hello.

That's certainly not what Justin had told Dr. Taylor at the hospital. It made me wonder what kind of smoothies he'd concocted for Kendall to drink without telling her what was really in them. And if he'd done that, what else was he capable of?

"I'd rather cut off my right arm than harm a woman."

What a bunch of hogwash, I mused, considering what I knew about him already. Justin's modus operandi did little else but hurt susceptible females. Honestly, the guy should've gone to Hollywood. His performances were deserving of the Oscar. Or at least the Oscar Meyer, since the guy was so full of baloney.

I wondered what it felt like, to be such a smooth liar. To

have it come so easily that you didn't blink, didn't even flinch, when you looked someone in the eye and told untruth after untruth.

"Justin wasn't who you thought he was," I said, perhaps recklessly, but part of me believed she needed to hear it. It would come out sooner or later, wouldn't it? In the Tuesday edition of the Park Cities paper, as a matter of fact. "There are things about him you don't know."

I nearly said, *"Things your mother never knew,"* but that wasn't the truth. According to Cissy, Marilee had known about Justin all along.

She shut her eyes. "I don't want to hear."

"He was a con man, Kendall. A gigolo. He slept with rich, older women to get money and cars and whatever else they'd give him. He's done it all over the state, maybe beyond the border. He's the male equivalent of a bimbo . . ."

"Stop." She jerked her hand from my grasp and dropped the Snoopy to her lap, putting her palms over her ears. "Stop, please, stop."

So I did.

Gently, I took her hands and peeled them away from her head, and I didn't let go.

"Look at me," I said.

She blinked and tears splashed past her lashes, running fast down her cheeks and onto the Snoopy doll.

"You love him, don't you?" I asked, watching the way her face crumpled, the way the tears fell harder still as she nodded. "He took care of you." Paid attention to her when no one else would.

"Yes."

"You figured he'd marry you someday, didn't you?"

"Who told you that?" She blinked and glanced down in her lap. "He said it would work out with us," she whispered, "that he'd take care of things with Mummy, that it wouldn't be long until we could be together for always." Her eyes lifted again, and the pain in them was all too clear. "I believed him, Andy. I'm such a fool."

Take care of things with Mummy, huh?

Or just "take care" of Mummy?

My guts twisted inside, and I hated Justin for what he'd done, for lying to someone barely old enough to understand what love meant. Kendall was no middle-aged woman with a passel of failed relationships in her past. Hadn't he even fathomed the kind of damage he could do to her? The kind that couldn't be undone.

Did he betray her?

Hell, yes.

But I couldn't say it, not when she was so obviously hurting.

"It doesn't matter now, does it? He's gone forever," she choked out. "And Mummy's gone. How? How can that be possible? It can't be real . . . it can't be. I would feel it if she were dead. I'd know it in here." She pressed a hand between her breasts.

I felt my own eyes prick with tears. I hated being so helpless.

"Why did this happen?" she cried, her skin flushing purple. "Mummy didn't have to die . . . she didn't have to go and leave me all alone. Why, Andy? *Why?*"

She suddenly came uncoiled, springing up to throw herself into my arms, grabbing onto me and burying her face against me, so that I could do nothing but embrace her as she cried uncontrollably, ripping out my heart with every broken sound.

"Hush"—I smoothed her tangled hair—"sweetie, hush."

"Hurt . . . me. Mummy . . . help."

The garbled words she'd whispered from her hospital bed suddenly seemed to make sense. Kendall was hurting, deep inside, and had needed her mother to help her. Only Marilee had more important things on her mind. And now she was dead.

My skin prickled with gooseflesh, and I fought to maintain what composure I had left as I curled the rumpled bedclothes into my fist.

"Don't leave me," she wailed. *"Please, don't leave me alone."*

"I won't," I said and meant it. I would take her back to Mother's. I couldn't leave her in this house. Someone had to watch her, to make sure she didn't do anything rash, make sure she took her medication.

Cissy was right. I was doing it again. Picking up strays, getting attached to them out of pity, unable to walk away.

I was in over my head with Kendall Mabry, I realized. Way too deep.

And I didn't know how to get out.

Chapter 23

I called ahead and warned my mother that I was bringing Kendall back to the house on Beverly. The girl had nowhere else to go, and I wasn't about to desert her in that big old empty mansion. Cissy was worried that it might upset Kendall more to be under the same roof where her mother passed, but I knew it wouldn't matter, not tonight. Especially not after Beth Taylor administered a sedative once I'd gotten the girl tucked into my old bed.

"I'll check on her in the morning, ladies," Dr. Taylor assured us before she went home.

Ready to hit the road myself, I promised my mother and Sandy that I'd be back early, too. I felt bad about leaving Kendall, but there wasn't much room in my tiny condo. And Sandy was a much better nursemaid than I could ever hope to be. Besides, I aimed to get down to Mother's before Kendall even woke up. She wouldn't have a chance to miss me.

Sandy kissed my creased forehead and told me not to worry so much.

Cissy gave me one of her long looks and sighed. "I feel like I'm operating a halfway house." Okay, so it wasn't the first time she'd done this kind of favor for me, and I'm sure she'd find a way to make me pay her back. She always did. "Why don't you stay overnight, too, Andrea? I don't think you should be driving home. It's late, and you're tired."

It wasn't even eight o'clock. The late summer sky was still awash with blue. It wouldn't blush pink for another half hour.

"I'll be fine," I said, because it wasn't the hour that worried her or how exhausted I was. It was seeing me go after what had transpired. If she could, I knew, she'd guard me like the hounds of hell for the rest of my life.

"See you in the morning," I said and hugged her, and she hung on tight. I could smell her Joy on my skin even after I drew away.

"Be careful," she called from the door. "Put on your seat belt and drive slowly, please."

Her concern was enough to make me tear-up. But I slipped on my Ray-Bans, hiding my eyes, and waved as I steered the Jeep around her circular drive.

I saw her figure in the rearview until trees obscured it. I had a feeling she would stand there for a few moments after.

When I pulled onto my street in Far North Dallas a good twenty-five minutes later, a red Acura coupe sat in my parking spot. Lucky for Malone, it wasn't the last space, so I pulled into the empty slot beside it.

He perched on my front steps, his face flushed with perspiration. His green Polo shirt sported widening stains.

God knows, there wasn't an antiperspirant made that could stop a man from sweating in the Texas heat.

He stood as I approached. I was glad he didn't lift a hand to wave.

"How long have you been here?"

"About an hour," he said, mopping sweat from his cheeks as I unlocked the front door. "I tried to call your cell, but you weren't answering."

"Oh, yeah, that." I pushed wide the door and he followed me in.

"Is everything all right? You're not mad at me? Allie and I were working, Andy, really. She's just a colleague. I mean, we used to date before, but"—he stopped talking, suddenly deeply interested in the magnets on my refrigerator.

"Before what?" I dumped my keys on the kitchen counter and swung around to face him.

He ceased fiddling with the Take-Out Taxi menu and looked at me. "Before I met you, Andy. But it wasn't anything serious, really. At least it didn't mean anything to me."

I swallowed hard, not sure how I felt about him having dated a blond colleague with a perky voice who went over to his place on the weekend to work on his briefs. But I had a past, too, right? It wasn't fair to think he didn't. It's not as though we were an unblemished fifteen.

"Are you mad?" His glasses had slipped down his nose. His hair was ruffled, and his clothes were rumpled from sitting outside, waiting for me.

"I'm not mad," I said quietly. "I just think sometimes it's better to stick to the don't-ask, don't-tell policy, you know? If I don't ask, you don't tell. And vice versa."

He blinked and shoved his specs higher. "You're serious?"

"Yes."

His eyes brightened. "I can live with that."

"Okay." I dove into the fridge and fetched two bottles of water, passing one to Malone. He drank it like a dehydrated camel. "It wasn't about Allie, not really," I tried to explain. "I've got a lot on my mind," I said and played with the bottle cap, screwing and unscrewing it. "The past couple of days have been a nightmare. You should've been at Mother's for the Diet Club taping. No, strike that. You didn't want to be there. It was beyond awful."

He set the empty bottle down with an "ahhh" and swiped the back of his arm across his mouth. Then he reached for me, toyed with my fingers. "I'll hang around tonight if that'll help."

"Actually"—I drew my fingers away, earning an anxious look—"I'd sort of like to be alone, if you don't mind." I'd been around people for the past twenty-four hours, and I needed some solo time. I was sure he'd understand.

"So you want me to leave?"

"I guess so."

"Even though you just got home?"

"Don't take this wrong, Malone, please." I tucked my hair behind my ears. "But consider that I just spent the better part of the afternoon stuck at Mother's, watching a woman die and being questioned by the Highland Park police. As if that wasn't enough, I went over to Marilee's and sat with Kendall Mabry while she cried about being unloved and abandoned."

I barely got it out before I felt the prick of tears at my eyes and the tightness in my throat.

"Whoa, Andy, are you all right?"

I blinked away the threat of tears, forcing myself to smile. But even I could feel how shaky it was. "Just give me some time to myself, okay?"

"Yeah, sure, if that's what you want."

"I do."

He stepped around the counter and gingerly took me in his arms, giving me a hug. I didn't care that he smelled slightly ripe, and I hung onto him for a long moment, just standing quietly there with him. He planted a soft little kiss on my nose before he let loose. "Call if you need me? Any hour. I mean it."

I nodded.

He paused and nodded in return, before he left. Grudgingly.

When the door clicked shut, I turned to the sink, switched the cold water on, and hung my head over to cry. I let it all out, until my guts cramped up and my nose plugged up with snot. Then I rinsed my face in the faucet and dried off with a paper towel.

I braced my hands on the edge of the stainless steel and took in a deep breath.

Keep busy, I told myself. Being useful always made me feel better, less helpless.

After I plugged my cell phone into the charger, I checked my voice mail messages on my land line, finding quite a few from Malone and several from someone at Twinkle Productions, telling me that further shooting on *The Sweet Life* had been suspended indefinitely—well, duh—and that they were faxing a press release to the media, a copy of which was attached in an MSWord document. They would appreciate my putting it up on the Web site for visitors to read. I was informed I could pick up a check at the studio on Monday for my most recent hours billed.

Funny, but a paycheck was the last thing on my mind.

I went to the computer and booted it up, strangely comforted by the gentle whir as the programs loaded. The touch of my fingers on the keyboard as I connected with the Web felt so damned normal that a sense of calm settled through me.

After doing the last job I'd ever do for Marilee, I stayed online and surfed the Net, checking the local news links. Finding just about what I'd expected, plenty of coverage of Marilee's sudden demise. So I switched my agenda and started Googling, thinking of what Kendall had said about doing research for her mother on the Web, looking up recipes and such.

I did a search for "Justin Gable" instead.

And I didn't come up empty.

I clicked through several pages that linked to society columns, even finding a few photographs with captions that described Justin as being "on the arm of" this woman or that and tracking down mentions of earlier liaisons, prior to his dallying with socialites in Houston and San Antonio. He'd been busy in Miami, too, I realized, and in Scottsdale before that.

Leaning back into my chair, I stared at the enlarged black-and-white photograph on the computer screen, ignoring the grainy quality and focusing on Justin's eyes. How cool he looked. Like he hadn't a care in the world, and I guess he hadn't. Certainly, not while he had Sugar Mamas to pay his bills and keep him in hot wheels and Armani. As long as he could do his thing without attracting the attention of the law, he obviously didn't worry about sticking around anywhere for too long.

What a piece of work, I thought, running a hand through my uncombed hair.

If he'd done this . . . if he'd killed Marilee with an overdose of ma huang . . . if he'd nearly killed Kendall . . . I hoped the cops would find him fast. I hoped they'd lock him up and throw away the key. A human wrecking ball, that's what he was, and I wanted him to rot in hell for the damage he'd caused.

I rubbed my eyes, wrung out from the day's events and from what little sleep I'd gotten the night before.

The enlarged newspaper photo of Justin turned blurry with my exhaustion, so I shut off the computer and went to bed, despite the fact that the hands of the clock had yet to strike ten; thinking as I did that "tomorrow was another day," as Scarlett O'Hara had opined after any number of messes.

And thank God for that.

Geese.

A whole flock of them from the sounds of it, honking loudly, persistently, breaking into my deep and dreamless sleep and causing my eyes to slowly crack open.

Honk, honk. Honk, honk.

I buried my head in the pillow, wishing someone would please run the damned things over so I could sink back into peaceful oblivion. Hardly a fitting thought for someone who'd once been a goose liberator, but I was bone-tired and in no mood to celebrate nature.

Honk, honk. Honk, honk.

For Pete's sake.

My eyelids flapped up, and I pushed the sheet down, swinging my legs over the edge of the bed. Grabbing my glasses from the nightstand, I banged my thigh on the footboard as I stumbled around my double bed and headed toward the window. When I peered through the shutters, I saw no geese on my small patch of lawn. No birds at all making that horrible racket.

Just Janet Graham in her gray VW Jetta, parked directly in front of my condo. She caught me spying and waved through the front windshield, gesturing for me to hurry up, laying on the horn again for good measure.

Honk, honk!

Could she be drunk? But it was only—I checked the alarm clock—half past seven. Or was she trying to annoy me and wake up the whole frigging neighborhood?

I'd fallen asleep in my T-shirt and panties, so I quickly pulled on a pair of shorts and ran outside, braless (as if anyone would notice). She rolled down her window as I approached.

"Morning, sunshine," she said and smiled, pushing her cat's-eye shades up onto her forehead. Her bright orange hair was pulled back from her face in two tiny, spiky pigtails.

"It barely qualifies as morning," I grumbled, glancing back at my condo building to see Charlie Tompkins watching from his next-door window and Penny George from upstairs, peeking from between her drapes. "You've just about woken up everyone on the block."

"Well, I thought you'd be waiting for me, sugar. Didn't you get my message on your cell phone?"

"What message?" I hadn't checked the voice mail on my cell since I'd turned it off on the way to Marilee's house the day before.

"About going to Gunner with me this morning. Well, don't worry. We'll still make it by the time the nursing home allows visitors. But you'd better go change." She wrinkled her nose. "Your hair's a rat's nest, and where are your shoes?" she asked, checking out my attire disapprovingly before lowering her sunglasses down to her nose again. "You're not even wearing a bra . . . or should I say, a Band-Aid." I crossed my arms as her eyes went to my barely there chest.

"Very funny." I grunted, which only seemed to make her grin go wider.

"I think you'd better go back inside and try again, girlfriend. I'll wait out here."

"Wait for what?" Did she actually think I was going anywhere? The sun hadn't even risen over the rooftops. I could still get in a few more hours of shut-eye.

"C'mon, please, don't tell me you're changing your mind? You promised to go with me, to check on Marilee's old aunt, remember?"

Okay, I do recall her telling me she thought she'd tracked down Doreen Haggerty, but I definitely don't recall promising to take a trip out to Gunner with her. Especially not at seven o'clock on a Sunday morning.

"It's an hour there and an hour back, maybe an hour or so to talk to her, so you'll be back by lunch," Janet said, giving me the full court press.

"But I have to be at Mother's . . ."

"For what?" Her plucked brows arched above the rims of her Donna Karan shades. "Is something going on that I should know about?"

"No, no." At least, not that I was aware of. "It's just that"—I paused to consider how much to say. It wasn't that I didn't trust Janet, but I didn't figure it was wise to share with a reporter—any reporter—that Kendall Mabry was staying at Cissy's house. Part of me felt that Kendall's life was still in danger as long as Justin was on the loose. So the fewer who knew the girl was there, the better.

"It's just what?"

I did the simplest thing to evade her questions. I caved. "All right, all right. I'll come with you. But give me ten minutes to dress and call my mother. Unless you want to sit out with your AC running, you're welcome to come in."

"I've got the new Wilco and plenty of gas, so I'll just leave my seat belt on and see you in ten minutes, or else I'll start honking again," she said, wiggling her fingers at me—her nails cranberry to match her silk top—and her window rolled up with a whir.

I nearly tapped on the glass to remind her that carbon dioxide emissions from a stationary vehicle doubled that of a moving one, as if the ozone layer wasn't thinning fast enough, rather like Matt Lauer's hair. But I knew she wouldn't care.

So I hurried back into the condo and spent five minutes doing a quickie sponge bath and applying plenty of Secret antiperspirant. I put in my contacts and brushed my chin-length hair before pulling it back with a twisty. Despite the heat, I tugged on jeans to avoid being mistaken for a cactus since I had no time to shave my legs.

With five minutes to spare, I phoned Mother's house. Before the initial ring had even completed its trill, I heard a click as the phone was picked up and a voice I barely recognized barked, "For heaven's sake, stop harassin' us!"

"Mother, it's me."

Cissy didn't have Caller ID. She didn't like technology. Had never learned how to program a VCR even before she'd replaced it with a DVD.

"Andrea." She sighed. "Thank God."

With those two words alone, my blood pressure edged upward. "What's wrong? Is Kendall okay?"

"Yes, yes, she's fine. Still sleeping, and I'm hoping she'll stay out like a light until Beth drops by to check on her in a few hours."

My eyelid twitched. "So what's the problem?"

"I've had to call the police once already . . ."

"The police?" My heart made a beeline for my esophagus. "What happened? Is anyone hurt?"

"Well, not yet. Though I'm tempted to take the hose to the lot of them."

"The lot of whom?"

"The television crews, darlin'. They're all over my front lawn and blocking the driveway. Well, anyway, they were before the police shooed them off the property, though those nasty buggers keep tryin' to inch their way back up. It's like a circus out there. And my phone has been ringing off the hook, everyone askin' about Marilee dying on my carpet. How on earth do they get access to unlisted numbers? I do declare. There's no such thing as privacy."

"The media?" That was her big problem? "Are you serious?"

"Don't use that tone with me, Andrea, like I'm overreacting. It's downright irritating, and not just for me. They're blocking Beverly with their trucks. The neighbors aren't the least bit happy about that. Oh, Lord, is that *Entertainment Tonight*? I think I see Mary Hart. . . ."

It was all I could do not to laugh, purely with relief. I felt reassured that trucks with cameramen and reporters were hanging around outside my mother's house. If Justin somehow learned Kendall was staying there, he surely wouldn't have the nerve to show his face and risk appearing on the news. The police would be all over him faster than Britney Spears could disrobe.

"You're coming over, aren't you?" Cissy asked.

"I'll be there sometime around noon, okay? I have to go somewhere with Janet first."

"With Janet Graham? Where?"

"To Gunner."

"Where on earth is Gunner?"

"It's a speck on the map between here and Tyler, about an hour's drive. I'll be back before noon," I said. "I promise."

"What's in Gunner, might I ask?"

"Marilee's aunt."

"Marilee's aunt?" she repeated.

"I'll explain when I see you."

Honk, honk.

Janet laid on the horn again, and I glanced at the kitchen clock. I'd run over my ten-minute time limit.

"I've got to go," I said.

"What about Kendall?"

"Keep an eye on her, please, and don't let her leave the

house. If she needs me, have her call me on my cell phone, and tell her I meant every word I said."

Honk, honk.

"Andrea . . ."

"Bye, Mother."

I hung up, snatched my cell from the charger (making sure it was turned on), shoved it inside my purse, and hurried out the door.

Fifteen minutes later, securely belted into Janet's car, I braced my hands against the dash as she sped east on Highway 20. Wilco blasted from the stereo speakers, and she sang along at the top of her lungs, making me wish I'd worn earplugs. Alicia Keys she was not (she was more like Way-Off Keys).

At least I didn't have to worry about small talk, I thought, as I risked peeling my palms off the dashboard and resting them in my lap. I watched the endless stream of scrubby trees and billboards rush by, before my eyelids drooped.

Janet screeched something about a casino queen being mean, before I tuned her out and drifted off.

The next thing I knew, her fingers were poking me in the ribs. "Wake up, sleepy. C'mon, we're here. Doreen awaits."

I wiped drool from my chin and gingerly raised my head from where I'd wedged it between the window and the seatback. Wincing, I did a neck roll, bones and cartilage crunching as I worked out the kinks. As I unfastened my safety belt, I squinted out the windshield to find the VW parked in front of a whitewashed one-story building.

A square wooden sign surrounded by wilted petunias read:

PECAN GROVE RETIREMENT HOME.

As I dragged myself from the Jetta, I surveyed our sur-roundings but there was no pecan grove in sight, only a faded square of asphalt that served as the parking lot and a gray haze of exhaust from cars on the highway rushing by.

Well, it sounded nice.

After an hour of riding in an air-conditioned box, I wel-comed the warm breath of outdoors. Besides, it wasn't much past eight, so it couldn't have been more than eighty-five degrees, ninety tops.

A few chickadees hopped around the ground nearby, poking at a flattened box of popcorn. Planters potted with red geraniums added color to the front porch, where a pair of gentleman in white undershirts played checkers.

"Morning, ladies," the pair of them said, tipping imagi-nary hats at us as we ascended the wheelchair ramp, and Janet reciprocated their greetings.

When I opened my mouth, all that emerged was a yawn.

So much for all the gold stars I'd earned in my junior eti-quette classes (but then I'd been five-years old at the time and got regular afternoon naps).

Once inside the front doors, Janet marched straight to the front desk, manned by a dark-skinned woman in white with her hair wound atop her head in the shape of a tor-pedo. She peered at Janet over a pair of spectacles perched low on her nose.

"Doreen Haggerty?" she was saying when I got near enough to hear. "Oh, you're the writer who called up yes-terday asking about her. Just a sec, hon, all right?" She picked up a handset and tapped a number into her phone.

"Angelina, do you know if Doreen's done with breakfast yet? She is? I'll send her visitors back. Thanks, hon."

I saw her nametag read: EDNA DUPOIS.

She hung up the phone and touched the gravity-defying beehive of brown spinning high above her broad forehead. It was mighty impressive, though I resisted the urge to comment on it. Sometimes those kind of things can backfire.

"Go on around the corner," she said, looking at Janet, "up the hallway and take a right at the last door before the rec room, all right?"

"Thank you, Nurse Dupois," Janet chirped, friendly as could be, earning a "you're very welcome, hon," from Miss Edna herself.

I yawned again and felt my ears pop.

"This way, sleepy." Janet tugged on my hand, propelling me forward, which was a good thing since I'd already forgotten the instructions Edna had given us.

It was a widely known fact that I was directionally dysfunctional. My mother could find her way from Corpus Christi to Wichita Falls without a map. If I tried the same thing, I'd end up in the Gulf of Mexico, having taken a U-turn at Padre. As my daddy used to say, my mental knapsack was missing its compass.

After she'd dragged me through one hallway after another, Janet released me in front of an opened door, through which the strains of a televised Sunday service emanated. A voice cried out for us to repent, and Janet hesitated, tugging at the hem of her skirt to make sure it covered her thighs before she knocked on the doorjamb.

"Miss Doreen?" she said, stepping inside the room, and

I followed so closely behind that I nearly tripped over her heels when she stopped, grabbed my arm, and pointed.

A tiny birdlike woman reclined in a La-Z-Boy chair, the thin frizz of her head tipped back on a pillow, her eyes closed, and mouth wide open. While the TV preacher called for her to "lift up her voice and shout 'hallelujah,' " she snored instead, a noise not unlike the whistle of a teakettle.

"Miss Doreen?" Janet said again and bravely walked over to the television set and turned it down. Perhaps it was the softening of the preacher's voice, but the snoring abruptly stopped, and the tiny woman shot straight up, her bulbous eyes blinking.

"Who's there?" she asked in a shaky East Texas twang and reached to the tray table beside her, clutching at a pair of glasses that she promptly stuck on her face. The frames were black and round, and the lenses magnified her eyes about fifty times over. If I hadn't known better, I would've sworn she was Mr. Magoo in the flesh. "Do I know you?"

Janet took the lead, stepping forward with her right hand outstretched. "No, ma'am, we haven't met. I'm Janet Graham, the society editor with the *Park Cities Press* newspaper from Dallas." She flicked her wrist in my direction. "That's Andrea, my associate."

"Society editor from Dallas?" Doreen repeated, not paying me the slightest attention.

Hey, even I was impressed.

Janet pulled a straight-backed chair up beside the La-Z-Boy. "I've come to ask you a few questions, ma'am, about your niece Marilee."

"Marilee?" The wizened face screwed up further. "Why? What's she done now? Does she still have that TV show in the city? Did she get herself fired?"

Janet glanced over her shoulder at me, giving me an "uh-oh" look, and I realized, too, that no one had told Doreen Haggerty that her niece was dead. Though maybe no one even knew she existed. It had taken Janet weeks to run down an address on her.

When I shrugged, Janet turned back around and said, "I'm actually writing a story about Marilee, and I'm trying to find out more about her early years, like what happened when she left Stybr to live with you when she was sixteen."

The big eyes behind the round glasses blinked, and the blue-veined arms crossed defensively. "Oh, no, no, I don't talk about that, not with anyone. It's family business, and Marilee made me sign a paper that I wouldn't tell, not so long as she lived. Or else she said she'd stop my monthly checks, and they'd kick me out of this place." The loose skin beneath her chin trembled. "And I couldn't afford to go nowhere else 'cept those cesspools for folks on Medicaid. You ever set foot in one of them places?"

"No, ma'am, I haven't," I heard Janet say.

I walked across the tiny room to the only window with its cheerful yellow calico curtains, avoiding Janet's eyes, because I didn't want to be a party to what I knew was coming next.

"Well, Miss Doreen, you don't have to worry about those checks anymore," I heard Janet say as I gazed out upon a small courtyard with a shuffleboard deck. "And you don't have to stick to any contract you signed with Marilee, because"—she cleared her throat, and I felt mine close up—"I'm sorry to be the one to tell you this, but your niece passed yesterday."

"She passed what? A stone? I had me one of those, and it hurt worse'n hell."

"No, she didn't pass a stone, Ms. Doreen. She passed *away*," Janet explained, and I winced, afraid of what would happen next, how the poor woman would react.

"Marilee's dead?"

"As a doornail. I'm so very sorry."

"You're sure about this?"

"Yes."

I stood on the sidelines, watching Janet do her best to convince the woman about Marilee's demise, though I was starting to think Doreen Haggerty would demand a death certificate as evidence.

"You're positive?"

"Yes, ma'am, I'm 100 percent positive," Janet insisted. "I was present when it happened, ma'am." Her cheeks were pink with her effort. "Again, I'm so sorry for your loss."

"Well, I'll be damned." Doreen leaned back in her easy chair, glassy-eyed with disbelief, her lips moving as she murmured to herself, words I couldn't hear.

I cringed inwardly, wondering what kind of damage hearing the news from a stranger would do to the woman. I expected the sound of sobs, maybe moaning or a pitiful wail, but not the whoop of relief that blew past Doreen's lips.

"Well, I'll be damned." She slapped a hand against a

polyester covered thigh. "And I thought only the good died young. That girl was ornery as her pa."

I heard the preacher on the television shout, "Say, Amen, brothers and sisters! Say, Amen!"

"Amen, amen, amen!" Doreen chanted like a mantra, and I turned away from the window to see her reach for Janet with a clawlike hand.

"Well, that changes everything, don't it?" She squinted behind those huge magnifying lenses. "So what is it you want to know about my dear departed niece? 'Cuz there ain't no cause to keep quiet now, is there? And I've got a mind like a steel trap."

Chapter 24

Once she got started, Doreen Haggerty didn't stop talking for over an hour.

The story that unfolded from her chapped lips wasn't pretty, and the ending wasn't anything close to "happily ever after." It was more like a big fat question mark. But neither Janet nor I stirred until she was finished, right as Nurse Edna strode into the room with her torpedo-shaped 'do, clutching a container of Metamucil and announcing it was time for Miss Doreen's midmorning fiber.

After Janet had kissed the old woman's cheeks and thanked her profusely, we departed in the Jetta. No Wilco blasting on the stereo this time. Just a tension-filled silence. Behind those cat's-eye shades, I knew Janet's mind was going a mile a minute, already writing her bombshell of a feature on the life and times of Marilee Mabry.

Exposing Marilee's dirty laundry to the world.

Ensuring that two lives would never be the same.

I wasn't so sure how I felt about that.

So I gazed out the window, barely seeing the blur of pasture, trees, and road signs, watching a picture come together in my head, pieces I hadn't realized fit so neatly together. Or maybe not so neatly, considering all the jagged edges.

I heard the shaky voice of Doreen Haggerty as I replayed snatches of her monologue over and over again.

"... *her good for nothing daddy left her alone on the farm for days or weeks at a time, though nobody told me what was goin' on until it was too late to do any good because the girl went and got herself pregnant by a boy headin' off to the Army. A Negro boy, if you can picture that, and she was afraid to tell a soul until she knew she was in trouble. So she came to me until it was over. Bore herself a child with dark eyes and black nappy hair to remind her of her sin. Mari cried and cried and cried, knowin' she couldn't take that baby home or everyone would know what kind of a girl she was ... that she was no better than trash ... oh, it might not sound like such a tragedy now, with teenagers havin' babies like they're dolls to play with and everybody actin' like they're colorblind ... but it was thirty years ago ... mixing races like that wasn't tolerated, not in Stybr ... she wouldn't have been able to show her face in that town again and her father would've beat her to a pulp had he known what she'd done ... so we did the only thing we could've ... once it was born, delivered in my house by my hands, we turned the child over to a foundling home that didn't ask too many questions ... we prayed together and washed our hands of the whole mess like it had never happened ... I didn't think Mari was ever gonna tell the baby's father, but she must've or else he got wind of it somehow ... 'cuz he came looking for his daughter some years after and I couldn't tell him where she was because I didn't know and Mari didn't know either . . . besides Mari had moved on by then and didn't want to look back . . ."*

The young black soldier who'd fathered Marilee's baby was named Ronald Hull.

Beth Taylor's brother.

Renata's deceased daddy.

Oh, what a tangled web we weave, I mused, still finding it hard to believe.

Renata Taylor was Marilee's by birth.

A daughter she'd been too afraid to keep; a child she'd kept mum about for thirty years. My God, how much pain she'd caused with her deception!

How Ronald must've wept when he'd learned he had a baby somewhere out there. It was a miracle he'd even found her without much of a trail to follow. But he had tracked her down eventually. Sometime after he'd been discharged from the Army and before he'd been killed in a car wreck—at least according to Kevin Snodgrass's article—at which point Beth and Richard Taylor had raised the little girl as their own.

I couldn't imagine they hadn't felt angry at Marilee for what she'd done, for the lies she'd told that had kept a child hidden from its rightful family for so long.

I leaned my head against the seat rest and sighed, sure that Marilee had assumed her secret would die with her and Miss Doreen.

But now Janet and I knew what had transpired.

And we weren't the only ones.

My cell started ringing as Janet pulled onto my quiet street in Prestonwood, and I eyed the number on the CallerID before I picked up.

Mother.

"What's wrong?" I asked, as Janet guided the VW into the parking lot.

"Hey, sweetie, mind if I ask where you are?" Only the most seasoned expert could have picked up on the slight rise in her smooth-as-silk drawl, a subtle signal of inward panic.

"We're in front of my condo . . ."

"Well, get in your car and get down here this instant," she lowered her voice to a hiss, no longer bothering to hide her nerves. "Marilee's lawyer dropped in, the deputy chief is back, Gilbert Mabry showed up on my doorstep demanding his daughter go home with him, and Kendall's refusing to talk to anyone."

"Where's Sandy?" I asked.

"She's visiting her mother at the Blue Belle Home for the Aged like she does the third Sunday of every month, Andrea, for goodness' sake."

"Geez, I forgot, okay?" I glanced at Janet, who was watching me with interest. "I'll be right there. Give me twenty minutes."

"Make it fifteen," Mother said and disconnected.

Yes, ma'am.

I slipped the phone into my purse, unhooked myself from the belt, and reached for the door.

"Anything I should know about?" Janet asked as I pushed on the handle and let in the noon heat.

"Just Cissy, freaking out," I said and rolled my eyes. "She's got a mouse trapped under the refrigerator. She's scared to come down from a chair. So I've gotta run down there and rescue it before she calls an exterminator to annihilate the poor thing."

"Uh-huh." She looked skeptical.

"Well, it's been a real, um, trip," I said and closed the door, giving her a wave from the other side of the window.

Before she'd even backed out of the space, I rushed over to my Jeep and hopped in, though I waited until the Jetta disappeared from the parking lot before I put her in gear and peeled rubber all the way to Beverly.

Cissy must've been watching for me out the window, as she appeared on the doorstep, waving impatiently as I parked behind a pair of squad cars, a red Lexus, and the Mercedes with the vanity plates that I knew belonged to Dr. Taylor. If the media had been swarming earlier, the police had done a brilliant job of dispersing them. I'd only spotted one television van with a satellite on its roof settled across the street.

"Thank God you're here!" As soon as I was near enough, Mother—appropriately funereal in black silk top and pants—caught my arm and drew me into the foyer. "I was beginning to think you'd never arrive."

Though it had taken no more than fifteen minutes—as she'd demanded—and involved my tearing through a couple yellow lights and traveling a wee bit over the speed limit.

"They're all having tea and cookies in the sunroom," she leaned near to inform me as she ushered me through the front hallway, away from the cordoned-off living room and toward the rear of the house. "I finally got Kendall to dress and come downstairs."

"How's she doing?" I asked.

Cissy made a face. "She hasn't eaten a thing, even refusing Sandy's chocolate chip pancakes. I think she'd stay in bed with the drapes drawn all day if I'd let her. Poor child. Someone from Twinkle Productions phoned to say they're shutting down the studio for a while, until they figure out what to do. I took the call when Kendall wouldn't. They said they're arranging a memorial service for the crew to attend, so they can have some kind of closure."

I couldn't blame them for locking up the studio. They had no cause to rush repairs, not since taping was suspended indefinitely. I wondered if they could save *The Sweet Life* without Marilee, or if they'd have to shut down forever.

"You said Marilee's lawyer was here?"

"Yes, about an hour ago." Her footsteps faltered, and she stood still, her brow settling into a half-dozen creases. "I'm apparently the executrix of Marilee's estate," she said, and I couldn't stop my mouth from hanging open. "I don't imagine there were many people she trusted, and I'm just thankful that Justin Gable didn't talk her into putting him in charge of her affairs before she died. Because she had talked about changing her will in the last few weeks, giving that con man a share of her assets, babbling on about how he reenergized her sex life, for pity's sake. Thank heavens she didn't get around to doing it."

"She didn't leave him anything?"

"As a matter of fact, she didn't, not in the will, anyway. He'll get nothing more than what she'd already given him, like the car, new clothes, watches, and what not." She frowned and touched the gold bauble clipped on her earlobe. "Mari's bequests are quite simple, really. Basically, all of her worldly goods go to her surviving heir, which would be Kendall, naturally."

Or not.

"Oh, God," came out of my mouth before I realized that I'd said it.

Mother stopped fiddling with her earring and eyed me strangely. "What is it Andrea? Do you have something to say on the subject?"

"No, I mean, yes."

Rats.

With a sigh, I hurriedly confessed to what had gone on at the Pecan Grove Retirement Home in Gunner, Texas.

Cissy frowned, but didn't interrupt. Though, when I'd finished, she quietly asked, "Are you sure this old woman's brain wasn't addled?"

"She was as coherent as you or I." Though maybe that wasn't saying much.

Mother hesitated, putting a finger to her lips before declaring, "I can't believe Marilee never breathed a word of this. I never imagined she had another child. And it's Beth Taylor's girl, Renata? Who's actually her niece by blood?"

It sounded like a soap opera, putting it that way.

"There'll be DNA tests, of course."

"Of course."

"But, yes, I believe it. It fits, don't you see?"

My mother sighed. "I wish now that I hadn't talked to Kendall already about her mother's will, but I figured she'd learn soon enough, what with the formal reading being tomorrow afternoon."

"You're right. She has no clue she's not the sole surviving heir," I said

"Oh, dear," Cissy breathed. "What a mess. Marilee has another daughter," she repeated, as if saying it again made it real. Then she clutched at my arm. "Does Beth realize who Renata's birth mother was?"

"She must." It didn't make sense any other way. "I've got a feeling that's why they moved to Dallas, to find Marilee."

I thought of how Dr. Taylor had slipped up at the hospital when Kendall was admitted, saying, "*since her daughters have been positively diagnosed*" before correcting herself, claiming weariness for the mistake. Only it hadn't been a mistake. She had known the truth but she'd kept it to herself.

"What about Renata?"

"I'd guess she knows, too."

"So Kendall's the only one out of the loop?"

I nodded.

"Well, then we have to remedy the situation," Cissy said, her normally placid expression showing strain. "It seems as good a time as any to tell Kendall she has a sister. Better she hear it now than read about it on the front page of the *Park Cities Press*. You did say Janet was doing a feature?"

"A three-part series." And a book, I would've added, but I had crossed my heart and sworn not to tell.

"You okay, sweetie?" she peered into my face. "You look green."

That's exactly how I felt. Kermit had nothing on me.

"I'm fine," I assured her. I'd been saying that a lot lately and not meaning it. One of those little white lies that nobody counted.

"Then let's get this over with, shall we?" She tucked her hand in the crook of my elbow and propelled me the rest of the distance to the sunroom. Her heels clicked staccato-sharp on the tiles. My sneakers squeaked as I dragged my feet, wincing at the thought of what—and who—awaited us.

Heads turned as we entered, and I surveyed the group that had gathered at Mother's, rather like the cast of characters attending the Mad Hatter's tea party. Though no one seemed to be doing much sipping. The cups looked full, the plate of cookies untouched. With all the poisoning going on, I couldn't blame them.

Deputy Chief Anna Dean stood by the windows overlooking Mother's roses.

Dr. Taylor and Renata sat side by side on the wicker sofa.

Kendall Mabry curled on the chaise longue, hair tied in a ragged ponytail, wearing a robe borrowed from my mother, pink silk with an embroidered *C* at her right breast.

Behind her, Gilbert Mabry leaned against the wall, arms crossed, bland features puckered with distress.

The notable missing player from this drama was Justin Gable. I assumed, by his absence, that he was still on the lam. I wondered just how far he'd been able to run without his passport.

I figured that's why the second in command of the Highland Park police had made an appearance at Mother's house on Sunday noon, doubtless to give us an update on Justin's whereabouts.

"Nice of you to join us, Ms. Kendricks," the deputy chief said and gave me the thinnest of smiles.

"I was out of town this morning," I said by way of apology, though I didn't know why I should feel guilty for being late to this impromptu gathering. "Hello." I nodded at Beth and Renata. Gil Mabry squinted at me, ostensibly trying to figure out who I was. Did he even recall running into me at the studio yesterday after his and Marilee's shouting match?

My gaze settled on Kendall. "Are you okay?" I mouthed.

She bit her bottom lip, fighting tears. I could hardy believe what the past twenty-four hours had done to the tough-as-brass girl. She looked as miserable as any human could. Probably wishing she'd fought less with her mother. Probably wishing for a lot of things she couldn't have.

I took a step toward her, but Mother kept hold of my arm, resigning me to a position near the French doors. Which might not be too bad should I need to make a quick escape.

"Andrea has something she'd like to share," Cissy said to the room at large. "It's important . . ."

The deputy chief cleared her throat. "If you don't mind, ma'am, I'd like to get a word in first."

Mother gave her the floor, much to my relief.

Anna Dean hooked her thumbs in her utility belt and moved in from the window. "I had promised y'all I'd keep you informed on what the preliminary reports told us about what happened to Marilee Mabry. So that's why I'm here." She squared her shoulders, looking very much like a petite General Patton. "We've compared initial toxicity results to what Dr. Taylor and the hospital lab found in your bloodstream, Ms. Mabry." Her chin jerked toward Kendall. "And it appears that there was a foreign substance added to the recipe for the Death by Chocolate which Marilee Mabry consumed."

"Ma huang," I said without thinking, and the deputy chief glanced at me.

"Yes, that exactly. A highly potent form of ephedra, yes,

in a toxic dosage," she explained. "And we've matched the chemical composition with a bottle of liquid ma huang found among Justin Gable's belongings, left behind at the Mabry house."

"Justin killed my mother?" Kendall's hand went to her throat, and I could see in her face that she didn't believe it. "No, there's no way."

"We've got corroborating statements from the crew of *The Sweet Life* that Mr. Gable was in the kitchen while the cake was being prepared. So, yes, he is our prime suspect," the deputy chief said and added, "We've issued a warrant for his arrest, and I've put out an APB on his BMW, as of this morning. We'll have him in custody soon, I'll wager. We've got the city police and the state troopers in on this, too."

"Oh, my God," Kendall breathed.

"Don't fret, Ms. Mabry, please," Anna Dean said, lowering her voice. "So far as I understand it, no one but family knows you're here, so you're safe for the time being. I've got a squad car keeping an eye on your mother's house around the clock, in case he returns to pick up that passport of his. In fact, I'm heading over there next, to check out a call from the caretaker."

"The caretaker?" Kendall curled her fingers beneath her chin and stared at the policewoman, her eyes wide as pennies. "Is it the animals?"

"Just something fishy in, er, the catfish pond."

"There's nothing wrong with the pond . . . nothing wrong. Why can't you just leave it alone? Why can't this all just go away? I want to go back." Kendall's voice shook, and I saw the way she dug her nails into the flesh of her hands. She would draw blood if she kept that up. "Please," she whispered to no one, "let me go back."

"It'd be better if you stayed here, Ms. Mabry," the policewoman insisted, but I had a feeling that's not what Kendall meant. She wanted to go back in time, before her mother passed away, before Justin took off and left her.

Back.

I took a step toward her; but Cissy held on to my arm.

"You're right, it might be nothing," the deputy chief went on. "The groundskeeper noticed an oily substance on the surface of the pond this morning. A few of the fish were floaters, so he's worried about contamination. He thinks it could be vandalism. We'll see if we can't figure out whether maybe someone pitched a gas can in there or rolled an oil drum. He figures the tractor may've been used. There are tracks leading up to the edge."

Kendall moaned.

My first thought was Justin. What if he was lurking around, angry enough to sabotage Marilee's property?

The girl must've figured that, too; as I noticed the gleam of sweat on her face, worry pinching her features.

"You think that's all it is, right? Vandalism?" I piped up, hoping to reassure Kendall that it could be as simple as a prank, teenaged mischief.

"Like I've said before, Ms. Kendricks"—Anna Dean shot me a narrow smile—"I don't like to jump to conclusions. We'll take a look at the pond and figure out . . ."

"Enough about the pond, for heaven's sake!" My mother's voice cut across the room, stunning the rest of us to silence. "There's a killer running loose, and you're worried about catfish?" Cissy pointed—actually pointed—at the deputy chief. I'm sure Emily Post rolled over in her grave. "The boy poisoned a cake . . . an entire cake that I nearly ate . . . that my friends could have eaten. He could've killed us all, and you're concerned about a few dead fish?"

Anna Dean shifted her steely gaze in Cissy's direction. "From what the lab tells me, Mrs. Kendricks, the level of ephedra wouldn't have done in a healthy human being with no cardiac risks. But Marilee Mabry had a congenital heart arrhythmia, like her daughter. Mr. Gable had specifically targeted her, not you or your friends."

"Marilee had a what? What the hell are you talking about?" Gilbert Mabry asked, reminding us that he was there. He peeled himself from the wall and gripped the wicker frame of the chaise longue that held Kendall. "This arrhythmia Kendall was diagnosed with . . . Marilee had it, too?"

"It's called long QT syndrome," Beth Taylor told him. "It's often passed down from parent to child."

"But Marilee was strong as an ox." Gilbert scratched his head. "I saw her with my own eyes yesterday morning, and she was full of spit and vinegar."

A rather polite way to say she'd bitched him out, I mused.

"She might've been full of spit and vinegar, but she wasn't strong. At least her heart wasn't." Dr. Taylor clutched her daughter's hand, while Renata sat still. "The arrhythmia isn't something you see on the outside. Sometimes those afflicted get a sense of what their bodies can handle, they realize their limitations, and they can avoid complications. But it's like lightning. No one can anticipate when a fatal arrhythmia could occur. But when it's properly diagnosed, it can be treated with medication."

"So Marilee had this problem all along?"

Beth nodded. "She undoubtedly shared the same gene mutation. We'll have proof positive when the final reports return in a few weeks."

"If the tests aren't back, how can you sound so certain?" Gilbert Mabry looked as confused as before. "Are you guessing or is there something you're not telling us?"

The same thought had crossed my mind.

How could Dr. Taylor and the deputy chief be so sure Marilee had the LQTS without the results of the gene tests?

Unless—*oh, whoa.*

The answer seemed suddenly obvious.

I looked at Beth and the young woman beside her.

"Renata has long QT syndrome, doesn't she? Because she's Marilee's daughter by birth," I said, barely hearing my own voice. The thump-thump of my heart filled my ears, pounding like horse's hooves. "Both her children inherited the gene mutation from her, not from their fathers. Your brother Ronald didn't have it, did he, Dr. Taylor? That's how you knew that Marilee had the syndrome, as soon as Kendall was diagnosed. It's the only thing that makes sense."

"Her children?" Gilbert Mabry's cheeks flushed purple. "What in the hell are you saying?"

"No." Kendall shook her head, adamant. "Mummy didn't have another baby. I'm her only little girl."

"Yes, she did. She really did," I said, as Cissy squeezed my arm, urging me to finish what I'd started. "Renata Taylor is your half-sister. Your mother was just sixteen when

she gave birth, and the circumstances were very . . . difficult . . . for everyone." I half-expected Beth Taylor to con-
tribute to the conversation, but she didn't. "I can't say
whether what was done was right or wrong, but it happened all the same. Now maybe that the truth is out, some
of the damage can be undone."

Kendall unwound her legs from beneath her, setting bare
feet on the ground, toes curling against the tiles. She drew
the robe tighter around her, staring unabashedly at Renata,
and I couldn't blame her. "My sister?" she murmured as
she studied the other woman. "How can that be? She's not
even . . . we're not even the same color."

"Renata's father was African American," I spelled it out
plainly, "but her mother—*your* mother—was white. Marilee's blood runs through both of your veins."

Kendall touched the mole on her cheek, as if realizing
she and Renata shared the same small mark on their skin.

Renata sat ramrod-straight, her cut-glass features so
stoic, that I wondered if she resented Kendall's remarks,
her reaction; if she felt angry at the other girl because Marilee had kept Kendall but let her go. Though I hoped not,
for both their sakes.

"You *are* sisters," I said again, because I thought each
woman needed to hear it more than once. "You're not
alone, Kendall. You have family."

"Of course she has family." Gilbert came around the
chaise and took hold of his daughter's shoulder. "She has
me and Amber Lynn." He flicked a hand toward Renata, the
sunlight setting sparks to the plump gold Rolex at his wrist.
"I've heard all I want to hear, and now I'm taking my baby

home. She's mourning her mother. She certainly doesn't need . . . this! Look at what you've done to her already. She's a mess."

Tears streaked down Kendall's pale cheeks, staining the pale pink silk of the borrowed robe.

"Come on." Gilbert's voice softened and he reached for her arm. "Come on, princess, let's go home."

But Kendall didn't move. She didn't reply, didn't even acknowledge her father had spoken.

"Princess, get up, please. Daddy wants to take you home." He tugged at her, but Kendall refused to budge.

"She may stay with me as long as she wants," my mother said, just shy of snapping. "She's old enough to make up her own mind of where she wants to be."

"And just who do you think you are, lady, the queen of Sheba?"

"Stop it!" Kendall cried and turned her tear-stained face toward her father. "Why did you even come here? You can't help me now that Mummy's dead. You didn't want me for all these years, but suddenly you want to take me home to live with you and Amber?" Pain distorted her face. "You never loved us, did you? You never cared about anyone but yourself."

"You're wrong, princess, listen . . ."

"No, you listen!" she screeched and swatted him away. She jumped out of the chair and turned on him, cheeks red with rage. "Why don't you go back home to your whore and let me be? It's your fault that Mummy had to work so hard she didn't have time to mother me," she sobbed and ran out of the room, her bare feet slapping on the tiles and pink silk trailing behind her.

I started after her, but Cissy stopped me.

"Let her go, Andrea," she said firmly. "This is a lot for the poor child to digest in one sitting."

Gilbert Mabry made a lunge after Kendall as well, and Mother stopped him cold.

"Don't even think of it."

He scowled, but put up no fuss. Maybe it was because the deputy chief was right there with a holster at her hip. Or maybe it was Mother's tone of voice.

Cissy wasn't done with him yet. "I do believe, sir, that it's time I showed you out. Kendall will call if she needs you. Shall we?" She inclined her head toward the French doors and he followed, red with embarrassment.

I turned back to the room, so full before and now half-empty.

"If you don't mind," I said to the remaining threesome of Renata, Beth, and the deputy chief, "I think I'll check on Kendall."

Renata let go of her mother's hand and slowly rose from the wicker sofa, her lips pursed tight.

"No, Andy. I should go. She's my blood, after all." Renata sounded so cool, so calm when she said it, and I wondered if she'd been testing those words in her head for a while. I wondered how long she had known the truth? Weeks, months? How hard it must've been for her to stay silent.

"Are you sure?"

"Yes, I'm sure." She glanced down at her aunt, who nodded and wiped tears from her face.

When I looked at Renata, really looked at her, I could fully see the resemblance to Kendall that had seemed merely incidental before: the shape of the eyes, the wide mouth, and small mole on the cheek. It was all there, so obvious now. As subtle as the similarities truly were, they seemed glaring, knowing what I knew now.

"Kendall's staying in my old room upstairs," I said. "Third door on the left."

"Thank you."

Without another word, she left.

As I watched her go, a panic settled in my belly, as the full impact hit me, of what this revelation could mean when it went public. I had a bad, bad feeling, deep in my bones, that things were far from finished.

"I should have come clean before," Beth Taylor murmured, removing a tissue from her handbag to dab at her cheeks. "Before Marilee was dead, so Renata could have known her birth mother, no matter what kind of person she was."

But she had known Marilee.

She'd seen the good, the bad, and the ugly. Okay, the bad and the ugly, anyway. Maybe it had saved her a lot of pain, I thought, knowing what living in Marilee's shadow had done to Kendall.

Beth dried her eyes and looked at me. "I only told Renata the truth a few months back, when I realized Marilee's show was going national. It was like a sign, for me. I couldn't live with myself, keeping it from her any longer. It took Ron five years to find his baby girl . . . five years of giving up his career in the Army and his life in order to get her home. And it was rough on him, really rough. On Renata, too. She'd been in four foster homes by the time he got to her."

"I'm sorry," I said. I'd been apologizing a lot lately, for things that weren't my fault.

Beth sniffed into her tissue. "At least the worst is over."

But I didn't agree.

"It's not over," I said and turned to the deputy chief.

"Something else you'd like to confess, Ms. Kendricks?"

If that was a dig, I was willing to ignore it.

"I'm not sure how to put this"—I spoke slowly, though my pulse raced—"but I've got a really bad feeling that Kendall isn't safe. If Justin tried to kill her once, he might take another shot. Only this time, he might succeed."

Though I was beginning to wonder if Kendall wasn't more of a threat to herself than Justin Gable would ever be.

Chapter 25

 Mother was pouring herself a very stiff cognac when I took off, trailing the deputy chief and another squad car over to Marilee's house, where I'd been dispensed to collect some of Kendall's things.

Thankfully, Anna Dean seemed to find my fears founded, enough to advise that Kendall remain at Mother's, which necessitated my schlepping to Preston Hollow . . . when all I wanted was lunch and a big margarita.

Maybe there was something to Mother's early happy hours of late. Must be the stress triggering a sudden yen for booze, when neither of us normally did much partaking of anything stronger than hot tea (Earl Grey for her, organic green for me).

Though the deputy chief assured me that Marilee's staff had returned—a few of them anyway—I didn't see a soul once I drove past the gates where the media had set up camp. While Anna Dean took a stroll around back with her boys in blue, I entered the quiet of the mansion and crept up the stairs to Kendall's room.

If I'd had a hankering to poke around, I guess I could've. I didn't see anyone upstairs to stop me from peeking into whatever room had been Justin's or detouring into Marilee's boudoir.

But I didn't.

I wanted to get the heck out of there as soon as I'd packed up Kendall's clothes and toiletries, things she'd left behind in the haste to get her to Mother's. She'd made me a list, which I'd folded and stuck in my purse for safekeeping.

On the second-floor landing, I took a right at the top of the hallway, homing in on the room at the very end. Kendall said it overlooked the spread out back so she could hear the crow of roosters before the sun arose each morning.

Not the kind of alarm clock I'd want, but each to her own.

I pushed open the door, gearing myself for décor that was over the top, all black and chrome or even Vegas red and glitter. I would've expected as much from a teenager whose very existence had been geared toward rebelling against everything her mummy stood for (i.e., good taste).

When I flipped on the switch, I looked around and my jaw fell.

Pale walls the soft pink of cotton candy with crisp white trim. The furniture would've looked perfectly suitable for a cottage on the beach, all white wicker and distressed wood. Floral Laura Ashley comforter, shams, and drapes with a matching border above a molded chair rail. White wicker shelves filled with enough dolls and stuffed animals to stock a Toys 'R'Us.

Was Kendall reliving her childhood or just a serious pack rat?

Even more odd were the wall decorations, framed covers of local magazines that had featured Marilee's smiling face, as well as feature articles from the *Morning News* and other Texas papers. Either she was prouder of her mummy than she'd let on, or she was torturing herself. I couldn't decide which.

I had the same reaction as when I'd first glimpsed a rack filled with Isaac Mizrahi clothes at Target: *what's up with that?*

Once my astonishment faded a bit, I set about packing the smallest of the Louis Vuitton suitcases fetched from a spacious walk-in closet. Underwear, pajamas, jeans, and tees, her makeup kit from atop the mirrored vanity, expensive lotions and potions from La Prairie situated neatly around the marbled sink.

As instructed, I popped open her medicine cabinet to locate her birth-control pills, found the pink pack easily but lingered to eyeball the labels on the dozens of brown prescription bottles and silver tubes lined up on the slender shelves.

Prozac, Zoloft, Paxil, Effexor, Celexa . . . just about every antidepressant on the market was present and accounted for, not to mention Xanax, Librium, and Valium for antianxiety, Ambien and Soma for sleep, Prevacid for stomach acid, Lamisil for toenail fungus. I noted different doctors' names on many of the bottles, each probably unaware of the other.

Hell's bells.

It's a wonder the girl wasn't in a coma.

If Justin's herbal remedies had kept Kendall away from her well-stocked medicine cabinet, I could understand why Marilee had thought him a miracle worker. But what if Kendall needed to be medicated? What if she had clinical depression and her brain required a synthetic pill to fix an imbalance, to keep her wires uncrossed and prevent her from feeling such emotional extremes?

Justin certainly hadn't done either of them any favors in the end, had he?

I shut the mirrored cabinet, turned off the bathroom light, and tucked the toiletries into the opened suitcase on the bed. As I zipped the bag closed, I glanced sideways and spied Kendall's computer, a sleek Titanium laptop lying atop the wicker desk.

Was I supposed to bring that back with me?

I pulled the list from the handbag slung crisscross over my shoulders. Like Santa, I checked it twice, but "computer" wasn't on it.

Still, I sidled over to take a look, unable to resist stroking the cool metal cover as if it were a kitten. For the hell of it, I picked it up—wow, so much lighter than my Gateway model—then I set it back down and opened it, pressing the power button and giving it a whirl.

The latest Windows program booted, and a photograph appeared to wallpaper the background. It was a young girl dressed as a princess with tulle skirt, glittering tiara, and silver wand. Kendall, I realized, at maybe eight or nine years old. Before her parents had divorced. She smiled, showing missing teeth, looking elated in the moment, blissfully unaware of her future.

So sad, really.

I thought of the pill bottles in the bathroom. The scars at her wrists. The way she'd starved herself with anorexia and purged herself with bulimia.

The girl was not a happy camper.

Calling Kendall "confused" didn't even begin to describe her, and I wondered how she would come through this. She was already so fragile, psychologically.

"Can you drive a tractor, Andy? Because I can. And I can milk a cow and muck a stall, too. Not something everyone knows how to do. Hell, I can probably do all the things Mummy professes to doing so expertly on her show. Except I'm the real deal. Don't you think that's kind of ironic?"

Kendall would miss Marilee, despite their troubles. Sometimes I think people who fought the most, felt the void most.

"You know, I could've done Mummy's Web site, if she'd let me . . . I do all her research on the Internet, looking up recipes and stuff. I'm an expert at Googling. Can't be much harder to put up web pages."

I was sorely tempted to get into Kendall's files, but they were password protected. Not that I would have invaded her privacy anyway.

But I did connect to the Internet, as her screen name password was saved. I was curious about Kendall's research for Marilee, wondering what sites she'd recently Googled. I pulled down the queue from her cache and began clicking my way through them.

The most recent links led to information about long QT syndrome and drug interactions, listings of potential fatally herbs, like ephedra. I ignored the prickle at my neck, telling myself it made sense that she'd delve into the subject after being diagnosed. It didn't mean anything sinister.

Then I clicked on the next page listed in her cache.

And the one after that.

My eyes widened, recognizing them.

Society pages from papers in Texas and beyond with photos of Justin with his old paramours, or mere mentions of him attending a soiree "on the arm" of this socialite or that. The same ones I'd stumbled upon last night after Googling for Justin Gable.

I went into the program files on the hard drive, checking the dates on the cookies left behind by Kendall's visits to each site.

My mouth dried to cotton.

Kendall had viewed those pages weeks ago.

How could that be? When I'd brought up his past with her last night, she'd denied knowing anything. Isn't that what she'd told me?

I tried to remember her reaction, after my stating, *"He was a con man, Kendall. A gigolo. He slept with rich, older women to get money and cars and whatever else they'd give him. He's done it all over the state, maybe beyond the border. He's the male equivalent of a bimbo . . ."*

She had told me to "stop." She'd said she didn't want to listen to me.

But she hadn't denied it, hadn't insisted I was lying.

Because she already knew, I realized.

"I make sure Kendall's lies don't get out of hand . . ."

". . . she did this to hurt me . . . to pay me back . . . what am I going to do with her? What?"

Who was Kendall Mabry, really? What did I truly know about her? Had my sympathy for her clouded my judgment? Was I missing something?

If I hacked into her files, maybe I could learn more about . . .

No.

I shut off the laptop and clicked it closed.

"Used? How do you know I'm not the one doing the using, huh?"

Who was using whom?

Suddenly, I wasn't so sure.

I walked to the windows that overlooked Marilee's backyard farm. Figures in blue conversed with a man in coveralls by the edge of the fishpond, the smooth gray surface of the water like an animal skin, bouncing the sun off its back.

From where I stood, I couldn't see much of anything, not with the glare.

I closed my eyes, and I heard Kendall's voice:

"There's nothing wrong with .the pond . . . nothing wrong. Why can't you just leave it alone? Why can't this all just go away?"

Why so panicky?

What about the pond made her so nervous? The poor little catfish floating to the surface?

For some reason, I didn't think that was it.

"We also located his passport and around a thousand dollars cash stuffed down into a pair of Tony Lamas in the closet."

That had never made sense to me. Why Justin had run off without his passport and a wad of cash. Why throw your underwear into a duffel bag and leave your ticket out behind?

"Justin killed my mother? No, there's no way."

Maybe Justin was a lot closer than anyone realized.

A thought flashed in my head, a "what if" so horrific, I quickly pushed it aside, a shiver running through me.

I touched my fingers to my temples, rubbing, wishing for once that I didn't have that "vivid imagination" I'd been accused of having throughout my life.

For once, I wished I'd been dull.

Then I wouldn't have had the knot in my stomach.

The pain in my chest.

I wouldn't have had this awful suspicion that I'd been taken in as much as anybody. That I'd been deceived without being told a single lie.

I had to get back to Mother's.

Without further hesitation, I scooped up the suitcase and hauled it to the Jeep, stuffing it behind the seat before I hopped in.

My heart beat so fast and so loud, it was all I could hear as I drove.

I think I'd known what I'd find well before I ever walked through Cissy's front door and saw my old bed upstairs empty; before I woke my mother from her Cognac-induced nap to discover her car keys were missing, the Lexus vanished from the garage.

Kendall was gone.

And I knew exactly where she was.

Chapter 26

 Ring around the rosey, pocket full of posies, ashes, ashes, we all fall down.

    I'm not sure why that childish refrain kept running through my head as I drove to Marilee's studio in Addison, but it did. Maybe because it's how I thought of Kendall: going round and round in circles before falling so fast she had nothing to grab to stop herself from hitting rock bottom. She'd been trying to tell us all along what she'd done—without exactly saying it—and, like so many other times in her past, no one had listened.

    When I pulled into the parking lot off Midway, the neat square building with the green awning stood alone in the sea of black asphalt. How odd to see it so deserted, especially after the pandemonium of the party and the glut of repair trucks that clogged the lot just yesterday morning. I found myself wondering again if the show would continue in some other format or if all of Marilee's crew would lose their jobs.

One woman's death—even a woman not well liked—had affected so many.

I steered the Jeep around the back and spotted Mother's champagne Lexus, tucked close to the rear exit that I'd become so familiar with since Marilee's bash.

After I slotted the Wrangler beside it, I shifted into Park and stayed put for a few minutes, getting my thoughts in order and making a few phone calls. I couldn't do what needed to be done alone. I needed help.

Then I gathered my purse and my wits, turned off the car and headed in, prepared to face the ghost that Marilee had left behind.

The back hallway was dark, though a light streamed from the door to Marilee's office. I had no misgivings as I moved toward it. I wasn't sure exactly what I'd find, but I was determined to do this part alone.

"Kendall?" I called before I entered the room. "It's Andy. Are you here?"

I looked around, but didn't see her. Clothes were scattered on the carpet, and I toed a familiar-looking sweatshirt left in a heap. One of mine. A pair of paint-splattered sweatpants and tattered Stan Smith sneakers lay on the floor, closer to the bathroom.

"Kendall?" I knocked at the door, hoping to God I wouldn't spot her sprawled on the tiles. But I needn't have worried. Except for the strong smell of disinfectant, the space was empty.

When I turned around, Marilee's computer monitor flickered as the screen saver came on, the sudden change of color and motion catching my eye. I felt myself drawn toward it.

When I touched the mouse, the screen came alive, and I realized the web cams were switched on, though the live video stream was off. I studied the monitor, checking through the different zones, noting that the lights were on throughout the studio, everywhere but the kitchen set where the fire damage was done.

I stopped the slide show of frames, seeing something.

Seeing someone.

There on the living room set, seated on the sofa, gesturing in a way that suggested a conversation . . . only no one else was around. Just a slender figure in tan slacks and blouse, ash-blond hair barely touching her shoulders.

Marilee?

My throat closed up.

No, that was impossible.

I blinked, but she was still there.

Then I saw the silver bracelets, both forearms were thick with them. Bracelets that covered old scars on her wrists.

I walked over to Marilee's closet and opened the doors to reveal the rows of mannequin heads topped with various ash-blond wigs.

One head was bare.

I glanced back at the computer screen and swallowed, that figure-eight knot tying itself in my gut again.

"I want to go back . . . take me back."

Back in time.

But Kendall couldn't erase the damage she'd done. She couldn't bring her mummy home. So she was doing the only thing she could to make her live again.

She was trying to be Marilee.

I dried sweaty palms on my jeans, wishing I could wipe

away my nerves so easily. I left the office and started up the long hallway, past the unmanned cubicles, past the test kitchen and into the studio.

The sound of Kendall's voice floated toward me as I approached, carrying on a dialogue that only she could hear. Every now and then, laughter punctuated her words or the pause in between, and I felt my heart wrench.

I paused at the edge of the living room set, squinted up at the spotlight shining down upon the young woman—the girl—dressed in her mother's clothes, wearing a wig so like her mother's hair.

". . . well, I agree, Nate," she was saying. "When you're decoratin' your bedroom, it should reflect who you are, and you should surround yourself with colors and things that reflect your personality."

I took a step up, onto the stage, the boards creaking.

She clammed up suddenly.

"Kendall," I said. "Please, don't do this."

She turned her head, her dark eyes brightening at the sight of me. She grinned, her mouth painted with Marilee's red lipstick. "Andy! Did you come to watch the taping? I'm rehearsing for a show about decorating bedrooms."

"No, I didn't come to watch a taping." I moved closer, stopping behind an armchair and gripping it hard. "I want to talk, about your mother."

"Mummy?" Beneath the wig, her forehead crinkled. "But Mummy's gone, Andy. You said so yourself, remember? That's why I'm taking over now. Because there's no one else to do it, and I know everything. I know better than anyone."

Slowly, I circled the chair, my hand on the armrest, needing the support it gave my wobbly knees.

"How did it happen?" I asked her. "Did you mean to hurt her, Kendall? Did you rig the boom mike to fall that day? What about the brown recluse spider in your mother's shoes? Or the ma huang in the champagne? It was meant for her to drink, because you knew how even a little caffeine made her jittery. Did you imagine it would knock her off her feet for a while? Hold up taping? Only you ingested the ephedra and ended up in the hospital. Then you found out about your heart ailment, and you must've realized she had it, too."

The grin died from her lips. Her dark eyes darted about. "Why are you saying these things, Andy? Don't embarrass me," she whispered. "Not in front of the crew."

"But no one else is here, Kendall," I said and swung my arm around me. "There's no one but us." I squinted against the spotlight, seeing only shadows beyond the stage. "So you can be honest. You don't have to lie. Tell me what really went on. Convince me it was an accident. Don't let me believe you're a killer." I swallowed, wishing my mouth weren't bone dry, making it even harder to get the words out. "You didn't mean for it to happen. It was a mistake, right?"

"Yes." She grew rigid, sitting ramrod straight. Except for the hands in her lap, which kneaded together. "It was a mistake."

"She wasn't supposed to die, was she?" I lowered my voice, keeping it soft, as if speaking to a child, a little girl who'd erred gravely.

"I just wanted Mummy to be sick." Her chin trembled, and a rush of tears spilled from her eyes. "Sick enough so that I could take care of her. I wanted her to *need* me, for once. To rely on me. Then everything else would disappear. I wanted to make them all disappear, so she would finally have to see me." Her eyes narrowed, jaw clenching. "If I didn't do something, she would've pushed me even farther away. She would've let him come between us forever."

"Justin?" I asked.

"Yes, yes, Justin!"

"I'll bet you wish you'd never brought him into your lives, don't you? After you'd met him at the gym, after you'd brought him home, you thought he would romance your mother and then leave her, like he did all those other women. You'd researched his past on the Web, and you knew what he'd done. You wanted to be there for Marilee when he broke her heart. But instead, he decided to stay."

"Mummy didn't love him, not really, but she liked having him around," she whispered, her fingers curling into fists. Trails of black and blue from her makeup bruised her eyes, left dark streaks on her cheeks. "Justin liked the celebrity of being with Mummy. He liked hanging around the set and running errands for her." She wiped a silk sleeve across her face, only making more of a mess. "He said he might even ask Mummy to marry him someday, that they had fun together and he was tired of moving around. When I told him we could be together, he laughed and said he didn't want me. That I was just a diversion." She jerked up her chin, and I read the rage in her eyes. "He left me on the floor of her bathroom when I got sick that night . . . he left me there, Andy. I would've died if you hadn't found me. He would've had her all to himself." She drew in a deep breath and shook her head. "That's when I knew . . . when I made up my mind."

"So you took care of him."

"Yes." She seemed to calm down as she said it. Her hands relaxing in her lap.

She had murdered Justin, I told myself, only now truly believing it. And it had been no accident, not from what Deputy Chief Dean had relayed, only minutes earlier.

The police had sent a diver into the catfish pond and found the silver BMW Roadster, Justin belted into the passenger seat, and the tracks of the tractor indicated the car had been pushed the final few feet into the water. They were awaiting the crane when I'd spoken to Anna Dean from my cell in the studio parking lot. An autopsy of the body would doubtless show he'd been drugged. I had a feeling Kendall had made him a sleeping pill smoothie, maybe even here at the studio, when everyone else had packed up and gone to Mother's for the taping. She had already decided then that he had to go, even before she made her mummy "sick" with the ma huang in the chocolate cake.

"Mummy, come back, please," Kendall breathed and pulled the wig from her head and cradled it, her own dark hair falling to her shoulders, the streak of white-blond catching across her face. "I'm so sorry . . . so sorry . . . I didn't mean to hurt you, Mummy, believe me." She drew her knees to her chest and started sobbing in earnest, vicious shuddering sobs that broke my heart.

I wanted to reach for her, to hold her, but I couldn't.

Not this time.

Instead, I wrapped my arms around myself and closed my eyes, sick with disappointment and anger and guilt. Disgusted at Kendall for what she'd done and at the people who'd surrounded her, wondering how many times she'd cried out for their attention and had been ignored.

She had needed love and had killed to get it.

If I—if anyone—had only listened.

A hand touched my shoulder, and I turned, opening my eyes to see my mother's face, the sadness in her eyes reflecting mine.

"Come, Andrea," she said softly. "Beth has made arrangements for Kendall. You have to let go."

I saw Dr. Taylor approaching the stage with a bespectacled man, and I knew that they would take Kendall somewhere she'd be safe, where she could heal her mind and soul. I only hoped the courts would let her seek the treatment she needed instead of punishing her. I think she'd punished herself enough.

"Sweetie?"

Cissy reached for my hand, and I held on.

"Yes," I said and leaned on her. "Please, take me home."

Epilogue

Two Weeks Later

 "You sure Cissy actually included me in this invitation?"

"Yeah, sure," I lied and brushed invisible lint off the shoulder of Brian's crisp button-down shirt. We stood between the terra cotta lions that guarded Mother's door, putting off ringing the bell for a minute. "Besides," I said and caught my thumbs beneath his collar, looking spot-on at him, "I told her I wouldn't come to dinner tonight without you."

He swallowed. "So you forced her to invite me? Is that it?"

I shrugged. "It was either that or risk her hooking me up with some rich cattle rancher's unmarried son who probably suffers from halitosis as well as serious issues with commitment."

"Wow," he said, adding dryly, "You sure know how to make a guy feel special, Andy."

"You are." I smiled and went up on my tiptoes to plant a soft kiss on his lips. "Special, I mean."

Malone had gone out of his way to help Kendall, arranging for that colleague of his, Allie whatever her name was, to work with him on a deal with the D.A.'s office so that Kendall wouldn't have to go through a trial. What she needed was psychiatric help, years of it, and Brian assured me he was doing everything in his power—and the power of Abramawitz, Reynolds, Goldberg, and Hunt—to get the job done.

Somehow, I believed he would.

"Who else did you say was coming?" he asked, his eyes so blue behind the preppy glasses. "Anyone I know?"

"Renata Taylor," I told him.

"Marilee's daughter? The one who ended up getting everything?"

"Yes, that one. And a friend of hers, Carson Caruthers. He was the food editor for *The Sweet Life*. They're actually working on a new show for Twinkle Productions called *The Bald Chef*. I think it has 'hit' written all over it."

They'd asked me to design a Web site, but I'd declined. I aimed to stick to nonprofits from now on. So much less drama. And never a murder as yet.

"Oh, and Dr. Taylor and her husband."

"The couple in the newspaper article?"

"Yes." I sighed. "But don't bring it up, okay? I don't know how they feel, but Mother was hugely embarrassed about it."

"Understandably," Brian murmured.

Unfortunately, he'd seen the copy of Kevin Snodgrass's piece, as had the rest of Dallas and the world, since MSNBC picked up on it and posted it on their Web site, basically to poke fun at it. But it had made Beth and Richard Taylor local celebrities. They'd been on every morning talk show in the Metroplex.

Isn't it ironic, don't you think?

"Ready?"

He nodded.

"Brace yourself." I pressed a finger to the doorbell.

Malone shifted behind me, listening to the muted chimes before the door groaned open, revealing Mother in all her glory. This time, in pink Chanel and gray pearls.

"Darling," she said, and I stepped up for her air kisses. She turned to Brian. "Mr. Malone, what a surprise. I wish I'd known you were coming." Her eyes narrowed on me. "I'll tell Sandy to set an extra place."

"But Andy said . . ."—he swallowed and looked at me frantically, as in *"what have you done?"*

"Hey, Mother"—I took Brian's hand and twined his fingers in mine—"guess who's coming to dinner?"

As we slipped inside past her, I heard her murmur, "Obviously, it's not Sidney Poitier."

Enter
THE GOOD GIRL'S GUIDE TO MURDER
Sweepstakes

Win a basket filled with the Debutante Dropout's favorite things, including a gift certificate for M. Avery Designs— tucked inside an Emily cosmetics bag!

Andrea Kendricks might not like the designer labels her mother wears, but she isn't averse to pampering herself now and then—like after tracking down a killer. Beyond bags from funky maverydesigns.com, Andy counts these among her "must-haves" (and she's put them in a big ol' basket for the sweepstakes winner): bath goodies, chocolates, CDs by Def Leppard and YoYo Ma, and much more!

Additional prizes will be awarded, so you'll have plenty of chances to win. Just answer this simple question relating to the storyline of THE GOOD GIRL'S GUIDE TO MURDER and the gift from Andy can be yours!

QUESTION: What is the name of Marilee Mabry's television show?

Send your answers, along with your full name and street address, via email to:
DebDropout@aol.com.

Deadline for entries is June 15, 2005.
The winners will be drawn randomly from all entries received and will be notified by mail.
No purchase necessary.
For more information, visit www.susanmcbride.com.

GGM 0205